# Guardian Angel

Book Four in the Master of Illusion Series

*Anne Rouen*

First published 2018 by Lynn Newberry, writing as Anne Rouen
PO Box 116, Manilla NSW 2346

**National Library of Australia Cataloguing-in-Publication
entry:**

 A catalogue record for this
book is available from the
National Library of Australia

Cover Images:
'Vintage WW2 Portrait' — Copyright: Jay P. Morgan — via
Getty Images

'France Background'— Copyright: Durva — via Getty Images

'View of Castle Against Sky'— Copyright: Laurence Marx /
EyeEm
— via Getty Images

Editing & Cover Design by Web Etch Design and Editing

Printed by CreateSpace, An Amazon.com Company
Also available on Kindle and other online stores

# DEDICATION

Guardian Angel is dedicated to my beautiful friend
Diane, who, having read a fledgling manuscript and
believed in its possibilities, encouraged me to pursue my
dream.
This book represents the culmination of that dream, and
I thank her with all my heart.

# PROLOGUE

**2 June 1930**

Armand Delaine sat in the baroque magnificence of the Opéra Magique on the eve of his departure for New York, absorbed in the harmony of the two most glorious voices he had ever heard: those of the divine Angel of Song and her son, *le beau* Nicolas—*le dernier cri* in Paris, and in Armand's judgement, the world.

His father had followed a story written over a lifetime and, scenting an even bigger one, was loath to let it go. 'The late Madame Dupont,' he told him, 'made some intriguing statements regarding the child, Nicolas de Beaulieu. It is your task to prove or disprove them. I want you to follow him wherever he goes and write his biography, which, in due course, the house of Delaine shall publish. Times are lean, but I believe I shall contrive to clothe and sustain you as befits a respectable man of letters.'

The words 'respectable man of letters' gave Armand an idea. He wanted to show his father that his son had innovatory skills as well as literary ones. And that he could adequately clothe and feed himself. In line with this bid for independence, he jumped at his parent's wry suggestion that he adopt his mother's maiden name, Lemaitre. Being young and bookish, Armand asked no questions—then.

He made representation to the marquis de Beaulieu to such good purpose that he was now touring with them as secretary to the marquise, the sensational diva, Angelique and tutor to their equally gifted son, Nicolas.

He then made a secret vow: 'I, Armand Delaine alias Lemaitre, am determined to seek out and unravel the mystery that my father, the publisher, so yearns to reveal.' He obtained a peculiar satisfaction in the knowledge that whatever the story, he himself was to be a part of it: an essential character in an unknown plot. A shaft of excitement tingled his spine at the prospect of a lifetime of adventure with these talented people, for although he knew already *how* he would write it, he didn't know just *what* he would write.

# 1 IL DIVO

**18 August 1930**

*Our last evening in New York. My diva is stunning as always. And my pupil is excited. He occupies centrestage alone tonight. Strangely enough, I don't think he has any nerves. I could write so much about the beautiful Angelique, but this is meant to be the story of Beau Nicolas and not the hopeless yearnings of Armand Lemaitre for the Angel of Song.*

Nicolas de Beaulieu stood at the front of the stage, bowing to his fans: the elite and privileged of New York.

It was his first solo, and he straightened in triumph before a standing ovation. He'd taken encore after encore, and he could not bear to leave them: These people who adored him so openly. He felt their love wash over him like warm breakers on a tropical shore. He was overwhelmed by it; his heart almost bursting with the love he felt in return.

His mother joined him, taking his hand as she smiled and bowed to their public. 'We will sing *Éternité d'amour* and then we will go,' she said. 'It is fitting that you sing it with me. Angelpapa wrote it for Godmama's opera ballet *Le Perdu*. It was our favourite duet.'

'I know.'

'How do you know?'

'Perhaps you have told me before … More than once.'

'If we weren't in front of an audience, I would box your ears!'

His lip lifted and his eyes flashed sapphire-blue—a strangely adult amusement lurking at the back of them. 'If we weren't in front of an audience, my dear Mama, I would not dare.'

'Cheek!' she said, smiling at the audience.

'But after we have sung and you still wish it, you may do so with my good will.'

She almost laughed, but *au fond*, she was shocked, too. *Do other ten year olds speak like this?* 'As if I would! Come, now! On the count …'

He was scanning the audience as if looking for someone. His mother squeezed his hand, nudging him into another bow, after which he resumed his scrutiny.

Angelique blew a kiss to the audience and left the stage, but Nicolas lingered behind. 'Come!' she whispered, beckoning from the wings.

Nicolas bowed, took a last look around the standing, wildly cheering audience and went to where his mother, father and Armand were waiting for him. Armand was going to take him to supper at the Waldorf while Mama and Papa went to a reception at the French Embassy on this, their last night in New York.

'Godmama and Monsieur Dupont weren't there tonight,' he said. 'I looked most carefully.'

'So that is why you were ogling the audience!' exclaimed Angelique. 'Oh, Nicolas!' She laughed, but Armand stood, stricken.

'Godmama? … Monsieur Dupont?' he repeated.

'Madame Dupont was my godmama: my mother's godmother. She reared me when … Never mind. On our last tour, Nicolas thought he saw her sitting in the audience with her husband Monsieur Dupont.' Tears sprang into the beautiful eyes. 'On the day she died, as it turned out.'

'I didn't "thought" I saw her,' corrected Nicolas. 'I *did* see her ... them.' He surveyed Armand. 'What do you think of that?'

Armand stared. *Her godmother? Madame Dupont had reared this beautiful creature? My God! And her diaries are about to be published!* He swallowed. 'Most ... unusual.' Averting his eyes from the sight of his idol's husband cradling her to him and offering her a handkerchief, he said to Nicolas, 'Come along, now. You can tell me all about it over supper.'

'*Oui, bien, bien!*' Nicolas ran to kiss his parents. 'Goodnight, Mama and Papa.'

'Goodnight, my darling.' Angelique smiled through her tears. '*Merci*, Armand.'

Armand did not hear the marquis echo her sentiments. The words 'goodnight, my darling' reverberated in his head. He pretended that they were for him.

He was preoccupied during supper, lingering over a shrimp cocktail while his charge tucked into delicate sandwiches, cakes and lemonade. He tried to make the effort to question Nicolas about his sightings. But it was no use: the diaries loomed large in his thoughts. He began to wish that he'd paid more attention to what his father had said about the publishing date. Armand understood it to be after he'd found out what he could about Nicolas. So, perhaps there would be time, yet.

'Armand? Armand!' Nicolas turned a menu card into a paper aeroplane and launched it at his mentor.

He started, brushing it off his collar. 'I beg your pardon?' He took one glance at his pupil's fun-filled eyes. 'Now, look here, young man!'

'No! You look here.' Nicolas stabbed a finger either side of his own nose. 'Armand, dear old chap. Can we have some ice-cream? Please?'

'What? After that exhibition? I doubt it!'

'Please? You were away with the fairies. I only wanted to wake you up. Please?'

'Oh, very well! I expect you'll have nightmares, though. Or be sick.'

'*Merci*. I won't.' Nicolas stood up, waving his napkin like a semaphore at the maître d'hôtel. '*Eh bien*, Monsieur! *Ici, s'il vous plaît!*'

Armand laughed. 'That's the head waiter you're treating like that. Serve you right if he ignores you!'

But the maître d'hôtel not only did not ignore him, he beckoned to a minion with a trolley of desserts, another with a tray of coffee and wended his stately way through the tables. He bowed to Nicolas. 'Ice-cream, Monsieur? Or strawberries, perhaps? Which would you like?'

Nicolas fixed him with his great blue eyes. 'Could I possibly have ice-cream *and* strawberries, please, Monsieur? If it is not too greedy?'

'You are a growing boy. Of course you may have both.' He lowered his voice. 'An *extra* helping of ice-cream?'

'*Bien sûr*, Monsieur! You are a trump!'

Suppressing an exclamation, Armand grew red with embarrassment.

The maître d'hôtel turned. 'Coffee, Monsieur?' he murmured, beckoning the second waiter. 'You are to be congratulated on such a spirited young charge.' He turned back to Nicolas. 'You are happy with our service, Monsieur?'

'But, yes! It is perfection. Thank you.'

'It was an absolute pleasure.' The head waiter bowed and left them.

Armand surveyed the ecstatic expression as his pupil spooned in huge dollops of strawberries and ice-cream. 'Incorrigible!' he said, dropping three lumps of sugar in his coffee and forgetting to stir it.

Everyday life was something Armand had contrived to escape. Until now. His head in his books; he'd never given a thought to how real flesh-and-blood people might feel. *Selfish! I've been selfish*, he thought, suffering agonies of remorse.

In true journalistic style, he'd been prepared to sacrifice all for a story, seeing himself as an investigator and chronicler of an ongoing mystery. He'd no idea that he would not simply be an observer—that he would be forced into the maelstrom of the lives of the de Beaulieus—that he would fall hopelessly, deliriously, in love. He'd also had no idea that this family was so close to Madame Dupont. How could he? His father had been so secretive about the diaries.

He'd known Angelique was the daughter of the reclusive comte de Villefontaine and that she'd married the heir of the powerful duc de Belvoir, but he knew nothing of her relationship to Madame Dupont, since his father had not allowed him to read the manuscript. All he'd really known was that Madame Dupont had noticed something unusual about the child, Nicolas, that his father wanted to follow up. *If only I'd thought!* he told himself, writhing inside. *I would have seen ...*

'Are you unwell, Armand?'

Armand looked up to see his charge eyeing him anxiously.

'No.' He stirred. 'Just ... thinking.'

'*Eh bien*,' said Nicolas. 'They must be troubling thoughts. You look ill, Armand. Come back to our rooms, and I will read you a bedtime story to take them away.'

'Thank you.' Armand was touched by the boy's insight and compassion. He couldn't very well tell Nicolas that Angelique's disclosure had shocked him; or that what had shocked him even more was that he, Armand, cared.

§

They came home to France on the *Olympic*, as always. Nicolas was quite used to sea travel by now, having toured the world, singing with his mother from the time he was three. He turned to his tutor as they sailed out of New York harbour. 'I love the *Olympic*. Do not you, Armand?'

'Yes, she's a grand old lady. Showing her age a little now, of course.'

'Armand? Is ... is that why you seemed troubled last night.' The boy hesitated, took a deep breath and rushed on: 'Are you worried that, perhaps, we cannot pay you?'

'No, no, of course not!' A tiny smile lightened the tutor's rather grim expression. 'What questions you do ask, Nicolas. Why would I be worried about something like that?'

'This morning, I heard a lady ask Mama why she still sailed on the *Olympic* when the *Île de France* was now all the fashion for those who could afford it. And do you know what she said, Armand?'

'No, what did she say?'

'She said, "But, Madame, that is *exactly* why!"' Anxious eyes studied the tutor's wan face. 'What did she mean, Armand? Can we not afford it, do you think?'

'Oh, I wouldn't think that would be the case, at all,' said Armand, thinking of packed houses and the dock full of waving fans. 'No, no, remember what your papa told you? Your mama needs to rest after her performances. Surely, you saw how tired she was this morning?'

'Yes.' Nicolas mulled this over. Relief sprang into the sombre blue eyes. 'Oh, I *see*. You mean, she would have to be social when she wants to sleep?'

'That is exactly what I mean, so there is no need to worry. And now,' Armand looked at his watch, 'I am going to get a book, sit in a deckchair and read in the sun.'

'*Bon.*' Nicolas, his fears relieved, stood at the rail on the promenade deck, contemplating the ocean. Water, as far as he could see ... It could become boring, he supposed, such an expanse, except that it was always heaving and moving like a living creature. Who knew what lurked beneath the surface? It had always attracted him and continued to do so. But there was one thing that endlessly fascinated him that he'd pondered often from his earliest voyage: what made the wake that boiled out from under the ship, spreading out behind it like a highway?

Nicolas had asked his father.

'It's the turbines,' he said.

'What is a turbine?' countered Nicolas. 'And, please, don't say an engine. I know it is not an engine.'

'I think you know more than I do, *mon fils*. Perhaps I mean propellers? Yes, the propellers beat the water and move the ship along.'

'But how, Papa? How do they do that?'

'Oh, my son,' laughed Etienne. 'I am not an engineer. Perhaps you should ask Armand.' With a shrug of the shoulders, he walked away.

*How does beating the water into foam propel the ship?* Nicolas thought that if he could just see them, these propellers, perhaps he would understand what they did.

He took a quick glance around the deck. His mother was lying on a chaise longue in the sun with her eyes closed. She had on becoming white lounging pyjamas with a halter top. He watched her for a moment. It was true that Mama was always so exhausted at the end of a tour. As Armand had reminded him, Papa said she used this time on the ship to recuperate and must not be disturbed.

Nicolas didn't know why his father fussed so over Mama. When they sang together, she was good fun, lit with an inner glow after each recital. She appeared to have boundless energy until the tour was over. Then she just seemed to collapse.

'Mama lives on her nerves,' explained his father. 'That is why we must take the greatest care of her.'

Nicolas looked at his mother carefully. Yes, she was asleep. His eyes sought his tutor. *Good.* Armand had his head in a book, as usual, when he was at leisure. His gaze swivelled the other way. Papa was leaning on a bollard, paring a broken fingernail. Nicolas made a split-second decision. Now was as good a time as any to see what he wanted to see.

Leaping for the rail, Nicolas heaved himself on to it and leant over, grinning at his mother's frantic scream.

'Etienne, Etienne, look! He will fall! No, no! God save my baby!'

*Baby? I am not a baby!* He wriggled farther, craning to see … *No, just a little farther* … Then both hands slipped. He was falling, grasping wildly at nothing. Suddenly, he felt a broad chest against his shoulder, taking his weight, easing him back. Invisible hands grasped his—guided them to the rail—held them there until he got his bearings. Angel had come to his rescue, as always. His fright evaporated. He was fine. *Now, to see …*

Two arms went round him from behind. 'Careful, my son,' murmured his father, depositing him on the deck. 'We don't want to lose you …'

'Oh, Papa! Why did you do that? I was quite safe ——'

'*Tiens!* You were safe? I would hate to see you in danger, then!'

'I only wanted to see the ocean. How it ——'

'You can see it with both feet on the deck, can you not? It is all around.'

'No, I meant coming out from *under* the ship. The propellers.'

'You must not upset your mother, my son. *Les femmes,* they worry when they see their children dangling over the ship's rail. Why it should be …?'

Nicolas chuckled.

'You can laugh.' His father put a loving hand on his shoulder. 'Do not forget your mother's nerves.'

Instantly, Nicolas was remorseful. 'I am sorry, Papa.' He ran to hug his mother. 'Dearest Mama, I did not mean to distress you.'

'I know.' She wrapped her arms around him. '*Mon petit ange* is a little thoughtless. Also, a little devil, I fear.' Since she alleviated this accusation with a kiss on his brow, Nicolas was unworried. 'You will go with Armand while I have my sleep in the sun. I cannot rest if I am thinking about you falling into the ocean.' With another hug, she put him away. 'Armand, *ici!*'

'You called, Madame?' Armand snapped shut his book and rose; his pale cheeks tinged with pink.

'Yes. You must take your pupil in hand. He is endangering his life because, *if you please*, he wants to know what happens to the water beneath the ship!'

'Aha! The young genius!' Armand beamed. 'Always wanting to find out things.' He was genuinely enthused by the intellectual prowess of his pupil. 'But he does not need to endanger his life to do so.' He bowed to Angelique. 'Pray excuse us, Madame. Come with me, young man. We will do a scientific study of how ships move in the ocean. Also, we may well inform ourselves of the finer definitions of a propeller and a turbine.' He put an arm around Nicolas's shoulders and began to walk him away. 'What would you say if I told you that in my cabin is a big picture book, some balsawood and a fretsaw? We will make our very own *Olympic* and float it in the pool. Then you will see …'

'Oh, yes!' cried Nicolas, skipping ahead. 'Yes, yes, yes!'

*Thank God for Armand,* thought Angelique, smiling at these antics, *always getting into the spirit of things. Nicolas will be safe with him.* 'Armand, you are an angel! Positively!' she called after him. Watching her son's eccentric progress through the palm court, she did not see Armand redden at the gushing compliment. Angelique sighed and rolled over, calling Etienne to rub sweet-smelling coconut oil into her back and shoulders.

§

Armand glanced around his spacious cabin. He could

not fault his employers for generosity, even though they were inclined to leave Nicolas with him unless they were either on stage or about to go on. It seemed that they found their son exhausting. He looked at the young boy. Even from here he could feel his energy and vitality. He pointed. 'Over there: the smaller trunk.'

Going to stand beside his pupil, he indicated the necessary items. Only once did he mention the cause of this diversion. 'You are not usually heedless of your safety, *mon brave*, and you are far from stupid. Why did you do it?'

'Do what?'

'Come, now! You know.'

Nicolas grinned. 'I wanted to know how propellers work. Can you keep a secret, Armand?'

The tutor suppressed a groan, avoiding the bright, questioning gaze. 'That doesn't explain your reckless behaviour. I suppose you wanted your mother's attention?'

Nicolas considered him, briefly. His mother's attention was just what he hadn't wanted. He shook his head. 'Guess again.'

'Pass me that book ... No, not that one, the other ... Right. It is in here, somewhere ...'

'Don't you want to know, Armand?'

'If you wish to tell me: yes, I do. But not if you want to play silly games.'

'You're in a mood, aren't you?'

The tutor raised his head. Grey eyes clashed with blue.

'Very well.' Nicolas capitulated. 'Have you ever had a secret friend, Armand?'

Armand blushed.

'Why, what did I say?'

'Nothing. Go on ...'

'*Have* you?'

'An imaginary friend as a small child, do you mean? I expect I did.'

'Don't you remember?'

'No.'

'I have a secret friend. I've had him *depuis longtemps*—as long as I can remember. But he is not imaginary. He is real!'

'Ah ...'

'His name is Angel. He tells me things and ...' Nicolas paused for effect. 'He rescues me whenever I am in danger!'

The tutor blanched. 'You are *not* serious!'

'*Oui,* I am. He saved me when my hands slipped off the rail today.'

'I saw no-one but your father. He was the one who rushed to your aid.'

'Silly! Angel is invisible.'

'Oh ... And you think he will rescue you whenever you put yourself in mortal danger?'

'*Oui,* he will. He has promised.' The statement was quiet, assured.

'It is a dangerous theory, *mon brave.* I would not put it to the test too often if I were you.'

Nicolas flicked him a glance, then began to read, '*RMS Olympic.* Scale model dimensions ...'

# 2 SCANDAL

**Four thirty am, 25 August 1930**

*Today the ship docks, and we return to Paris. I must, must convince Father to cancel the publication of Madame Dupont's diaries. If I cannot, my heart trembles at my fate. I think of glorious amethyst eyes: how it would slay me if they looked upon me with reproach or reproof.*

The ship docked at Cherbourg in the early hours. Nicolas, half-asleep, was shepherded by Armand down the gangway and across the pier, avoiding the sudden crowd: families reuniting; porters with great trolleys of luggage. Very soon, they found themselves in their private carriage on the *New York Express* to Paris.

Armand took Nicolas to their compartment and settled him in the top bunk where he went straight to sleep. The tutor flung himself down on the lower one, returning to the problem that had scarified his emotions since their last evening in New York. *I cannot bear to hurt her!* 'Angelique …' he whispered the name with hopeless longing, closing his eyes on the vision: her long, golden hair; her alluring scent; her willowy beauty; her glorious smile; her voice: to die for.

There was no getting away from it: he'd always known his father meant to publish the diaries of Madame Dupont. How could he have acquiesced in such infamy?

He felt guilty, smirched: as if he were the worst traitor. The duc, so gentle and dignified; the marquis, a quiet wall of strength; his heroine, fragile and nervy; Nicolas, bright and confident: Armand knew that they would be shattered by this. Nothing would ever be the same for them. *Do we have the right?* he asked himself.

For the first time, he thought of the reasons behind his father's suggestion of a name change. Armand was certain to be dismissed if his real name were known. He clenched his fists. If only he could get to Paris in time to stop publication, convince his father that it would hurt too many people to be justified. No-one could know the ferment that raged behind the scholarly brow; the pale, austere expression.

Suddenly, he knew it was not just Angelique he loved, but all of them.

The automobile ride from the Gare Saint-Lazare seemed to be unconscionably slow. When they reached their apartments in the hôtel du Bois, Armand begged leave to make an urgent visit to his father.

'Of course,' said Etienne. 'You have been away a long time. You must take a week to yourself.'

'*Merci*, Monsieur, but a day or two will suffice.'

'Nonsense! You have devoted all your time to Nicolas. If you are not exhausted, then you should be. There will be no argument: you must take a week.'

Armand's conscience flayed him at his employer's generosity.

§

The duc greeted his family lovingly. He was thin and looked distraught, as Angelique noticed. 'But, Papa-duc: what have you been doing to yourself? You look all-in!'

'Do I, my child? Well, that is no wonder. You see, I have received a great shock. You and Etienne must prepare for one, also.'

Etienne moved to hold Angelique firmly in his arms. 'What is it, Papa?'

'These.' The duc picked up a set of three red leather-bound volumes. 'We're all in them: you, me, the marquis du Bois, La Belle …' His voice softened for an instant, then sharpened again. 'Even Nicolas! The scandal will encompass us all!'

'Scandal?' asked Angelique, bewildered. 'What scandal?'

'One that should have been forgotten, but for the unscrupulous theft of Madame Dupont's diaries!'

'Godmama's diaries? Why? Whatever can be in them?'

'Don't …' said Etienne, looking at his father's face.

Angelique moved to free herself from his suddenly tightened embrace. 'Monsieur Bernaud's son, François, came to see me the day I returned from our tour … after Godmama died. He was asking about her diaries. It seems her instructions were that they be taken from her drawer and placed with her in the Dupont vault.' She wrung her hands; her face reflecting the duc's grief. 'I took him to her room—it was so lonely there …' The beautiful eyes filled with sudden tears. She took a moment to go on. 'And … showed him the drawer where she kept them. But it was empty. We searched the whole house and did not find them. And so, we could not …'

The duc ran his fingers over the tooled leather. 'This was the last thing Ma Belle … Madame Dupont would have wanted: to hurt us. She ———'

'When did you get them, Papa?' Etienne interrupted the melancholy speech.

'Yesterday,' said the duc. 'Your sister, Elise, sent them to me from our Embassy in London. She said that some kind acquaintance had given them to her, saying that our family should know what is being bandied about in all the salons about us! I read it last night. Which is why I look so tired, probably.'

'I see,' said Etienne. 'No hope of stopping it, then?'

'No. I have tried. It is too late.'

Angelique picked up a volume. '*The Diaries of Madame Dupont*. Author unknown,' she read. 'Anonymous? But who could it be? Someone who knew Godmama? Well enough to know where she kept her diaries? A servant, perhaps?'

'No,' said Etienne. 'All the servants were loyal. They would never have ———'

'*Vive* La Reine!' muttered Nicolas, hunching over a semiquaver he was forming on a music scoresheet.

The duc spun around. '*What* did you say?'

'*Vive* ... La Reine ...' he faltered, looking from one shocked face to another.

'Why?' asked his father in a soft voice.

Nicolas shrugged. 'I don't know. When Mama asked who could have written the book, it just popped into my head; so, I said it. Have I done something wrong?'

'No, no, my angel!' Angelique smoothed his hair. 'We forgot you were here, so quiet as you were. Go along to the piano, now, for your practice.'

'Cèline: the Countess Kireyevsky, of course!' said the duc, clapping a hand to his brow. 'There is no-one else who would do it! In her heyday as a ballerina, she was called "The Queen of Dance", La Reine, for short. Though, how the child knew ...?'

Nicolas lingered just beyond the doorway, sneaking back in when he saw he'd been forgotten by his mother. She was staring at his grand-père. 'When François Bernaud asked the countess if she had them, she said she knew nothing about them. She also said that they were hers by right, since she was Godmama's only child; and if they were found, she wanted them. François said, "No: If they were found, they were to be placed in Godmama's casket, as per the instructions in her will."'

'And what did Cèline say to that?'

'She just smiled nastily and said that it was just as well

that they were missing, then.' Angelique's eyes clouded with puzzlement. 'I couldn't make her out, at all … Oh, and she said to ask the nurses. But when François finally tracked one of them down, Nurse Jacques said the other, Nurse LeFevre, had given Madame's diaries to her daughter. When he took it up with the countess, *she* said the nurses were lying and it was obvious that they had stolen them.'

'I cannot see the nurses doing it,' said Etienne, rubbing his chin.

'*Non, bien sûr,*' agreed the duc. 'They were good women.' He thought it over. 'No, on balance, if one had to decide who the liar was, it would have to be Cèline.'

'But would she not honour her mother's wishes?' asked Angelique.

'She never did, that I knew of.'

'Why would she do such a thing?'

The duc lifted a shoulder. 'For money or spite. Or both. Her life was governed by greed and malice. It was apparent, even from her childhood. She hated your guardian, my child.'

'But … Why?'

'Jealousy, perhaps? A form of insanity? She took after her father, in that respect.'

'Her father?' queried Etienne. 'You're not saying Monsieur Dupont …?'

'No. She was not Monsieur Dupont's child.' The duc tapped a volume. 'It is all in here. She even admits to attempted murder. The child of a murderer. La Belle was … *raped,*' he whispered the word.

'I know. Angelpapa told me,' said Angelique. 'Poor Godmama.'

'In that case,' said Etienne. 'Won't it be as bad for Cèline as it is for us?'

'Yes, Papa-duc: why would she allow that to come out?'

'I don't know. But, I believe, to court notoriety; the

way a mass murderer tries to admit to more killings than he actually does. She may also wish it to be known that she is the daughter of a prince. *And,*' he added dryly, 'it will bring publicity to the Opéra Magique. The more people come to sightsee and indulge their curiosity, the more money it will make.'

'And, perhaps,' said Etienne, 'there is a psychological factor: no-one will point the finger at her as the author, reasoning that she would be the last person to want the diaries published.'

'I should never have agreed to her taking over the management of the theatre when Godmama's staff retired!'

'You had little choice in the matter, my love, since we were still in America. It was a crisis, and the countess stepped in. We were grateful enough at the time. And the Opéra Magique is doing well under her management.'

'Yes, her reforms have brought full houses,' said the duc, with a frown. 'There is no doubt of that. But lately, I have heard it whispered that she went after the old management with a hatchet, so to speak, making it so difficult for them that they had to resign.'

'Do you mean that they did not retire voluntarily, due to age and ill-health, as we thought?' gasped Angelique. 'You are saying that they were forced into it by the countess?'

'*Oui.* My information is that her demands were intolerable. They did try to withstand her but eventually gave in. Some ulterior motive there must be, but I don't quite see it yet.'

'Control,' said Etienne. 'The woman must be a megalomaniac!'

'Oh, poor dear Mathilde, Monsieur Merignac and Jeanne! Something must be done for them, at once! If only I'd known!' Angelique's eyes flashed. 'I have a good mind never to sing there again! She is a harpy and a thief! A criminal!'

'I understand your loyalty to Madame Dupont's old retainers, my dear love. And we will do something for them, never fear. I will set it in motion before the day is out; I promise you. But you are making the wrong decision.'

'Why? You don't, *surely*, think we should allow her to get away with this, do you?' demanded Angelique.

'I think the scandal will be forgotten a lot faster if we all put a brave face on it and go on as usual.'

'You're right,' agreed the duc. He addressed his daughter-in-law: 'The Opéra Magique is half-yours, my dear. You can have as much say as Cèline.'

'Yes,' affirmed Etienne. 'And perhaps we should look into the question of its management more closely when we have time; although, she does seem to be quite efficient. But we have bookings for recitals to honour. It is your fans we should be thinking of, not the Countess Kireyevsky! Besides, we cannot prove she did this.'

'We just know,' murmured Nicolas, inscribing a neat fanfare on his scoresheet.

'Oh!' Angelique swooped. 'Give me that! I sent you to practise at the piano.'

'Mama?' The big blue eyes were sad, entreating. 'I miss Armand ... When will he come back?'

But, for once, his mother stood firm. 'In a week. Go, now!'

§

Armand greeted his father with an expression of doom.

'Why the long face? Has the world ended?'

'Not yet, but I think it is about to. For me, at any rate.' He took a deep breath and squared his shoulders. 'Father, I have come to beg you not to publish those manuscripts based on the diaries of Madame Dupont.'

'What?'

'Please, Father! Madame Dupont was the godmother of my employer's wife: she even reared her! Angelique, the marquise de Beaulieu—she will be distraught—her nerves are not strong. You do not know ...'

'What *are* you rambling on about?'

'The great diva: Angelique! The Angel of Song! Of course, you know who I am talking about! She is magnificent! She ——' He stopped for breath.

'Ah, now I understand!' Monsieur Delaine regarded this unusual animation in his son with a rueful eye. 'You have fallen in love, *mon fils*?'

Armand's colour rose. 'And what if I have?'

'I am sorry for you.'

'You need not be! To serve her is all I ask.'

'Ah, my son ... I have read of such devotion.' The publisher scratched his top lip with a forefinger. 'And quite recently, too.'

Armand grasped his father's hands. '*Mon père*, you must listen to me! These manuscripts: they must not be published. They must *not!*'

'My son, you are too late. It has already been done. Everyone who is anyone in Paris has bought them.'

'No! Why did you not wait for my contribution? Why did you break your schedule?'

The publisher's lips tightened. 'Because, unlike you, I don't live with my head in the clouds! Times are hard. I couldn't afford not to.' He viewed his son's distraught appearance with compassion. 'I am sorry. It was a difficult decision, but one that had to be made. You see, if the house of Delaine is to survive, something had to be done, and quickly. That is why I couldn't wait.' He jingled the coins in his pocket. 'The diaries were a windfall in that respect.'

Armand tore his hair. 'Survive? *Survive?* If it is a matter of survival ...?' He controlled himself with an effort, whispering, 'So, for the house of Delaine to survive, it is fitting that we destroy the house of de Beaulieu?' He flung himself blindly around the room. 'Let it not be!' he shouted. In that moment, he was so consumed with revulsion that he decided to keep the name Lemaitre.

'*Mon fils*, control yourself! I did what I had to do. It is done and cannot be undone.'

Armand sank into an armchair in misery. 'I would rather die myself than distress that beautiful angel.'

'Melodramatic nonsense!' snapped his father. 'Here! Read them for yourself and then tell me they should not have been published. *If* you dare!' He threw the volumes at him and strode out, as angry at the pricking of his own conscience as at the theatrics of his son.

# 3 DISMISSAL

*Time is running out. How shall I face these people I love? As a traitor? God forbid! Yet, I do not see myself as a hero—even an anonymous one.*

'So, Madame: you are satisfied with Lanvin's vision for you, as faithfully transcribed by me?' Madame Minette, one of a team of sketchers employed by the great designer Lanvin, touched the elegant creation on the sketchblock reverently.

'Oh, yes! It is perfection, Madame. I cannot wait to see it made up!' Angelique looked up, startled, as Nicolas bounced into the room.

'Mama!' He stopped, executing a bow that delighted her visitor. 'Oh, I do beg your pardon, Madame Minette! I am sorry, Mama, I did not know you were busy!'

'It is perfectly all right, my dear one. We are almost finished. What is it?'

'I have had my piano lesson, and Monsieur Merignac wants to take me to the Bibliothèque-Musée de l'Opéra. May we have the car, Mama, *s'il vous plaît?*'

'Of course, Petit. Mary is over in the hospice with her husband. Tell her I said you may go.'

'*Bien! Merci*, Mama.' He turned a friendly gaze on the sketcher from Lanvin. 'Our chauffeur is a lady. Have you

25

ever heard of that, Madame?'

'*Never*, Monsieur! You are *très avant-garde, n'est-ce pas?*' said the woman; her eyes twinkling. 'Do you like this gown your mama has chosen to wear when she sings with you? She will look beautiful, *hein?*'

Nicolas came forward to cast a critical eye over the flowing creation with Lanvin's signature embroidery: in this instance, stylised roses cascading from the shoulder and repeated from the waistline down one side and across the front of the dress. 'The material?' he asked.

'White silk,' replied Madame Minette, hugely entertained. 'You approve?'

'Mmm! And the embroidery?'

'Seed pearls, crystals and silver thread. What do you think?'

'*Épatante!* But Mama always looks beautiful.'

His mother laughed. 'Little flatterer! Go along now. And mind you don't tire Monsieur Merignac. Not too much standing, *hein?*'

'No, Mama. Monsieur Merignac is …' Nicolas threw wide his arms. 'Oh, *ancien!*' At the couturière's chuckle, he sent his mother a speculative glance. 'I *do* miss Armand!'

Angelique made a shooing gesture and he ran out.

'What a beautiful child! So full of spirit and *espièglerie!* You are to be congratulated, Madame. No wonder he is so popular with audiences.'

'He is wonderful! But such a *handful* without Armand.'

'You've let him go then?'

'What? Who?'

'Armand Delaine: You've dismissed him? I thought you would. It was only to be expected.'

'I'm sorry? I don't know anyone called Armand Delaine.'

'Your child's tutor. Your secretary.'

'Oh, Armand!' Angelique laughed. 'Armand Lemaitre, you mean? No, no, he is on holiday. We will be glad to have him back. Nicolas asks after him every day.'

Madame Minette pursed her lips; she seemed to consider before she spoke. 'Madame, normally I would not say this, but you are too long-standing and valued a client for me to pass over it. I am sorry to have to tell you this, but that young man has been deceiving you … One sees why, of course.'

'Armand has been deceiving us? But why?'

'He is the son of … *the* publisher. You know …' Madame Minette paused delicately.

'No!' Angelique turned quite pale; her hand going to her exquisitely draped neckline. So, not only had her couturière read the book, but Armand was a traitor, insinuating himself into their lives to spy on them. It was too much. She began to fight for breath.

'Madame, I am sorry. What can I do?'

'Smelling … salts,' gasped Angelique. 'In … that drawer … over there.'

'Here,' said Madame Minette, regretting that she had spoken. If Lanvin ever heard of this indiscretion, it would be the end of her career. 'Try to take deep breaths, Madame. In a moment, I will ring for your maid.'

'No.' Angelique inhaled deeply and waved a hand. 'I am feeling better now.' She visibly pulled herself together, smiling at her visitor. 'Thank you for your help, Madame. I am sorry ——'

'No, no. I am the one who is sorry, believe me. But I thought you should know …'

'Yes, indeed, Madame, and I am grateful. You may tell Lanvin that I am thrilled with her design. I look forward to the fitting.'

Madame Minette took the hint and left, wearing a very troubled expression.

Angelique waited only until the front door closed behind the woman before voicing her distress: 'Etienne! *Etienne*! Oh, someone *find* him for me!'

'*Doucement*, Madame.' Justin, the butler, appeared silently. 'I have sent the groom with a message for

Monsieur le marquis. He will not be long delayed. A small dose of your nerve tonic, Madame? I have it here. I have sent for your maid, also.'

'Thank you.' Angelique sank into an armchair and drank the cordial; her chest heaving. The knowledge that Armand—on whom she relied so heavily to care for Nicolas and smooth over the difficulties that accompanied fame—had lied and betrayed them was enough to starve her of air whenever she thought about it. Her fingers convulsed on the bottle of smelling salts.

Her maid hurried in. 'I am so sorry, Madame. I went to get your new *parfum*, *Joy* by Monsieur Patou, while you were with Madame Minette; and I had to wait and wait. Shall I take you up to your boudoir? Do you wish to try it?'

'No.' Angelique waved dismissal. 'I will wait … here.' She turned as the door opened. 'Etienne?'

The marquis strode swiftly to her side. 'What is it, my love?'

'Oh, Etienne, I cannot, *cannot* believe it!'

'Cannot believe what, *Chérie*?'

'I cannot believe that Armand is a traitor!'

'Armand a traitor? What nonsense is this? Come now, you are working yourself up for nothing, my darling.'

'No.' She clung to his hands and told him what Madame Minette had said to her.

He was silent, gripping her fingers, staring out the window, a rigid set to his lips. He looked at her. 'You know what this means, don't you?'

'But Nicolas is so attached to him!'

'All the more reason to let him go.'

'But *poor* Nicolas!'

'We will just have to make sure we spend more time with him.'

She didn't quite meet his eyes. Her love for Nicolas was as strong as ever. It was just that he was *so* tiring.

§

Upon Armand's return, the butler met him, expressionless. 'Monsieur le marquis wishes to see you in his study, Monsieur. Immediately.'

'Yes, thank you, Justin.' Armand wondered if it were possible to feel any more wretched than he did already. Sooner than he wanted, he faced the study door. He knocked and was bidden to enter.

'Ah, Armand ...' The quiet tones of the marquis de Beaulieu were oddly intimidating. 'Just the person to answer a question that has been bothering me. Before we go any further, I will ask it of you: is your name Lemaitre or is it Delaine?'

Armand's breath caught in his throat. He flushed to the roots of his hair. 'It was Delaine, Monsieur, but it is now Lemaitre. *Je regrette* ...'

'So do I.'

'Believe me, Monsieur, I tried to stop it. I would not, for the *world* ... It was why I asked for leave. But I was too late, the book had already been published. I beg your forgiveness and that of Madame la marquise ...'

'It is possibly too late for that, also,' murmured Etienne.

Armand ducked his head. 'Yes.' His throat worked. 'I must tender my resignation, Monsieur.'

'You have a month's wages owing.'

'No! I cannot take your money! Pardon, Monsieur.' He swallowed. 'I am desolated to have hurt your family. Those I love ——' He stopped abruptly, gasped, *'Adieu,'* and bounded for the door.

The marquis sighed and went out after him.

# 4 LEFT BEHIND

**1 September 1930**

*My father should be pleased: our coffers are overflowing. I feel we are vultures, feeding off misery. How can I live without her, my Diva? And Nicolas? How shall I survive without these beautiful people? I saw in the newspapers that they are going on tour, to England, this time. How I wish I could turn back the clock and be with them!*

The duc retreated to his château in Provence to escape the interrupted conversations in the salons; the sudden silences whenever he came within earshot. He spent much of his time behind the locked door of his study.

Etienne, Angelique and Nicolas honoured the first of their obligations to perform at the Opéra Magique, but when Nicolas came down with a sore throat they cancelled the other two and followed the duc to Belvoir. Anxiety over their son made them put off their decision to question the countess about her role in the resignation of the theatre staff. Had they been party to the furious tirade the cancellations brought down over the head of the unfortunate count and anyone unlucky or unwise enough to step into the path of the countess, they may have rethought their priority.

'We will take a short break before our tour of England,' said Etienne. 'It will be good for Nicolas to play with the village children.'

'I should go with you to England,' said the duc. 'It is a long time since I saw my cousin and friend, King George. He is not well, I believe.'

'Yes, do come, Papa-duc. There will be plenty of room for you.'

'Thank you, my dear. We will see.'

Nicolas grew well and spent his time outdoors with the children of Belvoir village until the day an outbreak of measles was reported. After this he was confined to the château, watched anxiously by his mother.

'I miss Armand,' he said. 'When will he come back?'

'Something has come up,' said his mother. 'He is too busy to return to us.' She shrugged. 'I am afraid we must do without him.'

All was going to plan until a few days before they were due to depart. Nicolas developed a dry cough but was otherwise well. On the morning of departure, he woke up with a headache and a temperature. He refused to get up when his mother came to call him. 'Mama, I feel too sick to travel,' he complained.

'Look at you!' she cried. 'Covered in spots! Oh, Nicolas, you have the *measles*!'

'He'll have to be quarantined,' said his father. 'We will have to leave you behind, my son.'

'Can you not wait for me to get better?'

'Sadly, no. We have engagements in a few days.'

'Perhaps I can come, then, and stay in the hotel with Grand-père until the spots go?'

'Oh, my darling,' said Angelique. 'You cannot come with us.' With a sudden inspiration, she took off her locket, slipping the chain over his head. 'There,' she said. 'You will wear my Angelpapa's locket until I come back. It contains one of your grandmamma's curls. Yes: Katarina, but you must not call her that! I wear it in memory of the love my Angelpapa had for me; just the same love that I have for you. You will wear it until I come back, and each time you touch it, you will remember that I love you … Oh, so much.' She put a cool hand on his forehead and smoothed his black locks. 'Do not despair. The time will pass quickly.'

'I will miss you and Papa.'

'I know. We will miss you, too.'

'It would help if I could have Armand.'

His parents looked at each other helplessly.

'Be brave, *mon fils*,' said Etienne. 'You don't want Armand to catch the measles. We won't be away long.'

When the duc heard what had happened, he said, 'Never mind, Nicolas. I will stay here with you. It is up to you and I to hold the fort, eh?'

After a week of misery, Nicolas began to feel better. He went to stand before his favourite portrait in the picture gallery, his hand clasping the locket: the little forget-me-nots with their sapphire centres and diamond leaves pressing into his fingers. 'Grandmamma: Katarina,' he murmured. Suddenly, he remembered his secret friend. 'Angel,' he said, concentrating hard, but there was no invisible presence beside him when he said the name. It seemed that everybody had left him.

A tread on the stairs roused Nicolas's curiosity, and he ran to look over the gallery railing. It was his grandfather, on his daily journey to his private sanctum. Nicolas followed. He'd often done so but had never made it past the locked study door. This time it hadn't latched properly, and Nicolas eased it open and slipped in.

The boy ducked down behind the ornate desk to watch the duc press the centre of a carved lotus flower on the bookcase. He almost gave himself away with a gasp of astonishment as the wall of books slid away to reveal another room. When the duc went inside, the bookcase slid back. Nicolas moved to lie down behind the sofa and wait.

After what seemed forever, the aperture opened silently, the duc crossed the room and went out. Nicolas heard the key turn in the lock. Now, what? Faced with the prospect of being incarcerated until the duc returned, perhaps in a day or two, he was taken aback. But the lure of the secret room and the prospect of adventure suppressed his fear.

His heart thumped, and the blood sang in his ears as he reached for the flower centre his grandfather had pressed. He sprang over the threshold, and the bookcase slid back behind him. But he didn't notice, fascinated by the full-length portrait of a ballerina. *Belle, she is belle,* he thought, examining the delicate features, the perfection of her attitude. Yet, deep within himself, he was certain that this exquisite creature was the sweet lady known to him as Godmama. And, young as he was, he knew that the glorious ballerina depicted in the portrait was his grandfather's secret love.

Nicolas didn't question these things but made his way around the tower room, taking in everything with his bright, inquisitive gaze. 'La Belle,' he read in a newspaper clipping preserved under glass. So Godmama had been famous like him and Mama: *épatante!* Strange that she had never given him any inkling of it. He climbed the spiral staircase a little way, viewing walls full of sketches. He approved them, knowing without question that they had been done by his grandfather.

Suddenly, loneliness surged over him; he felt frightened, overwhelmed. *Angel, Angel, where are you?* he cried in his mind. *Angel, you promised!* But no comforting, invisible presence came to him.

'I want Mama,' he whimpered, clasping the locket so that it hurt his hand. He went to stand before the portrait to try to dispel the coldness, the loneliness, but it was no use. *How beautiful was Godmama,* he thought and began to cry.

'So, there you are,' said a voice behind him. 'I have been looking for you.'

'Oh, Grand-père. I am sorry ...' Nicolas sobbed.

'There, there …' The duc put an arm around him. 'You are lucky that I left my spectacles behind; otherwise, I may not have thought to come here. There they are, over on that display table.'

Nicolas disengaged himself to fetch them, thankful that his grandfather did not seem angry or reproachful.

'Thank you, *mon fils*.' The duc pocketed them and steered him towards the opening. 'Come, let us go to luncheon. Then, perhaps, we will take a ride around the estate, *hein*?'

Nicolas looked at his grandfather with love and gratitude. He knew without being told that he had discovered something that the duc would prefer to keep a secret, yet he asked nothing. With an innate integrity and sensitivity beyond his years, the boy determined, then and there, that he would never reveal the duc's secret; never go back into the tower room unless he was invited.

§

Etienne and Angelique, though missing Nicolas, decided to look on this tour as a second honeymoon. They had not been away alone together for over seven years.

After Angelique's recital at the Royal Albert Hall, the King held a reception for them. 'Meet Sir Sefton Brancker, Director of Civil Aviation, and Lord Thomson, my Air Minister, both great fans of yours, Madame.'

Angelique bowed and thanked them. Etienne shook hands.

'These gentlemen are about to make aviation history,' continued the King, 'we are soon to launch a luxury passenger liner of the skies. I think your guardian would have approved, Madame.'

'The marquis du Bois designed an airship, I think.' remarked Etienne.

'Oh, all manner of mechanical inventions,' replied

Angelique. 'He probably did.'

The King smiled. 'I wonder what he would think of our R101?' He glanced at Lord Thomson; a quizzical gleam in his eye. 'Could we?'

'Oh, most certainly! We shall be honoured. There is plenty of room, you know.'

King George turned to Angelique. 'How would you feel about a trip to Karachi on our airship's maiden voyage? Perhaps we could arrange for you to sing to the viceroy?'

'Your Majesty is inspired!' exclaimed Sir Sefton. 'Irwin will be charmed, utterly charmed. It will give him something else to think about besides Gandhi!'

Everyone laughed, except Thomson. Anglo-Indian relations were giving him a headache at the moment. Etienne and Angelique looked at each other. Their hosts waited in expectant silence.

'How stupendous,' said Angelique, with her glorious smile, 'to be a part of history! I should adore it.'

'Then that is settled,' said Etienne. 'Thank you very much, gentlemen.'

§

'It is such a shame Nicolas could not come with us,' said Angelique, viewing grey skies and the panorama below from the promenade deck of the airship. 'He would love this!'

'Yes, a pity, indeed. Never mind, there will be other times.' Etienne ushered her to a striped canvas deckchair and stretched out in the one beside her. 'How tiny the people look from up here! How small is the world! This is a most impressive way to travel. I could become used to it—very quickly.'

'Yes. So beautiful and so quiet! Almost angelic! Here in the clouds, away from the bustle of the world. Perhaps it would become boring for Nicolas?'

'I don't think so,' Etienne smiled. 'Without doubt, he would be down with the engineers, finding out how it moves through the air!'

'Too true!' Her laughter pealed out.

'Even your laughter is musical, Madame,' said Lord Thomson, coming up silently. 'May I invite you both to dine with us?' He presented his arm. In the white and gold dining room, he appeared to take great pleasure in pointing out the use of aluminium cutlery and wicker furniture to reduce the weight for lift. 'Lift,' he added, with a rueful smile. 'The word has given us nightmares! But not any more, I am happy to say!' He looked around with pride.

They retired to the airy lounge for coffee and conversation. Angelique sang them her latest song and a couple of old favourites before Lord Thomson called a halt. 'You are too good, Madame,' he told her. 'We must not impose on your generosity any longer. Let us have a nightcap.' He signalled to a waiter with a tray of drinks. When they had been served, he said, 'There is some bad weather at the moment, but I do not want you to worry. There may be some rolling …' he shrugged.

'Like a ship in heavy seas?' suggested Angelique.

'Something like that, Madame, though not nearly as bad. She may dive a little or rise due to air currents. She is built for it: very strong and sturdy. My engineers have it all under control.' He finished his drink and rose. 'I am so little worried by it that I am going to bed. Tomorrow—today, I should say—ought to be fine and fair. I beg you will excuse me.'

'We are the last up,' said Etienne, when the air minister had gone. 'Everyone has retired for the night.'

'Let's take a stroll on the promenade deck and watch the storm.'

'Very well,' said Etienne, falling into step and tucking his arm around her. 'How awe-inspiring!' he gasped at a brilliant lightning display.

'Yes,' she whispered, nestling into his body. 'Simply amazing!'

After a while, he said, 'I think we should retire now.'

'I don't feel sleepy.'

'No? We are so used to late nights, I suppose.' He bent to kiss her earlobe. 'There are other reasons for going to bed …'

'So there are! I had almost forgotten!' Mischief edged her smile. 'We need a bottle of champagne to set the mood … and grapes and canapés. But of course, we are beginning with this romantic stroll in the heavens.'

'Siren!' He pulled her to him. They kissed deeply. 'I don't need anything to set *my* mood—only you!'

Her lips curved tenderly, but she protested, 'No, no! The proper sequence! We must have our wine and grapes.'

'Oh? An orgy? I see!'

'Silly!' Her eyes gleamed with secret promises.

'When I have all these things organised for your pleasure, my dearest love, I shall return to claim you …' He added, in a melodramatic whisper, 'In the best operatic tradition!'

'*En avant, mon chevalier.* My heart pines …' She erupted into delicious laughter, then became serious. 'It is true, what I just said. Oh, Etienne …' Her lips sought his. They were silent, locked together in their own delightful world.

'I love you more than life itself.' He tightened his hold, suddenly overcome. 'To be with you for all eternity. That is all I wish for.'

'All?' Tender laughter infused the question. She held his face between her hands. '*All?*'

'It is a lot to ask, *bien sûr*! But you are right, my wicked one. Tonight, I wish for something else! Back soon!' He kissed her again and strode away.

Her eyes followed his tall, slender figure, then turned back to the storm. *Love with Etienne*, she thought, *calm and protective like this airship; erupting into splendour like the storm; moments of exquisite pleasure …* Her lips softened in anticipation. *Hurry back, my dear, dear love.*

Rain lashed the windows; the airship dived and rose again. The electrical display was spectacularly terrifying, but Angelique felt no fear, only awe at the power of nature. A bolt of lightning plunged through the heart of a cloud, illuminating the deck with an eerie blue glow. 'Such majesty!' she whispered. 'Such awesome majesty!'

There was movement beside her. 'Etienne? You're back already?' She turned her head, her eyes widening. 'Angelpapa! *You're* here!' Crying and laughing all at once, she threw herself into the arms of the man who had supported her for most of her life. 'But why are you here? I have not seen you for years!'

'We have come for you, my angel.'

'We? Oh, Godmama!' She moved from his arms to embrace the dainty lady who stood at his back. 'I did not know you were there. How wonderful it is to see you both! Angelpapa, you look so *well!* And Godmama looks so young and pretty.'

The tall, handsome man smiled and held out his hand. 'Come with me, my darling. It is time for us to go.'

'But: Etienne?'

'He is coming, too.' He spoke to his companion. 'Elise?'

Madame Dupont turned gracefully. 'But certainly: I will go to fetch him.'

Strong, comforting fingers closed over Angelique's. 'Come along, Petite: Etienne will be with us soon.'

# 5 THE POWER OF MUSIC

**6 October 1930**

*I have decided that my life is over. No more life: no more
love. It died with my adored one in a fiery inferno. My body
may exist in time, but I no longer live.*

The duc stood before the great studded front doors of the
château; his head bowed over a telegram. Harsh, dry sobs
shook his spare frame. White and stricken, he raised his
face to the heavens, crumpling the telegram in his fist. 'My
God …' he whispered in agony. 'Could you not have
taken *me* and left my son and *ma belle-fille* to raise their
child? Why did you do this? Why?'

'Grand-père!' Nicolas ran to embrace him. 'What is
it?'

The duc held the boy close. 'Oh, my dear child, you
must be brave. Your mama and papa have gone on a long
journey. One from which they will not be able to return.
You see, God requires your mama to sing with his angels;
and your papa has gone to take care of her. Ah, *mon Dieu,
mon Dieu!*' he lamented softly. 'Come, Child, we must tell
your grandmother. Although, perhaps mercifully, she will
not understand.'

Nicolas barely understood himself, but the old man's
grief overwhelmed and frightened him. Holding his
grandfather's hand, Nicolas cried the first of many lonely

41

tears. At first, he felt disbelief, but gradually it was borne in on him that his beloved parents were never coming back.

News of the crash of the British airship just south of Beauvais spread across the country. The nation mourned the death of their beloved soprano, Angelique, and her charming husband, the marquis de Beaulieu. Cards and letters of condolence poured in from all over the world. The duc dealt with them by throwing them into a room and shutting the door.

Later, Nicolas's Aunt Elise and Uncle Philippe arrived from the French Embassy in London; their eyes red-rimmed and sad. They were driven down by his Uncle Christian, a gentle giant, inarticulate in his grief. Yet, he had an aura of kindness that drew his nephew to him. Nicolas knew his father's sister and mother's oldest brother better than his Uncle Christian because he had occasionally met them after performances, but his Uncle Christian never went into society, living as closely as possible to the land he farmed on the de Villefontaine estate. There was another brother, Luc, but this was the first Nicolas had heard of him. There was speculation as to whether he would arrive to complete the family gathering, but he didn't.

Aunt Elise wanted to take Nicolas back to London with her, but the duc wouldn't allow it. 'Belvoir is his home,' he said, 'the one constant in his young life. It must not be taken from him as well. And, of course, he is my heir.'

Aunt Elise began to sob when he said that, and Nicolas held his breath. He liked his aunt, but he didn't want to leave his grandfather. It was with relief that he heard the duc say, 'Yes, it is a hard thing to come to terms with, my dear. But you have your own family. You are married to the head of the de Villefontaines, and you must take care of them. It is your sacred duty.'

'But of course, I will have time for Nicolas and you and Mama!'

'Of course, my dear, *cela va sans dire*. And I thank you for your kindness. But, you see, I, *and* Belvoir, have only Nicolas. He will remain with me.' The duc made soothing noises and held her until she stopped crying. His most immediate fear allayed, her nephew managed to slip away before anyone noticed him.

Nicolas was dressed in a formal suit and taken, in a big black limousine, to attend a memorial service. He stood with his family to accept an endless number of solemn greetings. People called him the marquis de Beaulieu and spoke of him as the duc's heir. He wanted to say, 'No! You are mistaken! That is my papa!' He thought that when he was older, he would refuse to allow anyone to call him Monsieur le marquis. *I am Nicolas,* he thought, trying to blink away tears. *Mama and Papa call me Nicolas.*

He was asked if he would sing a hymn for his mama and papa. Almost, he couldn't do it, but suddenly, Angel was there beside him. His secret friend had come back when he most needed him. For just long enough, joy overcame grief. Nicolas sang *Panis Angelicus.* His voice— pure, sweet, angelic—had the congregation in tears. Finally, for his mother, he sang their favourite song *Éternité d'amour.* And then he broke down.

§

During the day, Nicolas was kept busy with music lessons, singing lessons, schooling and riding lessons; but at bedtime, he remembered. Every night he held onto the locket and sobbed his heart out. Even with Angel there, he cried.

'I understand,' said his secret friend. 'It is good to cry. One must cry for those one has lost. But remember: it is not forever.'

'It feels like forever,' said Nicolas.

'Yes, it does now,' agreed Angel. 'Tomorrow you will

ask your grand-père to let Armand come back to you. He is grieving, too.'

'Armand is grieving?'

'Yes, he understands how you feel. In a short time, he will come back. Then, for just a little while, you will no longer need me.'

'I will always need you!'

'Soon, you will grow up. You will forget to talk to your secret friend.'

'No, never! I will never forget you!'

'You will. But it doesn't matter. I will always come when you need me, and a time is coming that you *will* need me. Remember to listen to your inner voice. That is how I will help you. Promise?'

'I promise.'

'Good. Now, I must leave you for a little while.'

'No! Don't leave me! Please!'

'Many things require my attention. Occasionally, I will have to come and go. Don't worry: my promise to you is that I will always be with you when you need me.'

Nicolas felt a warm, loving hand sweep over his hair, invisible arms go round him in a comforting hug. Then he knew that he was alone. He clasped his locket and cried himself to sleep.

In the morning, he asked his grandfather if Armand could come back.

The duc regarded him sadly, 'I will think about it if you will be good enough to sit with your grandmother for a while.'

'Yes, Grand-père. I will play the piano for her. Why does she never speak to me?' Nicolas vaguely remembered a kind, gentle lady who hugged him and gave him sweets when he was little; but his grandmother hadn't recognised him for a long time now.

The duc's eyes filled with pain. He shrugged. 'An illness of old age, my child. There is nothing we can do except to see that she has every need and comfort provided. Even though she does not seem to notice, I am sure that she will appreciate you playing for her. She was no mean proponent herself, once.'

It was no chore to Nicolas to carry out his grandfather's request. He particularly liked the baby grand piano in his grandmamma's sitting room and often played several tunes when he visited, chatting to her in between, knowing better than to expect an answer.

He walked up to the still, silent figure wrapped in shawls in the armchair by the fire and touched her hand. 'Hello, Grandmamma, I am here to play some music for you.'

As expected, he received no sign of recognition and seated himself at the piano.

He played a Strauss waltz, followed by a Chopin *étude*. 'Did you like those, Grandmamma,' he asked, almost falling off the stool when she said, 'Etienne'.

'No, Grandmamma, I am Nicolas.'

'Etienne, have you had your music lesson today?'

'Nicolas. Yes, Grandmamma.'

'Play something for me.'

He began a Mozart piece from *Così fan tutte*.

'No, not that! Beethoven's *Fifth Symphony*: first movement. Can you do that?'

'I am just learning it, but I will try.' He went well for a while, then stumbled.

'No, no! Not like that.' The old lady threw aside her shawls. 'Help me!'

Nicolas helped her to the piano stool.

'Up here, beside me,' she said, patting the seat. 'See: like this. Now you try ... *Bien, bien!*' Her light eyes glowed with pleasure and kindness. For the first time in years, Nicolas saw what a beautiful person his grandmamma had been.

When the duc returned from his cogitations, they were playing *Chopsticks* together and laughing like old friends. Astonishment held him silent.

'Hello, my dear,' said the duchesse. 'Etienne is improving, is he not?'

'Indeed, he is, my love,' he said, helping her back to her chair and replacing the shawls. 'You were playing delightfully. Just like old times.'

But the duchesse did not answer. She had gone back to the lonely place she'd inhabited for so long.

'This is important,' said the duc when he had Nicolas alone. 'What did you do?'

The boy shrugged. 'Just … started playing the piano. Grandmamma began talking to me. She thinks I am Papa.'

'It doesn't matter,' said the duc quickly. 'And then what?'

'I made a mistake and Grandmamma got up to show me how it went. I, um … I had to help her out of her chair and over to the piano.'

'A miracle! It is the first time she has moved or spoken for well over a year.' The duc grasped Nicolas's shoulders. 'You will do this for her every day?'

'But, yes, Grand-père. If it helps!'

'I don't know how. But I suspect it does.' He knelt to look into his grandson's eyes. 'I am going to Paris to see your grandmamma's physician and tell him of this remarkable development. You will be a good boy and look after your grandmamma while I am gone. *Bien*!' He rose and smiled. 'I have also made an appointment to meet with Armand …'

For a second, the old Nicolas emerged from the solemn little boy. '*Eh bien,* Grand-père: you are a *trump*!' He whirled around the room. 'That will be just the cat's pyjamas!'

The duc laughed. "I don't know what that means, but I take it you are pleased?'

'*Aux anges*, Grand-père! *Merci*! *Merci*!'

'*Très bon*. I will see you in a few days.'

'With Armand?'

'Perhaps,' amended his grandfather, 'with Armand.'

§

Armand met the duc in a private corner of the Café de Flore. A red tide surged into the cheeks of the sensitive young man, across his high forehead and up to his hairline. He lowered his eyes. 'Monsieur le duc,' he muttered, briefly taking the proffered hand, 'you wished to speak with me?'

'*Oui.*' The duc surveyed him kindly. 'Thank you for coming. This meeting must, of necessity, be awkward for us both. But, perhaps, we can find some common ground?'

'Monsieur, if you could but forgive ———?'

The duc held up his hand. 'Not yet. Coffee?' He called a waiter and gave the order, then looked over the younger man. 'We must discuss our common ground. Is there one, do you think?'

Armand hesitated, his colour receding as suddenly as it had come, leaving him sickly white. 'Monsieur, dare I presume …?'

The duc nodded. 'Go ahead. I am listening. For Nicolas's sake.'

Coffee was brought to the table. Armand did not speak until the *garçon* left. 'Is … could Nicolas be our common ground?'

'Perhaps. I am waiting for you to convince me of that.'

'Yes, Monsieur.' Armand gulped. 'When I saw how … Monsieur, I tried to stop a … certain publication. I had not then read it.'

'And you have now?'

'*Oui*, Monsieur.'

'I … see.' The duc studied an engraving absent-mindedly, then met the other's eyes with piercing candour. 'You have changed your mind since you read it?

You, too, are a jackal after scandal?'

'No, no, Monsieur! *Never!* You must not think that! It is not a scandal but an epic!' The young man's grey eyes glowed with fervour. 'A powerful and inspirational story of love!' He gestured. 'Comparable with Romeo and Juliet; Tristan and Isolde; Siegfried and Brünnhilde. You have done nothing to be ashamed of. You conducted yourself honourably. Monsieur ———'

The duc grasped his wrist, holding his eyes with painful intensity. 'What do you know of love? You have, yourself, experienced love?'

Armand nodded.

The grip intensified. 'Who do you love?'

The young man dropped his gaze. 'She ... she is dead, Monsieur.'

'Ah ...' The duc released him. 'I see ... Yes, I see. But, just the same, there is great scandal attached to this publication.'

'Monsieur.' Armand leant across the table. 'If there was scandal, it was not yours. It belonged to a man of whom the world was well rid.'

'Perhaps ... Yes, that is true. The world *was* well rid of him.' The duc studied his long, white fingers. 'Other hands than mine were responsible for that.' He began to sound frustrated. 'These hands that have never held the pen to write a word in defence of my love; never worked to dispel the injustice visited on the innocent ...'

'They have held pencil and brush to create images that showed your adoration. They have held the reins that melded together a great estate and kept your loved ones safe all these years.' Armand leant forward to touch the duc's sleeve. 'Let it go, Monsieur. As I said before: It is a powerful love story: An epic. It deserves to be told. I did not understand until I ...' He was about to say, 'fell in love,' but substituted with 'read it'.

The duc's eyes filled with pain. 'I suppose it is a record of those whom I have loved ... and lost.'

Burdened with his own grief, Armand remained silent.

The duc straightened. 'I sent for you because Nicolas is lonely. It is not right for him to have a grieving old man and a woman out of her senses as his only companions. Will you come back to us?'

'But certainly, Monsieur. I thank you for asking. I, too, have been lonely.'

'And grieving, I think? No, do not answer. I know what it is like to be one of the thousands that adore a beautiful performer.' The duc sighed and stood up. He held out his hand to Armand. 'You will come as soon as is possible? *Bien.*'

Armand watched him walk away, then followed. Neither of them had touched their coffee.

# 6 REINSTATED

**6 November 1930**

*So, I will have Nicolas once more. How different is this
world to the former? All the bright things, all the good
things, all the beautiful things have gone. We that are left
must now support each other in our grief.*

Nicolas was pathetically overjoyed when his grandfather
returned with Armand. He showed his tutor the mountain
of sympathy cards and letters of condolence from all over
the world.

'*Eh bien*, here is work!' exclaimed Armand. 'Have you
answered any?'

Nicolas shook his head. 'Grand-père threw them all in
here, out of his sight.'

'I understand, but now we must face it. We will do
them together.'

'But there are too many!'

'So,' said Armand. 'You see how everybody loved your
mama and papa? They love you like that, too. Now, let us
get started. We have to answer them all, you know. Your
fans will expect it.' He was relieved: here was a way to
keep Nicolas busy for months to come.

Nicolas cavilled at first, but when he read the messages
of sympathy and support from his fans, he was comforted,
and since he had Armand, didn't feel quite so alone. He

stopped thinking about his secret friend and, as Angel had predicted, more or less forgot his existence. At least, for the time it took to answer the mountain of letters and cards.

At ten, Nicolas had a good grasp of the language; but it creased his brow to find the number of answers expected of him and even more to understand the meaning of some of his fan mail. One he took to his grandfather to decipher. 'Grand-père, what does this mean?' Nicolas pointed out a phrase in his letter.

The duc spluttered over his after-lunch coffee. '*Mon Dieu*! Where did you get this?'

'One of my fans sent it. A lady.'

'Hmm. Send Armand to me. Where are you going now?'

'To answer this letter.' Nicolas picked it up. 'When I find out what it means.'

'No, you are not!' said the duc, plucking the scented sheet out of his hand. 'I will answer it. Have you played for Grandmamma yet?'

'*Non*. I will go now.'

'*Bon*. Send Armand to me first.'

'*Oui*.' Nicolas sped off on his errand.

While he was playing the piano for his grandmother, the duc lay down certain rules before Armand. 'The child must be protected. I am not going to explain this filth to him and neither are you. His mail must be censored in future, by you, before he sees it.'

Armand's face was red. 'Yes, Monsieur. But, as I told Nicolas, I don't know what it means, either.'

'Good answer,' replied the duc, balling up the letter and throwing it into the fire. 'Anything else you don't understand can go the way of this one. But either you or I must read his mail first. One wonders about some of the minds in this world!' He left Armand and went to see how Nicolas was getting on with the duchesse.

'Nothing, Grand-père,' said Nicolas, with a

disappointed shrug.

'Never mind.' The duc took his wife's hand. 'We'll try again, tomorrow, *hein*? Where are you going?'

'To explore the east tower, if I may?' Nicolas's favourite place was this tower. It commanded stunning views of the surrounding terrain and fired his imagination.

'Go on, then. But be careful.' The duc remained, holding the hand of the duchesse. 'My poor Catherine,' he mourned. 'Poor, imprisoned soul.'

§

Angel came back into Nicolas's life in a totally unexpected manner.

After a history lesson about this very château, Nicolas had been as eager as ever to spend time in the east tower. He stood on the crenellated roof, surveying the vast expanse of fields, hills and valleys; the little hamlets with their church spires; the winding roads; the high, snow-topped mountains in the background.

In his imagination, he was Dominique, duc de Belvoir during the French Revolution, commanding his people in defence of the château. He thought about how his people had been loyal to him—resisting attempts on the part of the revolutionaries to arrest him—how he'd hidden another duc who'd escaped from the Bastille and helped smuggle him out of the country.

He imagined a great horde charging the portcullis, shaking the bars, screaming threats—the majority foiled by the rising drawbridge—the duc's own people gathering in the courtyard: the clamour, the shouting, the people of Belvoir taking up arms, the challenge and subsequent withdrawal.

*Go down to the picture gallery.*

Nicolas jumped. 'What?' Then he thought, *Inner voice!* 'Angel? Is that you?'

*Yes. Go to the picture gallery.*

'Why?'

*I'll tell you when you get there.*

The boy obeyed, negotiating the spiral stone staircase at death-defying speed; traversing numerous corridors and stairs until he arrived in the long, narrow, well-lit space that occupied the whole length of one wing of the château. He waited, breathing hard.

*The portrait between Katarina and Angelique.*

'But, that is ———'

*One thing to remember, mon brave: speak to me in thoughts. Otherwise, idiots will say that you are fou and lock you up.*

*Yes.* Nicolas concentrated. *Angel? You are the marquis du Bois? Mama called you Angelpapa.*

*She did, indeed. I am all of those, including the Master of Illusion.*

*But … I have always known you as Angel. What shall I call you?*

*Angel will suffice. That is my role where you are concerned.*

*What do you mean?*

*I was your mother's guardian, and now I am yours.*

*You saved me on the ship. Why did you not save Mama and Papa on the airship?*

*There are some things that cannot be changed. You must understand that: they are already written. Destiny. It took me a long time to accept that. But something is about to happen that can be changed. Don't worry. Trust what I tell you. Concentrate on the portrait. Look into my eyes.*

Nicolas looked into the commanding, sapphire-blue eyes—so like his own—little though he knew it. He fancied that they were alive: all-encompassing, all-knowing. He felt as if he were drowning in them: disappearing, submerging. He reefed his gaze away to study the strong, yet fine, aristocratic features: the shining black hair, the little touch of humour about the mouth. He saw a leader and was satisfied. *What must I do?*

*Listen to me.*

*Eh bien, I am listening …*

*Look well at the portrait. Memorise my features. When you need me, concentrate, visualise me standing beside you. Feel my strength, add it to yours. Open your mind to me. Together, we will be formidable! Do you understand, now, how I can help you?*

The boy hesitantly touched the painted surface. *I … think so.*

*No matter, you will.*

Nicolas glanced at the images of his mother and father. 'Mama, I … Papa, I miss you so …' Tears scalded. His hand grasped the locket until it hurt. He bowed his head and sobbed.

A wave of love swept over him, soothing his grief. *Be calm, my son. Be patient. They are not far away. When you have done what you have to do, you will see them again.*

He mopped his tears with a sleeve. Suddenly, he could look at the portraits and feel love and comfort as he always had with that of his grandmother, Katarina. He gazed into his mother's beautiful amethyst eyes and his father's warm golden-hazel ones and felt them near. He let go of the locket to grip invisible hands—one he knew was his mother's and one his father's—and was immeasurably comforted.

With Angel's help, he had accepted the loss of his parents and was at peace. And, paradoxically, in that moment of peace, they had returned to him. Nicolas understood none of these things, except that it no longer hurt him to think of them. On the contrary: he felt surrounded by their love.

# 7 THE PRICE OF LOYALTY

21 September 1931

*Nicolas seems to have accepted his loss and become his usual ebullient self. I would that the duc and I could do the same.*

Nicolas sat at the piano playing for his grandmother. So far, she had made no sign of recognition. He was very proud that he'd learnt the whole first movement of Beethoven's *Fifth Symphony* just for her. 'You would like to hear it, Grandmamma? *Bien.*' He began the majestic chords. 'You liked that, Grandmamma?' he asked, when he'd finished. But his grandmother sat expressionless, unmoving. Nicolas drooped; his pleasure gone. 'I will play it again,' he said, turning back to the keyboard and addressing it with more gusto.

*Make a mistake. Fumble a note or two.*

Nicolas's fingers crashed on the keyboard.

The duchesse winced. 'No, no, Etienne, not like that. Let me help you.' As before, Nicolas assisted her to the piano and they played duets, the duchesse warm and complimentary about his progress. At the end, she kissed his forehead and called him her clever little Etienne. He adored the feel of her lips, her warm sweetness, the way she held him in her arms.

Nicolas could hardly wait to tell the good news to his

grandfather, tearing down the corridor to his study, halting in astonishment at the spare figure standing in the shadows by the door.

'Shh.' Armand held a warning finger to his lips.

'*Quoi*?' whispered Nicolas.

'Listen.' Armand jerked his head at the raised voice behind the closed door.

'I do not, do not, believe it!' said the duc. 'What have you been about to let a thing like this happen?'

'I am sorry, Monsieur. It is the wording of the document. Had I been the one to draw it up …'

'François Bernaud,' breathed Nicolas in Armand's ear. 'Mama's lawyer. What is it about?'

'You, I think. Shh.'

'Very well. I understand,' said the duc. 'And there is nothing you can do?'

'No, Monsieur, *je regrette* … After a twelve-month period of mourning, which is now almost expired, Nicolas must perform once per week during the season in the Opéra Magique for a period of ten years. The Countess Kireyevsky is enforcing it.'

'Ten years! I know Nicolas has inherited his mother's half-share in the opera house, and, with it, her responsibilities to the place. But I am his guardian until he turns twenty-one. Do I not have a say?'

'Regrettably not, Monsieur. Not unless you wish Nicolas to forfeit his part-ownership of the Opéra Magique. It all hinges on the omission of a clause that under no circumstances would I have allowed. However, I was out of the country at the time. And because the Countess Kireyevsky has taken over the management of the Opéra Magique, she has the casting vote on any decision made by the owners. In other words: her word is law, she can make any demand she chooses and there is nothing you or I can do about it.'

'*Mon Dieu*! That woman is a she-wolf! But there are only two owners. How can she have a greater vote?'

'When Madame Dupont left her share of the Opéra Magique to her daughter, she had a document drawn up, giving equal say to three people: the two owners and the theatre manager. Knowing her daughter, she felt that this would prevent difficulties in case of unresolvable differences between the two owners. I would have made sure to add that the theatre manager must not be one of the owners. But, as I said ...'

'Yes, I understand. And you are sure that there is nothing you can do? You have explored all avenues?'

'*Oui*, Monsieur. I am so sorry.'

The door opened suddenly. Nicolas and Armand stepped back, red-faced.

'*Tiens!*' remarked the duc. 'How did you two know that I wanted you? Monsieur Bernaud shall explain your duties for the foreseeable future.' He turned his head so that they would not see that the lightness of his tone was belied by the pain in his eyes and the grim set to his mouth.

§

'Nicolas, your grandfather wants you, tout de suite, in your grandmamma's sitting room. The physicians have come,' said Armand. 'Hurry!'

Nicolas knocked and entered. A number of solemn gentlemen stood around the walls. His grandfather was frowning. 'Nicolas, will you show these gentlemen what you do to, er, "wake up" your grandmother? The gentlemen want you to act as if they are not there.'

'But certainly, Grand-père.' Nicolas bowed to the gentlemen and went to touch his grandmother's unresponsive hand. 'Hello, Grandmamma. I am here to play you some music. You will like that, *hein*?' He seated himself at the piano, played a waltz and a polka, then launched into the *Beethoven Fifth*, making a mistake at the usual place. He waited for his grandmother to react, but she sat unheeding. He played it again and again, crashing chords, playing wrong notes; but the duchesse noticed nothing.

Dismayed, Nicolas met the duc's eyes and rose from the piano. What had gone wrong? This method had never failed. He and his grandfather had been confident that they had the answer. He looked at the gentlemen. They were beginning to make impatient mutterings to the effect of wasted time. They took a whispered leave of the duc, with much shoulder patting, eloquent with sympathy for his obviously wishful thinking, as well as irritation for being sent on a wild-goose chase. One touched Nicolas on the head and smiled at him as he passed.

When the noise of their vehicles had receded into the distance, the duchesse came to life. 'I would not, for the world, point out your errors in front of those prosy looking gentlemen, Etienne,' she said. 'But now we must correct your mistakes.' She smiled kindly. 'It must have been nerves. I have never heard you play so many wrong notes. Come along, back to the piano.'

'*Mon Dieu!*' Not trusting himself to say more, the duc threw his hands in the air and left the room. Nicolas and the duchesse spent a very agreeable half-hour together.

It was their last. A day later, the duchesse succumbed to pneumonia and slipped away during the night, very quickly and silently.

'A happy release,' said the duc, wiping his eyes.

*If it is so happy*, wondered Nicolas, rubbing away tears of his own, *why is he crying?*

*It is not a tragedy. She is free, at last.*

Nicolas did not understand, but he was not about to question the judgement of Angel. It might be happy, he supposed, except that he missed his grandmother already. He loved the way she smiled, the warmth in her eyes when the music brought her to life, her wonderful loyalty that would not allow her to admit a mistake in one she loved.

Because she was a loving person: Nicolas knew that. When the music freed her, she could be herself. His soul craved a loving, feminine touch. The tears came in earnest.

Nicolas played Beethoven's *Fifth Symphony* at his grandmother's funeral service in the chapel. At the end, he felt a sudden rush of euphoria. A vision came to him of light, animated eyes; a delightful smile; a warm, loving presence; a sense of joy.

*You see?*

Suddenly, Nicolas could see what Angel meant. His grandmother was able to be herself all the time, instead of just now and again.

# 8 LA REINE

**12 October 1931**

*Nicolas and I are off to visit the queen. The duc is
indisposed and cannot come with us. Since Her Majesty
would not countenance a postponement of the meeting, I
have his strict instructions to protect the boy. Only, who is
going to protect me from being mauled by the 'she-wolf'?
That is what I want to know!*

Nicolas faced the Countess Kireyevsky with a strange fear
in his heart. Her thin lips smiled, showing gold teeth, but
no smile was echoed in her eyes: cold, ice-blue.
Expensively dressed, skilfully made-up, she smelled of
Chanel No.5 and cigarette smoke.

What was it about her that repelled him? He studied
her fearfully: her hair, swept up in a chignon, was a
classically elegant silver blonde; her slim figure, swathed
in softly falling silk and satin, was always chic, perhaps
even regal, in the creations of her favourite designer,
Chanel. Her features, despite her age and the fine lines
around her mouth, were still attractive. Nicolas was aware
of a kind of baleful energy emanating from her,
suffocating when one stood close. It was all that he could
do, not to step back.

Glad of his tutor's presence at his side, Nicolas
blanched when the countess flicked a malicious glance at

Armand and said, 'I believe we do not need you, Monsieur. My nephew and I ——'

'With respect, Madame. I must take issue with your statement. Nicolas is not related to you.' Armand became breathless, losing the thread. 'He, er, is not your nephew. I-I mean … you cannot be his aunt.'

'Such an awkward young man,' murmured the countess, her lips curving at his rush of colour. 'Splitting hairs, too.' She brushed him off with a careless wave and addressed Nicolas. 'My mother reared me first, and then your mother. That makes us sisters. Of course I am your aunt! If not by blood, then by the closeness of our two families.' She stood back, playing with the string of amber beads she wore. Her voice became caressing. 'And I know that you miss your mother and have no lady in your life to care for you in that way.'

Angel intervened. *Cunning! Agree with her.*

'Yes, Aunt.'

Armand began again, 'With respect, Madame ——'

'Enough! You may wait in the foyer!'

I beg your pardon, Madame. But I must ——' Armand's larynx bobbed painfully. He was afraid to argue with this domineering woman, but the duc had given him precise instructions.

'*You* are a servant! Do you dare to bandy words with the Countess Kireyevsky?'

'I am the servant of the duc de Belvoir, Madame. He has told me that, under no circumstances, must I leave Nicolas alone with … you.' Armand could hardly get out the last word. A painful silence ensued.

The countess stood tall; her eyes narrowing to slits.

Nicolas could see no resemblance whatsoever to the lady he'd called Godmama, even though this terrifying woman was supposed to be her daughter.

*Angel? What shall I do?*

*Tell Armand to go. She will only do him harm.*

*What about me?*

*You, she dares not harm … Yet.*

Nicolas placed a hand on his tutor's arm. 'Please, Armand. If my "aunt" wants to speak to me, I will listen to her. Please, do as she says.'

Armand glanced from the triumphant, cat-with-the-cream smile of the countess to his pupil's worried expression. How strangely grown-up and touchingly wise this young boy seemed. *Sometimes, Nicolas has such dignity for one so young*, he thought. *Just now and then, I realise the heritage he is born to.* He raised his brows. 'I cannot disobey your grandfather's orders, Nicolas. But I will sit over here out of earshot. If the countess permits …?'

A bored wave of the hand signified assent.

Armand looked hard at Nicolas. 'You are sure?'

*Yes.*

'Yes, Armand.'

Armand sat unobtrusively behind a handsome lacquered screen, painted with birds of paradise and butterflies—but his ears were good. He heard everything. Even things that he wished he couldn't hear.

The countess's voice was honeyed, 'I have invited you here because I know you are a lonely little boy.'

*I am not little!* was Nicolas's first indignant thought.

*Shh!*

'Now: I have found a way for you, so that you will no longer be lonely. You will like that?'

'Oh … Oh yes, Aunt.'

'Ah, good. I have had the most marvellous idea. Nicolai and I, we have no children, and you—poor little boy—have no parents. So, we, the count and I, have decided to adopt you as our very own. Is that not wonderful?'

'B-but …' stammered Nicolas.

'You like this idea of mine, *hein*?'

*Say yes.*

*Quoi?*

*Say it!*

'Yes, Aunt. *Merci.*'

'Ah, *très bon.* I have the perfect apartment for you. It has a secret entrance. Perfect privacy for a rising star. You may keep your tutor—Armand, is it not? There is room for him in your apartment. It once belonged to a tenor just like you.'

*It belonged to me.*

'I am a soprano, Madame.'

Cèline's metallic laughter rang out. 'Oh, dear little boy!' She tried to gather Nicolas into her arms.

He winced, evading her touch.

She straightened, eyes hardening. 'You will not always be a soprano, Child. Have you not heard what happens to little boys' voices when they begin to grow up? That is why we must make the most of what you have! Why you must come here to live with me and sing every night.'

Nicolas felt clammy and rather sick. 'Madame, *je regrette* … that I cannot. My grand-père is old. While he lives, he needs me. He has no-one else.'

*As if she would care! Don't worry; the duc will not allow it.*

'Well, well, you are a good little boy. Your grandfather will see reason. I will write to him now while you go along to the stage to practise. Nicolai is waiting for you. Make the most of the time you have with him because you will be performing together next week.' The countess stepped back and clapped her hands. 'Armand, *ici*! Take your charge to Count Kireyevsky on the stage and come back here so that I may dictate a letter to the duc saying that Nicolas wishes to live with me.'

*Salope!*

'*Quoi?*' Startled, Nicolas spoke aloud.

The countess cuffed him about the ears. 'Stupid boy! Have you not listened to a word I said? Go to the stage, at once!'

Nicolas stared, unable to take in her chameleon-like change. Armand touched his sleeve. They turned, as one, to the door.

# 9 TWO GUARDIAN ANGELS

**19 October 1931**

*I am now certain that I am going mad! How to even write
it? But, this evening, I could swear that I am so attuned to
Nicolas that I can hear his thoughts; and it is as if there are
two people I am listening to, not one. To hear
conversations in one's head? We all know what that means!*

*And tonight—I blanch to think of it!—I swear I caught a
glimpse of a man standing beside him on the stage. What
was worse was that I recognised him from a portrait in the
gallery at Belvoir—the marquis du Bois! And he died more
than a decade ago!*

*I will be in the insane asylum if I keep going like this.
Surely, it is midsummer madness with me!*

*And the countess? What a dragon! I feel in my heart that
she means trouble for Nicolas. She makes me shudder when
she comes near, and she's always getting me to write letters
for her, leaning over my shoulder, breathing into my ear—
Urrgh!*

*I don't want to know what Nicolas thinks, or who else is in
his head with him! I have enough trouble with what is in my
own head!*

The painted lips of the countess dropped phrases of affability: 'You have come to stay, this time, dear boy?'

Nicolas schooled his expression to bland apology. 'I am sorry, Madame ... Aunt. Grand-père says I must live with him until I am twenty-one. After which time, I may take up your most kind offer. I have come to sing tonight.'

'Ah, indeed, indeed. Your apartment will be waiting for you, *mon fils*. You have warmed up your voice? Come along then; I will take you to wait in the wings with your tutor.' She sent Armand a look that made him feel ill. 'This dance is about to finish, and then you may go on. He can wait for you here.'

The introductory ballet ended. The dancers filed past Nicolas. One attracted his notice, at once. She had chestnut hair, plaited into a becoming coronet, bright blue eyes, a pert nose and a cheeky, conspiratorial smile.

'Oh, there's Lisette! Excuse me, Madame. Sette! Settie!' He ran to her. '*Belle dame!*'

The pretty ballerina smiled and held out her arms. 'Beau Nicolas, *mon chou*! How wonderful to see you! You're still as cute as ever, *hein?*' The ballerina gave him a motherly kiss on the brow and a warm hug, which he returned with fervour.

'Am I big enough yet, Settie?'

'Hmm. Let me see ...' The ballerina held him at arm's length, looking him over with warm, twinkling eyes. 'Almost. Not quite. Soon, *mon ami.*' She kissed him again. Then, folding him closer, she whispered, 'I am sorry about your mama and papa, *Chéri*. But we are troupers, *hein?* We do not let our troubles be seen. The show must go on, *n'est-ce pas?*' She stepped back. 'Break a leg, as we say.'

He nodded, taking in her plain costume. 'Why weren't you dancing prima?'

'Because I did break a leg: an ankle, rather, and some toes. I'll tell you about it later.' She looked up to meet a reptilian gaze. Icy fingers groped her spine. 'You'd better go,' she whispered. 'The countess is looking at us. I think she wants you. I'm going to watch you sing, if I can. *À bientôt, Chéri.*' Lisette hugged him again and turned away.

Nicolas watched her go out of sight, then turned to face the older woman's speculative glance. 'You want me now, Madame?'

'*Prochainement.* You like Lisette?' she asked, smiling at him in a disquieting fashion. 'She has *espièglerie, n'est-ce pas?*'

'*Oui,* Madame. She is lots of fun to be with.'

'*Eh bien,* we must see that you spend time with her.'

'Yes, Madame. I love Lisette. She is *belle.* I am going to marry her, one day. As soon as I grow up.'

'Ah, then we must help you to grow up quickly.' The countess spoke dryly.

Nicolas didn't understand her tone and began to look around for the count.

'It is no use looking for Nicolai! Did I not tell you?' She laughed and waved her fan. 'How remiss of me! Poor Nicolai: he is indisposed. You will have to go on without him. When you hear the cue, you must go to centrestage and sing solo. But you can do that.' She turned and spoke over her shoulder. 'Forgive me, I must leave you now. A full house awaits you, so do not let me down!'

'No, Mad——— Aunt.' Nicolas watched her hurry away, consternation in his breast. 'Armand,' he whispered. 'Did you hear that? How can I face them alone? Without Mama?' Nicolas began to shake. He was afraid that he would break down as he had in the church. *What is wrong with me?* Never, in his life, had he been a victim of stage fright, but never had he been on stage in front of an audience without his mother close by, even though he had sung alone. She'd always been there to encourage him.

Armand held him by the shoulders. 'Steady, *mon gar.* Listen to me: Your public love you. Remember all the letters they sent you? This is how you can repay their kindness, return their love. And besides, you must fulfil your part of the contract. You don't want the countess to win, do you? Take your inheritance?'

'No. But I don't know how I can do it.'

A rustle of silk, a clicking of beads and the countess reappeared. 'Why are you not on stage?' she hissed. 'Herr Schmidt-Hesse is waiting for you.'

'And that's another thing ...' Nicolas whispered to Armand, 'I don't like that new German conductor! He is not at all *sympathique*.' He showed the countess a face of misery. 'I am sorry, Madame, I ... I cannot go out there and sing alone!'

'Of course you can! If not, I will sue you for everything you are worth!'

'Please, Madame ———'

She turned her fury on Armand. '*Chut!*' Tall, terrifying, she grasped Nicolas by the lapels of his formal suit. 'If you do not, you will be finished! *Finished!* Think about *that!*' She pushed him back so violently that he cannoned into his tutor.

*You are not alone. I am with you. Come, we will sing it together.*

Nicolas took a deep breath and smoothed his lapels. 'Very well, Madame.' He turned, squared his shoulders, tried to visualise Angel and stepped out on the stage. The orchestra began his introduction; the red and gold velvet curtain rolled back. Nicolas smiled and bowed to his audience. In return, he received a standing ovation.

*Eh bien, you see? You do not need me.*

*I do. Please?*

*Very well. On the count ...*

Suddenly, all Nicolas's confidence returned. He felt warm and loved, as if his mother stood on one side and his secret friend, the other. Angel's strength infused him. He opened his mouth and glorious notes streamed out. Sooner than he thought, it was over.

The crowd surged off their seats. 'Beau Nicolas!' they chanted. 'Beau Nicolas!'

*You did well, Nicolas. Superbe!*

'Thank you!' he said aloud to Angel. "Thank you, thank you, thank you!' But it didn't matter because the audience thought he was speaking to them and cheered even harder. As long ago, Nicolas felt their love wash over him. He went back for several encores, finally singing *Éternité d'amour.*

*That is enough. Do not go back.*

Armand was waiting in the wings to convey the same sentiments. 'Come, you have fulfilled your obligations. You have conducted yourself bravely. We will go home now.'

The countess intercepted them on the way to a side entrance. 'You did well, Nicolas. Your fans have been looking for you. Next time you come, you will stay behind to meet some of them backstage and sign their autograph books, *hein*? *Bien*. Goodnight.'

§

'Some of the other girls are leaving,' said one of a group of ballerinas draped about the top few steps of the third-floor staircase, smoking and conversing in tense low voices.

'Yes, but … I have heard that it is much the same wherever you go. There are expectations …'

'Expectations? Expectations are not the same as the demands that are being made on us! One can say no to expectations, but apparently not to La Reine. Do as she says or get out! Well, *I* am getting out!' said a third, in a furious undervoice.

'Hush! Here comes the old dragon now! Whatever can she want at this hour?'

'I hope it is not another "client" for one of us. I cannot bear ——'

The countess came to the landing and peered upwards. 'Lisette? Is Lisette there? Send her down to me.'

71

A tall, dark ballerina elbowed Lisette. 'You heard! Go on.'

'Lucky you!' said the one who was leaving.

'Shut up!' whispered Lisette, with a warning grimace. She raised her voice, 'Coming, Madame. I'll just get a wrap.'

'Very well. I shall be in my salon. Do not keep me waiting.'

'No, Your Majesty,' mouthed Lisette, to the concealed amusement of her friends.

'Be careful!' said the tall ballerina. 'She'll probably chop off your head if you say the wrong thing.'

'Shh. She'll chop off *all* our heads if she hears you.' Lisette ran up the stairs and, in a few seconds, down again, wrapping her sylph-like figure in a crocheted shawl.

'You wanted me, Madame?'

'Ah, Lisette. Yes, come in. I have a little "after-hours" job for you. Very pleasant. But first: what were you girls discussing on the stairs? You all looked so serious.'

Lisette studied the jewelled bows on the toes of the countess's expensive shoes and knit her brows. She knew someone had to speak up for the ballerinas. Lisette did not want to be the one, but the countess seemed to be in a good mood and here was her chance. 'Madame, we were discussing the new requirements of our positions. With respect, Madame, our previous ballet mistress, Madame Merignac, never suggested ... In fact, such liaisons were frowned upon, unless ... of the heart.' She coloured at the countess's amused glance. 'Some of us feel that we cannot ... That it is demeaning to us as dancers to be expected _____'

'Nonsense! Why should you think that?'

'But, Madame, you were a ballerina. You must know what it is like to be importuned after a performance; how unpleasant it is to be pawed about by some drunken ... roué!'

'*Chut!*' The countess got up and prowled around,

snapping her fan open and shut. 'I had sense enough to marry young, didn't I? No-one asks a married woman what she does in her boudoir.'

The ballerina stared. 'Madame! But …?'

The countess interpreted Lisette's shocked silence. 'Why not? If the price is high enough? It must be exclusive, of course. *Very* exclusive. And discreet. But we are not talking about me. We are discussing a service that is in great demand. *Eh bien*, if a commodity is in demand and we are providing it, that is good business. Extra little luxuries for you; extra for me.'

'But there are houses that provide this service!'

'Aha, but they do not have dancers, do they? It is the grace and beauty of the female form—the extreme athleticism of the dancers—that fascinates and arouses the gentlemen.' The countess's eyes gleamed as she extolled these virtues, but lost their animation as she continued, 'Then they go on to these houses you mentioned and make do with those lesser trollops. Where is the sense in that? This way we keep them. Double the profit. For a very high figure—and I *do* mean a very high figure—a discerning gentleman may have that which his eyes have desired.'

'Madame, we have trained since we were children to provide this beauty that you speak of. But it is a fine art: to look at and admire, not to touch. This idea of yours: it is ruining our lives! Believe me, these extra luxuries you promise do not compensate us for ——'

'Enough!' The countess snapped shut her fan. 'If you cannot, any longer, fulfil the requirements of your position, then …' She pointed the carved ivory sticks. 'There is the door!'

Lisette bit her lip. She knew she should walk away. But to what? Starvation on the street? Who was going to employ a dancer who could no longer dance *en pointe*? 'I am sorry, Madame.' She took a deep breath. 'What is it that you require of me?'

'That is better!' The countess's humour was magically restored. 'It is simple and easy. There is a young gentleman—no drunken roué, I might add—who has taken a fancy to you. *Quite* a fancy. In fact, he is ripe ...' Her cold blue eyes rested on the ballerina. Lisette felt, as usual, touched by evil. 'If you do as I say here, you will not be required to be available to other clients.'

'Very well, Madame.'

Her obvious relief made the countess smile unpleasantly. 'You will instruct this young man in every worldly pleasure: to be a connoisseur of wine, to hold his liquor, to smoke elegantly, to be awakened to the joys of aphrodisiacs like cocaine.'

'But ... cocaine? Cocaine is not ——'

'It provides euphoria, heightened energy, does it not?' The countess dropped her fan to reach for a cigarette in an elegant holder. Lighting it, she added, 'You will, of course, instruct him in the arts of the boudoir: the delights of love.'

'May I know who it is, first, Madame?'

'*Mais certainement!* It is our young superstar, Nicolas de Beaulieu.'

'But he is no more than a child!' gasped the ballerina. 'A child, Madame! Unawakened.'

'Then, it is for you to open his eyes.' She drew on her cigarette, expelling the smoke in Lisette's face. 'You will make him dependent on you ... Then you will insist that he comes here to live—with you!'

'Madame, *please!*' Lisette stretched out an imploring hand.

'Enough of this stupidity! This maudlin sentiment! He has said that he wants to marry you. He told it to me himself!'

'But ... but ——' Lisette was stunned.

'And when you are with him, you shall wear only white. I will provide your raiment.'

'But, Madame.' The ballerina finally found her voice.

'I think you are operating under an error. Nicolas has been saying that he wants to marry me since he was a little boy. It seems I look like some portrait or other that he is enamoured of.'

The countess studied her. 'Hmm. Yes, there is a resemblance, now you come to mention it: the hair colour, the eyes, the face shape. Although, she was a namby-pamby, milk-and-water miss if ever there was one! At least you have a bit of spirit. Or I thought you did. Katarina …' She clenched her hand in sudden spite. 'I don't know why all the men were in love with her. The comte: as namby-pamby as she was! And *Angel* …' Her face distorted into a mask of hatred.

*She's mad! The woman is mad! Who is this Angel she speaks of? And with such venom!* Frightened, Lisette whispered, 'Madame, it is just a joke I have with Nicolas; a standing joke between us.'

The countess sighed, seeming to come back from somewhere. 'Nevertheless, you will appear to take him seriously. You will instruct him in the art of love.'

'Madame, please! You don't know what you are saying! He is only a baby!'

'Then it will take as long as it takes. He will grow older; there is nothing more certain. There are ways to encourage him. He will soon get the idea. If you are the first, you will have a hold over him.'

Lisette gasped, but the countess, apparently unaware of having said anything atrocious, smiled and drew on her cigarette.

'But, that's … depravity!'

'Nonsense! A man of the world needs to know these things.'

'No, Madame, I beg of you … Let him grow up, fall in love and discover them naturally. As for the other evils of society …' The ballerina shrugged. 'There is plenty of time before he need make up his mind about them.'

The countess went on as if Lisette hadn't spoken, 'A

little extra knowledge in the boudoir never goes astray.'

Lisette felt ill with horror. The woman was crazy—*fou*. There was no doubt about it. She was obviously bent on ruining the life of a young boy. *But why?*

'Madame, forgive me, but I do not understand why you would wish to do such a thing to Nicolas? Why do you wish him to live here with me? And why would you want an innocent child to be exposed to vice at such a tender age?'

'That is not your business! You will do as I say! Or you will be out in the street!' In a sudden, vicious move, the countess pitched the cigarette out of its holder and ground it under her heel. '*And* I will see that you do not obtain employment in any other opera house.' She tossed the ebony holder into an ashtray and looked up. '*Tu comprends*?'

Again, Lisette felt the touch of evil. She shivered, drawing her shawl about her.

The countess picked up her fan. 'Next time he comes to sing, you will be waiting in his dressing-room with feminine comforts. I leave it entirely up to you. If you are there, dressed for the part, *bon*. If not …' She drew the fan across her throat, lifted her shoulders and swayed out of the room. Without looking back, she said, 'Pick up that cigarette butt before you go.'

Lisette stooped, picked what was left of the cigarette out of the carpet and flung it across the salon. Avoiding the other ballerinas, she went up a back staircase to her room, where she lay thinking and smoking for a long time. They weren't supposed to smoke in their rooms, but, tonight, she didn't care. Her face crumpled at the thought of that beautiful, clear-eyed boy: innocent, full of fun, adored by friends and fans, now so vulnerable in his loss. If she told the countess what to do with her depraved suggestion, that evil hag would find another, not so caring, to carry out her dirty work for her. Lisette was sure of that.

A sleepless night decided her. Who knew how far the

countess might go with her grotesque fantasy? The old witch could say what she liked, but what Nicolas needed was mothering. She stubbed out her last cigarette and turned her face into the pillow. If that dragon wanted the poor child to have feminine comforts, then she, Lisette, would provide them—in the sacred role of mother.

It was the only way she could think of to protect him from evil.

# 10 A PRETTY BALLERINA

**26 October 1931**

*Nicolas sings at the Opéra Magique again tonight. He
seems to have found a friend: a pretty ballerina. Her
presence and joie de vivre appears to have worked wonders
for him. Will he be onstage alone? Or will a ghost be with
him? But my biggest fear is: will the countess try to get me
alone again like she did last time?*

Nicolas's next appearance saw him step out onto the stage
with confidence. When the curtain began to open, he
wavered for one tiny second. *Angel?*

*I am here.*

Visualising the man in the portrait standing beside
him, Nicolas sang solo and then with the baritone Count
Kireyevsky. His final encore was a solo that again met
with a standing ovation.

When Nicolas came backstage to meet Armand, the
countess was waiting for him. 'I want Armand. You go up
to your dressing-room and wait for him. Lisette will look
after you until he comes.'

'*Très bon*, Madame!' In his joy, Nicolas did not notice
how Armand shrank and paled.

The countess watched his face light up and nodded.
'Go along now.'

'Are … Will the fans be there, Madame?'

'Not tonight. Next time.'

'*Bon.*' Nicolas tore up the stairs to the dressing-room that used to be his mother's; and before that, the Master's. *Angel's*, thought Nicolas, bursting into the room. 'Sette! Settie! You are here! Oh, you do look pretty in that!' He went straight into her arms. 'How soft you feel!'

'Do I, *mon brave*?' Lisette kissed his hair. 'Come, let me take your coat and undo your tie … there!' She held up a dressing gown for him to shrug into. 'You are hungry after your performance? Supper first?' She indicated a table loaded with sandwiches, pastries, cakes and various drinks and cordials attractive to children. 'Or make-up removal?'

'Supper first, *s'il vous plaît.*' His eyes glistened at the feast. 'That looks scrumptious! How did you know that I was starving?'

'I wonder!' She looked amused. 'Where do you want to start?'

'The quiche, please.' He waited while she cut him a slice. 'What about you, Settie? Will you have some.'

'No, thank you for asking. I've had mine. I have not just come back from a performance. Eat up.' She moved around the table, pouring him blackcurrant juice, finally serving him with a large piece of chocolate cake topped with strawberries and crème fraîche. 'Your favourite, I think?'

'Mmm, thank you.' Halfway through, he said, 'Settie, you won't be offended? I cannot eat it all.'

'*Mais non*! You've done well. A valiant effort, *mon cher.*' Lisette pulled out a chair from the dressing table in front of the mirror. 'Sit here, my soldier, while I remove your stage make-up, *hein*?'

He submitted. 'You're good at this.'

'Plenty of practise, *mon ami.*'

He sat, watching her in the mirror while she scooped up lumps of cold cream and spread it on sections of his face, removing it with cottonwool. 'Do you remember when we signed each other's autograph books, Sette?'

'Of course, I do, *Chéri*!' Lisette had been unashamedly admiring of Nicolas and he'd basked in her compliments: 'You have a voice, Maestro. *Bien sûr*, you have a voice!' Amidst much chaffing and laughter, they'd signed each other's autograph books. 'I keep yours in a special place,' she said. 'Turn your head a little. This way. *Bien*.'

'Grand-père said he's seen you dance. He says you are very good.'

'Not any more, Petit.'

'You must not call me Petit, Settie. I have grown a lot. I am big now; bigger even than you.'

'So you are, *Chéri*: big and handsome! Sit still while I get this pancake off your top lip. Do this.' She pulled a face. He laughed and complied, eyeing his reflection.

As soon as she finished, he asked, 'How did you break your ankle, Sette? You said you would tell me.'

'I broke my ankle and my toes in a skiing fall, and I cannot dance *en pointe* any more. So ...' Her face twisted. 'No more prima spot for poor Lisette.'

'That's a shame! You are *belle, très belle*!'

'Thank you, my sweet. That is very charming of you.'

'I told my grand-père.'

'Did you?'

'*Oui*. I told him I love you, too.'

Her hand stilled momentarily. 'And what did he say?'

'He said that one could not help falling in love with a beautiful ballerina and that I had good taste.'

'That is so kind! He must be a lovely grand-père.'

'He is.'

Lisette giggled.

'What are you laughing at?'

'There is a big lump of *maquillage* in your right ear! Who put this make-up on?'

'*Moi*.'

'Oh, Nicolas! You went on stage like that? No matter: it would not have been noticed. Next time, I shall do it for you. Sit still, now. There! Nice and clean.' Lisette tossed the soiled cotton into a bin. 'All finished.' She smiled. 'And what have you been doing with yourself lately, *mon brave*?'

'Oh, lots of things, Settie, mostly learning. Did you know that I like to design things?'

'*Tiens*! What things?'

'Oh, houses, buildings, machines, things like that; and I like to play and compose music.'

'Ooh, *brave*! You're very accomplished, *n'est-ce pas*?'

'You think so? I love music the most. Do you love music, Sette?'

'Of course! I am a dancer …' Her smile faded. 'Of a sort.'

Nicolas did not miss the change in expression, concern leapt into his eyes. 'Settie? I think that now you cannot dance prima, you might need me to take care of you. You might need to marry me soon. What do you think?'

'Oh, Nicolas!' She kissed his brow, smoothing his hair the way his mother used to. There was a break in her voice. She, too, found Nicolas's surprising insight touching. 'I think you will find a beautiful young girl, one day. Then you will throw me, like a rag doll, on the scrap heap.'

'Never!' he said. 'Never!'

'Never?' She smiled. 'What would you do if I married Armand?'

He looked at her speculatively, a little dismayed. 'Would you?'

'I might … When you throw me over.'

Nicolas chuckled. 'You're funny, Sette!'

'No! Am I?'

'Hmm-mm. Settie? May I have a hug?'

'Of course, you can, *Chéri*!' Lisette sat on the couch, patting the cushion. 'Come, sit here beside me.'

Nicolas lay in her arms, nestling his cheek against the white satin *peignoir* that had been provided by the countess. 'Mama had one of these,' he said, touching the embroidered lapel. 'She always held me like this and kissed me on the forehead.' Tears sprang into the great blue eyes. 'I know I'm a trooper, but I miss her, Settie.' He turned his head into her shoulder. 'I do miss her so ...'

'Oh, you poor little boy!' gasped Lisette. 'You poor, poor little boy. Come here.' She kissed his brow over and over, holding him tightly, sobbing with him, until— exhausted from his tears—Nicolas closed his eyes.

Armand, finally released by the countess, came in. He seemed surprised to see the ballerina on the chaise longue with her arms around the sleeping Nicolas.

Lisette smiled. 'He is all in, Monsieur. He has just fallen asleep. Poor baby: he misses his mother.'

'Er, yes.' Armand reddened. *So do I. Especially after what I have just been through*! He shuddered at the memory.

Lisette, rising carefully, her eyes on Nicolas, did not notice. 'I don't want to wake him. You will look after him now, hein? Tell him I will see him next time.'

'Er, yes. Lisette, isn't it?'

'*Oui. Au revoir*, Monsieur.' Lisette let herself out of the room with a last look at Nicolas. Head down, brushing away tears, she did not see the countess until she almost ran into her. Lisette stepped back. 'I am sorry, Madame. I didn't see you there.'

'How did you go?'

Lisette's tone was guarded, subdued: 'He went to sleep in my arms, Madame.'

'Good, good,' leered the countess. 'Don't they all?'

'He's just a poor little child that misses his mother!' flashed Lisette, before she could stop herself.

The countess laughed. 'Well, of course, he does! What else are we going to use to hold onto him until he is a little older?'

'Oh ... You evil toad!' whispered Lisette, hardly able to speak for the fury that boiled in her breast. 'How can you be so ... disgusting? What you want me to do is a crime. Shame! Shame on you! Oh ...' She flinched as the countess slashed her across the face with her closed fan.

'I warned you! You stupid slut! Out! Get out! Now!'

Lisette straightened, head high, disregarding the trickling blood and pain that almost made her faint. 'With the greatest of pleasure, Madame!' Pride took her down the stairs, across the foyer and through the great front door without falter. It was only once she was out of the sight of the countess that she sank to the marble steps and cried, pressing the back of one finger to her bloodied cheek. The tears seeped into the wound, making it sting unbearably. She wished she'd had the wit not to lose her temper with La Reine, because who would help Nicolas now? She made a little, helpless gesture of despair, turning at the sound of hurried footsteps to see the tutor loom above her.

'Lisette!' He stopped, mid-career. 'But, good Lord! Whatever is the matter? Oh, you've hurt your face! It's bleeding! Here …' Armand pressed a clean handkerchief into her hand. 'Use that.'

'*Merci.*' The ballerina held it to her cheek. 'The countess hit me with her fan. She has thrown me out … on the street.'

'What a terrible woman!' He shuddered. 'Why on earth …?'

'Because I refuse to commit a sin against a child!'

'*Comment?*'

'Please …' She tossed him a silver cigarette case and lighter. 'I need a cigarette. Have one yourself.'

'Well, I don't really …' Armand sat down awkwardly on the step, lit two cigarettes and handed one to Lisette. She drew on it with a long sigh. He looked as if he didn't know what to do with his, or what to say, either. Carefully, he stubbed out the bright tip. 'Is this, uh … Is this about … Nicolas?'

'*Oui.*' She expelled the smoke and grasped his hand, her eyes urgent. 'Nicolas is in danger here! Please … You must do something before it is too late!'

Armand, embarrassed by her touch, was even more alarmed by her words. 'Wh-what do you mean? Are you trying to tell me ———?'

'Listen!' She told him what the countess had demanded of her and what the woman had threatened if Lisette refused. 'And now I am out on the street and that poor, sweet child will be at the mercy of that gorgon and perhaps another who does not have a conscience. You are the only one who can help him.'

Armand was silent. He couldn't leave Lisette out here alone, and there was obviously something very wrong with the management of the Opéra Magique. Despite having had a lucky escape himself, he had no way to determine the degree of danger to Nicolas. But it wasn't up to him. He cleared his throat. 'There is only one man who can do something about this. I must take you to the duc de Belvoir.' He stood up—suddenly decisive—his shyness overcome. 'I will fetch the car and come back for Nicolas. Get your things and meet me here when you are ready.'

'She won't let me get my things.'

Armand grimaced. 'I dare not face her, either. Wait here, then. I won't be a moment.' He strode into the square, signalled to the driver of a big black Daimler and ran back into the opera house, returning a short time later with a yawning companion. 'Come along, Nicolas: Where are your manners? We have a lady with us. Your friend, Lisette, is coming to talk to your grand-père.'

Nicolas gave her his arm and a sleepy smile. 'Oh good, Settie! He will like that. You can sit in the back with me. Armand can ride in the front with Mary.' He noticed the handkerchief she held to her face. Anxiety entered his voice. 'Did you hurt yourself? You're bleeding!'

'It is nothing. I bumped my cheek on the door. Armand lent me his handkerchief so it wouldn't drip onto my dressing-gown. Look it has stopped now.' She showed him the cut.

'No, it hasn't.' He frowned at the blood welling from her cheek.

Lisette smiled at the worry in his eyes. 'Then it will soon. We artists are tough. Remember?'

'I remember.' Nicolas pressed her arm.

They were just getting into the vehicle when a limousine drew up at the steps and a woman in furs alighted.

Lisette put a hand on Armand's sleeve. 'Can you wait a little minute, Monsieur? That is Anna, our present prima donna. She might consent to pack some things for me and bring them down … Anna!' Lisette began to run.

The blonde woman turned and waited. The others watched Lisette's agitated explanation; the calming gestures of the prima ballerina before she vanished into the Opéra Magique. The limousine drove away and Mary pulled over to the steps. The seconds ticked by. Then Anna was back with a large carpetbag and a dressing case. Armand got out and took them from her, averting his eyes as the ballerinas took emotional leave of each other.

As they approached the hôtel du Bois, Lisette indicated her dressing-gown. 'May I have a moment to change out of this, Monsieur, before I must meet the duc?'

'It's pretty, Sette,' Nicolas assured her. 'Grand-père will like it.'

'It is not *comme il faut* for the salon, *Chéri*. Only the dressing-room.'

Mary spoke rarely, but when she did, everyone listened. They loved the way she spoke French with her soft Welsh accent. 'Master Nic should be in his bed, Armand. Why don't I drop you two at the front entrance? Then take Mademoiselle with me to the hospice to change and have her injury seen to. I'll bring her back through the house to the salon as soon as she is ready.'

'Yes, that will be best, I think,' agreed Armand.

'That's good, Mary,' murmured Nicolas, 'if you will take care of Sette for me. I am so tired …'

'Of course, you are, *Chéri*.' Lisette kissed his brow. 'You've had a big night. See you soon, *hein*?'

Armand steered his charge through the front entrance, and Mary drove smoothly around to the door of the hospice.

'The late marquis du Bois and Madame Dupont turned most of this house into a hospital during the Great War. This wing remains a hospice, and I have an apartment upstairs. My husband is in here. He never recovered from his war wounds,' explained Mary, taking Lisette to a nurse to have her wound attended.

'I'm sorry,' murmured Lisette, her brow furrowed. 'One question, Madame: You said, "The late marquis du Bois". This is not the home of the duc de Belvoir?'

'No, but he is here. The house was left to Nicolas's mother and now belongs to him, but the duc has made it his headquarters in Paris. He feels that Nicolas, having lost his parents, must be allowed to keep his home.'

'Ah, *le pauvre*, yes. Then the duc is here?'

'Oh, yes, he is here.' Mary waited for the nurse to finish her ministrations before showing Lisette into a cloakroom. 'Leave your bags here. A porter will take them over later.'

When Lisette appeared, exquisitely dressed, Mary led her through what seemed like miles of corridors to knock on a door and converse with a large, sombrely dressed butler. 'I will leave you now,' she said to Lisette. 'Justin will look after you.'

'But certainly. Come along to the salon, Mademoiselle.'

Lisette followed the substantial figure, wondering how the duc would react to her story. If he did not believe her, or if he refused to accept her because of what she'd become, what would happen to Nicolas?

# 11 THE DUC TAKES CHARGE

**27 October 1931**

*I have never heard such a dreadful thing. La Reine is definitely mad! I cannot even write what she tried to do to me! The count does not care, either. I never saw anyone so apathetic. He told me that while she has her attention on me, she is leaving him alone; and that is all he cares about. He says that all he wants is peace and doesn't care how he gets it. No wonder: she is a hag! It is whispered around the back of the stage that she has another madness called nymphomania, and I believe it! And the evil she wishes to visit on Nicolas? Eh bien, there is only one man in the world who can pull her up!*

Lisette was relieved to see Armand seated in an armchair. He jumped up when he saw her, came to the door and escorted her in to the room. 'If you please, Monsieur, this is the lady I was telling you about: Mademoiselle Lisette …?' He looked a question.

'Lavoisier.' Lisette came forward, holding out a hand. 'I am happy to make your acquaintance, Monsieur.' She almost curtsied, so evident was the nobility of the man she faced, but stopped herself. *This is France. We are all equal here.*

The duc greeted her with a gentle courtesy that immediately set her at ease. 'I understand that I have to thank you for taking care of my grandson. We will get to that presently. But first, I think you have something that you wish to tell me?'

'*Oui*, Monsieur. Armand has told me that you are the proper person to relate this to. But I beg your forgiveness, Monsieur. It is sordid in the extreme.'

The duc waved a hand. '*De rien*, Mademoiselle, there is nothing to forgive! You would like some refreshment first? A little wine, perhaps?'

'No, thank you, Monsieur.'

'Then, I am listening, Mademoiselle.'

Lisette took a deep breath. 'When the Countess Kireyevsky took over the theatre management, at first, she did not make too many changes, only good ones; so that we grew to depend on her judgement. She has always been autocratic—will take advice from no-one—but lately, she has changed. She has moved all of us to rooms in the opera house and has closed the *Académie Mirage* to cut costs, she says. She seems driven ... I don't know ...' The ballerina's worried eyes sought to explain what her words could not.

'In what way has her behaviour changed, Mademoiselle?'

'That is it. It is inexplicable, really.' She shrugged. 'Madame suddenly decided that the Opéra Magique must offer more services than the entertainments an opera house usually provides.'

'No!' said the duc. 'You do not mean ...?'

'The countess has made it quite plain that unless we are prepared to give gentlemen the ...' Lisette hesitated, flushed and lowered her eyes, 'pleasures that they desire in our rooms after the performance, there will no longer be a position for us at the Opéra Magique.'

The duc straightened in shock. 'Cèline has become an *entremetteuse*? And has turned the Opéra Magique into *un bordel? Une maison close? Mon Dieu!*' He got up to pace back and forth.

'I think she has gone mad, Monsieur.'

'*Vraiment?*' He swung around to face her. 'That is your considered opinion, *n'est-ce pas?*'

'*Oui*, Monsieur. *Je regrette …*'

'It is more than possible, Mademoiselle.' The duc was looking grim. 'Please continue.'

'I tried to leave, Monsieur, but I injured my toes and ankle and could not dance for several months. The countess pretended to be sympathetic: gave me time off with full remuneration. She said I could think of it as a holiday. But then, she began to demand recompense or she would throw me out in the street as I was, saying that the kind of dancing I was to do wouldn't stress my ankle.' Lisette paused, the suggestive chuckle of the countess ringing unpleasantly in her ears. 'I did as she said, but believe me, I am not proud of it, Monsieur.'

'Poor, poor child! It is a scandal. Worse even than …' He indicated her swollen, dressed cheek. 'She has done this to you?'

'*Oui*, Monsieur. I may be so much dirt, but there is a sin that I will not commit. So …' She shrugged. 'I am out on the street, and Armand has brought me to tell you my story.'

'Armand was right to bring you to me,' he assured her. 'But there is one thing you will *not* do. As a dancer, you have an exquisite gift: an ethereal beauty of body and soul. You will never again refer to yourself as dirt. You understand? *Bien.*' The duc looked at her closely. 'But I know you! Were you not principal dancer at the Opéra Magique …? Now, let me see … the year before last? Nicolas has talked about you: *Lisette*, of course! Are you not the one he's been wanting to marry since he was four or five?'

'Yes, Monsieur.' Lisette's tense expression changed to one of tender amusement. 'He is a faithful suitor, that one.'

'Indeed!' said the duc with a charming smile. 'I do apologise for not having recognised you sooner, Mademoiselle. That year began ——' The duc stopped himself from saying, 'A nightmare of grief and confusion that still goes on today', squared his shoulders and changed the drift. 'You were a very lovely dancer.' He smiled again. 'I must applaud my grandson's good taste.'

'*Merci*, Monsieur. It is a joke I have had with Nicolas since our first meeting. It seems I remind him of someone he loves.'

'Ah, yes: the portrait of the late comtesse de Villefontaine. He was enamoured of it long before he was old enough to understand she was his grandmother. Permit me to tell you that there is a distinct likeness. Now, if it will not distress you too much, will you recount to me this sin that the countess has told you to commit?'

'Monsieur, it has to do with this very thing we are talking about. I tried to explain it to her, but ...' Lisette told him exactly what the Countess Kireyevsky had demanded of her.

'*Incroyable*! Such depravity!' The duc went white, swayed and grasped the back of a chair.

'Monsieur, you look ill!' Armand hurried to take his arm.

'That is not surprising. I am sick to the very core of my being! Never have I heard ...'

'May we assist you to the chair?' asked Lisette, at his other side.

'*Non, merci.*' The duc held a handkerchief to his lips. 'I shall recover presently.' He took a few deep breaths and, when his colour returned, spoke to the ballerina. 'You may rest assured that the countess will *not* get away with this. But you, Mademoiselle ... what will you do now?'

Lisette dropped her eyes. 'I do not know, Monsieur. My ankle, you see, is not strong enough to do more than dance in the main corps—in the background. And my toes … There is only one other avenue open to me. I do not wish to take it, but … one must eat.'

'Will you go back to the Opéra Magique as a dancer? If I make it possible for you?'

'Monsieur, my career is very close to the end. I feel it here in my heart. Despite months of practise, I have not been able to attain my previous high level of dance. And the countess! I do not think I can …'

'I understand. Do you read and write?'

'Oh, yes, Monsieur.'

'And you sew?'

'I make all my own clothes, including my hats.'

The duc eyed her fashionable, tastefully designed suit and chic little hat with approval. 'Forgive me, Mademoiselle, for this question: if you had a respectable job, would you consider any other, let us say, *less* respectable offer?'

'*Never*, Monsieur! I will be only too glad to escape a way of life that has become a living hell.'

'Poor young lady!' The duc's eyes were full of sympathy. But then his expression lightened. 'I have an idea: do you feel that you could teach?' He waved a hand. 'Dance? Deportment?'

'*Mais oui*, I suppose so …' Lisette thought for a moment, then looked up, joy in her face. 'Oh, yes! Yes, I could.'

'*Bien, bien*. Then, here is your job: You will help Armand answer the fan mail—a sort of under-secretary, if you will. You will keep Nicolas's stage costumes furbished up and make sure he is neat and tidy and made-up for his performances. Then, when we go to Belvoir for the summer, you will teach the village children, and Nicolas, dance and deportment.' The duc came closer. 'What do you say?'

'Oh yes, Monsieur. *Merci*.'

'*Bien*.' The duc bowed. 'May I say how thankful I am to you for saving my grandson?' He took her hand and kissed it. 'You will not have to demean yourself in *my* house, Mademoiselle.'

'Thank you, Monsieur.' She hesitated. 'Nicolas isn't … he only wants the love of a mother. And despite that evil … it is the only kind of love I have shown him.'

'I know that without you telling me. Nicolas needs a mother figure. It has made him vulnerable. I have no objection if you wish to continue in that role.'

'*Merci*, Monsieur. I will be very happy to do so.'

§

The duc met the countess in her newly decorated salon on the ground floor of the Opéra Magique. He briefly closed his eyes at the harsh modernity that accorded ill with its baroque surroundings and made his way to the countess, who stood motionless beside a small table on which reposed a silver ashtray with a gazelle *couchant*, a matching cigarette box and a long decorative holder. Clasping a carved ivory fan in a black-gloved hand, she made no move towards him; her thin lips curling at his approach.

'Ah, Monsieur le duc! You make your appearance at last, *hein*?' The countess looked him over with unconcealed mockery. 'To what do I owe this *great* pleasure?'

'Madame.' The duc fancied he saw knowledge and spite in the narrowed blue eyes and bowed with chilling hauteur. 'I have come because I have heard some *extraordinary* tales about this house, and I wish to know the facts behind them.'

'So, Monsieur: what have you heard? All good, I trust? We are doing very well in these hard times. Very well, indeed!' The countess flourished her fan, deliberately aping the style of her mother—watching his reaction with amusement—enjoying his revulsion in her own perverse way.

'That is not how it was put to me, Madame,' replied the duc. 'In fact, it was something quite different. May I?' he said gently, removing the fan from her suddenly flaccid grip and placing it on the table. 'I am afraid I cannot bear to watch you do that.'

'My mother ——'

'You dare to speak your mother's name to me after what *you* have done?' The duc's voice vibrated with anger, though he did not raise it.

The countess tossed her head. 'Why not? I have done nothing wrong.'

'Nothing wrong? *Nothing wrong?* You published your mother's diaries. In direct contravention of her wishes!'

The countess laughed, reached for her ornate holder, and concentrated on inserting and lighting a cigarette. 'You will have to prove that, Monsieur.'

He sidestepped the smoke she expelled and waited for her attention. 'No matter. I know that it was you. But not content with disrespecting your mother's wishes, I hear that you have further tarnished her memory by turning her beautiful Opéra Magique into a house of ill repute. Is this true, Madame?'

'*Mais non*, Monsieur!' She narrowed her eyes. 'Where *on earth* did you hear that?'

'It does not matter. So there is no truth in it, then?'

'No, Monsieur. None at all.'

The duc drew from his pocket a wad of notes, closely watching the woman's reaction. 'And if I happen to have seen a dancer that I … desire?'

'This is an opera house, Monsieur.' She shrugged. 'Nothing more. You must go to another type of house if that is your requirement. Your informant has obviously been mistaken.'

'I wonder,' he murmured, moving to the table and setting down roll after roll of notes. 'I have heard that this house is most exclusive. How exclusive?' The pile continued to grow.

Tension heightened. The hand of the countess trembled as she raised her cigarette holder to her lips. 'I have already told you, Monsieur: there is no such service here.'

The duc watched her impassively as he placed yet another wad. 'Everything has its price, Madame. Tell me when I have reached this one.' He set down another and another. 'Now, perhaps?'

She gritted her teeth. 'Monsieur, I have told you: this is an opera house, nothing more.'

'Ah, yes. I heard you.' He took a little chamois drawstring bag from his inner coat pocket and poured its contents onto the table, smiling inwardly as he heard a sharp intake of breath.

'*Mon Dieu!*' gasped the countess, greed flaming in her eyes.

The duc waited, idly stirring the diamonds with a forefinger, so that they flashed with a myriad rainbow lights.

The countess moistened her lips and sucked hard on her cigarette holder.

The duc waited patiently while she coughed, waved away the smoke and took another draw.

Finally, as if forced, she spoke. 'Times are hard, Monsieur. Perhaps ... *something* ... could be arranged for a man who desires a ballerina as much as that.'

The duc sighed and straightened. 'So ... it *is* true? And you *are* lying.'

'No, Monsieur.' The countess ashed her cigarette. She glanced slyly from him to the bounty on the table. 'For those who ... *sufficiently* ... appreciate beauty, it is just an extra service, that is all.'

'Into which you *coerce* your dancers ...'

'No, Monsieur! Certainly not!

'You lie. I know that you do.' The very quietness of the duc made him all the more formidable. His implacable calm, icy dignity; the condemnation in his eyes silenced the countess. 'There was only ever one ballerina I desired,' he said, picking up the notes and returning them to his pocket. 'I thought you would know that.' He glanced from her thwarted expression to the seductive glitter of the diamonds on the table. 'It seems that I read the diaries more carefully than you.' Scooping the bright stones back into the bag, he pulled tight the string. The silence lengthened while he waited. When the countess did not speak, he went on, 'Monsieur Dupont never permitted such usage of his ballerinas. To him they were exquisite, precious creatures to be protected and adored.'

'Papa ...' she whispered. A dim recollection from her childhood almost brought tears: Monsieur Dupont she had truly loved and never forgotten, despite losing him before she was three years old.

'Not your papa—as we both know—as everyone now knows, thanks to you.' The duc was brutal in his quiet way. 'There is poetic justice here: By your actions you have tarnished his memory, too, ruined it for yourself. Because until you read the diaries, you did not know that the one person in the world you loved was not your father, did you?'

The countess flinched and made a strangled cry. 'Do not ...' She bowed her head, blindly stubbing out her cigarette, dropping the ebony holder with a clatter on to the ashtray.

'No,' said the duc. 'Because ... If he had been, your hereditary instincts would not have allowed you to behave in this despicable fashion. You have acted on your own whim— always; listening to no-one; causing misery and evil to all that you touch, including these beautiful creatures at your mercy—and I tell you now that you have gone your length.' The golden-hazel eyes, usually so warm, were hard as tiger's eye. 'What do you have to say in defence of yourself?'

The countess did not lift her head. She made a gesture

that could be construed as helplessness, remorse, excuse or even grief at the mention of Monsieur Dupont.

'Nothing? *Vraiment?*' The duc was not fooled. The gentle, sensitive artist was gone. In his place stood the ruler of a great estate: one who expected to be obeyed. 'In that case, you will attend to me,' his voice rose a little. 'You are listening? *Bien,*' he said at her nod, lowering it again. 'If a ballerina consents to a liaison with a patron by her own free choice then, *eh bien,* it is her own decision.' He shrugged. 'It may be a bad decision, but it is hers to make. It must not be a requirement of the position.' He paused, and his glance held bitterness. 'You have Nicolas over a barrel, and I allowed him to sing because I would not risk his inheritance; but now things have changed. I have been informed of your scurrilous and infamous plot against my grandson, and I tell you, here and now, that your machinations will come to nothing. Lift your head and look at me when I speak!'

At last the countess raised her head and looked down her nose with an arrogance that reminded the duc of his late cousin, the Black Prince. He ignored the frisson that went down his spine, resuming his quiet tone, 'I will *not* have my grandson's inheritance turned into a bordello. You will observe the so-called niceties—the mores of society, however double-faced they may be—or I will have you closed down.'

Spite flashed in her eyes; triumph that lasted less than a second. The countess began to speak but the duc forestalled her.

'*And* I will do it in a way that will give you no redress. There is no money in playing to an empty house, Madame.' He waited for that to sink in, surveying her with a contempt and revulsion that made her flush and bite her lip: a reaction that she had not expected from herself, and it enraged her.

Noting the fury in her narrowed eyes, the duc was satisfied that his thrust had gone home. He was the undisputed leader of fashion and a connoisseur of note when it came to *les beaux-arts*. If he declared a house below standard or *démodé*, then *le beau monde* would ostracise it. His next words, measured and softly biting, flicked the countess on the raw: 'You may live off your mother's toil and beauty, but I will *not* have it mired in this fashion.'

She gasped but said nothing.

The duc gave an order, 'Call your ballerinas.'

'*Mais …*'

'Call them.'

Baffled by his air of chilling authority, the countess inclined her head and went out.

The ballerinas filed in, looking nervous. The duc's eyes softened and warmed as he looked upon these delicate creatures so dear to his heart. The countess did not return.

'Mesdemoiselles,' began the duc, smiling at each of them, 'I have been a patron of this house for many years and have a profound admiration for the grace and elegance of the ballet. I now stand proxy to one of its owners, and in that guise, I wish to assure each and every one of you that your contract here is as a dancer. Nothing more, nothing less. Despite what you have previously been told, your beauty is for the stage alone and must not be compromised by fear or coercion. For art to shine in its true glory, the artist must be free to express it with joy, unconstrained.' His warm, golden-hazel eyes held all the respect and admiration the ballerinas could have wished; and his next words did nothing to dispel the illusion: 'Your personal conduct must be at your own discretion. Should anything else be required of you, I will wish to hear about it.' His smile encompassed them. 'That is all.'

The duc bowed and turned away. But as he left them, his expression set in grave lines. He was not enjoying his thoughts. Memories, good and bad, crowded in on him, overlain by the feeling the countess had given him when she had raised her head and looked at him with a venom that reminded him of a man who was pure evil.

It was then he realised that his visit to the Opéra Magique had not allayed any of his anxieties about Nicolas. *Au contraire,* it had only increased them.

# 12 THE DOPPLEGÄNGER

**2 May 1932**

*The duc has been closeted with Monsieur Bernaud several times over these last months in an attempt to free Nicolas from his contract with the Opéra Magique. Lisette made a signed affidavit in an attempt to help. True to form, the countess has utterly denied Lisette's accusations, claiming that she has always been a liar and a troublemaker. Since it is only Lisette's word against hers, this testimony cannot be used to break the contract.*

*The main problem with this contract, as I understand it, is that any failure of Nicolas to be onstage at his appointed times will allow the countess to sue him for loss of income, to the sum of his inheritance, no provision being made for illness or misadventure. I don't understand how she got away with it, but she has. Only one little thing has come out of it. Monsieur Bernaud has discovered that there is no actual mention of Nicolas having to sing. He must just 'perform' onstage, whatever that means. How this helps I have not the wit to fathom. However it is, Nicolas must not miss a performance date.*

*Lisette inadvertently solved the problem. Upon hearing of it, she remarked in her flippant way that what Nicolas needed was a double. Whereupon the duc clapped a hand to his head, made a stifled exclamation and strode to the telephone.*

'I have asked you to find a double for Nicolas, and you have brought to me a blond?' The duc raised his brows in disbelief at Monsieur Lorraine, the musician he had sent on this crucial errand. 'Gervais, isn't it?' he said, glancing kindly at the lad whose profusion of flaxen curls dominated a cherubic face. 'You are a boy soprano?'

'*Oui,* Monsieur.' Sapphire-blue eyes, uncannily like his grandson's, briefly looked into his.

'He has a voice of power and quality, Monsieur,' interrupted the musician. 'Would you like to hear him?'

'Not yet.' The duc turned back to the boy. 'Where do you sing, Gervais?'

Again, the musician answered for him: 'That is the great part, Monsieur. He is an orphan from a church in the poor quarter. None of *le beau monde* will have ever heard him or be likely to.'

The duc ignored him and spoke to the boy: 'I am sorry for this misunderstanding; and I am certain that your voice is all that it is claimed to be, Gervais; but I asked Monsieur Lorraine to find me a dark-haired boy. I am afraid that we have importuned you for no good reason, *mon fils.* Regrettably, I do not see how you can be of use to us.'

The boy, robust and angelically fair, blinked rapidly, dropping his eyes to conceal his disappointment. He began to search his pockets for a handkerchief.

'*Doucement,* my child.' Monsieur Lorraine gave him one and put a comforting hand on his shoulder. He turned to the duc. 'Monsieur, he is the only one with the voice … height, build, face shape: it was the best that I could do. We have searched the whole country. We considered going into Italy for the dark hair, but the skin tone and eye colour …' The man shrugged. 'Hair can be dyed,

Monsieur, and if you have a good make-up artist … But there is no disguise for a voice.'

'Very true.' The duc rang the bell. 'Take this young boy to Lisette and ask her what she thinks of your choice. Tell her that I shall be along presently to hear her verdict and to let me know when she is ready. My servant will show you the way.' The answering footman bowed and escorted them from the room.

A short time later, the duc made a rare appearance in Nicolas's dressing-room at the hôtel du Bois. There, he found Lisette, the two boys, Armand and the musician, Monsieur Lorraine. He raised his eyebrows at their various expressions.

Lisette was selecting a number of pots from a drawer of the dressing table, glancing from one boy to the other with intense concentration: Nicolas looked surprised and pleased, Gervais nervous and uncertain, Monsieur Lorraine tense and unhappy and Armand, frankly, astonished.

The duc broke the silence: 'You have made your decision, Lisette? If, by some chance, we are called upon to use this young lad, Gervais, are we able to do so with anything approaching credibility?'

'I think so, Monsieur, but I have asked you to come along and witness the transformation for yourself.' She smiled, glancing, as had the duc, at the surrounding faces. 'You are thinking that I will need to be something of a magician, *non*? But I will show you the power of make-up. Nicolas and Gerry are not unalike, you know.' Her eyes questioned the duc. 'You do not see it?'

'Not at first glance, no,' replied the duc, standing back to view the boys. 'But do go on. I must confess the hair colour has me bedevilled. I expect you mean to dye it?'

'No, Monsieur.' The ballerina resumed her serious air. 'It will not do just to dye Gerry's hair. It is thick and curly; whereas, Nicolas's is straight, giving his head a sleek contour. Also, we do not want Gerry to lose his identity when he sings on his own account. He must not just disappear from his church, *n'est-ce pas?*'

'No, indeed! You are quite right. We must not have anyone looking for him,' agreed the duc, much struck.

'We will need the services of a good wigmaker. Then, with a wig the same as Nicolas's hair, I can make Gerry up to look so like him that it will not be noticed when he is onstage. If the audience is expecting Nicolas, then it is Nicolas they will see. But enough chatter. I will show you what I mean.' She went to the boys, shepherding them towards the dressing table. 'Come here, Gerry. Stand next to Nicolas in front of the mirror. That's it, *bon.*'

The two boys looked at each other and then at themselves in the mirror. Two almost identical sets of deep blue eyes twinkled back: one below a pair of black brows, the other beneath a set so fair that they were practically invisible.

Lisette threaded her small fingers through Gervais's hair, pulling it back from his forehead. 'You see, Monsieur, how alike they are, apart from colouring?'

The duc tipped his head to one side, considering. 'They have the same eyes, height and build. But I must confess ...'

'You do not see it yet? *Eh bien,* I will show you.' With remarkable dexterity, Lisette drew arched black brows on the fair face and expertly darkened the lashes, then, with a quick twist, tied a matching kerchief about the head of each boy, hiding the hair. She stepped back with the air of a conjurer.

'*Extraordinary* ...' breathed the duc.

Nicolas laughed delightedly, clasping the other boy's hand. '*Eh bien,* we are twins, Gerry. *Foudroyant!*'

Gervais smiled back. Nobody could tell that he was older than Nicolas (thirteen), and all his singing had been in churches and cathedrals. Here was his chance to break into opera. '*Foudroyant,* yes!' he agreed, returning the handshake. 'We look like twin pirates, *n'est-ce pas?*' He turned to the duc. 'I thank you from the bottom of my heart, Monsieur, for this chance that you have given me.'

'*De rien, mon fils*! You are part of the team: Nicolas's team. It seems to be growing by the day,' he added dryly. He studied the two boys, so alike in their make-up and the natural joy that shone from their faces. Then he looked at Lisette. 'Go ahead and order the wig,' he said. 'And, of course, we will tell no-one. This is a card that will be best kept up our sleeve. There is nothing wrong with Nicolas having a young musical friend to keep him company and do his lessons with.'

'*Mais oui*, Monsieur. Without the wig and make-up, no-one will notice how alike they are. You proved that yourself.'

'So I did.' The duc laughed.

'Gervais will continue to sing at his church and will learn Nicolas's songs in secret,' said the musician. 'We have agreed on that?'

'Yes, he will live here with Nicolas and be taken to his church on Sundays to sing. As long as he keeps his real purpose here a secret.' He turned to the boy. 'Do you hear that, Gervais? If you cannot keep it secret, the job will not be yours.'

'*J'écoute*, Monsieur. I will not let you down. Our secret will never be known because of me.'

The duc sighed. He now felt that he had another string to his bow. This would take the pressure off Nicolas and give him a companion of similar age: another thing the duc had been worried about.

Gervais moved in to the room next to Nicolas. Lisette and Armand took charge of them both, and Nicolas almost had the family he craved. He found out that Gervais was an orphan, brought up by nuns, and felt an even closer bond.

Nicolas was confident—bright and bouncy—a natural leader. Gervais was quieter, but ready to join in anything Nicolas proposed. They became inseparable, uncannily alike in their speech and actions. Gervais had taken his promise to the duc more seriously than anyone envisioned.

Armand shook his head. 'Two of them,' he said to Lisette, 'are more than twice as much trouble as one.'

'They are good for you,' she replied. 'At least you know that you are alive.'

Armand stared after her as she walked away. 'Wait! Wh-what do you mean?'

'What I say.' She turned her head to give him a mischievous smile. 'I always mean what I say. *À bientôt,* Monsieur.'

Armand stood, perplexed. He'd never understand Lisette. She made him blush, laughed at him, made him blush even more and laughed at him again. But she was kind and wonderful with the boys, encouraging their sense of adventure, at the same time, quelling their pranks before they got out of hand. Yes, Lisette was wonderful. He wished he understood her. He wished he could feel more for her. Whenever he tried to feel something for someone living, a beautiful ghost got in the way. Yet, he acknowledged to himself, Lisette only treated him in the same way she treated the boys. At the thought of her warmth, he flushed again.

Once per week, Nicolas, accompanied by Armand, turned up at the Opéra Magique. Nicolas sang alone or with the count, signed photos and autograph books for his fans, then went home unobtrusively through a side entrance where the car was always waiting. The fact that the countess was not in sight did not prevent both him and Armand from looking nervously about for her.

Armand had not spoken to the countess since the night she had hit Lisette, but he still shuddered at the memory of those gloved fingers stealing about his neck, fondling his hair; her lips close enough to his earlobe to feel her moist, tobacco-laden breath as she whispered her dictation, followed by suggestions that made him go hot and cold and wonder, desperately, how he might escape.

But now, it seemed, the countess wanted to have nothing to do with them: either absent or at the other end of the opera house whenever he and Nicolas were present. Occasionally, they saw her gesturing with her fan, or her long cigarette holder, in conversation with a patron; but she never once glanced their way. It was as if they no longer existed. Almost, they began to enjoy their visits.

Armand knew that Nicolas had a complex and all-consuming relationship with his audience. Once onstage, it was difficult to get him to leave them. So far, it had not been necessary for a substitution to be made. *At least,* thought Armand, *Nicolas enjoys himself onstage, while I do my best to hide …*

### 15 May 1934

*I have begun to get a few worries about the behaviour of Gervais. There has been a sudden change in his attitude, which is understandable, at this stage of his manhood. He is fifteen, more than a year older than Nicolas, but the traits he is beginning to exhibit are unfortunately dark. I fear that he has begun to bully Nicolas. I believe I caught him at it today, but Nicolas denied it. That, of course, is to be expected. Nicolas's loyalty, along with his open, caring and friendly nature, is one of his most admirable attributes; and I don't want him to be used in this way. I must keep a better eye on them.*

After two years of waiting, with Nicolas never missing a performance, Gervais became moody and temperamental. He was beginning to make excuses not to be with Nicolas, showing a preference to get away by himself. 'To read,' he said. 'I don't want to play any more. Little boys' games. I am sorry.'

Puzzled by his attitude, Nicolas got on with his own interests, but he sometimes caught his understudy in a vindictive stare that made him feel uncomfortable. Gervais, miffed at being so thoroughly ignored, began to use ridicule, practical jokes and cruel taunts against him whenever they were alone together. Nicolas shrugged them off as a bull might brush away an irritating fly. Only once did he retaliate.

His blue eyes alive with malice, Gervais lunged for the chain of Nicolas's locket, pulling it hard against his throat. 'You're wearing a necklace,' he jeered. 'Little girl!'

'Leave go, Gerry. You're hurting me.'

'It's my turn to have it. Give it me!'

'Stop it, Gerry. You know it was Mama's, and I never take it off.'

'Oh, diddums! Little baby, wearing Mama's jewellery.' Gervais pulled harder so that the chain bit into Nicolas's neck. 'You're going to take it off now, then.'

Nicolas knocked him down, surprising both of them.

Sending him a covert look, Gervais picked himself up off the floor and, head down, sped out of the room.

'I'm sorry, Gerry,' Nicolas called after him. 'I didn't mean to hit you so hard. I didn't mean to hit you at all. You shouldn't have ———'

Gervais slammed the door.

'———Tried to take my locket,' muttered Nicolas, feeling like a brute. Over the top of Gervais's running footsteps, he could imagine his grandfather saying, 'Violence solves nothing, Nicolas. It is the ploy of the ignorant; indefensible in a man of character and education.'

*I must apologise to Gerry,* he thought. *I had no right to hit him, no matter how much he provoked me.*

Gervais received Nicolas's apology in cold silence, rejoicing at the weapon the younger boy had placed in his hands. He could, and did, use Nicolas's genuine remorse to find subtle ways to bully him and, occasionally, subjected him to a pinch or a hold that made him protest at the pain.

After one of these episodes, in answer to Nicolas's agonised 'why?' Gervais said, 'You have everything, and I have nothing.'

Nicolas shrugged his bewilderment. 'We eat, dress and live the same way. What do I have that you don't?'

'You don't understand. It is not what you have. It is what you are. I am nothing.'

'No. Never! You are just like me.'

'Like you?' He stared at Nicolas with contempt. 'Why would I want to be like you? You are just a child. A selfish child!'

'No, I'm not!' Nicolas showed his hurt. 'I don't know what you mean?'

'I mean that you have never once given me the opportunity to sing onstage. And I am growing older. Soon, my voice will break. You are selfish. Selfish! I want my chance!' He grabbed Nicolas by the collar, then reefed his arm up behind his back. 'Give me my chance!' he shouted, twisting it unbearably.

Nicolas gasped at the pain, trying, without success, to free himself.

'Boys! What is all the noise about?' Armand appeared in the doorway as Gervais let Nicolas's arm fall and stepped away, breathing hard.

'Nothing,' said Nicolas. 'We were just playing, weren't we, Gerry?'

'Then do it quietly.' The tutor withdrew after a meaningful look at each of them.

Nicolas's blue gaze was straight and regretful. 'I'm sorry, Gerry. I can't pretend.'

'Yes, you can,' hissed the other. 'And it's Gervais. Do you hear? From now on you will call me Gervais.'

Nicolas went away, miserable. He'd never seen Gerry behave quite so badly. Maybe he should pretend he was ill; let him have his chance onstage to know what it felt like to have the love of a whole audience. *But it is me they want. Gerry will only be getting something meant for me. Because everyone will think he is me. It won't be for him, so how can it be right?*

*Nicolas.*

*Angel? What should I do? Gerry is so angry.*

*Allow him to take your place tonight, as he wishes.*

*But ... Nothing is wrong with me.*

*It will not hurt you to be generous to him. Besides, you have overused your voice, and it will be all the better for a rest. Tell Lisette you think you are getting a sore throat, and let the boy have his way.*

*But ...*

*You are not a selfish person, Nicolas. Stay at home tonight.*

When Lisette came to dress and make him up, Nicolas told her his throat didn't feel right. That was no lie: the tension in it was unbearable. He felt miserable and put upon. Even Angel had as good as told him he was selfish not to let Gerry sing, just this once.

Lisette felt his forehead. 'You look a trifle downcast, *mon chou.* Perhaps you are sickening for something? Your throat is sore?'

'N-no. Just ...'

'Not quite right, *hein?*'

'Yes.' It was a relief not to have to lie to Lisette.

'Then we must take no risks. I will call Gerry.'

'He says we must call him Gervais.'

'Oh!' Lisette exploded into laughter. 'Gerry is getting too big for his boots. A cockerel learning to crow! Let us see what happens when he tells *me* to call him Gervais.'

But Gervais made no such demand of Lisette, anxiously complying with all her directions. Nicolas watched her make him up with a horrid sensation in his stomach that he didn't realise was jealousy. It increased to sickening proportions as Gervais bid him a cocky goodnight and went off with Armand, leaving him behind.

'Come,' said Lisette, with an understanding hug. 'An early night for you, *jeune* Monsieur. We must rest your voice. *And* keep you out of sight.'

§

Gervais got a peculiar thrill out of impersonating Nicolas. He had memorised his gestures, favourite sayings and was word perfect. His excitement at the adulation Nicolas almost took for granted knew no bounds. He began to toy with the idea of forcing Nicolas to allow him to sing more often. From his experiences at the orphanage, he knew of one or two quite excruciating holds that would cause the victim to promise anything for release and decided, then and there, to try them on the other boy at the first opportunity.

At the end of the performance, Armand hustled him out a side door, avoiding the fans. There was one thing that Gervais could not copy, no matter how hard he tried: Nicolas's handwriting.

'Whew! Thank goodness that's over. I was so nervous. But you did well. Very well.'

'*I* am Nicolas de Beaulieu! And tonight, I had the audience at my feet,' exulted the boy. '*I* am a *succès fou*.'

'Indeed, you are. It was a brilliant performance. You are a first-class actor as well as a singer, *mon brave*.'

'*Merci*, Armand.' He sounded so uncannily like Nicolas that the tutor was shaken. 'Up there on the stage: It was *épatant!* So exciting! I can't explain …'

'I expect someone else knows exactly what you mean,' said the tutor, looking around in vain for the car and realising that they were a little earlier than usual.

'No, he doesn't. It was the danger of being recognised. Wondering if I'd be found out. But no-one knew,' gloated Gervais.

Armand looked hard at the glowing eyes; the tension evident in the young body. 'I felt that, too. But I did *not* enjoy it. Ah well, we're safe now.' The words were hardly out of his mouth when he was hit with a tremendous blow from behind and fell heavily to the cobblestones.

A black-clad figure threw a rope around the neck of the boy, drawing it tight in a slipknot. Gervais thrashed about, desperate to free himself. Just as he went unconscious, there was a roar, an arc of light and the big limousine turned in to the narrow street. The masked figure looked up, gave a last vicious jerk on the rope, then ran back into the opera house as Mary leapt out of the car to release the ligature and allow the boy to breathe. Having been an ambulance driver in the Great War, she had the necessary knowledge to resuscitate him. When he was breathing harshly, but evenly, she helped him into the back seat and turned her attention to Armand.

'Monsieur! Monsieur! Wake up. We must get Nicolas home. He has been throttled.'

The tutor groaned and came round, staggering to his feet with a hand to the back of his head. He had difficulty grasping Mary's instructions and leaned groggily against the stone wall of the opera house and then over the bonnet of the limousine. Somehow, the chauffeur persuaded him into the car and took them straight to the hospice and the attention of Doctor Martin.

When the tidings were carried to the duc, he hurried in to the ward where Gervais and Armand lay in neighbouring beds. The doctor straightened from her examination of Gervais. 'Bad news, Monsieur. Oh yes, the boy will live,' she assured him, after one glance at his ashen face. 'It is not as bad as all that. I have sedated him for the pain and my examination. You have Mary to thank that he is alive at all. But the strangling has damaged the larynx. His vocal cords have been subjected to such trauma that … he will not sing again, Monsieur. He will regain speech of a kind, but his singing voice has gone forever, I am afraid.'

'*Non! Le pauvre* …' The duc appeared to be in shock. 'What about Armand? How is he?'

'He has suffered a relatively mild concussion, as far as I can tell. I will keep him here under observation for a few days to make sure there is no bleeding on the brain. Always a possibility with blunt force trauma.

'But look here, Monsieur. It is not Nicolas, but his friend, Gervais.' Doctor Martin smoothed back the black hair to show a flaxen curl protruding over the boy's ear. Gently, she removed the wig. 'What do you make of this? An impersonation?'

The duc flushed. 'He is not only Nicolas's friend, but his understudy. It is because ...' He explained the conditions of the contract that had forced such secrecy.

'It is well for Nicolas then,' said Doctor Martin with a direct look from her cool grey eyes. 'One cannot say the same for his understudy.'

'But, Madame,' protested the duc. 'It was not for this purpose, *je vous assure!* Had I known, I would have provided them with bodyguards. Poor child! His career finished! I must do something for him. Does he know?'

'No, Monsieur. Not as yet. I told him I must sedate him for the examination.'

The duc nodded and moved to look down on Armand. 'Is he still unconscious?'

'Sleeping, Monsieur. I have also given him something for the pain. One must be careful, of course.' The doctor ushered him out of the ward. 'Come back tomorrow, Monsieur. You will be able to speak with them then.'

When Armand awoke it was to Nicolas and Lisette bending over him, arguing in whispers.

'Armand? Are you awake?'

'Shh,' admonished Lisette. 'Let him sleep.'

'He's awake, I know. Armand? See, I told you,' he added, as Armand half-opened an eye.

'Would you like a drink, Monsieur?' asked Lisette. 'How is your head?'

'Please.' Armand opened both eyes and sipped cautiously at the cup she held for him. 'Thank you. My head? It hurts.' He moved a little, wincing as he touched the back of his bandaged head. 'What ... happened?'

'Someone hit you with a brick, *mon cher*. You have been lucky. Very lucky.'

'*Eh bien,* if this is luck …' Recollection came all at once. He looked around. 'Gervais?'

'In the next bed: there. Gerry has been lucky, also. But not quite as lucky as you. He has lost his singing voice.'

A sob came from the other bed.

'Oh, I *am* sorry,' said Armand. 'What happened?'

'He has been throttled.'

'Oh, that's too bad. Damage to the vocal cords?'

Lisette nodded. 'But he is lucky, too. Because if Mary had not come along to undo the rope and revive him, he would be dead.'

'I wish I was!' The words came in a harsh whisper. Gervais sat up and pointed at Nicolas; his eyes wild. 'It is *your* fault! Why did you have to make me go on *that* night?'

'But ——' began Nicolas, astonished.

'Never mind,' said Armand, looking at the distraught face. 'Now is not the time.'

Gervais sent him a venomous look. 'I blame *you*, too. You wouldn't let me stay and talk to the fans!' He tried to say more, but his whisper failed; and he sank back on his pillows.

'No talking now, either,' Lisette reminded him. 'Doctor Martin said you must not hurt your vocal cords any further. Remember?'

'What does it matter if I can never sing again? I hate you,' the boy rasped out, turning away. 'I hate you all!

Feeling terrible, Nicolas went to his room. *Angel?*
*Nicolas?*
*Did you know that this would happen?*
*Yes, I knew.*
*I feel as though I have betrayed my friend.*
*Why?*
*You knew, and you did not tell me.*
*I had a good reason. You will know that reason in time. Then you may judge whether it was right or wrong.*

Nicolas bowed his head and sobbed.

Gervais maintained his resentment: a truculent, snarling fury, particularly towards Nicolas, against whom it often erupted into violence. His animosity towards everyone in the household was so intense that the duc decided it would be best for them all, including Gervais, to send him to Belvoir with Monsieur Lorraine to be taught piano, in the hope of giving him the light of a new career.

The duc, horrified that his actions had helped to turn a happy, healthy, growing boy into a depressed and violent adolescent, settled enough money on him to provide a large allowance. It was a sum far more generous than was strictly necessary.

Nicolas realised that, whatever had been the cause, he had lost his friend and was saddened; although, he didn't miss what Gerry had become. He continued his weekly performances at the Opéra Magique with only one change. He and Armand were accompanied everywhere by two deceptively ox-like companions. These gentlemen may have appeared bovine, but they moved with a cat-like grace. There was also a sinister bulge under the jacket of each, just below the armpit.

# 13 BIRTHDAY CELEBRATIONS

**2 February 1935**

*The countess is combining her birthday celebration with a celebration of the music of Wagner at the opening performance of Tristan and Isolde. It is now seventy years since this opera was first performed in Munich (the home town of Herr Schmidt-Hesse), and the countess is making much of it. According to her, the count is throwing this celebration for her. According to the count, he knows nothing about it!*

*There will be champagne on arrival for the guests and at nine-thirty, during the interval between the first and second acts; wherever we are, we must stop what we are doing and drink the health of the countess.*

*Drink the health of the countess? I would rather drink to her demise! Elaborate and pretentious nonsense! And I am not going to do it. For such a purpose, the champagne would choke me; I am certain!*

The countess greeted them at the door. She glanced slyly at the bodyguards and commented that Nicolas should be safe with such men of substance. 'There have been a few changes, as tonight is a special occasion. Nicolas, I want you to go to your dressing-room until I call you. With your men, of course.' The countess called Armand back. 'You may take this opportunity, if you will, to look over the books. There has been some slight discrepancy.' She shrugged and waved her cigarette holder. 'Just a tiresome *betise*, but I cannot find it. Perhaps you will have more success. Then, you may join us in the foyer for cocktails before the performance. Nicolas will survive without your vigilance for a few minutes.'

The few minutes became an hour as Armand wrestled with a complication he had not so far seen in the books of the opera house. *Still,* he thought, *it does not matter how long this takes. Nicolas will be safe with his minders.* He did not doubt it. His only concern was to escape the attentions of the countess, and it seemed, the luck was with him. She appeared to have other things on her mind tonight and left him quite alone.

In the dressing-room, Nicolas found a feast awaiting him. There was a big jug of lemonade and another of his favourite blackcurrant juice; the table laden with any number of delicious cakes and pastries. His eyes shone at the treats in store. 'Messieurs,' he said to the bodyguards. 'Look at this! I wish you will join me. Do you prefer lemonade or blackcurrant juice?'

One of the bodyguards had his head under the chaise longue, the other, engaged in peering behind the curtains, briefly emerged. '*Merci, jeune* Monsieur. Just as soon as we make sure that we are the only ones here, *hein?*'

Nicolas offered to pour their drinks, and they opted for lemonade. 'Sit down, Messieurs. I will serve you tonight. This is a real feast.' He cleared a tray, added two brimming glasses, two plates of cakes and pastries, and carried it to them.

'Thank you, *jeune* Monsieur. You are a gentleman.'

When Nicolas had poured his blackcurrant juice, they raised their glasses in a toast before downing the contents in two swallows.

'More, Messieurs?' enquired Nicolas, astonished. At their nod, he brought the jug.

He ate a vol-au-vent, swallowed a large mouthful of his drink and shuddered. He took another sip and put it down. The bittersweet taste set his teeth on edge. When he turned back to his minders, he noticed that they had dozed off. Feeling unaccountably weary himself, he staggered to the chaise longue and fell upon it.

Behind the mirror, in what was once the Master's apartment, waited a poor, shrivelled creature that no longer held any resemblance to the pretty young girl she once was. There were sores eating away her nose and lips, suppurating in her scruffy, thinning hair and in other places hidden beneath the crossover robe she wore belted tightly around her skeletal frame. Ugly, ill, embittered, she existed only to wreak vengeance on those she held responsible for her state of living death.

Remembering the day she'd gone on a picnic in the woods with her friends—without telling them her devastating secret—that she was subject to epileptic seizures, her face screwed up in pain. She couldn't bear the rejection in the faces of those she told. And so, she had not. It still pierced her soul to think of what had happened. She had awoken out of unconsciousness after grand mal to find a heavy man grunting and writhing on top of her, thrusting into her; his hand over her mouth so that she couldn't scream her pain. *Such tearing pain!* Not that screaming would have helped: all her friends had run away and left her, out of fear of her condition.

It was only later she discovered that, not only had this despicable monster taken advantage of her vulnerability, he had also given her a filthy disease. She could have had treatment, but she didn't, vowing revenge for the evil that had been wrought on her. It had been many years since anyone had found her attractive enough not to puke at the thought, but when she was young and pretty, she had hooked in quite a few.

Now (she could hardly believe it), she'd been hired to put the kiss of death on a beautiful young man: a boy— not even into his manhood. The instructions that had accompanied an unbelievable sum had been clear. The boy would be sleeping. He would know nothing. She picked up the silver stiletto paperknife that had been left for her on the desk and shuffled to the door.

The woman slid aside the mirror and went to stand over the unconscious boy. She thought he looked beautiful. The ripe-peach bloom on his cheeks; dark, curved lashes resting on pale skin; his lips so soft and vulnerable. His hair so black and glossy. She reached out claw-like fingers to touch the silken strands. Poor young thing. He had not yet had the chance to hurt women. But he would grow up into a hateful beast. Her maternal expression changed to revulsion and back again. If she killed him now, he would always be like this: young, innocent, beautiful. In the madness of her disease, she thought it so much better to give him a quick death than to condemn him to a life like hers.

She loosened her belt and, with surprising agility, stepped onto the chaise longue, straddling his inert body in a way she had done many times in her chosen profession, and raised the stiletto, ready to plunge it into his heart. It would take all her strength, and she must not make a mistake. She threw back her head—the dagger held high in both hands—arching her body for extra drive.

Suddenly, an expression of absolute horror widened her eyes, twisting her face into a dreadful parody of humanity. Involuntarily, her mouth gaped to emit a scream, high and shrill. A scream of anguish.

Nicolas, awakened out of his light stupor by the terrible noise, saw the monstrous face above him, the bleeding sores on lips and sagging breasts, the knife about to pierce his heart. He cried out and tried to move aside, but his body would not answer. The combined effects of the weight of the woman and the drug he had imbibed held him down. Paralysed, he waited for the end.

Whatever the woman saw terrified her completely. She threw her arms wide, tossing the knife, her face set in a rigid grimace. In slow motion, she arched backwards to fall off him and lay convulsing on the floor; her robe in disarray.

Nicolas tried to sit up, but waves of nausea and dizziness forced him back. This, plus the horror and bewilderment, was too much; and he collapsed, moaning.

*It is all right, Nicolas,* said his inner voice. *You are safe now.*

*Angel? I was so afraid. What did she see that made her scream?*

*She saw her life pass before her eyes. She saw what she had become.*

Nicolas averted his gaze from the horrifying figure on the floor that stiffened in tendon-cracking catalepsy for terrible moments, then relaxed to lay uncannily still. *Is ... is she dead?*

*Yes, she is dead.*

Nicolas's eyes widened. Then he closed them. He swallowed. *Did ... did you kill her?*

*No. She died of a medical condition. But do not despair. You are safe. It will not hurt you to learn to overcome fear and disgust. Besides, others had to be alerted to what is going on in this house. Now they will take the necessary precautions.*

'I am *so* sick of coming here,' whispered Nicolas.

*Patience, mon ami. It will all come to an end. Sooner than you think—or want. For now, you must apply yourself to your music and education. Au revoir, mon brave.*

'Angel?' But there was no answer. Nicolas turned his face into the cushion to stifle heartbroken sobs.

Armand, beginning to mount the stairs, caught a scream that sounded like a woman being murdered. He bounded up the rest of them, fumbled for what seemed like an eternity for the key to the dressing-room and threw open the door. His startled glance swept the room, taking in the incongruous figure of a dreadful old hag in a satin robe lying on the floor: her disfigured face set in the rictus of death; her robe disarranged to reveal things that should not be revealed; the open door where the mirror should be; the bodyguards apparently asleep in their armchairs and Nicolas, huddled, sobbing and heartbroken on the chaise longue. Then, he stumbled over the knife. 'My God! Nicolas! Nicolas, what has happened? Are you all right?'

'I don't know … I think so. I woke up to find … *her* … sitting on me, holding up a knife. And then she … she …'

'*Doucement, mon pauvre.* We must have some help.' Armand went to the phone on the coffee table, gave the number he wanted to the telephonist and waited. He spoke urgently for a few seconds, dropped the receiver into its cradle and turned back to Nicolas. 'Doctor Martin is on her way. How do you feel now?'

'Armand,' he said in a small voice. 'I think I am going to be *sick.*'

'Hold hard, *mon fils.*' The tutor guided him to the basin in the adjoining bathroom, dealt competently with his *extremis* and brought him back to the chaise longue, carefully avoiding the hideous remains on the carpet. 'We will both be better if we do not have to look at *her,*' he said, picking up a rug to cast it over the corpse.

The calm presence of Doctor Martin reassured them. She took the pulses of the bodyguards, lifted an eyelid of each to peer into unseeing eyes and talked softly to Nicolas while she checked his vital signs.

'What about …?' Nicolas moved his head slightly towards the frightful thing on the floor.

'The living first,' said Doctor Martin. 'Take a deep breath. Now, another.' She put away her stethoscope, dipped a finger in each of the jugs on the table and just touched it to her tongue. 'You have all been drugged. You, only lightly.'

'I didn't drink much. It tasted … urgh!'

'Turn your head away, Nicolas.' Doctor Martin made only a cursory examination of the body, before replacing the rug. 'I know this woman. She has refused treatment from me, time out of mind.'

'Do you know what killed her?'

'Yes. She was a sufferer of epilepsy. She died, most probably, from a seizure.' Her eyes considered Nicolas. 'She has a disease. It is unlikely that it has been transmitted to you, so you need not worry. Do you have a change of clothing with you?'

'Yes,' said Armand. 'He has a spare formal suit.'

'Good,' she said, looking around. 'A bathroom? Yes, over there.' Having told Armand to help Nicolas to bathe, change his clothes and hand the ones he was wearing to her, she used the telephone to arrange for transport of the body and demand the immediate presence of the manager. She thanked Armand for the clothing and said she would take it with her to the laboratory. 'I will send an ambulance for these men. They should wake up naturally sooner or later, but it is as well to be careful. Nicolas has had a bad experience. You should take him home now. There will probably be nightmares. If they go on for too long or he cannot sleep at night, send for me.' She took another, more detailed look around the room. 'I will have a word with the manager before I go.'

The countess, when she arrived, seemed as horrified as anyone by the scene that met her eyes and palpably anxious to keep it a secret. She apologised volubly to Nicolas and assured him that she would increase the security of the house so that such a thing could never happen again. 'I would prefer not to involve the police. I don't want the reputation of the house to suffer.'

'I don't suppose we need the police,' said the doctor. 'It is obvious what has happened here. The woman has paid for her crime before she committed it. But there is a further crime. The drugging of the drinks.'

'No!' said the countess. 'I do not believe it! Who …?'

'You supplied the beverages, Madame?'

'No … yes. I ordered them to be brought up to the dressing-room. Naturally, I was looking after my star. He is still a child. Champagne would not be good for him. But as to who? Perhaps …?' She waved her cigarette holder at the covered remains.

'Perhaps.' Doctor Martin's penetrating gaze bored into hers. 'You will need to increase your vigilance, Madame. If you are lax enough to allow any old insane, syphilis-ridden prostitute to wander in off the street and attempt to murder your child star, your house will obtain an unsavoury reputation, police or no police.'

§

'Armand, must we tell Grand-père?' asked Nicolas, on the way home. 'And I don't want Settie to know! Please?'

The boy seemed so agitated that Armand murmured soothingly, 'We will not tell Lisette if you do not wish it, but we must let your grandfather know what has happened, I think.'

'Yes, but he is in England, remember?'

'I suppose we need not worry him before he returns from his holiday with your Aunt Elise,' replied Armand, frowning slightly. 'But he may think differently.'

'He is already worried about King George and wants to spend some time with him. If we tell him now, he will rush back and worry about both of us. *Please?*'

'Very well,' said Armand. 'It shall be as you wish.' He congratulated himself that his answer seemed to have calmed his pupil's nerves.

That night, Nicolas slept heavily due to the effects of the drug, but the next morning when he didn't come down to breakfast, Armand went to look for him. He found Nicolas in the bath, up to his chin in foam, scrubbing himself with a soap-filled sponge. 'This is an unusual place to find you at this hour, *mon fils*. How long have you been here?'

'Armand ...' Tears squeezed out from beneath closed eyelids. 'I don't know. I just cannot make myself clean.'

'There, there,' said the tutor, awkwardly.

The blue eyes opened to show a tortured expression. 'She had *sores*, Armand! They were eating away her face! And she ... had nothing on under her robe. She *sat* on me. Urgh!' Nicolas disappeared beneath the foam. Just as Armand was worried enough to reach in and haul him out, he emerged, spluttering. 'She was horrible! *Horrible!*' he said, meeting his mentor's gaze.

Armand, hurting at the pain in the boy's eyes, made soothing noises.

'She was going to kill me, Armand. Do you know that?'

'*Doucement, mon cher.* It was a terrible experience for you. But you are still alive and likely to remain so while you have us.'

'Yes. Thanks to ...'

'Angel? You think *he* saved you?'

'He said not, but I think so. He was there. And she saw something, and that's when she fell down in a fit.' He shuddered. 'Why did she do it, Armand? Why?'

'She was insane, *mon fils*. Remember what Doctor Martin said about her? She was a poor, pathetic creature, rather than an evil one. What she tried to do: it was not you, personally, she wanted to hurt. And since you were fully clothed, you are safe from the dreadful disease she carried.' Armand held out a big, fluffy white towel. 'Come out of the bath and down to breakfast, and we will talk.'

'No, you don't understand.' Nicolas resumed his scrubbing. 'I *cannot* make myself clean. I cannot!'

'Ah, *mon pauvre*. Come, now ...'

A few minutes of quiet persuasion, including the question that Lisette might come looking for him if he did not come down soon, got him out and dressed in a hurry. Armand could see that Nicolas was far more devastated than he had first thought. He was going to need a lot of understanding and possibly a man-to-man talk. *It is not as though I am any authority on the subject,* he thought, feeling inarticulate and unprepared.

Nicolas lost his bright confidence, became introspective and took refuge in his music. He baulked at the idea of going back to the Opéra Magique. The next night, the nightmares began.

'Something is very wrong with Nicolas,' said Lisette. 'I was up with him to all hours because he had a bad dream, but he wouldn't tell me what it was about.'

Armand reddened. How could he describe what had gone on to Lisette? Even if he hadn't promised Nicolas. It horrified him—made him ill even—to think about it. 'It is something very serious,' he acknowledged. 'But, please, don't ask me about it. Doctor Martin was there. She can tell you what you need to know. In fact, she said that he would have nightmares and to send for her if they go on for too long.'

Lisette, noticing his colour, put up her chin. 'I don't know what is going on, but you two should remember that I am *not* a fool. I will see Doctor Martin and you will tell Nicolas that I know all about it and not to worry.'

When she came back, she said, 'Poor Nicolas, he is lucky to be alive. What a dreadful experience for him! I do not know how you two thought you could hide such a thing from me. But I think it will help Nicolas to understand if you tell him about the birds and the bees, and how one can and cannot catch *a certain disease.*' At his expression, her laughter pealed out. 'Poor, dear Armand! You don't know, yourself, do you?'

At the end of the week, Nicolas was still unwilling to go back to the Opéra Magique, but he had an unexpected champion in Lisette. 'From now on, I am coming with you, countess or no countess. I will take charge of the dressing-room and no food or drink must pass any of our lips that I have not brought and personally broken the seal on. I don't know where this is going, but I don't like it.'

Eminently practical, Lisette brought a hammer and nails in her basket, and got the bodyguards to nail up the track so the mirror could not slide. 'We will inspect this every time we come, to make sure the nails have not been removed. That way, there will not be any more surprise visitors.'

Lisette's kindness and bravery reassured Nicolas, but privately, she struggled with the miasma of evil that met her in the foyer and followed her up the stairs to the dressing-room every time she entered the opera house.

By the time the duc returned, the terrible experience had assumed the status of an old nightmare, never to be forgotten, but tucked away in a hidden corner of their minds. And since his employer had come back looking worn and ill, Armand did not want to mention it for the sake of his health. No-one felt guilty about hiding it from him. They just wanted to make his life as easy as possible.

The bodyguards were apologetic, became fanatically vigilant and refused to eat or drink on duty. Armand and Nicolas depended on Lisette more and more for her commonsense approach. All of them believed wholeheartedly that Lisette's methods had ensured that there could be no more attempts on Nicolas's life.

Lisette, herself, was not so confident, but this she kept to herself. *This has to be the work of the countess,* she thought. *If only we can keep ahead of her!*

## 16 March 1935

*Nicolas is fifteen today, and we thank le bon Dieu that he has lived to see this day. Even if we are biased, Lisette and I think him the most beautiful young man, inside and out, that we have ever come across. We are both incredibly proud of the way he is growing up and so thankful that the evil designs of the countess have come to nothing. (No matter how much she prevaricates, I know she is behind this last attempt on his life). How terribly wicked and unjust it would have been for the world to have lost such a delightful personality. He is engaging and spirited, but he also has manners and charm, and a strangely touching adult compassion and understanding.*

*But it is suddenly becoming obvious that we are not the only ones to think so! We are having the weirdest problems, and none of us knows what to do. They are like ants invading a home. The bodyguards are afraid to touch them. And it is not solely because they scratch like cats! No, these big rough men have, most admirably, been taught not to touch them without their consent. But that does not help the situation!*

After almost a year at Belvoir, Gervais, according to his teacher's reports, was progressing with his training and looked set to succeed as a concert pianist. He refused an invitation to Nicolas's birthday party, remained at the château, and was cold and distant to Nicolas whenever they crossed paths. At the same time, Nicolas's predominantly female fan base began to exhibit a disquieting change, perplexing the bodyguards who knew what to do with men, but not women that flung themselves on the young singer, swooned in front of him, leapt into his car, and sneaked into the house through varied and original means.

Had it not been such a problem, Armand would have thought it funny to see how gingerly these great brutish men handled the *demoiselles*, almost pleading with them to behave. It fell to Lisette to point out to them, with sharp words and the occasional sharp slap, the error of their ways.

The young singer was also inundated with marriage proposals and letters expressing undying love and other more earthy sentiments. There was a great to-do when a young woman was found in Nicolas's garderobe; and an even bigger one when an enterprising *demoiselle* was dragged out from under his bed by Lisette and the housekeeper, and sped on her way by a few choice phrases.

Nicolas, concerned for them, went to Lisette. 'What is the matter with them, Sette? Are they ill?'

'It's nothing a good box on the ear won't fix. Don't worry about them! It is you I am worried about. Stupid little cows.'

'But why are they doing it?'

'No sense in their silly heads. You will understand when you're a bit older.'

'Oh, Sette. You're always saying that.'

'I know. Never mind: it's true.' She looked at his lithe young body, still smooth, yet with promise in its immaturity and thought, *No wonder!* Then, at the expression in his clear blue eyes and gave him a hug. 'Don't worry your head about them. They'll get over it.'

The duc knit his brow, made telephone calls, wrote letters and thanked the heavens when the Opéra Magique closed for the summer break. He whisked Nicolas and his entourage out of Paris and down to Belvoir as soon as he could. From there he made further telephone calls, then confounded them all by leaving again. 'I will be away for some days,' he told Nicolas. 'Do not leave the grounds of the château until I return. *Mon Dieu!*' He clapped a hand to his brow. 'I am too old for this! It is the first time Belvoir has had to lower the portcullis since 1793!'

Monsieur Lorraine hurried in to the hall. 'Monsieur le duc?' he asked.

'He has just left,' said Armand, returning with Nicolas from waving him farewell. 'Can I be of assistance, Monsieur?'

'Perhaps,' admitted the music teacher. 'Gervais has disappeared.'

# 14 THE VESTAL VIRGINS

**16 July 1935**

*The duc calls them Nicolas's Muses, Lisette calls them the Amazons (with a shudder), I call them the Vestal Virgins and the newspapers call them Avenging Angels. Nicolas has embraced them from the start, calling them his Dees or by diminutives of their names, Desi and Dani. They are identical twins and over six-feet tall! How he tells them apart is beyond me, but he says it is easy. Life has suddenly gotten interesting. Very interesting. But I wouldn't dare say so to Lisette!*

The duc alighted from his limousine and entered the château, accompanied by two statuesque blonde beauties clad in military-style trouser suits. Both he and the butler who met them were tall men, unused to women who could stand with them eye to eye. The duc smiled at the butler's noncommittal expression. He greeted him kindly, adding, 'I trust there have been no disturbances while I have been away, Justin?'

'No, Monsieur. It has been very quiet, except for a *Quatorze Juillet* celebration of dance in the courtyard—the large one.'

'Was there? Excellent! Lisette *has* been busy. I am only sorry that I missed it.' He included his companions with a gesture. 'Justin, meet Mesdemoiselles Désirée and

Danielle Swenson, Nicolas's new bodyguards. You may take them to the housekeeper. I believe she was given the message to prepare their rooms? *Bien.* Then you may tell Nicolas and Armand to come to my study.'

'Certainly, Monsieur. Coffee?'

'It will be most welcome. You may send some up to the young ladies, if they wish?'

'No, Monsieur. We drink only fresh fruit juice.'

'Oh, yes, I beg your pardon. I forgot. Do we have any orange juice, Justin?'

'Probably only lime or lemon, Monsieur.'

'Ladies?'

'Any, Monsieur. Whatever is in season.'

'*Bien,*' said the duc again. 'By the way, Justin, that other business has been settled satisfactorily.'

'I am very happy to hear it, Monsieur,' said the butler. '*Merci.* Now, if you young ladies would like to step this way …'

§

Nicolas and Armand found the duc seated behind his desk with a cup of coffee at his elbow. He gestured to a laden trolley. 'Help yourselves, gentlemen. I'll have one of those petits fours, thank you. Nicolas, you are now officially old enough to have coffee if you would prefer it to your usual, er …'

'Thank you, Grand-père.' Nicolas passed him a plate of little iced cakes. He would have preferred a cold blackcurrant juice, but he wouldn't say so for the world. Feeling very grown-up, he poured coffee for himself and Armand.

'Did you find Gervais, Monsieur?' asked the tutor, thanking Nicolas absently, as he received his cup.

'Sit anywhere,' said the duc; his gesture encompassing a chaise longue and a pair of armchairs. 'Yes, thankfully,

I did. He is in Nice at a small music school, tutoring the younger boys while he learns from the maître. I have ascertained that it is a reputable school with a good teacher. Monsieur Lorraine seemed impressed when he heard the name. I did ask Gervais to come back to us, but he said he wants to stay where he is because there will be venues for him to perform regularly. Therefore, I have made it possible for him to access his allowance from the Banque de France in Nice.'

'Does Gerry seem happy, Grand-père?'

'Not noticeably, no.' The duc shrugged. 'But perhaps, in time, the poor lad will find satisfaction and fulfilment as a concert pianist. We can only hope ...'

'Yes, indeed,' said Armand.

Nicolas said nothing, but his expression was pensive.

'Drink your coffee,' said the duc. 'We have things to do.'

Nicolas would normally ask, 'What things?' but he continued to look thoughtful as he sipped his coffee. He brightened when the duc told them he had a surprise for them. His blue eyes sparkling, he cried, '*Tiens!* What can it be?'

'Not *it*: they,' replied the duc. 'It may be easier to wait until they get here. The housekeeper is taking them on a tour of the château. Otherwise they are sure to get lost.'

'Guests! We have guests?'

'Wait and see,' said the duc. 'Ah, here they are. Come in, Mesdemoiselles.' He turned to his grandson. 'Nicolas, meet your Muses.'

§

Nicolas's engaging personality soon had his bodyguards enthralled, just like the rest of his fans.

'But, Monsieur, what do you want with these great big Amazons?' asked Lisette, spreading her arms and pouting when the duc had made the twins known to her, and Nicolas had taken them off to see the view from the east tower. She shuddered. 'They frighten me.'

'Let us hope they have the same effect on his female fans,' replied the duc, 'because that is the idea.'

'They'd frighten any female that wasn't …' prophesied Lisette, leaving her sentence unfinished.

'Have you thought, Monsieur,' said Armand, watching them walk off, one either side of Nicolas, arm in arm with him, lifting him off the floor to delighted chuckles, 'that they, too, might become enamoured of him? Or perhaps that, later, he may succumb to one or other of them?'

'Perhaps you are afraid for yourself, Armand?' said Lisette. 'You are partial to blondes are you not?' She laughed, a little cruelly, as Armand flushed and turned away.

'*Eh bien,* Mademoiselle,' admonished the duc, gently. 'You were right in your first premise. Instinctive, perhaps?' He flicked a speck from his sleeve, and his lips just quirked into a smile. 'Naturally, I had thought of that aspect. I have not, ahem, enquired too closely, you understand? They have told me, candidly, that they have not fully made up their minds one way or the other. But I believe that, at this time, they are leaning towards the teachings of Sappho.'

§

Only once did Lisette speak willingly to the Amazons to tell them something the duc still did not know about the Opéra Magique.

'You can leave it to us, Mademoiselle,' said Desi. 'We will take care of everything.'

'We *never* eat or drink on duty,' said Dani. 'It is our rule.'

'You can give us the refreshments for Nicolas. They will not leave our sight.'

'Until eaten by him. Unless you want to come with us?'

'Thank you, no. *Bien*. It is very kind of you.' Lisette hurried away before the bodyguards could see how relieved she was not to have to go back to the opera house.

§

One day, Nicolas came upon the twins practising their judo. Dressed in traditional white, loose, belted jackets and long pants, they took turns to throw each other down with athletic grace. Watching their several techniques, he was immediately enchanted. 'Oh, Dees, *please* ... Will you teach me that, too?'

'Of course, young Monsieur,' said Desi, with a bright smile. 'It will be a great pleasure.'

'Stand in the middle,' ordered Dani, all business. She held out her hands. 'Now, take hold of me, like this.'

In an instant, he was on the floor, chuckling in disbelief. 'How did you *do* that?' He leapt to his feet. 'Show me again! No, wait until I get Armand and Lisette. They must learn this, too.'

Armand had to be persuaded to take off his coat and roll up his sleeves for judo lessons. Once he got over his shyness, perhaps he might enjoy being tumbled on the carpet by a couple of beautiful women; but Lisette, making a wry face, was firm in her refusal.

'We women have our own methods of self-protection,' she said, with scant approval. 'They do *not* include throwing people all over the floor, which is *hardly* ladylike.'

'You mean hatpins?' asked Dani; her spectacular body towering over her.

'And other means,' said Lisette, stepping back.

'We have those, too,' Desi, pale Nordic eyes glowing, assured her. 'But being able to throw your attacker makes a huge difference. You should learn judo. It adds a whole new dimension to a woman's safety, *je vous assure*.'

'I am sure it does,' said Lisette, with irony. 'But no, thanks. I will make do with what I have.' She went out, head high, her skirts swishing around her shapely calves.

Nicolas and Armand regularly attended these training sessions, becoming quite accomplished in the art. Armand's reluctance to grapple with a female was daily becoming a thing of the past, and he entered into the spirit of it with gusto.

'It's fun, Settie,' said Nicolas. 'I can throw Desi, but not Dani. Yet! They say we are getting so good that we won't need them soon.'

'Do they? That's good,' said Lisette, examining her fingernails.

'Yes,' he enthused. 'Armand and I have been enjoying ourselves, haven't we, Armand?'

'Yes, I *had* noticed,' said Lisette, before Armand could answer. 'I don't see as much of either of you as I used to.'

'Then why don't you come with us?'

'Not on your life!'

'Why not?'

She sniffed and looked at the chandelier over their heads. 'I am sure I would find it *fort amusant* to be tossed around like a ragdoll by your Amazons, but I don't think I should risk damaging my weak ankle, do you?'

Nicolas and Armand glanced meaningfully at her high heels and then at each other, but that was all they could get out of her on the subject.

# 15 THE MAISON ROSE

**24 April 1936**

*I have just read something in the morning paper that has given us the shock of our lives. And I do not believe it. No, I do not believe it.*

A discreet messenger came early to the *manoir*, spoke briefly to the butler and was shown in to the dressing-room of the duc de Belvoir. The duc, being shaved by his man, was in his dressing-gown: a royal blue quilted satin. He signed to the man to sit down until he finished. When the hot towel had been removed and his shaven skin spritzed with witch-hazel, the duc dismissed the valet and turned to his informant.

'What do you have for me, old friend. It must be important for you to have come so early?'

'Regrettably, yes, Monsieur. You must see this before it is all over Paris,' said the man, handing over a folded newspaper. 'It is the front-page headline.'

'But ...' The duc stared at him in disbelief. 'Nicolas would not do such a thing.' He frowned. 'Besides, he was here last night. At least ...'

'*Je regrette*, Monsieur.' The visitor shook his head. 'The sightings have been verified by several witnesses who do not wish their whereabouts to be known, *tu comprends*? I made sure that there could be no mistake. The lad has been rampaging through the red-light district of Paris for over a month, Monsieur.'

The duc held up his hand. 'Thank you, Gabriel. I do not know what to do about this.'

'He's just a boy, Monsieur. Paris will forgive his, er, enthusiasm.' The messenger's lips curved. 'The young devil! Such stamina! *Bien sûr*! He is a tiger ———' he broke off, seeing the pained expression on the duc's face; and once more became the correct, slightly regretful servant. 'I am sorry to be the bearer of such news, Monsieur.'

'Thank you, I depend on it. I must dress. You will leave in the usual way? *Bien.*'

The duc went down to breakfast wearing a grim expression, lay the newspaper in front of Nicolas, sat down and poured himself coffee. 'Well? What do you have to say to me?'

Nicolas stared at the headline and shook his head. 'No, Grand-père. This cannot be right. I have not been there. Whenever I am out at night, I come straight home with Armand and my Dees.'

'May I see?' Armand held out his hand for the paper. '*Depraved Young Singer Haunts rue Saint-Denis. Beau Nicolas: Precious, Precocious, Promiscuous. Mon Dieu!* What is this?' His eyebrows flew up. '*Of late, a certain young star has been frequenting houses famous for their notoriety, including, it is whispered, the Maison Rose. We find it amusing that he has managed to evade his Avenging Angels for some devilish doings ...*' He glanced from Nicolas to the duc. 'Of course, it could not be Nicolas.'

'I assure you, Grand-père, I have not been out at night. Could it be ... Gerry?'

'*Mais certainement*! That must be it! Find Lisette while I go and talk to your Muses.'

§

The two bodyguards listened to what the duc had to say, then told him their strategy for guarding Nicolas at night. Since the duc couldn't tell them apart, he listened without comment to both.

'At night, we take turns at guarding him, Monsieur. We each have our watch.'

'One of us always sleeps in a trundle bed across his doorway.'

'We are light sleepers, Monsieur. Even if the watcher fell asleep, we would hear him if he tried to open his door.'

'Third-floor windows, Monsieur, with shutters. No-one can get in or out that way.'

'We have taught Nicolas judo, Monsieur. Not to be a human fly.'

'No, Monsieur, not possible. On our oath.' Here, they each spat on a palm and shook hands.

The duc's face never moved a muscle. 'Thank you, Mesdemoiselles.'

Lisette was waiting when he returned to the dining room. 'You wanted to know what I think of this, Monsieur?' She flicked the page with the back of one small hand. 'Absolute rubbish! Ridiculous to think that it might be Nicolas!' she said, her eyes fulminating. 'It has to be that little ... Gerry.' She turned. 'The wig disappeared, you know. I could not find it after Gerry left. And he is a year-or-so older than Nicolas. Of course it is him!' She stood, head on one side, her mouth twisting while she thought. Suddenly straightening, she said, 'Monsieur, will you give me a week's leave? I think I know how to solve this.'

The duc hesitated. 'I don't want you to put yourself in danger.'

'I will be careful, Monsieur. This must be stopped before Nicolas's reputation is ruined. Because that is the object: to bring Nicolas down.'

'Yes, you must be right. Why else?' He sighed. 'What are you going to do? And, more to the point, how are you going to do it?'

'Leave both these things to me, Monsieur,' she replied, her eyes twinkling. 'The less that is known about it, the better. The only thing is: I will need money.' She hesitated, then looked him squarely in the face. 'A very large sum of money.'

'*Eh bien*,' said the duc and gave her what she requested. He asked no more questions, but Nicolas plainly did not want her to go.

'I love you, *Chéri*, but I have to have a holiday sometime,' she told him.

'Where are you going?'

'I don't know yet. On an adventure.' She blew him a kiss. 'I'll tell you all about it when I return.' Armand, she glanced at, but did not speak to.

Lisette went to the kind of place she'd escaped, thanks to the duc. An old mansion, shabby in daylight, but grand and mysterious at night. It was run by a retired ballerina she knew. '*Bonjour*, Madame. Do you remember me? Lisette.'

'Well, well, little Lisette!' Madame Eugénie invited her in to a cluttered salon. 'I could not count the years since I saw you last. You are still dancing, *hein*?'

Lisette shook her head. '*Non*, Madame. I have had to retire.'

'So, you come to me looking for a job—here at the Maison Rose?'

'Not at this point in time, Madame.' *Dieu merci.* Lisette managed to repress a shudder. 'I am searching for Nicolas de Beaulieu. I have read that he has been haunting all the houses in this street. Does he come here?'

'That may be privileged information, my dear. Why do you want him?'

'I have a yen for him. You understand?' Lisette spread her hands.

Madame Eugénie showed broken teeth. 'He is handsome, I will give you that. But a little young. More like an eager puppy than a hero in the boudoir, I would say.'

'I have this *fantaisie* that haunts my dreams, night after night. A *fantaisie* that I meet him here, at a *bal masqué,* and we spend the night together.'

Madame Eugénie threw back her head and laughed, revealing the full extent of her dental problems. 'A *fantaisie* such as that, my dear, is not impossible. No, not impossible. *But ...*' Her expression became calculating. 'It will cost you much.'

'But, naturally,' murmured Lisette. 'And the cost will be ... How much?'

The *entremetteuse* looked at her closely and named an exorbitant sum, opening her eyes when Lisette, without bothering to bargain, reached into her bag and placed the notes before her. 'You have come into money, *hein?*'

'But, yes.' Lisette met the woman's frankly curious glance. 'A duc.'

'Ooh! And you want to jeopardise your good fortune? You *cannot* be such an *idiote!*'

'He is old, you understand? But that is why it must be a masked ball, so that I may be disguised.' She played with the clasp of her handbag. 'I have heard that this young man is ——'

'Oh, yes! He has the stamina, *bien sûr!*' Madame Eugénie chuckled. 'No doubt, everything you miss. He comes here most nights. I will invite him for tomorrow. Be here at ten in the evening.' She scrabbled around on the littered coffee table. 'Bring this with you, or you will not get past the front door. Come as the Sleeping Princess. I will look out for you.'

'*Bien*, thank you.' Lisette took the grubby card, then hesitated. 'He must not know who I am, Madame.'

'But certainly not! The fee covers absolute discretion. You do not want to risk what you have for a night of passion, *hein?* Quite rightly, too. I will tell him you are a friend come from Chartres to visit me and that I desire him to show you a good time.'

'*Merci*, Madame. *À bientôt.*'

'You are lucky you don't have to do this for a living,' Madame Eugénie called after her, with a touch of envy.

'*Je sais*,' replied Lisette. 'Thanks be to God and my duc.'

Next, Lisette went to the wigmaker she knew and obtained a blonde wig of long, flowing curls. A little later, she entered a select establishment in the rue de Rivoli. 'I am going to a masked ball as the Sleeping Princess. I want something that appears to be nightwear, but is evening costume … not too revealing, but …' she said in answer to the proprietor's question.

'I understand, Madame. You want to hint at what you have, eh? Not flaunt it to the world.'

'You put that very well, Madame. It must only be the very slightest of hints.'

'Either the one you want to impress is eager, or you are modest,' said the woman. 'Not like most who come here.'

'It might be both, I think,' murmured Lisette.

'I beg your pardon, Madame: I didn't quite catch that.'

Lisette raised her voice. 'It must be pearl pink.'

'I don't think I can help you there, Madame. The pink has been very popular. But come this way.' The woman showed her in to a cave-like room full of shimmering fabrics. 'I have an oyster satin, or this very beautiful white silk gown and matching silver embroidered robe. You see, the gown is a little revealing, but the robe is as modest as you wish. Perfect layering, *non*?' The woman gave a discreet smile.

Lisette shook her head at the oyster satin, agreed with the woman over the white silk, but said, 'You do not have this in another colour, Madame? Blue, perhaps?'

'*Je regrette*, Madame. Only the white. This is all I have until the silk merchant comes.'

Lisette looked a question.

'The day after tomorrow.'

'Oh.' For a moment, she was troubled. 'White is *not* a colour I prefer.'

'Madame has the colouring to wear it. It would become her very well,' advised the woman. '*Je vous assure* …'

'*Eh bien*, at this short notice, there is nothing else to do.' Lisette shrugged. 'May I try them?'

'But certainly. If there is any adjustment to be made it can be done quite quickly. Within the day.'

§

At ten the next evening, a richly attired Sleeping Princess presented her ticket to the villainous-looking man on the door and was ushered in to the hall she'd had no time to admire the previous day. When her eyes adjusted to the darkness, she could make out its gracious proportions, enhanced by pillars at intervals supporting decorative arches. Dimly-lit by one or two lights in a magnificent but grubby chandelier, a truly beautiful, ornate staircase rose from the depths of the passage. The doorman, pointing, told to her to go up to the next floor and wait at the head of the stairs. Music and a confused babble of voices grew louder as she reached the landing.

Here, she was intercepted by an elderly Marie Antoinette. 'Come in, my dear. There is a gentleman here waiting to meet you,' she said, leading her in to a ballroom crowded with masked figures. It was even more dimly lit than the hall, smoky from candles, incense and cigarettes.

Just inside the door, a young man in a *tricorne* and long brown wig tied with a black riband stood easily in his uniform, one hand tucked in the front of his coat, surveying the room. He turned as Madame Eugénie came up to him. 'Napoléon Bonaparte, Madame. At his very young and virile best!'

'Monsieur Bonaparte,' said Lisette, with an empty

giggle, giving him her hand to kiss. 'I believe I am your Joséphine?' *How can I be so inane?* she wondered.

'My Sleeping Princess, adorable Aurora!' He spoke in a husky, sexy voice; took both hands and held her away from him for a moment to look at her through the half-closed eyes of the connoisseur; kissed her fingers and led her onto the dance floor. Taking her in his arms, he gave her a provocative glance. 'It shall be my great privilege to awaken you to unforeseen pleasures.'

*Ooh, the little ...* '*Eh bien*, you have a ready tongue for one so young.'

'What makes you think that I am young?'

She shrugged. 'The unmasked bits. They look young.'

The sapphire-blue eyes glittered behind the mask. 'Perhaps I am not so young, Madame. I have other "bits", as you call them. But you will be surprised when we unmask.'

'*Vraiment?* Why?' She looked around, nodding acknowledgement as a portly Nero apologised for treading on her robe. Both he and the ample Hebrew slave girl he was clutching smiled at them and resumed their passionate embrace.

'If I tell you, it will not be a surprise.' Gervais pulled her closer, dancing in a very intimate manner. Young, strong, virile. His lips found her earlobe, then began to nuzzle into her neck.

*The young devil,* she thought, pulling away with a flirtatious giggle. 'No, no, Monsieur. You go too fast for me.' *Listen to me: an empty-headed coquette ...* Little though she relished it, she had a part to play.

'I can tell you like it,' he whispered, reaching for her again. His bold eyes roved over her. 'I can't wait to unmask you ... completely!'

*Tiens!* she thought. *Gerry's libido is out of control. A well-placed knee would do him the world of good!* 'There is plenty of time for that, Monsieur,' she said, removing a wandering hand and holding it. *No wonder Nicolas is getting such a bad reputation.* Then, a little later, pushing him away: *I don't know how much longer I can put up with this!*

He was stung by her withdrawal, pulling her to him aggressively. 'I will have you tonight. Make no mistake about that! When you see who I am, you will want me.'

'Will I?' Her lip curled. 'You seem very sure about that.'

'Oh, yes. They all do.'

'Do they?' Lisette's anger faded, replaced by a kind of tenderness. She put up a finger to touch his chin. 'That's nice, Monsieur.' In that moment, she felt a great sadness for him: he felt so unwanted for himself that he had to ride on the fame of another for acceptance. She allowed him a couple of liberties, then gently freed herself. 'Later, *mon cher.*'

Now, she must steel herself for what she had to do. *Poor Gerry. Poor, lonely boy. But he must be stopped before he does Nicolas any more harm.*

Gervais led her in to supper, fed her tidbits, altogether behaving in a very lover-like and attentive manner. *Bien sûr! I should feel that I am getting my money's worth,* she thought, thankful that the only person she recognised was Madame Eugénie, who winked and nudged her whenever she went past.

'Come back to the ballroom,' said Napoleon, kissing her cheek, because she'd strategically turned her head. 'It will soon be midnight. Then you will see me as I am. I am impatient to awaken my beautiful Aurora. Are you looking forward to it?'

'Oh, yes, Monsieur. I can hardly wait!' she gushed, successfully foiling another attempt to kiss her. *And that is the truth,* she thought. *I must end this charade, even though I know it will be dangerous—to both of us.* She concentrated on her companion, responding to his innuendo with an arch stupidity that made her grit her teeth.

At midnight, the music stopped.

'And now the unmasking. On the count of three,'

called Madame Eugénie with relish, tugging on the light cord. The light threw them all into garish relief.

Staying his partner's hand, Napoleon removed his own hat and wig and looked around at the other couples congregating on the dance floor, laughing and shrieking as they unmasked each other, blinking in the sudden light. One after another, they fell silent, staring at him in amazement.

*A little carefully. He was careful to remove only one of his wigs,* thought Lisette, holding on to her mask. Gervais was still too taken up with his own effect on the other revellers to attempt to remove hers. In a strangely grotesque way, he reminded her of Nicolas with his audience. *A parody,* she thought. *A poor, sad little parody.* Once again, she was stricken at what she had to do.

'Nicolas de Beaulieu!' The whisper went around the room. Lisette looked at the excited faces and turned her attention to the boy.

He stood, tall and strong; triumphant; proud as he enjoyed the acclaim, looking with interest from face to face. Even Lisette couldn't tell the difference now. Gone was the parody. He *was* Nicolas de Beaulieu, down to the smallest gesture. 'Surprised?' He reached for Lisette's mask as he spoke. 'And now, you. Time to wake up!'

It was her cue. 'But, Monsieur, you are still in disguise,' she shouted, dodging his attempts to unmask her. 'Let me help you.' Her hand grasped his smooth black hair and tore it from his head. 'Look, everyone! Monsieur Gervais l'Abbaye!'

For countless seconds, shock held him immobilised, a sudden wave of colour suffusing his fair skin. Scarlet with chagrin, he clapped the wig and *tricorne* he held over cropped blonde locks that were kept too short to curl, glanced around, hunted and desperate for an escape as the exclamations grew louder and louder.

The guests milled around, pointing. 'Look he's an impostor!'

'It's not Nicolas de Beaulieu, at all.'

'We've been misled!'

'Impostor!'

'He doesn't even have black hair!'

'*Who* did she say he was?'

Madame Eugénie stood open-mouthed. An impostor? But Lisette would demand her money back! *Only if she can find me,* thought the *entremetteuse,* vanishing behind a curtain to unlock a secret door. She hurried away to a staircase at the back of the house. *I'll come back only when I am certain she has gone.*

Lisette blanked out her pity for the boy's humiliation. *And now for the dénouement,* she thought, reaching for her own mask, aware that in his pain he might well lash out— hurt for hurt.

Gervais recognised her at once, even with long blonde curls. 'I'll kill you for this,' he whispered, blanching with fury. And there was no mistaking the murder in his eyes.

She tucked the black wig into her bodice, turned and ran for the door.

# 16 A SIXTH SENSE

**25 April 1936**

*For some occurrences, there are premonitions. And for others, just as devastating, there are no warnings at all.*

Not all that many doors away, around in the rue de Rivoli, Nicolas was at supper with Armand and his bodyguards. Since he had his Dees, who, perforce, ate or drank nothing while on duty, they'd got into the habit of finding a different café or restaurant every week to frequent after his performance at the Opéra Magique. Sometimes they were invited to the house of a discreet friend of the duc but, more often, went café hopping. This was not quite as random as it sounded. At sixteen, Nicolas was allowed a certain amount of freedom, but the cafés and restaurants were all carefully vetted beforehand for guarantees of privacy and protection from fans, even if this fact was prudently kept from the young star.

'Let's try them all. Can we?' Nicolas had asked his tutor. 'I don't want my Dees to faint from hunger.'

'No, nor you, either,' had said Armand, tongue-in-cheek.

'Now you come to mention it: I *am* starving,' admitted his pupil, with a deprecating grin.

'I knew it.' But he privately acknowledged that Nicolas's main concern was for the wellbeing of the

149

bodyguards. 'I don't see why not. But we cannot keep Mary up waiting for us until all hours. We'll have to either walk home or call a cab.'

Most nights they walked. Nicolas's Avenging Angels were, by now, legendary; and Nicolas and Armand had become quite proficient at martial arts. Since a skirmish with a street gang, which they had all hugely enjoyed—and which had ended with the vanquishing of the would-be robbers—the word had got out. From then on, none had dared to attack them. Fortunately, this was another event the duc had not heard of, so their itinerary continued, uninterrupted by restrictions. There was one more item of note: Armand was now the shortest of the group by more than half a head.

Tonight, they were sitting at their table in a private room, laughing and chatting over the remains of supper, when Nicolas jumped as if hit by a bolt of electricity. He shouted, 'Where?', leapt to his feet and flew out the door. The bodyguards rose, as one, to follow. Outside, he looked back. 'Come on, you two. *Vite*! Sette is in trouble!' Not bothering to see if they followed, he sprinted around the corner into the rue Saint-Denis. *Where now?*

*Maison Rose*, said his inner voice. *Along here, on the right.*

Just then, a door flew open and a woman in white with long blonde hair rushed out. Her pursuer, grasping her robe, dragged her back inside the house. The doorman, entering the spirit of the hunt, leered at her and slammed the door in her face. Desperate to escape, she shrugged out of her robe and doubled back towards the staircase.

Nicolas, shouting, '*Ici*! *Ici*!' was banging on the knocker like a madman.

The doorman, beginning to open to him, took one look at his face and tried to shut it again.

Nicolas yelled, 'She's in there! I can hear her. Open the door! *Vite*! *Vite*!'

'Stand aside, *jeune* Monsieur!' said Dani, leaping for the door; her twin right beside her.

'Hurry!' groaned Nicolas, chafing at the sounds inside. He could hear, but not see, her attacker catch Lisette a little way up the staircase, jerk her back and throw her down. Her temple came into collision with one of the newel posts, and she slid to the floor, subsiding into a stupor. Gervais dragged her away from the stairs and began to search her inert body for the wig: his passport to fame and acceptance.

At the same time, the combined weight of the bodyguards prevailed against the doorman, and the door burst open, catapulting them in and slamming him into the wall; Nicolas right behind them.

The doorman was a big man. 'No you don't!' he growled. 'I won't stand for ——' Staring in disbelief at the women, he grabbed Nicolas in a vicious headlock.

Dani turned back, gave him an elbow in the throat that glazed his eyes; and he reeled against the wall, gagging. Nicolas dropped to the floor, and she helped him up. The doorman was showing signs of recovery, so Desi, with supreme indifference, kicked him in the groin before turning back to her charge. The man collapsed to the floor, moaning.

Nicolas pointed farther down the hall. In the gloom, they could just make out a figure tearing at the bodice of an unconscious woman. Gervais, oblivious to the uproar, had only one thing on his mind; and the bodyguards thought they knew what it was. With a dual muttered exclamation, they leapt from Nicolas's side and went for him.

Gervais, intent on his purpose, never knew what hit him. One minute, he was head down, inhaling must from the grimy carpet; the next, eyeballing a cobwebby chandelier. He bounced off walls, cracking the plaster, showering them with dust and breaking his nose—all against a background of lewd merriment from the ballroom above and the rasping commentary of the doorman, who'd overcome his pain enough to cower against the wall with his knees drawn up.

'It's cruel, it is, the way those two are bashing him about,' he muttered, as Gervais's body smashed into the wall, yet again. 'Hey! You two had better stop that before you kill him!'

Dani straightened; her light eyes glowing like a white tiger's. 'Will that be a problem for you, Monsieur?'

'No,' he said, shrinking against the wall. 'But it might be for you, the amount of damage you're doing.' His gaze went to Desi, effortlessly holding Gervais with his arm twisted up behind his back, and he fell silent.

Dani smiled. 'I doubt it.' She dropped down beside Nicolas who was bending over the unconscious figure. 'Is this her, Monsieur?'

Nicolas, paying no attention, called, 'Sette? Settie? Are you all right?' His face crumpled. 'She doesn't answer. She can't be dead! No, Sette: you *can't* be dead!'

A strong white hand reached past him to feel for a pulse. '*Doucement, jeune* Monsieur. She is not dead. See the swelling on her forehead? She has banged her head on something, probably the stairs. We must get a doctor.' Dani stood up. 'I will go up and tell the *entremetteuse* to call one.'

They heard the sudden roar of an engine and a car screech to a halt outside. There were running footsteps.

'Wait!' called Nicolas. 'Someone is coming! Don't leave her. It might be someone wishing to hurt her.'

They waited in mounting tension as the door swung open. A man stood in silhouette, temporarily blinded by the gloom. Against the light from the street, they could not see who it was.

'Come in, Monsieur,' invited the doorman. 'Add to the madness: why not?'

'Have you seen a young man and two ladies?'

'Armand! It is Armand,' whispered Nicolas. Relief made him sink down beside Lisette, almost overcome by faintness. 'Everything will be all right: it is Armand.'

'A young man and two ladies?' said the doorman. 'A young man and two giants, more like! They kicked down the door, then me; threw one of our clients all over the house. I don't know what they were. They may be females, though I think it unlikely. But, *bien sûr,* they are not ladies: I can tell you that! And if you've come to take them away, I'll be very much obliged to you!'

By this time, Armand's night vision had cleared. His startled gaze took in Gervais standing bruised, bleeding from the nose and covered in plaster dust. In the dispassionate hold of one of the twins, he looked battered and defeated. Then the tutor's eyes went to the woman with long blonde curls lying so still in a shimmering white dress, and his heart contracted. He truly thought he would die, that his heart would never take another beat.

'Armand! Armand, *ici*! Settie has been hurt,' called Nicolas; his eyes eloquent with distress.

'Lisette? No ...' Armand crossed the space with long strides, fell to his knees and gathered her into his arms.

'Careful,' warned Dani.

'Let Dani help you,' added Desi, shifting her grip on Gervais so that he winced.

'*No*! She is mine!' Armand lifted her gently and carried her to the door. 'Open up. Quickly!' he ordered the doorman. 'Why didn't you stop this?'

The doorman was defensive: 'He's paid for his ticket; not like you lot. The goings on in here, well ... You just learn to take no notice.'

'He knocked her unconscious! He was taking advantage of a woman he'd attacked!'

'Ah, but you wouldn't know, would you? It might all be play-acting, what they call ... you know ... I'm paid to keep me mouth shut about what goes on in here.'

'Hurry up and open the door, then,' said Armand. 'I've never heard a weaker or more cowardly excuse!'

'Now, just a minute ...' The doorman went purple about the collar, balled his right hand into a fist and stepped towards him.

'Would you like me to do it for you, Monsieur,' called Dani, springing forward.

'No.' The doorman moved aside and reefed open the door. 'Get out, the lot of you!'

'Samson?' called Madame Eugénie, peering fruitlessly from the landing above. 'What is going on down there?'

His sleek black head illuminated by the outside light, Nicolas turned from beyond the doorway and bowed. 'Nothing, Madame. We are just leaving. Thank you for your hospitality.'

Madame Eugénie blinked. *Nicolas de Beaulieu*? 'My God, he *was* here!' *Somewhere* ... She shrugged her bewilderment and went back into the steamy ballroom.

Outside, Armand was still giving orders. 'Get in the car, Nicolas, and I will pass her to you. Make sure she does not bump her head. There, that is right.' He settled himself in the back seat. 'Now, give her to me.'

'We will start walking with this *canaille*,' said Desi. 'Send the car back for us along the rue de Rivoli.'

'Yes,' said Armand. He called to the driver, 'The Hospice du Bois. *Vite!*'

'Armand?' Nicolas asked, 'Will Settie be all right? Is she breathing?'

Armand lowered his head to Lisette's. Her scent wafted upwards with the soft rise and fall of her breasts, filling his senses. It made him think of flowers in the fields; the woods after rain: fresh, sweet, adorable. His hand rested on her waist, absorbing her warmth, adjusting to the soft curve of her abdomen. A lump rose in his throat. 'Yes, she is breathing, *le bon Dieu merci!*'

'Oh, thank goodness!' whispered Nicolas. 'I thought we had lost her.' He was silent a minute. 'Armand? Why did you say "She is mine"?'

Armand cleared his throat. 'I don't think I said that. Did I?'

'Yes, you did.'

'Oh.'

'But she is mine, too, you know. I've known her for a lot longer than you.'

'I don't remember what I said. Perhaps it was the shock.' Armand lapsed into silence. He had made a life-shattering discovery. And he couldn't, quite yet, take it in.

'Armand? ... *Armand?*'

'Yes?'

'Did you think Sette looked like Mama?'

The tutor took a while to answer. 'At first, yes.' He turned his head away. 'Didn't you?'

'I see what you mean. I might have if ... The thing is: I already knew it was Settie.'

'Don't say it!' said Armand, glancing at him. 'Angel told you.'

'Yes. How did you know?'

'Just a guess.'

'He told me the Maison Rose, too. How did you know where to come?'

'I saw you run around the corner. And the Maison Rose had been mentioned in the paper. I thought I would start there.'

'*Bien* ... Armand?'

'*Oui?*'

'That was Gerry. How could he do that to Settie?'

Armand frowned. 'I don't know. He is very different from you and me. Perhaps Lisette will be able to tell us what happened. Later, when she comes round.'

At the hospice, Doctor Martin took over giving the orders; and she soon had Lisette diagnosed, treated and made comfortable. When the twins came in with Gervais, she frowned in disapproval. But when she heard the full story, sedated him and locked him in a room designed for patients who try to escape and self-harm, before sending a nurse to clean him up.

'Mademoiselle will be just fine,' she told the duc when he strode in a little later, 'but she will need at least two

155

days bed rest. She has quite a bit of bruising.'

'And the lad, Gervais?'

'He is in the brig, Monsieur.'

The duc nodded, understanding of her whimsical term for the padded cell. 'Is he much injured?'

'Nothing serious, apart from his nose. But I am about to straighten and dress it. You can see him tomorrow.'

That night, Armand could not sleep. For that first mad moment in the hall of the Maison Rose, he had thought it was Angelique lying there. He knew he had gone a little crazy. And then he'd made a discovery: it was Lisette's body he held as if he could never release her, Lisette's perfume that delighted his senses, Lisette's soft sweetness that made him ache with love for her.

At last, the beautiful ghost had been displaced by an even more delightful reality. *But I cannot tell her*, he thought, tossing and turning in misery. *She will only laugh at me.*

# 17 LESSONS OF LIFE

**27 April 1936**

*Gervais has come back into our lives in a strangely
dangerous and bewildering way. He looks so wholesome: a
fair young knight in shining armour. Yet, peer beneath the
burnished metal and a filthy dross appears. It does not
matter which way you look at it, his jealousy of Nicolas is
at the bottom of all he does. He wants to have what Nicolas
has; yet, at the same time, is impelled to destroy it.
Overlaying all this is his need for love, his feelings of
worthlessness and his brutality that makes him so
dangerous to defenceless women. Despite all this, I view
him as a catalyst for both good and evil because, had it not
been for him, I would never have seen what was under my
nose.*

Lisette was sitting up talking animatedly to the duc when
Armand and Nicolas came in. Nicolas carried a huge
bouquet of flowers. Lisette stopped what she was saying,
smiled at them both, kissed Nicolas and thanked him for
the flowers. She pretended not to notice Armand's colour
rise.

'Were you jealous, Sette?' asked Nicolas. 'Armand was
in here with a bang on the head once.'

'No, no. Believe me, I could have done without it,' she
twinkled. 'I would be happy to have let Armand's record

stand.'

'Would you?' Nicolas chuckled. 'Next, it will be my turn.'

'Heaven forfend!' said the duc. But he couldn't get the flippant words out of his mind. 'I must call another meeting with your Muses. In one hour; in my study. Go and tell them for me, would you? Both of you.' He smiled charmingly. 'Come back in ten minutes, *n'est-ce pas*?'

When they'd gone out of earshot, the duc said, 'You took a very grave risk, *ma fille*. We might have lost you. Had I any idea that Gervais would assault you, I would never have allowed you to do it.'

'To be fair, Monsieur, I don't think he meant to hurt me.'

The duc shook his head. 'There can be no excuse for the rough handling of ladies.'

'Strictly speaking, Monsieur, I don't think he thought I was that, either. I did do a fair imitation of someone who wasn't ... a lady.'

'That does not matter. There still can be no excuse.'

'What the Amazons told you they saw ———' She made a moue and met the duc's eyes. 'I am certain that he was only after the wig.'

'Hmm. If you say so. Speaking of which: was he successful?'

Lisette felt around under her pillow and pulled out what looked like a matted and tangled piece of black fur. 'It looks disgusting, doesn't it? Like a poor, sick animal. Perhaps, even, a dead one.'

The duc held it up between thumb and forefinger to examine it quizzically. 'I see what you mean, *ma fille*. We will get Doctor Martin to pronounce life extinct and then it shall be cremated.' He called a nurse. 'Lead me to the hospital incinerator, if you will be so good, Nurse.'

'Will I take it for you, Monsieur?' asked the nurse.

'*Non, merci*. It is not that I do not trust you, Nurse. I need to see with my own eyes that it cannot come back to haunt us. *Bien.*'

A short time later, the duc returned to Lisette, smiling. 'And that should be that.' He patted her hand. 'I do not know whether you were brave or foolish. But I don't know how to thank you.'

'It was the only way to ensure that Gerry can never do it again.'

'I appreciate your loyalty, *ma fille*, but shudder at the possible consequences. How sad that Gervais has changed so much: become so violent and antisocial. I feel responsible.'

'Monsieur.' Lisette touched his sleeve. 'What he is now, must always have been there, hidden, deep down, waiting for release by a certain set of circumstances. Gerry, though he looks angelic, is full of darkness.'

'Lucifer!' exclaimed the duc, whitening.

'Oh, I hope not!' Lisette moved in distress. 'What will happen to him, now?'

'I am thinking of giving him the choice between going into the military or facing the courts over what he has done to you. However, you are the one who has suffered—is suffering—and yours must be the decision.'

'Well, of course, poor boy, I did humiliate him in public. Who could blame him if he felt murderous! Yes, let him go into the army. The discipline will do him good.'

'It is like you to be so generous,' said the duc. 'I will go to speak with him now.' He turned his head. 'Here come your cicisbei,' he said with a smile, as Nicolas and Armand returned. 'Don't let them tire you.' He looked on with approval as Lisette held out a hand to each of them before going on his way. He'd omitted to tell Lisette that Gervais l'Abbaye would enter the military as a commissioned officer—funded by him.

Before he went to interview Gervais, the duc had one more question to run past Doctor Martin. 'I am getting a little worried, Doctor, about Nicolas. His voice has not yet broken.'

'How old is he, exactly?'

'Now, let me see … He has sixteen years, one month and eleven days.'

'Then it will happen soon. Any time between thirteen-and-a-half and sixteen-and-a-half is normal, Monsieur. I would not worry.'

'Perhaps he will be a countertenor?'

'Perhaps. But he is developing rapidly now. It won't be long before you know.' She hesitated. 'Has he been told about the birds and the bees?'

The duc coughed. 'I have not told him. Perhaps Armand …?' Under her steady gaze, he added, 'I will enquire. *Merci*, Doctor.' He bowed. 'And now I must deliver my message to our prisoner.'

'*Ma foi!*' said the duc, examining the facial injuries of the huddled figure on the bed. 'The Muses did let their talents loose on you, did they not? You must have upset them, *mon fils*.'

'It is not funny, Monsieur,' mumbled Gervais, turning his head to hide blackened eyes, a swollen jaw and plastered nose.

'No, indeed. You are quite right. Violence, in any form, is abhorrent. That is really why I have made this visit. That … and one other matter.'

The expression in the deep blue eyes became furtive. 'I suppose you don't like me pretending to be Nicolas.'

'You suppose right. And I like it even less when I hear that you have been masquerading as a Don Juan amongst the ladies of the night.'

Gervais hung his head and said nothing.

'Why did you do it? You are jealous of Nicolas and want to bring him down?' suggested the duc. 'Is that it?'

'Not … altogether, Monsieur.'

The duc raised his brows. 'Not … altogether? What does that mean?'

'It means … I suppose I am jealous, but I have not been visiting the Maison Rose and the other houses to hurt Nicolas.'

'Why, then? You must explain yourself, *mon fils.*'

The boy shrugged. 'You wouldn't understand.'

'I cannot understand if you do not tell me. One thing I will tell you: you are treading a very slippery path to continue on your present course.'

'I don't know what you mean?'

'Then I will put it bluntly: I advise you not to frequent the society of prostitutes.'

'But, I ——'

'Yes, *mon fils*? You what?'

'I must have ... love.'

'*Love*?' The duc was incredulous. 'You think that what you get in return for your money in these houses is *love*?'

'What else is it?'

The duc was shaken into silence. He could see that the boy was serious. He continued in a much more gentle tone: 'Love has many faces, *mon fils*, but what we speak of here is not one of them. I repeat: whatever else you find in these houses, it is not love, *je vous assure*!' The duc put a hand on the hunched shoulder. 'Listen, my son: I am going to show you something that will explain why it is that you must not continue on your present path to ruin.'

'I don't know what you mean. I must have love!' said Gervais, a little wildly. 'And I am happy to pay to get it.'

'You do not realise how much you will be required to pay for your desire: that the price will be too great. In more ways than you think!'

Gervais moved impatiently. 'You talk in riddles, Monsieur.'

'Do I? Then I must show you what I mean. I will return this afternoon to take you out. Make sure that you are ready to accompany me.' The duc rose to leave. 'By the way—your aggression—you have two choices over your violence towards one who has only given you kindness ——'

'*Kindness*?' Gervais's eyes snapped with fury. 'She

humiliated me in front of all those people! She has *ruined* my life!'

'No! That is your prerogative. You may go to prison for assault or into the army to make something of yourself. Which is it to be?' The duc stood, one eyebrow raised.

'The … army, I suppose,' muttered Gervais, in grudging tones.

The duc's eyebrow rose even more.

The fair skin attained a rosy hue. 'Thank you, Monsieur.'

The duc nodded acknowledgement. 'The person you should thank is Lisette. She is the one who has given you the choice. I would not have blamed her if she wanted to have you locked up. But, no, she has forgiven you. And that, my son, is love. One of its faces, at any rate.'

Gervais said nothing. His bewilderment was clear.

§

Later in the day, the duc sent for Armand, Nicolas and the Muses to accompany him and Gervais to an unfashionable quarter of Paris. But first, he spoke to Armand alone. 'It is more than time to talk to Nicolas, man to man. Have you done so?'

Armand's cheeks reddened. 'I am hardly qualified, Monsieur. The thing is: Nicolas has not asked.'

'Not even when Gervais …?'

'No, not even then.'

'By the time he does, it may be too late,' said the duc. 'He is developing very quickly: maturing by the day. You'd better leave it to me.'

Armand sighed thankfully. He wished that his father had bothered to do the same for him. There were things that puzzled him now that he did not dare think about. For example, how to approach and show his love to the woman of his dreams. Shyness bound him and held him inept. He felt cursed by his awkwardness.

The duc's method was a quick speech full of euphemism that bewildered all except Gervais. However, they got the gist of it. But the duc's pièce de résistance was a tour of two institutions, just as his father had done for him.

'This is what any gentleman of substance must know,' said the duc on the steps of the Magdalen. 'Many lures will be held out to the unwary—some harder to resist than others.' He stopped to greet and suitably reward the Mother Superior before proceeding. 'This is what happens to the associates of a man who cannot control his natural desires.'

They looked in on women of all ages, some nursing babies, others at various stages of pregnancy, some with illnesses that showed in their ravaged faces. The Dees held hands and leant a little more to the teachings of Sappho. Gervais strode on, unmoved.

Nicolas gave them all friendly smiles, but Armand was too embarrassed to look. A woman carrying a particularly beautiful infant passed them with a murmured apology. They both glanced at each other and thought at the same time: *This could be where Gervais came from.*

Gervais read their minds, and his eyes narrowed in fury and bitterness at this all too probable explanation of his origins. He completed the tour with lowered eyes and a sulky mien.

'And this,' said the duc, showing them in to a hospice for men infected with venereal disease, 'is what happens to the man.'

Nicolas took one look at the terrible lesions on the faces of the inmates and the madness engendered by syphilis and was promptly sick. Armand fared little better. Gervais surveyed them with contempt. For the bodyguards, walking behind them, the pendulum swung a little further.

As a deterrent for profligacy, it may have been masterly; but as a foundation for love and marriage,

Armand thought it woefully inadequate. He felt sorry for Nicolas, who had, by now, put two and two together about the illness of the terrible old woman who had tried to kill him; but there was nothing that he, Armand, could say to him.

Armand reflected on how strange it was that when these physical acts were done with love and consent, the poets wrote of them as a thing of beauty, precious moments, divine even. Yet the same things without that all-consuming love constituted evil abuse and exploitation. He could see why Nicolas was so distraught. The duc had meant well. Indeed, it was a good lesson. But now it only compounded Nicolas's misery.

Some time later, Nicolas went to Lisette. 'Sette?'

'What is it, *mon chou*? You seem troubled.'

'It is just that …' His hand went briefly to the locket at his throat and fell again. His eyes, dark and earnest, searched hers.

'What? You are growing so fast that you don't understand yourself any more?'

His expression relaxed. 'Yes, that's it. At least, it is a part of it.' He took her hand and held it up. 'You see where I have grown to?'

'I see it. I see it,' she agreed with a twinkle. 'You are not going to hold me to my promise, are you?'

'No.' He relaxed even more. 'But I thought you were going to hold me to mine.'

Lisette seemed to consider. 'I could, I suppose.' Then, she laughed: a lovely, warm, companionable laugh. 'You were just a gorgeous little boy who loved and admired someone. That was the highest expression of regard you could make, and I was very touched.'

'I will always love and admire you, Settie.'

'Thank you, *Chéri*. And I, you. But now that you are growing into a man, you suddenly realise that to offer marriage entails a lot more than you thought it did, *hein*?' She pinched Nicolas's cheek as he blushed. 'Now you know what is wrong with your female fans, *n'est-ce pas?* You go and find that beautiful girl that will knock you out.'

'But, how will I know?'

'I have just told you: she will knock you out.' Lisette smiled at his obvious puzzlement. 'You are not quite as grown up as you look, *mon chou.* But now that you have thrown me over ...' She sighed theatrically. 'I must make do with seconds.'

§

Finding Armand alone in his office, Lisette came over and sat on his desk.

Armand felt a hot tide of colour surge up his neck and moved uncomfortably. 'Hello, Lisette,' he mumbled, head down. 'May I offer you a chair?'

'No, I'm comfortable here.' She smiled a little wryly. 'Unless I am distracting you?'

'No, no. Not at all,' he disclaimed, ruining his page with an ink blot and having to start afresh. 'I won't be long,' he gasped. 'How may I ... serve you?'

Lisette swung one pretty foot. 'You can marry me if you like. Nicolas has thrown me over.'

Armand dropped his pen, heedless of the ink stain. 'But ...' he sputtered. 'I haven't asked ...'

'But you want to, don't you?' she prompted.

'Er ... hmm,' he gulped; his face on fire. He leant farther over the page to hide his embarrassment.

'Then, *alors*, I have had to do it for you if I don't want to wait until our dotage for you to mention it,' said Lisette, in a jaunty tone. She sat looking at his bowed head and realised that he was completely overwhelmed. When time passed, and he did not respond, she said, 'My friend. If you don't want to, it is all right to say no.' Her mouth twisted. 'You see, once—a while ago—I dreamt that you said, "She is mine!". And you held me as if you loved me.'

His head sank lower. He struggled to speak, miserably inarticulate.

'*Mon ami* ...' She reached out to touch his hair with her fingertips. 'Must I be wearing a white gown and a blonde wig for you to say and do something like that?'

'No! Oh, no!' he groaned, throwing back his chair and rising to pull her into his arms. The bands on his tongue suddenly loosed: 'God knows, I love you! I do! I was afraid to tell you.' He bent his head to kiss her eyelids, the tip of her pert nose, her soft mouth; and lost himself in her sweetness.

# 18 WEDDING BLUES

**30 June 1936**

*Today I am the happiest of men! It is a day I truly thought would never come to pass. I never knew it before, but it is true that one is not complete without that special person. And how lucky I am to have found her! But, how was I to know that it would be a life-changing event for Nicolas as well as myself?*

The wedding of Armand and Lisette was to be held this morning at Belvoir.

Early, before anyone else in the wedding party was up, Lisette's maid of honour, her younger sister, Antoinette, hurried into the rose garden, gathering flowers to decorate the chapel before the sun's rays scorched their delicate petals. She hummed a sweet, lilting tune as she worked. Antoinette was the singer in the family; Lisette, the dancer. None of the others had met her before, since she had been away singing in a music hall in the West End of London, but there was no mistaking who she was. She was a taller, paler version of Lisette, striking with her white skin, rose-gold hair and light cornflower-blue eyes. There were some family friends who teased her as being a ghostly version of Lisette, referring to her as a shade or apparition, which she accepted with humour and a few throwaway lines to do with haunting. Although, she did wonder why she was not just accepted for herself. Perhaps it was, in part, why she had moved to England and become an entertainer in her own right. She knew she should write more often but never spared the time in her mad rush to keep up her schedule.

Incredibly, Lisette understood, never complaining about the lack of answers to her letters. 'No news is good news,' she would say, with her impish smile. 'As long as you are well and enjoying yourself, *Chérie*, then that is all right with me.'

Antoinette took her baskets of flowers and went inside, nodding to the château staff setting up the long tables for the sumptuous feast ordered by the duc for the wedding breakfast. Her mind on the chic ensemble her sister had chosen for her to wear; she carried her baskets with a happy smile. It was like her sister to ensure that she was dressed to enhance her delicate colouring, in a rose-pink silk chiffon coat-dress with a matching hat, so that no-one would comment on how pale she looked. *My favourite colour,* she thought, with gratitude. *It is so like Lisette to consider the sensibilities of others. We will be foils for each other: the bright in the pale; the pale in the bright.*

In a small side-hall, she began to arrange the roses in the great bowls that had been provided. Finally satisfied, she carried them, one at a time, into the chapel and spent a long time placing them to their best advantage. Then, with a last look around, she returned to her room.

Later, when Lisette descended the stairs in her waltz-length gown of palest-pink silk organza, followed by her sister, the duc was waiting. He leant back with the stance of a connoisseur to admire the picture they made, then concentrated his attention on the bride.

Everything about her was perfection: from her stylish chignon to her dainty self-embroidered satin shoes. He smiled approval on the little spray of flowers decorating the wisp of a hat perched at a dashing angle above her right eye, from which a tiny veil spread like an aureole over her bright hair and pale forehead to just cover the tip of her nose and give her an air of mystery.

'Exquisite, my dear,' he murmured, touching a pearl bead on the shoulder of her charming little embroidered bolero. 'Did you do this … tambour embroidery, don't they call it?'

'*Oui*, Monsieur, to both.'

'Clever. And beautiful. Armand will be enchanted: absolutely enchanted!'

'Do you think so, Monsieur?' For the first time, Lisette's voice betrayed anxiety.

'Wedding nerves?' The duc smiled down at her. 'I do not just think so, *ma fille*: I *know* so.' He took her hand and tucked it into his arm, warmly acknowledging Antoinette as he did so. 'You also look enchanting, Mademoiselle. As an artist, I could not do better than the colour palette you create.'

'So, you do not think that I look like a ghost, Monsieur?' murmured Antoinette.

'A *ghost*?' The duc laughed. 'No, no, a sylph, perhaps?' He looked more closely, understanding with his particular sensitivity why she said what she did. 'Each of you, in your own way, is stunning. Make no mistake about that. But together? Ah, together you are sensational.' He smiled upon them both and spoke to the bride: 'Are you ready, my dear? Truly, Armand will not need me to tell him what a fortunate man he is. Come. This is *your* day.'

'It certainly is, Monsieur! But wait, just a little moment, *s'il vous plaît*.' Antoinette stopped them to make a last-minute adjustment to the bride's veil and tweak the folds of her hemline. 'Now, Monsieur, we are ready.'

'*Très bon*,' said the duc, setting a stately pace.

The groom, nattily dressed in a pearl grey morning suit, with a pale-pink self-embroidered waistcoat and bowtie, was attended by Nicolas as his best man.

Nicolas, just as smartly attired, heard him draw in his breath as the bride approached. He was not surprised.

Settie had an aura of sweetness and beauty that would take anyone's breath away. Always, he had thought her beautiful; but today she had a special radiance. He noticed that Armand was looking at her in the way that he had often seen his father look at his mother. The thought flashed through his mind that he might look at someone like that, one day. Nicolas began to wonder what it would feel like, but then the ceremony started. He concentrated on what the priest was saying. When it was time for his part, he hoped that he would not drop the ring.

The chased-gold band was successfully placed on Lisette's finger and all was going without a hitch. When the bride and groom were officially man and wife, Nicolas moved to the chorister's dais. His wedding gift to the couple was to sing *Éternité d'amour* for them as they walked down the aisle a married couple. His first notes were magnificent, soaring upwards to the Gothic arches. But when he took a breath to deliver an even higher note, there was a silence followed by a strange, deep squawk. He stopped, his face a study in humiliation and despair.

Lisette left Armand's side to run to him and take him in her arms. 'Don't despair,' she whispered, 'you are a man now, and we must wait for your grown-up voice.'

'I'm sorry, Settie,' he replied, wiping at a tear. 'I have spoilt your wedding ceremony.'

Lisette's heart went out to the tall young boy with his head bowed in misery. She hugged him. 'Nothing can spoil it,' she said. 'Nothing! You didn't know it was your time. Anyway, it is the thought that counts.' She smiled her beautiful smile. 'Go on, play the song on the organ for me, *hein*? I promise you that I will love it just as much.'

'So will I,' said Armand, coming up behind them. He put an arm around each of them. 'Mine and Lisette's wedding day. You become a man. A special day for all three of us.'

For a long moment, they clung together: a family

united in love. Then with a murmured 'Felicitations,' Nicolas kissed them both on each cheek and went to seat himself at the organ, while the newly married couple made their way back to the aisle to wait for the beginning chords.

The bridesmaid stood back, watching. A momentary wry expression was masked by her public face. For the first time in her life, she felt a pang of envy for her sister, quickly suppressed. She could not quite deal with the emotions behind it; knowing that, however much she loved Lisette, in future she would have to stay away. And even if she did know the song, not for the world would she spoil their moment by offering to sing.

During the wedding breakfast, Antoinette teased Nicolas out of his introspection; entertaining him with anecdotes and stories from her London musicals; distracting him when Lisette and Armand left for their honeymoon in an open car, followed by cheering villagers.

It was an unforgettable day.

§

Nicolas grieved the loss of his voice as if it were a dear friend. He didn't know who he was any more. His voice had been so much a part of him that he was now incomplete. Lost. It had been a vital connection to his mother. How often had they sung together, their voices soaring, blending so perfectly? It was the reason his fans all adored him. And now, he hardly dared open his mouth even to speak, not knowing what kind of horrible sound would emerge. He knew that there were a wide range of possibilities: all of them discordant.

Now, he had an inkling of what it must have meant to Gerry to lose his voice: and without the hope of regeneration. Suddenly, his whole body shook with fear. *What if I do not get my voice back? What if I can never sing again?*

*Hold hard, mon fils,* soothed his inner voice. *We must wait a little while.*

*Angel? What will happen? Will I be able to sing again?*

*Mais certainement. But do not try it just yet. You must be patient.* Angel repeated the advice given to him long ago by Monsieur Dupont. *For now, concentrate on your studies.*

*I will.*

*Bon. Meanwhile, it will not hurt you to apply your considerable musical talents to the piano.*

Nicolas absorbed the sage advice, and the piano became his only solace. Every day he went to his grandmother's sitting room and played his heart out. Sometimes, beside him on the piano stool, he sensed a warm, loving presence; caught a fleeting image of light eyes and a sweet smile; felt a feather-light kiss on his brow.

Sometimes, he was so bereft and lonely that he put his head down over the keyboard and sobbed. Other things were happening to him, too. Things he couldn't talk about. The duc, a reserved and private man, had intimated that just as *les femmes* must silently endure the mystery of their menses, so were there things that men must silently endure, too.

Nicolas wished that he could have gone with Armand and Lisette, who were touring Greece and Italy, combining Armand's love of the classics with Lisette's passion for art and dance. Antoinette stayed a few days, then went to the Riviera to meet with friends before going back to England to begin rehearsals for a rigorous production. 'I will be very busy,' she told him. 'Too busy to think. You will forgive me if I forget to write.'

Nicolas murmured something. His heart went out to her because he thought she seemed sad. Yet, it was a sadness that he had no means of understanding, and after she'd gone, he soon forgot it in the welter of his own troubles. He liked Antoinette and missed her, but nothing like he missed the Lemaitres. They would not be back before the opera season started. He wished fervently for them to return. Secretly, he was afraid that something would happen to them, and he would be left alone, again. He reached, subconsciously, for his locket, holding it through the folds of his linen shirt.

His misery was a little alleviated by the duc showing him an interesting feature of the ducal apartment. 'Here we have a medieval innovation that could be used as an escape, should the occupant be cornered in his room. Always an interesting conundrum for rulers in those days: to be up high and safe, but yet have an escape route should the unthinkable happen. Here in my dressing-room is such a thing. Where is it, do you think? Have a look and see if you can find it.' He beckoned Nicolas closer. 'I know that you are discreet; that you can keep a secret. And, indeed, I thank you for keeping mine.'

'*De rien*, Grand-père!' responded Nicolas, knowing that his grandfather was speaking of the time that he had sneaked in to the tower room. 'It is a secret that belongs to you and you alone. I know that I should not have …'

'Well, never mind. You were curious, after all. Unlike that other secret, this one belongs not only to the duc but his heir. And for a very good reason: when asleep in your bed, you do not want a clandestine visit from someone who does not have your, erm, *welfare* in mind!'

Nicolas shivered. 'No, *indeed*, Grand-père.'

'And since this particular trait is very hard to discern, discretion is mandatory. Do you swear that if you find this secret escape route, you will tell no-one?'

Loneliness forgotten, Nicolas solemnly swore to keep what he found a secret; and at the duc's leave, he ran to sound the panels, twisting, pushing and pulling anything that might be a hidden knob.

'Is it like your secret tower room?' he asked, looking in vain for a carved flower.

'Ah … not quite. A similar principle, I suppose,' replied the duc; his eyes agleam.

Having exhausted all possibilities in the dressing-room,

Nicolas stepped inside the big garderobe, squeezing through the duc's suits; his nostrils filled with the scent of lavender and cedar wood. He tapped the back of the wardrobe, searching with his fingers for anything that might be used as a latch; but the back wall was smooth, defying entry.

'I have searched and searched and I cannot find it, Grand-père.'

'Do you give up?'

'I do not like to, but …' The boy hung his head. 'Yes.'

'*Eh bien*. Come into my bedchamber. Do you see that *cartouche*? *Oui*, that one there by the door. Twist the head of the bird above it. Now go into my dressing-room and step inside the garderobe.'

'Look, there is no back wall! Oh, there is a staircase. *Formidable*, Grand-père. *Formidable*!' Nicolas emerged from behind the clothes; his eyes alive with excitement. 'Where does it go? Can we *explore* it?'

'*Mais certainement. Cela va sans dire.* Wait while I find a torch.' He smiled as he opened a drawer in a tallboy. 'Belvoir *does* have other secrets, but they will be revealed in good time.'

§

Too soon, it was time to go back to the Opéra Magique. Nicolas tried not to be afraid of what the countess would say—what his fans would think. Would they turn away in disgust when they learnt that he would not sing? Would never again sing in the beautiful voice they loved? Or worse: would they *ridicule* him? He was a little comforted to know that he would not have to face them alone. Feeling as if he were going to his own execution, he walked into the building accompanied by his grandfather, his lawyer and his bodyguards.

The countess was jubilant when she heard that

Nicolas's voice had broken. That was until Monsieur Bernaud pointed out that the wording of the contract said 'perform' not 'sing'.

Sourly, she ordered the grand piano be brought out onto the stage. Nicolas would perform as a concert pianist until further notice. 'Your fans want you, and they will have you,' she said, with her thin smile. 'I will tell Herr Schmidt-Hesse.'

§

'But he is not an accomplished enough player for a concert pianist,' objected the conductor with a cold stare. 'What claim to fame does he have in this area?'

'You will have to get used to it, Herr Schmidt,' replied the countess, with a droll look. 'As will I.'

Herr Schmidt-Hesse frowned. He hated people not using his full name. But what he hated even more was that he dare not say so to the countess. 'Very well. But I do not have to like it.'

'Let us face it, Monsieur: His fans will not care if he hits a wrong note now and again. They are just happy if he is there.'

'Hmm. If you do not disagree, I will put another musician up there with him as a duet. I have a young violin pupil: very gifted. I will bill them as Young Talent.'

'You do as you like, Mein Herr.' The countess could not help herself. 'Just as long as they don't play Wagner.' She waved an admonitory finger. 'He is not for the young, however accomplished.'

The conductor's face suffused. He bowed without returning an answer. Wagner was certainly his favourite composer, but who had demanded he play him almost exclusively, in the first place?

# 19 DUET

**1 September 1936**

*Back to real life again. But the enchantment is not over. It is stronger than ever. How did I not know that all the beautiful things I have read about love are as nothing beside its glorious reality? On a more earthly plane, Nicolas seems very pleased to have us back. I believe he has been fretting over his voice. Although, from what I can tell, his duets with a young musician have been a resounding success. Lisette and I are going to hear them tonight.*

Nicolas's partner onstage was a tall, skinny fourteen-year-old. She was shy and blushed dreadfully whenever Nicolas looked at her. She had large hazel-green eyes and a sprinkling of freckles over the bridge of her straight little nose. Long chestnut hair dragged back from her face and secured with a bow on the back of her head, emphasised her high forehead, making it seem too big for the rest of her face. Taken separately, her features were good, but none of them seemed to fit together; her sensitive mouth hardly able to contain her teeth, which, though large, were white and even. She moved awkwardly, spoke with a slight accent only when spoken to, but when she put bow to strings, her sound was just divine. Her violin said all the things that she herself could not, in ways that were inimitable.

Herr Schmidt-Hesse had introduced her as, 'Natalie Watson: My most gifted pupil. She is Australian.' And this had sent her into an embarrassed silence from which she could not be drawn by Nicolas's friendly request to tell him about herself and her country.

This constraint between them was only evident when they were not performing. As soon as they began to play together, it was apparent that they had an extraordinary musical connection.

Tonight, Nicolas was playing for Lisette and Armand. He came on stage and bowed, handsome in tails—returned to the wings to escort Natalie, dressed in an ice-blue silk Schiaparelli evening gown and clasping her violin and bow with trembling, white knuckled fingers—then seated himself at the piano. All to uproarious applause. He waited for Natalie to take up her stance and set his fingertips to the keys.

Again, their duet took on an extra dimension. They played with passion and beauty: a sensitivity beyond their years. Veteran music lovers were astounded. To Nicolas, it was a spiritual connection, as if they could read each other's mind and play effortlessly in perfect timing exactly what was in the other's thoughts. It was a liberating experience, a freedom, a beauty; something so perfect that he could not say what it was because there were no words to describe it.

They took curtain call after curtain call. Normally, Natalie would run off, red-faced, mumbling something as she fled; but tonight, Nicolas held onto her hand. He wanted to introduce her to Armand and Lisette, who had come backstage with the bodyguards to congratulate them.

Nicolas was so filled with joy at their performance that, in an extravagance of emotion, he kissed Natalie's hand and exclaimed, 'We are good together, *n'est-ce pas*? I cannot wait for our next practice session.'

The girl tried to say something, spun on her heel and ran off, fiery red.

Nicolas stared after her in horrified bewilderment. He turned to the others and spread his hands. 'But, what did I say?'

'Poor sweet!' said Lisette, looking at him with deep compassion. No-one was sure whether she meant Nicolas or Natalie. 'I will go after her.'

'I think she is shy,' said Desi.

'Awkward age,' added Dani.

'Yes,' agreed Desi. 'We were like that at that age. Weren't we Dani?'

'All legs, hair and teeth.' Dani shrugged. 'She will grow into herself, *jeune* Monsieur.'

*If she grows into herself as you have done, she will be a knock out!* Armand didn't dare say it. But he thought it.

The bodyguards smiled and retired into their usual enigmatic silence.

Lisette returned, shrugging, to place a hand on Nicolas's shoulder. 'I could not find her; I am sorry. But don't worry. She will get over it.'

'I think we should go and have coffee,' said Armand.

'Yes,' said Nicolas, in a flat voice. 'Are you coming, Sette?'

'As long as you give me your arm. Armand can go first and find us a table.' Lisette waited until the others were out of earshot. 'Is she the one, *Chéri*? The one who has bowled you over?'

'No. Oh no, nothing like that. It is just that when we play together, something happens. It lifts me high, higher than the angels. It is so joyous! So beautiful! I cannot ... explain.'

'You don't need to. Just enjoy it.' She looked into his shining eyes. 'Does it happen for her, too, do you think?'

He returned her glance: honest, puzzled. 'I don't know. She will not talk to me. I don't know why.'

'I think your Amazons are right. She is shy. Give it

time, *Chéri.* Now, we had better catch up to Armand. We have a lot to talk about, *n'est-ce pas*?' She smiled at Nicolas, and he basked in the warmth he'd been missing.

Impulsively, he hugged her. 'Oh, I have missed you, Settie! Both of you!'

§

Nicolas now looked forward to his weekly performance at the Opéra Magique. It enraptured him in ways he could never have imagined. Yet Natalie remained elusive, out of reach as a personality, unless she was drawing her bow across her violin strings. And then it happened. Whatever it was …

But whenever Nicolas tried to find out what it was between them that was so uplifting, he was foiled, both by Natalie's shyness and the rigid attitude of her teacher.

It was as if Herr Schmidt-Hesse suspected Nicolas of having designs on the girl, assuming the role of a domineering parent. 'You are here to play the piano. You have done that. Now go. I will not have you frightening my pupil,' he ordered, fixing Nicolas with an icy stare.

'But, Monsieur,' began Nicolas, 'can you not see how well we play together? I only want to thank her ———'

'And so you might well!' shouted the conductor; his neck bulging. 'It is not how well you play together! It is she that carries you! I will not allow you to importune her.' He turned possessively to the trembling girl. 'Do not let him distress you. Come along with me, my dear. That was a superb performance. Superb!'

Nicolas stared after them, hurt and humiliated. But he'd seen something else. Natalie was obedient to her teacher, but the distress in the great hazel-green eyes had been brought into being by his attack on Nicolas. He was sure of it. And the memory eased his pain.

During his months as a concert pianist, Nicolas's adult

voice emerged like a red emperor from its chrysalis. It was a fine, golden tenor: crystal clear and pure. But he said nothing because he wanted to keep playing with Natalie. He wanted to go on feeling the way he did when they were together on the stage, making music that took him to the angels.

When it became known that Nicolas had made a record, Herr Schmidt-Hesse stalked up to the countess. 'Do you realise, Madame, that de Beaulieu has regained his voice?'

'Has he?' The countess was uninterested. 'So? The duet with your scrawny pupil is a success.' She blew smoke in his face. 'I think we should carry on with that.'

The conductor almost lost his temper. 'He is not a concert pianist's bootlace! *My* pupil is doing everything in *that* duo!'

'Careful, Herr Schmidt.' The countess looked amused. 'Your slip is showing.' Her smile grew wider. 'That is *not* how the critics see it, Mein Herr. They are saying: not only are they both equally talented, but together they produce a synergy that cannot be equalled by any other duo—or either of them playing solo. They are *electric!* Don't tell me you cannot see that!'

'*She* is carrying him!'

'Nonsense! You are biased against him. The box office approves, Mein Herr. And if the box office approves, who are we to go against it, *hein*?' She blew a last, long stream of smoke, stubbed out her cigarette and walked away, leaving him baffled and furious.

But that was not the end of it. Merely the start of a string of complaints made by the conductor to the countess after each performance. The last was made with an aggressive raising of the voice: 'He is intimidating my pupil! He is making unwelcome advances!'

'What?' countered his employer. 'That scrawny little piece? When he could have his choice of all the debutantes in Paris? Don't make me laugh. As if any man would be interested in a beanpole like that! She has neither chic nor grace!'

'No, not yet.' Colour began to rise in the conductor's jowls. 'But he is not a man.'

The countess gave a little spurt of laughter. 'I would venture to suggest that he is more a man than *she* is a woman ... Mein Herr.'

'She will grow into a beauty! But enough of this! She has something more important: true talent!'

'And you are saying my performer does not?' The countess raised plucked eyebrows, taunting the conductor into open fury.

'No, Madame. I am saying that it will be better for both of them if he sings solo, and *my* pupil stays with me to further her studies!'

'You're jealous, Mein Herr? Over that scraggy chit? I had no idea you were such a *dirty* old man!'

Herr Schmidt-Hesse, puce to the ears, veins bulging in his forehead, stormed out, followed by the countess's mocking laughter.

But when the countess heard how well Nicolas's record was selling, she knit her brows, counted her box office takings and gave certain orders.

When Nicolas arrived, excited at the prospect of their duet, he was met, not by Natalie and the grand piano, but an empty stage. It was a shock. One he was forced to accommodate at the shortest of notice. For a moment, he felt as he had when he first had to step onstage without his mother. Then, a hand to his locket, he visualised Angel, took a deep breath and began his aria.

Nicolas sang in his new golden tenor voice. After the first bar, he had to stop and acknowledge a standing ovation: truly a testament to the beauty of his adult voice. Yet, despite the overwhelming approval of the audience, Nicolas was vaguely unsatisfied. Joy was there; his interaction with the audience was all it should be. But there was something missing: the euphoric mystery ingredient that lifted him higher than the angels when he and Natalie made music together.

When he found an opportunity, Nicolas asked the countess if he and Natalie could occasionally play together, but the countess was unresponsive. The audience was charmed by his solo; the box office takings went up, not down.

Herr Schmidt-Hesse refused to even speak to Nicolas, let alone reveal Natalie's address. The countess laughed and said she did not know it. Nicolas continued to lobby the countess, desperate to be reunited onstage with the only girl in the world who could raise him to celestial heights. But it was no use: Young Talent had played their last duet.

# 20 REVELATION

24 December 1936

*There have been many discordant notes at the Opéra Magique since the countess took over its management. But none more so than these ...*

The duc de Belvoir was holding what was increasingly becoming a rare event in the hôtel du Bois: his Christmas soiree. Lisette was his hostess, and almost every artist and musician of note was present. He moved easily amongst his guests. As always, a charming host. He glanced approvingly at his grandson, circulating as etiquette demanded, leaving smiles and animation in his wake. *Doing the pretty,* thought the duc. *And doing it well.*

The gentle murmur of conversation was suddenly jarred by a booming voice: 'Where is Herr Schmidt-Hesse? Ah, there you are, Sir!' The large gentleman, a veteran patron of the Opéra Magique, was not famed for his tact, especially after a few cognacs. 'I must speak with you about your penchant for Wagner, Monsieur. I know you are an expert on him, but some of us are nostalgic for the music played in years gone by.'

'Indeed, Monsieur?' The conductor stiffened. There were certain things that riled him, besides having his name shortened. One was criticism of his choice of music and another was a comparison of himself to any other musician. His colour mounting, he said, 'The countess prefers Wagner, Monsieur. You must appeal to her.'

Some imp of devilry wouldn't let Monsieur Bourrac leave him alone. *What a stuffed shirt,* he thought. *The stereotypical pompous Prussian!*

'But don't you agree that there should be variety? Oh, look! There is Monsieur Merignac over there. If only he were still our conductor! You could learn from him, you know.' The man raised his voice further. 'Join us, Monsieur Merignac, *s'il vous plaît?* I have just been telling your successor how nostalgic I have been for your music.'

Monsieur Merignac, his white hair a fuzzy halo around his thin, lined face, limped over with the aid of a walking stick and bowed to him. 'Thank you, Monsieur. But the music of Herr Schmidt-Hesse is not lacking, you know.' He replied in gentle reproof, bowing to the conductor. 'Not in any way.'

The fury in the German conductor's face was equally matched by contempt. He did not acknowledge the compliment.

The patron persisted, 'I have been saying to Herr Schmidt-Hesse that there should be a variety of composers in any house's program. What do you think, Monsieur Merignac?'

The old conductor stood silent, aware of the German conductor's mounting choler. Finally, he said softly, 'I think, Monsieur, although it is only my humble opinion, that it would be a pity to confine oneself solely to one composer, however compelling his work. There is, then, so much beauty that you miss ——'

'Jew! Filthy Jew! What would you know about beauty or music?' screamed the German, flecks of spittle adorning his chin. 'All the evils in the world are caused by the likes of you! You and your entire race should be expunged from the face of the earth!'

The buzz of conversation ceased like a snapped thread. Heads swivelled to where the two conductors stood staring at one another. Those looking into their faces saw that one was filled with hatred, the other with a melancholy dignity.

The shocked silence was broken by quiet footsteps. Monsieur Merignac felt a hand under his elbow. 'Come with me, Monsieur,' said the duc de Belvoir, softly. 'You do not have to be subjected to this.'

'Jews are an inferior race!' hissed the German as they walked away.

The duc turned a stern face. 'No, Monsieur. The fields of France have run with blood to prove that all men are equal. I would venture to add that the Jews are still God's people. Even though they made a terrible mistake all those years ago, being a just and compassionate God, will He not forgive them?'

'Pah! God? I do not believe in God.'

The duc bowed. 'Then, that is your misfortune.'

'Man is his own God.'

'*Eh bien*, if that is so, the world is condemned to misery. But that is beside the purpose.' The duc spoke even more quietly. 'You will not be here when I return, Monsieur. Such monstrous behaviour, as you have shown, is not welcome in my house.' He beckoned to Nicolas to bring his Muses. When they arrived, he said, 'Herr Schmidt-Hesse finds he has another engagement he must attend, *à l'instant*. Please, make sure that he is escorted safely to his car.'

Without looking back, the duc took Monsieur Merignac to his study, signalling his butler to follow with coffee and cognac. He made the old man comfortable in a chair in front of the fire, while Justin placed a table within easy reach, pouring cognac and coffee for each of them. Dismissing his butler, the duc sat opposite. 'I am desolated that you have been subject to such abuse in my grandson's house, Monsieur. Herr Schmidt-Hesse is *not* my countryman,' he said; his face white and set. 'But, as a fellow human being, I apologise.'

'It is not your fault, Monsieur.' Monsieur Merignac shrugged. 'This kind of thing: it has always been there in some degree. But it is increasing with the rise to power of this man, Hitler. Jews have always been blamed for everything, but with the Nazi movement it has reached unprecedented levels.'

'I am aware, of course, of the sad history of your race, Monsieur. As to this man Hitler, I did hear something of his attitude but have not paid close attention. An oversight I must rectify.' The duc looked distressed. 'Persecution of others is the greatest sin. I do not know why it happens.'

'Wherever we go, we are hounded, Monsieur. History will attest to that.' Monsieur Merignac played with the handle of his cup. After a second or two, the duc was astonished to see a little nostalgic smile break the downward curve of his lips. 'But there was a time—*la Belle Époque*—when things were good. People were accepted for their talents, no matter who they were. We laughed, we played, we fell in love ...' The old conductor sighed with sudden, deep sadness. 'I have outlived my time, Monsieur. I must go home to Jeanne. She worries if I am out late. She is more nurse to me now than wife. And I must not keep you from your guests. I thank you from the bottom of my heart for your kindness to an old man.' He met the duc's eyes. 'It will not be long, Monsieur.'

'Do not say so, Monsieur,' said his host, distressed. He pulled the bell. 'Wait here before the fire while I organise a car for you and someone to see you home.'

'Please, do not trouble, Monsieur. You must return to your guests.'

'*Eh bien,*' the duc assured him, with a sweet, sad smile, 'it is not a trouble. Not, in the slightest. And my other guests will be happy to wait on such a venerable gentleman as yourself, Monsieur.'

Monsieur Merignac did not die straightaway, but he did begin a noticeable decline. The duc had no doubt that the exchange with the German conductor—the *hatred* emanating from the man—had begun the process of his demise.

As he, Nicolas and Armand attended the old man's funeral on a bleak winter day, the duc determined to learn the extent of this evil that was invading even the houses of moderates in Europe. He'd found that the son of his late friend and cousin, King George, seemed enamoured by it. It was a bad business, and David seemed to have no grasp of the enormity of it. *Perhaps it is just as well he abdicated,* mused the duc. *David is not equipped to be king.*

Over the coming weeks, the duc sent out his spies to Nazi meetings. Sometime later, he attended a lecture by Hitler and came away troubled. *It sounds wonderful,* he thought, *while one is in there. The man is a consummate orator. It is only later that one begins to think and realise that he is, essentially, evil. The danger will be that some will not think. Like David … And what then?*

The duc's painful train of thought became an obsession, occupying every waking moment. Once before he had felt like this: he, Angel and countless other good men who'd spent the next four years in the deepest nightmare. He couldn't do now what he'd done then. He was just too old and frail. But he could ensure the safety of Nicolas and his people. He was not a fanciful man, but almost, he felt the spectre of Angel urging him on.

§

Upon Herr Schmidt-Hesse falling ill with influenza, the countess unexpectedly closed the Opéra Magique for a month and went on holiday to Majorca. The duc needed nothing more. He left for Belvoir the next day, telling Armand, Lisette and Nicolas to pack up the household and follow in their own time.

When they arrived, they found him supervising the packing and sewing of the portraits of his immediate family into padded waterproof sacking. 'I cannot take the old portraits, a mark will be left on the wall, but I can take all these recent ones where it is not so obvious.' It was as if he talked to himself. 'And if I do it now, when the time comes, this slight mark will have faded. People have been tortured for such things as a missing painting.'

'You're not going gaga, are you Grand-père?' asked Nicolas, voicing Armand's fleeting thought. Somehow, Nicolas could say such things without offence.

'I only wish I were,' said the duc, without resentment. 'But … I fear not.'

'What did you mean when you said, "When the time comes"? What time is coming? I don't understand.'

Armand put a restraining hand on Nicolas's arm. 'Do you know something, Monsieur, that we do not? What is it that you fear?'

Lisette came in to call them for lunch, and the duc, in greeting her, lost the opportunity to answer.

# 21 THE SECRET OF BELVOIR

**6 March 1937**

*Ever since our charming conductor's outburst against the Jews, my employer has been increasingly paranoid. Perhaps it is his age, I know not, but he is most definitely driven to take some sort of protective action against something he perceives as a threat. Today I have been privileged to witness one of the wonders of the natural world as well as the most amazing product of medieval ingenuity. Safe to say that not even in my wildest fantasy had I thought of something like this. It is, at the same time, a grim relic of the past, and a boy's greatest dream of adventure. I have never seen Nicolas's eyes so huge. And yet, I fancy, it has challenged him in a way that he is not yet ready for. Et moi aussi!*

At breakfast the duc told Armand and Nicolas that he had something to show them and to dress for hiking. 'And bring your jackets. It is a little chilly out today.' He seemed so tense and grim that, although they looked at each other, they didn't question him but hurried away to change their clothes.

'What is it, do you think?' asked Nicolas, when they were out of earshot. 'Has he gone gaga after all?'

Armand shook his head. 'No, but something is

191

worrying him, and we can help him by doing what he wants.'

'So, what does he want us to do?'

'We'll soon find out. But I think …'

'Yes? You think …?'

Armand seemed to hesitate. 'That whatever it is, we will find it interesting.'

'Evasive!' The straight gaze accused. 'You know something, don't you?'

'No, no. It is just an oblique reference I have come across now and again when I have been studying the old records of the château. Very cryptic. Do you know if there is anything … an oubliette, for example?'

'An oubliette? *Non.*' Nicolas was unequivocal, thinking of his escapades with Gervais in exploring the vast cellars of the château that his grandfather had described more than once as a rabbit warren, warning them not to get lost. 'I would know of something like that.'

'Then … what about a secret way of escape in case of a siege?'

'Yes …' Nicolas began, then remembered his long-ago promise to his grandfather and amended, 'perhaps there could be. The château is very old. We'd better hurry. *En avant.*' He dived into his room and, in a matter of minutes, dressed in a shooting jacket, breeches, boots and gaiters, was knocking on his tutor's door.

When the duc took them into his secret tower room, Nicolas began to feel that perhaps Armand had been right about an oubliette. After all, what did he really know of this room? He received a shock straight away. 'Grand-père, the ballerina is missing! Where is she?' As he spoke, he saw that the showcases and walls were empty. The vast quantity of memorabilia and sketches were no longer here.

'Over there.' His grandfather indicated a sacking-wrapped object, the size and shape of a small door, leaning against the wall. 'I managed the artifacts and the other paintings alone, but I am afraid that I will need your help with La Belle. You will notice that handles have been sewn into the sacking at either end for easy carrying.'

'That's a good job.' Armand took one end of the painting, directing Nicolas to take the other. 'It will not be so awkward to carry.'

Nicolas took the handle, lifting it easily. 'It is not heavy.'

'No, it is just too big for one person to handle,' said the duc, lighting a storm lantern. 'Come this way, if you please.' He went to the opposite wall of the tower, below the staircase, pulled out a hinged rock and pressed a concealed lever. A section of the wall, camouflaged by jagged edges of rock, swung out to reveal a small, dark room. 'The old treasury,' he said, indicating a large brass and silver-inlaid wooden coffer standing in the middle of a crimson turkey carpet. 'Leave the portrait there for a moment, and help me shift this. It is extraordinarily heavy.'

'Give me your place, Grand-père. Armand and I will do it.' They moved the chest up against the wall without too much effort.

'Hmm,' said the duc. 'You two make it look easy. It is a job for one; I can tell you. Now roll up the carpet and stand over here with me.'

When they obeyed, he twisted a knob of rock on the wall beside him, and the midsection of the board floor opened vertically on a central hinge to reveal a hidden spiral staircase descending into gloom.

'The lower part of *this* staircase,' said the duc, pointing upwards. 'Follow me with the portrait, and tread carefully on these old stairs. It will not be too awkward if you use the handles and stay as close as you can to the wall. By the way ...' A little ripple of amusement entered his voice. 'I have ascertained that it will fit.' He picked up the lantern, descended a few steps and turned. 'To all intents and purposes, we are now inside the walls of the château. This tower has been bricked up on all the lower levels. When we emerge, we will be on the mountainside below the château.'

'Oh! You were right, Armand,' said Nicolas, handing down the portrait to the tutor. 'It is a way of escape.' *Another one.* 'Our ancestors were devious, *hein?*'

The duc's lips quirked, but he said nothing, directing the lantern for them.

'Yes, so it seems. Or frightened.' Armand, negotiating the hewn rock slabs with his end of the burden, lurched suddenly, grasping with his free hand at a handrail fixed into the wall. 'Step carefully, Nicolas, these next few stairs are uneven.'

After what seemed like hours, but was really a matter of minutes, they came to a passage that was level for a few metres then began to descend. Light had filtered through the small slits that passed for windows in the bricked-up tower, but now it was pitch dark. And noticeably colder. Nicolas shivered and followed the golden lamplight.

The passage twisted and turned, always descending, with a number of other passages leading off in different directions. Here and there, were larger openings, some with piles of rubble, some without. The duc went on steadily before them, halting where the passage opened out into a cave on the mountainside below the château, hidden from sight by small trees and a dense growth of vines and shrubs.

'This is the most vulnerable part,' said the duc, gesturing towards the opening where daylight made a silver drapery. 'Our only Achilles heel. We will leave the portrait here for the moment. There is something I want to show you before we put it with the others.' He saw that Armand and Nicolas were looking at each other in amazement, and smiled. 'Not long now before all is revealed. Pick up that boulder, will you, Nicolas? And bring it with you,' he said, scooping up a stone and pocketing it. 'It shouldn't be too heavy. No? *Bien.* Come this way.'

Mystified, they followed him to the entrance. Nicolas recognised it as one of the rough, overgrown rocky areas on the eastern side of the mountain—too steep to explore on horseback.

'Here is where you must be careful not to show yourself.' The duc pushed aside a tangle of vines and slid, crabwise, through a narrow opening into a second cave. 'However, there seems to be enough shrubbery.'

The other two, inching after him, agreed that there was certainly enough shrubbery. Nicolas, balancing the boulder, was last to look up. Eyes widening, he followed Armand and the duc into a massive space.

The duc held the lantern high, swinging it around to allow them to observe the wondrous rock formations. 'Breathtaking, isn't it?' he murmured, shattering the awed silence.

'*Foudroyant!*' breathed Nicolas; his voice echoing eerily. He glanced all about him. '*Cette caverne est fantastique!*'

'Yes,' agreed Armand. 'It is a privilege to enter such an incredible space.'

'Do you think that this is what I have brought you here to see?' The duc led them across the cavern to a spectacular jutting formation, parallel to the back wall and curving around as if to join it in an amazing stalactite formation. He went right up to the wall before he turned left into an almost invisible space, continuing on a meandering path, weaving his way through the forest of magnificent natural sculptures without hesitation—even though the path was never clear until the last moment— through a triangular niche that narrowed high above them into a fissure. From somewhere nearby came the sound of dripping water: the artist at work.

'Almost there,' said the duc, vanishing behind a limestone drapery on their left like a fold in the cave wall.

When they caught up to him, he was standing in the archway of a flagstoned passage heading into the heart of the mountain.

'Unless you know this is here,' said the duc, patting the door pillar, 'It would be difficult to just stumble upon it.'

'I must confess that I could not see a way through the stalactites. Could you, Armand?'

'No, it all looks to be part of a rather solid wall.' Armand shook his head. 'Extraordinary … *se trompe-l'œil* on a grand and spectacular scale.'

Both Armand and Nicolas exclaimed at the workmanship: the precise, square construction of an underground corridor; its roof, a smooth, perfect arch.

'Definitely man-made!' commented Nicolas, as an aside.

'Indeed,' agreed Armand, with an answering twinkle. 'And by craftsmen who knew what they were doing, too!'

The duc appeared not to be listening. 'We must go carefully here,' he said, stopping to raise a warning hand. 'Don't walk on that big flagstone in the middle. You can give me that boulder now, Nicolas. Watch!' he commanded, stepping over to drop the boulder just where someone might tread. Instantly, the flagstone fell away from beneath it, spun over smoothly and snapped back into place as if nothing had happened. Seconds later, they heard a splash far below.

'Hinged in the centre and counterweighted,' remarked the duc. He edged around it, against the wall, motioning them to follow. 'It is imperative that you remember the first *big* flagstone. Remember not to tread on it.'

'I should *just* think I might!' whispered Nicolas.

'Indeed!' murmured Armand, white about the mouth.

'In fact,' added the duc, 'it would be advisable to adopt the policy of hugging the wall when traversing this corridor. Just to make sure …'

The walls of the passage became rough, with jagged floor-to-ceiling cracks, just before it ended in a heavy, nailed door with an iron ring at approximately shoulder height.

Again, the duc held them back. 'Watch what happens to anyone who touches that door.' He delved in his pocket for the stone and tossed it against the latch. The door opened smoothly outward. At the same time, a huge beam swung down from the roof, gathered impetus with its descent and swept through the opening. They shivered in the wind of its passing.

Nicolas glimpsed a deep chasm with a sparkling waterfall, a roiling pool; heard the roar of the water, before the door shut silently, and the beam went back into the roof with a satisfied 'clunk'.

'*Mon Dieu!*' gasped Armand. 'But how?'

'All counterweighted,' replied the duc. 'A very delicate balance. The marquis du Bois helped me restore it. That is, he gave me the design. He thought it less gruesome than the original blades and axes, while still achieving its object.'

'Eminently,' murmured Armand, shuddering.

Nicolas said nothing, sagging against the wall as he imagined what it might feel like to walk up to that door without thinking and be hurled into the depths of an underground maelstrom. To drown in darkness. Cold. Alone. He began to tremble.

*Don't worry,* soothed his inner voice. *I won't let you forget.*

'We'll go back for the portrait before I show you the rest,' said the duc, setting off back the way they'd come.

'The rest? What rest?' asked Nicolas, treading along the wall. 'This has to be a dead end.'

'The truest words that were ever spoken,' agreed Armand, in a hushed voice. 'For anyone who does not know the secret.'

'The portrait first,' said the duc, motioning with the lantern. 'Then we will see ...'

Heart-stopping minutes later, they were edging around the booby-trapped flagstone for the third time, halting a few metres back from the innocent-looking door.

'Death's doorway,' muttered Nicolas, shivering. He set

down his end of the portrait to stand near the left-hand wall with Armand and his grandfather. 'I still cannot see _____'

'*Doucement, mon fils*. All is about to be revealed. Do you see this crack in the wall? The middle one ... Here. This is our entrance.'

'Can that be an entrance to anything?' asked Nicolas, with a disbelieving glance at the narrow cleft. 'It is barely wide enough for an arm.'

'Fortunately, it is ... just,' said the duc, inserting his hand diagonally and stretching in until his shoulder met the rock. He fumbled at some unseen mechanism and nodded to his right. 'Pull this side out now.'

Nicolas grasped the jagged edge and pulled. Silently, a section of the wall swung out on a pivot, blocking the passage to the fatal doorway. He and Armand drew in astonished breaths as the duc stepped inside, holding up the lantern. They were looking at a fairytale cave—even bigger and more amazing than the last one.

'*Mais alors*!' Nicolas clapped his hands like an excited child; his fears subjugated for the moment. '*Foudroyant*! Grand-père, Look!' He pointed to a spectacular group of stalactites. 'They are like the lustres on a magnificent chandelier!'

The duc took them on a tour of the cave. Its roof was lost in darkness, but its walls were a confection of glittering structures: some as hard as icicles, others as soft and flowing as a silken robe. '*Et voilà*!' he said, bowing theatrically, the lamplight giving his eyebrows a Machiavellian aspect. 'The secret of Belvoir. Known only to its heirs. And those for whom it is necessary for their survival. This cave is called the Cavern of the King's Mantle. Do you see why?'

'Yes. Oh, yes!' Nicolas gasped at the great flowing rock structure that covered a vast expanse of wall with folds that made it look uncannily like a giant cloak with a long train and sparkling hemline. 'It seems to be edged with jewelled lace. What a tremendous secret! *Incroyable!*'

'And yet, strangely enough, this cavern is not the real secret. Only, perhaps, its great hall.' The duc's eyes gleamed proudly in the light. 'Bring the portrait, and I will show you my underground citadel.'

'Narrow is the path to life, but broad is the way that leads to destruction,' murmured Armand, thinking of the deadly passage that looked so civilised and the tiny crack in the rock that had led them here. 'That, or something very like it, was the biblical quote I read in the old records that set me thinking that there must be something. And here it is, *hein?*'

'You were able to work this out by studying the records?' The duc looked taken aback.

'Not this. A way of escape, perhaps, or an oubliette. But *this* ...' Armand turned right around, taking in the spectacle. 'It is beyond my wildest imaginings!'

'Grand-père?' Nicolas's voice held an edge of distress. He remembered his own attempts at cave exploration as a child: they were shallow and dirty, redolent of bat droppings and bird excrement, and held no attraction for him or his companions. *But something like this!* 'What if some child finds the passage and decides to explore? He will be killed and no-one will ever know what happened to him.'

'No, no, *mon fils.* Did you not notice me put up my hand to the right as we entered the passage—and at the same place when we went back for the painting?' The duc's eyes questioned each of his companions in turn.

'I can't say that I did,' replied Armand. 'I was too busy gawping.'

'*Non*, Grand-père.' Nicolas shook his head.

'You *cannot* think that I would allow the death of a child or a poor, innocent animal looking for shelter! Come now, *mes amis*, rid your minds of such macabre thoughts. Even if they would wander this far, which is doubtful—you know, very doubtful—there is a locking mechanism behind that smallest stone block where the arch meets the vertical stonework. But the flagstone responds to weight. Even if the mechanism were activated, a small animal or child would not have the weight to trip it. The door responds to a light touch, but only at a certain height: too high for either. The marquis du Bois took these things into consideration when he redesigned them. Come, I will show you.' The duc strode back along the passage to its entrance and pointed out a small rectangular block at shoulder height, recessed a little from its fellows. 'You see: when this block is depressed, like that, the mechanism is locked, the flagstone is safe and the door cannot be opened.' He pressed it a couple of times to show them, leaving it depressed.

Nicolas stared at the stone block, assimilating the import of his grandfather's words. His lip quivered. 'Do you mean to say, that when we came back through here with the painting, we were in no danger of plunging to our deaths?'

'Of course not! I would not allow you to take the risk, carrying a burden like that,' he replied, leading the way back to the great Cavern of the King's Mantle. 'I only activated it to show you. And I wanted to be sure that you remember it. Just in case …'

'In case of what?' asked Nicolas. 'I don't understand! Why, Grand-père? Why have this barbaric mechanism restored, at all?' *Frightening us and risking our lives. And for what?*

'Because …' The duc raised the lantern to look more closely at his grandson's white countenance with its huge, troubled eyes and spoke slowly, almost to himself. 'Even though we pride ourselves on being civilised men, sadly, there are times when, if a man does not kill, he himself will be killed. Kill or be killed: little though we may relish it, we must face the fact that there may come an occasion when there is no other choice. When you are pursued by such an enemy, it will be time to activate the mechanism.' His mouth drooped with sadness. 'I hope and pray that I am wrong, but I believe that the time is coming, and soon, when we will face such evil. When we do, I want you to be prepared.'

'But, Grand-père ...' Nicolas fell silent. *I could never kill anyone,* he thought. *Never. No matter what.* But how could he explain? Death had taken from him the two people he loved most in the world. He hated death! How could he be its instrument? In that moment, he was sure that, no matter the stakes, he could never take the life of another human being.

'Yes, *mon fils*?' prompted his grandfather. When Nicolas shook his head, he indicated the open section of wall. 'We will just shut this. There is not much use in having a hidden door if we leave it open.' The duc waited with the lantern while the other two complied, swinging the great rock on its pivot.

'I only hope we can find it again,' said Armand, as the section clicked into place.

'Oh, easily,' replied the duc, waving the lantern towards a metal drop latch. 'Here is the mechanism. Right here. You will notice that it is also at shoulder height.' His voice became animated. 'Let us say that you, Armand, are on the mountainside, pursued by a mortal enemy. You will slide into the cave, weave through the stalactite forest to the passage, hitting the stone block as you go past to activate the mechanism. You sidestep the flagstone, open the hidden door just enough to squeeze through, pulling it behind you. The latch drops and you are safe. Meanwhile, your enemy has finally managed to find the opening in the back of the cave. If he doesn't step on the flagstone: *Voilà!* The door will get him. You see?'

Both young men nodded, horrified beyond words. They could not see how a gentle, artistic, poetic, utterly civilised gentleman like the duc could condone such barbarity, let alone be animated by it. But they had not had to endure the dreadful years of battle with an implacable enemy: The terrible slaughter that had been the Great War. That shocking bloodbath that no-one ever had, or ever would, be able to make sense of.

'This great underground fortress,' continued the duc, 'was built by our medieval forefathers as a refuge for the people of Belvoir, in anticipation of a time when their very existence would be threatened. I do not know how many times it has been used in antiquity, but I reactivated it before the Great War, with the help of the marquis du Bois, when we could see what was coming. *Dieu merci,* we didn't need it then; but I feel in my bones that we will need it this time. And soon.'

'But, Grand-père …' objected Nicolas. *Humour him,* said his inner voice. *Old people have these fears. The memories of the carnage of the Great War cast long shadows. And he is, quite properly, preparing you to save your people. And what if he is right? Have you thought of that?*

The duc, with amazing energy for one in his eighties, led the way across the Cavern of the King's Mantle into a broad passage that was the beginning of a network of corridors, hewn in the precise manner of the great medieval buildings, with arched ceilings opening out at intervals into large chambers, reinforced by vaults with carved pillars.

Nicolas and Armand began to feel quite lost and disoriented with only the duc's lantern to guide them, as they looked into rooms with raised sleeping places carved in the rock walls; entered huge vaulted living spaces furnished with bench seats and tables hewn out of rock, with either fireplaces or braziers for heating; taking another passage cut into a far wall, repeating the process time and again, seemingly at random.

*It is so dark in here,* thought Nicolas. *And cold.* 'Grand-père!' he called at last, in desperation. 'How do you know where you are going?'

'Are you feeling lost?' enquired the duc, turning to shine his lantern on them. 'There is no need for concern. The layout is quite simple—once you know it. I will show you when we have stowed the painting.' He strode on, holding the lantern so that it made a mellow glow on straight walls and Gothic-arched ceilings. 'This is the main tunnel. It is wider and higher than the others—the arch more pointed—and all the other passages lead off it. It ends … here.' He halted before a studded door, frighteningly like the first one. 'No trap here,' he said, lifting the ring to push the door open. 'The end chamber. This side, a storeroom. And this side ——'

'A staircase!' exclaimed Nicolas. '*Mais*, where does it go?'

'*Un moment, s'il vous plaît*,' said the duc, preoccupied. He turned left into an alcove and opened a second studded door to reveal another huge, vaulted space: this time with rows of shelving, giant ceramic vessels and larger storage spaces—one packed with three huge trunks. 'Let us put this painting in the niche with the others. The costumes and the memorabilia are packed in those trunks there.'

'Never tell me, Grand-père,' exclaimed Nicolas, pointing to the trunks, 'that you brought *those* down here?'

'No, no. They were here. They came down in the Great War. All I had to do was pack them as I brought each article down. I used a small portmanteau for the most part. *Eh bien*,' he said, as they placed their burden to his satisfaction, 'I have done what I came here to do. La Belle and all the other portraits will be safe, thanks to your help.'

And even as they politely disclaimed, the younger men saw him shed his great energy like a no longer needed cloak. 'And now, the stairs: I am afraid that I am not up to climbing them today, but it is very simple. They lead to other levels laid out exactly like this one. All in all, there are five levels: two above this one, two below.'

'Amazing!' said Armand. 'How many people are able to be accommodated altogether, do you know?'

'Hundreds,' said the duc. 'Possibly thousands. But I do not know, exactly. Perhaps it can be yours and Nicolas's job to count the rooms and sleeping places and document it. In fact, that is the job I will give you: to make a scale map of my underground city. It will keep you busy until the Opéra Magique opens again.'

Nicolas was silent. He thought he would love this place. The idea of an underground city was mind-boggling. Those caves: fantastic! At first, it had seemed like the greatest adventure. He hadn't thought about how utterly dark and cold it would be with only a tiny lantern. *What if it goes out?* he wondered, suddenly feeling claustrophobic, as if he were entombed in the mountain. *Like the catacombs*, he thought. *Or a giant Egyptian pyramid.*

*But of course, it isn't!* said his inner voice. *This great city has been built to preserve the living, not the dead.*

*Why do I hate it?*

*You've never needed anywhere to hide … Yet.*

Nicolas felt a frisson pass down his spine. Why was that 'yet' so sinister? *That makes me feel afraid … I'm sorry.*

*It is permissible to feel fear. Fear is healthy. Acknowledge it, examine it: it is wise to know your enemy; then, put it behind you.*

*Is it possible?*

*Not only possible, but essential, mon fils. You must dominate your fears. Or they will dominate you.*

Nicolas mentally shook himself, making a conscious attempt to take Angel's advice. 'What about water, Grand-père? Is that what the amphorae are about?'

'No, they are storage vessels for oil and grain; flour, dried fruits, salted meats; things like that. There is another arrangement for water.'

'And air?' asked Armand. 'I fancy the air is sweeter here than normal for so far under the earth.'

'It is,' agreed the duc, pleased at his understanding. 'That also has been attended to by our gifted ancestors. Now, let us go back. We are looking for the sixth tunnel on the left.'

Counting suddenly made Nicolas feel better. And, as they turned into the required passage, he thought the air smelled fresher, too. His enthusiasm bounded back. This corridor, though narrower, shared the precise dimensions of the main thoroughfare. And it was a lighter colour, allowing the lamplight to penetrate farther. He put his hand out to run his fingers along the wall and touched something. Shocked, he called out to his grandfather to bring the lantern and showed the cord he held. 'Grandpère, this is an electric light switch!'

'If it is not another booby-trap,' muttered Armand. 'You are dreaming, Nicolas!'

'It is, isn't it?' Nicolas ignored him, pointing upwards; his voice a staccato of excitement. 'There's the conduit going along the wall. And there's the globe!'

'Indeed, you are right, *mon fils*,' said the duc. 'This area has been wired for electricity. Unfortunately, we have only been able to service a few rooms and corridors along this level because we are limited in the size of our generator.'

'Can it be?' Nicolas pulled the cord, but nothing happened. '*Mais non.*' He shrugged and walked on. Then, as if the light switch had worked on him, he exclaimed, 'Water! Air! Electricity!' and stopped, suddenly aware of a muted roar. 'I can hear something. Does all this have to do with the underground waterfall? And the waterfall: when the booby-trapped door opened, I could see it in the gloom. It wasn't pitch-black like in here. Does this mean it is open at the top? And if there is a waterfall, there must be a river. So, where does it come from? And where does it go?'

'*Eh bien*, you have many questions,' said his grandfather, suddenly invigorated and striding ahead. 'We must endeavour to find you some answers, *n'est-ce pas?*'

# 22 HELL OR HAVEN?

**Later, 6 March 1937**

*Our experiences this morning are so bizarre that I am sure
I will awaken to find that it has all been a dream. The duc
showed us his underground city with all the pride of a great
seigneur, (which he is, without question). And, indeed, he
has every right to be proud. To him, this great citadel is a
fortress; a last resort in times of siege; the ultimate haven.
But I wonder if it had the same effect on his heir? At times,
I was under the impression that Nicolas felt that he was in
the bowels of hell. That is, until he found a most
remarkable piece of engineering!*

'A *Fourneyron*!' shouted Nicolas, the last vestige of his fear
forgotten. 'Look, Armand! You know how we studied his
turbine? It is, is it not?'

'A very much more modern adaptation of it, certainly.
But yes, I believe so,' said Armand, bending down beside
Nicolas to study the machinery set up on the edge of the
waterfall. His brow wrinkled: Was this a turbine or a
waterwheel? It had elements of both. 'Partially, at any
rate.'

At first, they'd stood back from the ledge that jutted
out into the vast space carved by the water on its journey
into the earth, awed by the cataract that thundered down
the chasm it had carved, spritzing their faces with a fine

mist. As before, they could just make out the water in the gloom, where the passage opened out into a natural chamber. But then, in the lantern light, Nicolas had seen a stone balcony and set upon it a turbine, its rotary blades just now out of the water and turned side-on.

'Come over,' invited the duc. 'It is quite safe to walk on this parapet. You wanted answers, Nicolas, and here they are.' He held the lantern above the dynamo. 'It is time we shed a little light on the subject, don't you think?'

'Very funny, Grand-père,' muttered Nicolas, frustrated by the duc's circumlocution. He wished his grandfather would stop being mysterious and get on with it.

Perhaps the duc got his unspoken message. 'Pull this down,' he ordered, indicating a lever next to the machinery.

Armand obeyed, and the whole thing rotated on its base to bring the curved blades smoothly into the path of the water. Almost immediately, there was a hum, mostly indistinguishable above the rushing of the water. After a slight flickering, the cavern and passage lit up like a giant stage, with the waterfall as its magnificent backdrop.

'*Formidable!*' Nicolas's face showed all the excitement the duc could have wished. From a natural diversion of the water by a great jutting rock, part of the fall was collected into a man-made conduit, delivering water into a cistern at the edge of the parapet. Under this flow, the turbine spun efficiently above the reservoir.

'This one has been engineered with some characteristics of both turbine and waterwheel, due to the logistical difficulties of trying to enclose it,' said the duc. 'But it is efficient enough to provide this one area with electric lighting. And, of course, it has to be able to be shut down until needed, so that it doesn't wear out for nothing. The marquis du Bois designed it with both these objects in mind. And now, to the question of air. Look up!' he commanded. 'Tell me what you see.'

They both hung over the balcony and turned their faces upwards.

'A tiny spot of light,' said Nicolas. 'That must be where the water comes from. But, where is it?'

'That is a very good question. Do you know, Armand?'

'No, Monsieur. I cannot place it.' Armand wrinkled his brow, trying to think of a source that could be responsible for the spectacular display in front of them.

'It is the spring that was once used to fill the moat.'

'No!' said Nicolas. 'It cannot be! That spring is tiny!'

'*Je vous assure*,' replied the duc. 'It emerges for a short way just below the château and disappears underground amongst some large boulders. You know the place.'

'The Devil's Eye!' said Nicolas, blanching at the thought. Had not he and Gerry sneaked out once and tried to climb the boulders to see it for themselves after hearing of *l'œil du Diable* from one of the gardeners? *Thank God they were too steep!* 'I had no idea.'

'*Oui*. This, together with some other underground streams that join it, is what it becomes by the time it gets here.'

'*Incroyable!*' Armand voiced all their thoughts.

'Indeed! As to where it goes, we are not precisely sure. It is possible that it feeds the lake farther down the valley.'

'Yes,' agreed Armand. 'That would make sense.'

'A lake is an anticlimax after this amazing spectacle,' commented Nicolas.

'Precisely. Not only is it a wondrous sight, but you will see that, at once, it provides air, water and light for my underground fortress. Is that not a wonder in itself?' The duc set the storm lantern on the parapet. 'Come, I will show you around, and then we will go back. I have missed my morning coffee.'

'What?' said Armand, covering his reaction to the surroundings. 'Do you mean that you have had the forethought to provide air, light and water, but not *coffee*?'

'Very remiss of me,' agreed the duc. 'Replenishing the

storehouses must be the next item on my agenda.' He took them down a corridor built close to the waterfall, off which was a series of cubicles. 'The sanitation,' he said. 'Primitive, but effective.'

'You wouldn't want to stay in *here* long,' commented Armand, pushing open a door to be met by a blast of cold air.

'No.' Nicolas grinned. 'You'd have to find another place to read.'

The duc's eyes twinkled, but he remained oblivious to inference. 'I am afraid the bathing arrangements are not much better. You can wash here,' he said, indicating a stone basin where water continuously flowed in one side and out the other. 'It is fresh water for drinking, as well. But if you want warm water for bathing, it must be heated on a brazier or fireplace and poured into a tub.' He led the way to a sizeable room with a polished limestone floor. It was furnished with an oak desk, an assortment of chairs under covers and a large floor rug. The raised sleeping bench supported a rolled mattress and a number of folded military blankets. Several smaller rooms opened off this main chamber, which was one of the few with a fireplace. 'I envisage this as your quarters, if what I fear comes to pass,' he told Nicolas. 'I had it furnished for myself but never used it.'

'It is all in perfect condition,' remarked Armand, watching Nicolas stride around the chamber, switching on lights. 'One would think it had been furnished very recently.'

'The cold underground,' said the duc, 'is very conducive to preservation. Especially as this chamber is not damp. In medieval times, I am sure it must have been the apartment of an important man.'

'Yes,' said Armand. 'The polished limestone blocks for flooring. And some of these wall tiles are quite something, as well.'

'Oh, look! There's a harp in that corner,' said Nicolas.

'I don't believe it!'

'Musical entertainment for the troops?' suggested the tutor.

'Most important,' confirmed the duc. 'We couldn't get a piano down here. But a harp was easy. Can you play one?'

'No. What about you, Nicolas?'

'I don't know. I've never tried.'

'Perhaps you should learn it?'

'I might give it a try,' he agreed, continuing his exploration of the apartment. 'Grand-père?' Nicolas poked his head around a door. 'Can these be *radios* you have stored in here?'

'Yes,' said his grandfather, making his leisurely way across the chamber. 'I put them there after the war. You knew that here at Belvoir we were involved in intelligence? With, what was then, the new technology of radiotelephony?'

'*Were* you?' Two pairs of eyes turned to his with consummate interest.

'Do tell, Grand-père,' said Nicolas. 'We are all ears!'

'Later,' said the duc, with frustrating indifference. 'We must finish our tour and go back to the château. I am hungry, if you are not!' He went back for his lantern, but left the turbine working. 'We will leave the lights on until you finish your mapping, then we will put the turbine out of action until needed.'

They'd begun to get the idea of the layout of the underground fortress by the time they got back to the external chamber. But sliding behind the curtain of creeper fronds and entering the first chamber they'd come to on the way down, Nicolas was seized by a sudden fear. 'Grand-père, I am satisfied that the underground city is hidden from any who don't know the secret. But what is to stop anyone getting into the château from here, or laying in wait in one of the tunnels.'

'That is an excellent question,' said the duc, 'and one

which will be answered without a word. Follow me.' He set off across the cave. 'Compared to the other two, this cave is as a sparrow to a cock pheasant, is it not?' Near the far wall, he stopped and raised the lantern. 'Now tell me: which path shall I take?'

They stared at a veritable rabbit warren of tunnels, all branching and going off at angles.

'*Eh bien!*' gasped Nicolas. 'We are lost. I hope you know the way, Grand-père, otherwise we will have to go outside and climb the mountain.'

'*So* ...' said the duc. 'I take it that you are answered?' Without waiting for a reply, he took the right-hand tunnel. Smaller and narrower than the others, it looked as if it went nowhere, twisting and turning into dead ends, but eventually divided into two. 'Where now?'

They shrugged.

'Again, we take the right-hand tunnel.' He led the way upwards until the tunnel branched: this time, into a number of passages. 'More than two choices. What will we do?'

'We have no idea, Grand-père. Do we, Armand?'

Armand smiled. 'I don't think we need worry. I am sure your grandfather is about to tell us the secret.'

The duc swung around. 'Are you satisfied that *anyone* cannot find their way into the château without assistance?'

'Most assuredly, Grand-père.' Nicolas grinned. 'I am only sorry that I mentioned it.'

'Have you noticed anything different about these tunnels we are faced with here?'

'More of them? Bigger? Steeper in gradient?' suggested Nicolas. 'And someone has left a pile of rubble next to that one.'

'Shame on them,' quipped Armand. 'Very messy.' He turned to the duc. 'Or is it ...?'

'*Eh bien*, you are on the right track. It is very simple: when you are coming this way, you always take the right-hand tunnel, no matter how many choices there are;

except where you see a jumble of stones, like that. Then, you take the left. Or, if there is more than one choice, the far left. Naturally, on the way here, it is entirely the opposite.' He turned his head to look at them. 'There are, as you know, a number of caves in this mountain, most of them in the north face and mostly lacking in size and grandeur; but as far as I am aware, none of them lead anywhere. So, there are many possibilities to exhaust for those who have heard rumours, before they even stumble upon this one.'

They'd been climbing the whole time, and the duc fell silent until they passed through the level passage and entered the tower. 'I fear I must rest before we attempt these stairs,' he said, lowering himself onto a stone step and making room for the others. 'I have decided to leave the necessary mapping to you two and the replenishing of the storehouses to my agents.'

'Your agents, Grand-père?' Nicolas glanced meaningfully at his tutor before further questioning his grandfather. 'Do we know them?'

'No. That is the idea, you see,' replied the duc, with a twinkle. 'They are *secret* agents.'

'Oh, intrigue, *enfin!*' said Nicolas, alive to the inflection. 'But are you *serious*, Grand-père? I mean, what do they do? And why do they have to be secret?'

'They report to me. About everything: the state of the country ——'

'And what your grandson is doing?' Nicolas raised an eyebrow.

The duc smiled. 'That, too.'

'You mean: they are spies,' said Nicolas, flatly.

Armand preserved a discreet silence, rubbing at a mark on the polished leather of his boot. A slight frown creased his high forehead as he listened.

'I suppose you could call them that, yes. They were invaluable to me during the war, gathering intelligence to send to the powers that be, or,' amended the duc, 'that were. They are the only other people besides ourselves who know of this subterranean refuge. There were six of them, led by Gabriel and Michel. Unfortunately, Michel was killed on Armistice Day. Sadly, amongst the generals, there were crass fools, not to say, criminals, who kept sending their men into battle until eleven o'clock on that day; and Michel was caught in the crossfire. So now there are five. Gabriel is still their leader.' The duc glanced significantly at his grandson. 'By the way, he is the only other person who knows *all* the secrets of Belvoir.' He sighed and stood up. 'I will make him known to you both, tomorrow.'

# 23 THE GODDESS AND THE MUSES

**11 March 1938**

*So far Nicolas has evaded all the traps set for him and, at the moment, is living a charmed life with his Muses. Now that he is studying at the Sorbonne, he doesn't need me. In fact, he has grown past me; but the duc still employs me as his secretary. And Nicolas treats me as a friend—perhaps more than a friend—an older brother. Sometimes I feel that he views Lisette and I as his de facto parents.*

*He has grown tall, both deep chested and elegantly muscled. His temperament is still as even and beautiful as ever, and les femmes continue to fall before him as if scythed. He is courteous and gentle with them but says he feels nothing—just tells me he likes them all—but no-one, as yet, has 'knocked him out'. Do I envy him? Well, perhaps I would, were it not for my own wonderful Lisette: the perfect companion. My only wish for him is to find someone like her.*

*On another plane, it looks as though the duc was right, after all, to entertain the fears he has expressed in the past. His spies and the newspapers have both carried the same story.*

Nicolas lay on his stomach on the grass in a sheltered corner of the Tuileries Gardens, studying an aviation text. Beside him was a basket containing a vacuum flask of coffee and fresh croissants wrapped in a tea towel. He'd disdained a picnic blanket, leaving it folded. A little way over, backs against some shrubs, sat his bodyguards, ever vigilant.

Desi nudged her twin as a tall, elegant young woman in trousers passed close to Nicolas and dropped a book. 'Here we go again!' she sighed. 'I'd better ———'

'No, wait!' Dani held on to the hem of her jacket. 'Do you see who it is?'

'You're right,' whispered Desi, subsiding. They finished the rest of the conversation with their eyes.

'Hey, Mademoiselle!' Nicolas looked up in a friendly fashion. 'You've dropped your notes.' He reached for the book and stood up in one lithe move. The girl turned back, and Nicolas felt as though someone had punched him in the solar plexus. He'd never seen anyone so beautiful: she was a goddess. For a moment, he was struck dumb, frozen in time, holding out the notebook.

'Oh … thank you.' The goddess smiled, took the book and began to hurry away.

Nicolas knew that he couldn't let her go. There was something about her that teased him: a vague feeling that she reminded him of someone, yet he could not have said who. 'Please, don't go. Won't you stay?' His gesture encompassed the folded rug. 'Sit down a while?'

'Sorry,' said the young woman, giving him a cool glance from her hazel-green eyes. 'I can't. I have a class.'

'Oh, but …' Nicolas tried to wrest his gaze from hers, but could not. He felt as though he were being consumed, drowning in depths of mystery.

'You're staring,' she said, breaking the spell. 'It's rude.'

'Yes,' he agreed, charmingly apologetic; enchanted by her candour. He found it refreshingly different to the usual coquetry he encountered when dealing with *les femmes*. 'Do you mind?'

'It depends on the reason.' She tilted her chin. Her straight gaze gave no indication of her feelings.

'It is just that … you remind me of someone, and for the life of me, I cannot think who …'

The girl tossed her head so that her short chestnut curls flew back from her face. Her voice was tinged with contempt. 'If that's your pick-up line, I don't think much of it.'

'My *pick-up line*? But no, I …' Her directness had him momentarily lost for words. Then he thought he saw a lurking twinkle and smiled. '*Outrageous*, Mademoiselle! I assure you, I am not guilty. Please, won't you tell me your name? Mine is Nicolas.'

'Everyone knows *that*.' She glanced disparagingly at his bodyguards. 'Those two are a dead giveaway.'

'I'm sorry?' Why was this beautiful creature so prickly? He decided to try to lighten her hostility with another attempt at humour. 'You have the jump on me there, Mademoiselle, because I am desolated to admit that I cannot say that I know you.'

'No?' She arched a perfectly groomed, mocking eyebrow. Not for the world would she let him see how chagrined she was that he didn't remember her, or how flattered that he wanted to know her now … 'It's Natalie,' she said, shortly, turning away. 'And now, I really have to go.'

*Natalie!* He drew in a breath. *Natalie Watson: I cannot believe it!* Watching her glossy curls bounce on her collar as she crossed the lawn with her curiously mannish stride, her tailored jacket emphasising her tiny waist and slender curves, he experienced a yearning so profound it left him feeling winded. It was all he could do not to run after her and compel her to stop; agony to watch her walk away.

*How can I feel this way? And who is she like?* He wrinkled his brow: it wasn't the gawky fourteen-year-old that she reminded him of, but someone else. He could not believe a girl could change so much in two short years: The perfect oval of her face; her mouth, so tender in repose, yet twisting into mockery when he'd asked her name; the flawless perfection of her skin, with not the vestige of a freckle on the bridge of her straight little nose; her short hair styled into an artful tangle of curls. The way her coltish angularity had been transformed into slender, curvaceous elegance.

But the most incredible thing was how cool she was: how immeasurably superior and sophisticated. There had not been the slightest fluctuation of rose in her peaches-and-cream complexion. Comparing this goddess with the awkward adolescent—whose shyness rendered her inarticulate, whose teeth were too big and whose skin was either fiery red or sickly white—was like comparing an exotic orchid to a field daisy.

Then he remembered something else: whatever Natalie had been like then, her music always had the power to transport him to the angels.

All the rest of that day and night, he struggled with his feelings. How could Natalie have changed so much? How could he possibly feel like this when she had never previously disturbed his equilibrium—unless she picked up her violin. But there had been no question of that yesterday. Nothing like this had ever happened to him. He tossed and turned restlessly, glad when daylight came.

Early for breakfast, he was quiet and preoccupied, only giving a faint smile when Lisette quizzed him. He sipped a little coffee, toyed with a croissant, then prepared to leave the table. When she asked him why he was in such a hurry and what he was going to do that day, Lisette had to repeat herself before he answered.

'Oh, nothing much. I am going to class first, then to study in the Tuileries Gardens if it stays fine. If not, I will go to the library.'

'Admirable,' said Lisette, noting the shadows under his eyes. 'As long as you are not overdoing it? You're not sick?'

'No, no. In perfect health.'

'Is that so? You haven't fallen in love, by any chance?'

'No, of course not!' He stooped to kiss her cheek. 'When I do, you will be the first to know.'

'There is not a doubt of it, *Chéri*,' she said, hiding a smile. '*Je vous assure …*'

Armand came in and poured himself coffee. 'You're early today, Nicolas. What is the rush?'

'Nothing. I have some aerodynamic formulae to learn, that is all.'

'Curves,' said Armand, stirring sugar into his cup.

'What?' Nicolas raised a white face.

'In cross-section: the top of the wing compared to the underneath, curved for airflow and lift. That is what you're measuring, isn't it?'

'Oh! Oh, yes.' Nicolas laughed and went out.

Armand cocked an eyebrow at Lisette. 'What is going on with him? It is not like him to ——'

Lisette went up to him, set his cup on the table and pulled him to his feet by his tie. 'Nicolas,' she said, running her hands up the front of his crisp white shirt to his shoulders, 'has fallen in love.'

'Has he?' Armand put his arms around her, looking a little bemused. 'You don't say so? Who with?'

'That I do not know … *yet*.'

He laughed. 'How long will I give you?' Her answering smile made him lower his head. '*Eh bien*,' he sighed, against the warm invitation of her lips. 'I hope he will be as happy as I am.'

'*Et moi*,' whispered Lisette, kissing him again.

'I beg your pardon,' said the duc. 'I do apologise for breaking in on this scene of domestic bliss … No, no.' He held up a hand. 'It is I who must apologise, not you. Please, carry on.' He smiled upon them as they fell apart, embarrassed. 'Love must *never* be apologised for. There is not enough of it in the world. *Merci*,' he added, as Lisette placed a steaming cup of coffee before him. 'But where is Nicolas? Am I late?'

'No, Monsieur. Nicolas went early to his class.'

'Oh?' The duc raised his eyebrows. 'What is he studying?'

'Aerodynamics, I believe,' replied Armand.

'Ah-hah,' said the duc, 'I know: the curve of the wing, *alors*. For lift. Now, what is so funny, you two?'

'*Rien,* Monsieur,' gasped Armand, passing him the plate of croissants.

'It must be love,' said the duc, sitting back in tolerant amusement as they both went into paroxysms. '*Now* what have I said?'

§

Nicolas would never have admitted it to himself, but wherever he went, he kept a look out for Natalie. *Natalie* … He said her name silently, over and over, like a mantra. Until, at last, as if he'd conjured her up, he found her on his favourite patch of lawn in the Tuileries Gardens. She was reading the novel *David Golder* by Irène Némirovsky and did not seem to notice him.

'*Bonjour*, Mademoiselle.'

Natalie glanced up briefly and returned to her book. 'Hello.'

'May I sit?'

'Please yourself,' she said, closing her book with obvious reluctance.

'You are enjoying your novel? I have read it. It is very good.'

'Yes, she is an inspired writer,' agreed Natalie, playing with the bookmark.

After an awkward silence, Nicolas said, 'How is your music going?'

'Quite well, I hope. I had an exam yesterday. That's

why I'm reading today instead of studying.' In the longest
string of words he'd ever heard from her, she added, 'I
don't know if I passed.'

'You will. How do you find it here? Not homesick?'

'No.' Natalie dropped her mask. 'I feel as if this *is*
home. I love it.'

'Your parents: are they here with you?'

'No. I came over with some friends. When they went
back, I stayed on to study the violin.'

'But, don't you miss your family?'

'I do miss them at home, but I love it so much here
that I just can't make myself leave. These beautiful
gardens, the buildings, the cultural heritage, all the *history*
that makes up Paris, the artists on the hill, the ... Oh,
*everything*!'

'It is a bloody history, but I am glad that you approve
of us.'

'My mother is French.'

'No! Is she? I thought you were Australian.'

'I am. I was born in Australia.' The beautiful face had
come alive with her confidences. 'I wonder: have you
heard of the marquis du Bois?'

*Here is your chance!*

'Erm, yes. Yes, I have.'

'My father worked for him during the Great War, after
he recovered from his wounds. Something hush-hush in
military engineering.'

Nicolas tried to remember what he'd read of the Great
War when he'd sneaked a peek at Godmama's diaries. 'So,
your father must be ... let me see ... Hugh Watson?'

'Yes. How do you know?'

'I heard it somewhere. The marquis du Bois was a
friend of my grandfather.' *And my mother's guardian. And ...*

*I would leave it at that for now. She will not understand.*

'*Was* he?' asked Natalie, with even more animation.
'What a coincidence!'

'Yes, indeed. But, as they say, the world is small. How

did your parents meet?'

'When he was shot down over the English Channel, my father was picked up by a French fishing boat and taken to a hospital in Calais. My mother was his nurse. She said that they fell in love over the dressings. When the war was over, they married; and she came back to Australia with him.'

'Ah, a romance, *hein?*'

She flushed. 'Yes. They ... they are still in love with each other.'

'A marriage made in heaven,' he said, rejoicing to see her show emotion. *Like my own Mama and Papa's.* 'We would all hope to find one like that, *n'est-ce pas?*'

'No, I wouldn't.' Her prickles were back. 'I don't intend to get married—*ever!* I want my freedom, thanks.'

'But, does one preclude the other? I would have thought ——'

'What would you know?' Natalie leapt to her feet. 'An *aristo* like you!' She looked around. 'Your babysitters are here. What is it like to live in a goldfish bowl, surrounded by ...?' She gave a small sound like a sob. 'Sorry, I shouldn't have said that. I have to go!'

*You handled that well ...*

*What would you have done?*

*Patience, mon brave. Since you ask, I would be inclined to leave discussions of marriage until you are both a little more mature.*

Nicolas ran his fingers through his hair, jammed his hands in his pockets and slouched away. His bodyguards looked at each other and fell in behind him.

§

Days passed in a nightmare. Somehow, he managed to pass his exams, fulfil his obligations at the Opéra Magique and keep his fans enthralled—but it all meant nothing without Natalie.

The annexing of Austria by Herr Hitler on the twelfth of March completely escaped his notice. But not that of his grandfather, nor his tutor.

# 24 A CRUEL GAME

**28 October 1938**

*We are seriously worried about Nicolas. He has become hollow-eyed and pale, almost too lean. His fans sigh over his soulful good looks, calling them romantic and Byronic, and equally, his soulful songs. But I have begun to feel that he is extremely unhappy and unable to cope with the treatment he receives from the one he loves.*

*I have asked Lisette to intervene, but she says that we must leave them to work out their own lives. Until the day that Nicolas asks for help, and then we might think again. She thinks the girl is not as untouched by his love as she makes out. And that, au fond, she is still the frightened little girl that ran from us that night long ago.*

*As to that, I do not know: she seems frighteningly bold and sophisticated to me! But Lisette has powers of understanding way beyond my comprehension. All I know is that it hurts us all to stand back and watch the way this girl rides roughshod over Nicolas, blowing hot and cold to the point that it is making him ill.*

*All his life, Nicolas has been feted, fawned over, cosseted and petted by his fans; inundated since age fifteen with scores of marriage proposals. He has never experienced*

*the kind of rejection that he is being subjected to now. I
think he had a sort of rosy idea that when the girl of his
dreams came along, he would just have to reach out and
pluck her off the tree like a ripe plum.*

*This is a new experience for us all. And I can truthfully say
it is a nightmare.*

*L'Affaire Nicolas,* as his bodyguards privately called it,
transcribed an erratic course, either plunging him into
gloom or sending him *aux anges*, depending on the caprice
of his beloved. Sometimes, Natalie responded to Nicolas's
attempts at conversation and offers of coffee with
flattering interest, then with a wicked twinkle, would
either dig at him over his heritage or take offence at
something he said and leave abruptly. It took him a little
while to realise that her taunts arose from a kind of
perverse sense of humour, rather than a wish to hurt. At
least that is what he told himself.

At other times, the young violinist seemed preoccupied
and had to hurry away to keep an appointment or refused
his invitations with, what seemed to him, to be a lame
excuse. But sometimes, just often enough for him not to
lose hope completely, she flattered his ego by acting as if
she really admired him; and they would have an enjoyable
time and part sweetly.

He put his new-found love and yearnings into musical
compositions that Natalie never seemed to have time to
listen to, but which sent his fans *aux anges*. All his requests
to her to play a duet together were summarily nipped in
the bud after the first occasion when Nicolas met her
coming out of the Bibliothèque-Musée de l'Opéra.
According to prior agreement, Desi and Dani quickly
disappeared into the background, leaving them alone
together.

'How wonderful to meet you again, Mademoiselle.

Come and have coffee with me and tell me what you have been doing lately. The Café de la Paix is just around the corner—about a minute away. If that suits?'

'Yes. All right. I will,' said Natalie. 'Thank you.' She looked around. 'What about your babysitters?'

'Oh, my Dees? They've already gone for coffee.' He gave her a smile that his fans would willingly die for. 'They do get some free time, you know. I'll introduce you when they come back. They are great girls. A lot of fun when you get to know them. You'll like them.'

His words raised hackle. 'Feel free to speak for me, won't you?'

'I beg your pardon?' he asked, shepherding her along la rue Auber and right into the Place de l'Opéra where gaily striped umbrellas on a terrace advertised the business of a majestic building.

'Nothing.' She shrugged, stopping at the first empty table in front of the imposing façade. 'It is a lovely day.'

He laughed, signalled the waiter and pulled out a chair for her. 'Yes, yes, it is. Beautiful. What the poets might call a *Symphony of Spring*.'

'But it is *autumn*. Oh, you mean the words of your new song? *Every beautiful day, so the poets say, is a symphony of spring* … erm … I don't think I know any more.'

*When you're in love.* Nicolas had the presence of mind not to finish the line aloud. Her words produced a shaft of joy that he couldn't quite conceal. So, she was not so ignorant of his work as she had claimed. 'You've heard it then? What did you think?'

'I couldn't help but hear it. Everyone is singing it. Even those who shouldn't.'

'*Eh bien*, Mademoiselle, I see that you are a stickler for the truth.'

'It is best, don't you think? I hate pretence.'

'To a point, Mademoiselle. I think we all pretend a little. It is our way of surviving in society.'

'In your society, I do not doubt it,' said Natalie,

annoyed by the courteous, quiet reserve that hid his real self: the polite, well-bred, impenetrable air possessed by all the European nobles she'd met.

He raised an eyebrow but said nothing, distracted by the return of the waiter with their coffee.

Natalie accepted hers, declining an array of delicious cakes with a politeness that matched his; and they sat for a little while in silence.

'You were saying …?' he said, with an encouraging smile.

Natalie returned to her subject with alacrity. Over the rim of her coffee cup, she eyed askance the casual elegance of his dress and person. 'I don't agree with class distinction, and you shouldn't either. What happened to the cry of the revolution: Liberty, Equality, Fraternity?'

'Ah, Mademoiselle.' He seemed amused by her forthright declaration. 'So, as well as a feminist, you are a revolutionary, *hein*? Why have I not guessed it? We must discuss this further … But, since you are all for truth, I will admit that there was something else I wanted to discuss with you.' He looked at her in a way that his fans could only dream of. 'I missed our duets when they were cancelled. Could you find time for us to play together once more? For old times' sake?'

'*No!*' Natalie took a breath. 'I am sorry. I have no time. I ——' She slammed down her cup and leapt to her feet. 'I must go home. I forgot …'

'But certainly, if it upsets you …?' Nicolas rose, showing his concern.

'It doesn't upset me.' The words were forced through stiff lips.

*Who is pretending now?* 'Then you will meet me here for coffee, again? *Please?*'

'All right.'

'Tomorrow?'

'No, I can't, tomorrow.'

'The next day then?'

'All right. If I can.'

'*Bien,* I hope you can make it. But wait! I didn't ask you: where do you live?'

'With my French grandmother. Those friends I came over to France with: they brought me to stay with her. We live in the same apartment building as Herr Schmidt-Hesse. That is how I came to be his pupil. He heard me practising one day.'

'And, of course, he realised your talent.'

She lifted her shoulders. 'Herr Schmidt-Hesse is very hard to please. He is a perfectionist.'

*He is an evil, arrogant bigot. And he's known your address the whole time. Unforgivable!* 'As you say, Mademoiselle,' replied Nicolas, charmingly diffident. 'May I walk you home?'

'*No!*' Again she caught her breath. 'No, thank you. Goodbye.'

'You *will* come: the day after tomorrow?' He exerted all his considerable personal magnetism. In the past, it had caused damsels to swoon; but appeared to have limited effect on this one.

'Yes. Yes, I will come.' Natalie, beginning to rush away, called over her shoulder, 'Thank you for the coffee.'

'It was my very great pleasure, Mademoiselle.' As he stood, looking after her, concealing a sick disappointment, he was aware of movement by his side.

'We're back, Monsieur. Where now?'

§

Nicolas took more care over his appearance than usual, but arrived early at the rendezvous. He strode up and down, unable to sit still while he waited. His bodyguards, hovering discreetly in the background, sat down at the well-situated table. In a short while, they signalled to Nicolas, got up and strolled away. He took Dani's place and waited, leaping up as he saw the tall girl with chestnut hair weave her way through the morning coffee drinkers.

'Sorry, I'm late.' Natalie looked up briefly and lowered her eyes. Her arms were full of large, leather-bound books.

'*De rien*, Mademoiselle!' said Nicolas, pulling out a chair and moving towards her. 'Let me take those for you.'

'It is all right, thank you.' She dumped the load of books on the table and flexed her fingers. 'That's a relief.'

'I should think so. They must weigh a ton!'

'They do. Frau Schmidt-Hesse wanted them from the library. I said I would bring them to her, not realising how heavy they would be.'

'*Eh bien*,' he said, seating her. 'We must see what we can do. Coffee?'

'I think I would prefer hot chocolate, if you don't mind?'

'*Mais certainement*, Mademoiselle. Anything you want.'

'Then please call me Natalie.'

'I will be honoured,' he said, signalling a waiter.

'Oh, you *aristos*!' she mocked. 'Always *so* polite.'

His lip quirked. 'Is *politesse* a crime? If so, I have not heard of it?'

'No, no. It is just … Do you never shout or swear or get angry? Even when I tease?'

An answering gleam shone in his eyes. It was the best sign yet that she didn't mean the scarifying things she said. 'Never, Mademoiselle … Natalie. At least, not yet.' He gave his order to the waiter and sat back, outwardly relaxed. 'So, how is the Revolution going?'

'It went the way of all great theories: as soon as they put it into practice, they became tainted by the power and were corrupted themselves. Then *they* became the oppressors.'

'You are cynical this morning.'

'Yes, I have been studying the history of political movements in Europe.'

'That explains it, then. I understand perfectly.' He waited until their beverages were served, offered her the plate of *petits fours* before choosing one himself. 'These look delicious, don't you think?'

'Mmm. Scrumptious,' she agreed, picking one and taking a bite.

After a little silence, he said, 'So, your political movements: Does any one of them leap out at you? Apart from the Revolution, which you have just blown to smithereens.'

She shook her head and brushed a crumb from her lip. 'Not really, but I prefer socialism, myself. The theory, at any rate.'

'And you think socialists will be immune from the corrupting effects of power, *hein*?'

'No. I have to be honest: no-one seems to be immune from it. But I am thinking of joining the Communist Party … as the best of a bad bunch.' She finished her hot chocolate and rose. 'That was delicious, thank you. I'd better run. I promised Frau Schmidt-Hesse that I would have the books to her before lunch.'

Nicolas took them from her hands. 'And so you shall. Lead the way, Mademoiselle.'

Natalie looked as if she would dispute the matter, but acquiesced and pointed. 'This way.' She took him through narrow, winding streets that never saw sunlight due to towering stone buildings, finally turning into an airy, tree-lined avenue. 'This one, here,' she said, halting before a high wrought-iron gate that opened into the courtyard of a gracious old building. 'It used to belong to an *aristo* like you before the revolution, but since then, it has been turned into so many apartments that it is like a rabbit warren. So many of us: all wanting to live in a rich man's house! It isn't quite a ghetto, *but …* '

'The more things change, the more they stay the same?'

Natalie glanced at him from under her lashes. She was

torn between railing against his apparent acceptance of all she threw at him: the perfection of his social mask that never let her know what he was feeling, and a latent admiration for the depths of his understanding. '*Aristo!*' she taunted. 'If *you'd* been around back then, Madame la Guillotine would have *drunk* your blood.'

'And I suppose you would have been merciless enough to enjoy being my executioner? Or, perhaps, holding the basket to receive my head?'

'No, I …' Natalie managed to control a little spurt of laughter. 'Not quite.'

'I am relieved to hear it. But, you know, there *was* an ancestor of mine around at that time.'

'I suppose there must have been. Otherwise you would not be here now. What happened to him, do you know?'

'I do, as a matter of fact. He was saved by his people.'

'*Saved* by his people? That's a new one!'

'But true, nevertheless.'

'You mean he escaped to England under a load of cabbages?'

'By the hand of The *Scarlet Pimpernel?* No. As far as I know, his people smuggled him back to his château, lowered the portcullis and vowed to defend him to the last man.' His voice held affectionate amusement. 'I believe they quite liked him.'

'He was probably spuriously charming,' she hissed, 'like his descendant!'

He bowed. '*Merci du compliment!*'

She lifted the gate latch; a gleam in her eye. 'What makes you think I meant you?'

'*Eh bien* …' He threw back his head and laughed.

His laugh was infectious, and despite herself, she smiled and stretched out her arms for the books. 'Thank you. I must go in now.'

'Wait. Please. I have a party going to the Opéra Magique tomorrow night. Will you come?'

Once again, she was conscious of his charm: the charm

she so resented.

Before she could speak, he went on, 'I will have to leave the box for only a short while to do my aria, but Armand and Lisette will be with you while I am gone.'

'And your babysitters?'

The hard glitter in her eyes was answered by amused understanding in his. 'Out of sight; I promise you.'

'It is a tempting offer ...' She looked around as a door slammed and Herr Schmidt-Hesse stepped into the courtyard. 'I'm sorry; I can't come,' she gabbled in a whisper, snatching the books. 'I already have a date. You'd better go!'

'Give those books to me,' barked the conductor, 'and come inside, at once! Nanette wants you.' He held open the gate, ignoring Nicolas.

All the way home, Nicolas tried to analyse the expression in the hazel-green eyes: the look Natalie had given him before she turned to obey her mentor. He didn't waste a second thinking of the attitude of the conductor towards himself: he preferred not to be noticed by a Nazi. It was Natalie who filled his thoughts. She seemed so independent, so modern in her feminism. Yet, she'd wilted before the cold commands of Herr Schmidt-Hesse.

Two questions continued to hammer at his brain: Was she in danger from the overbearing conductor? And *who* was her date?

§

Nicolas moved to the front of the stage, bowed to his fans and looked down into the orchestra pit. He didn't know how long he stood there; his gaze riveted on the girl in the emerald-green gown who had come to stand beside the first violinist. As if she felt his eyes on her, she turned her head to meet them in a long, defiant stare, before returning her attention to the conductor. Nicolas was left stunned. Finally, the cheering roused him, and he bowed again and left the stage. Why hadn't Natalie told him she'd joined the Orchestra Magique? Why had she let him think she had a date?

He thought he might stay behind and ask her these things but he was waylaid by some fans. His last sight of Natalie was a back view of her leaving the opera house between the conductor and a man in uniform. They were too far away and the lights too dim to recognise the man.

§

For a week of agony, he waited every morning at 'their' cafe, unconscious of irony in the name blazoned on its façade, in the hope of meeting Natalie for coffee; but she did not come. Had something happened to her? Some accident? Or was it the man in uniform? Should he go to her apartment and try to find out if something was wrong? But then, there was the man in uniform. He was tempted to send the Dees to find out where she was, but he did not share his grandfather's penchant for surveillance. He could just imagine Natalie's contempt if she found that he'd resorted to spying on her. He stared into his coffee, feeling too nauseated to drink it.

'A penny for them?'

'Pardon? Oh, Natalie!' He leapt to his feet. 'I haven't seen you for a week. I was afraid something had happened to you.' Heart pounding, he pulled out a chair and seated her.

'Sorry. Busy.' Natalie looked up from arranging the pleats in her skirt. 'What's up?'

He made a moue. 'Nothing. Why?'

'You were looking very blue.'

'Was I? Oh ...' His face creased into its attractive smile. 'Perhaps it is for you to cheer me up, then.'

Natalie snapped upright.' Why should I?' she

demanded, with a little spurt of temper. 'I am not just here for you to use!'

'But, there is no question of——' He stared in disbelief at her reaction.

'Whatever indication you think I may have given to the contrary,' she spat, leaping up, 'I have no ambition to be a rich man's plaything! ... Ever!'

'What? Natalie, no! I did not mean ...' Shock left him grey and wordless. He tried again. 'Please stay and talk about this ... this misunderstanding.'

'I can't,' she said, striding away. 'Sorry, I don't have time to entertain spoilt playboys!'

He flinched at the cruelty in her voice, more than that, of her words. How could she say such things? He'd thought that their precarious relationship was stabilising into friendship. But now? Why did she treat him as an enemy? Throwing up barriers as if their meetings were some kind of competition: always fencing with him, misjudging him, twisting his words to give them meanings he had not thought of. Unjustified meanings he would never think of. Would *never* demean himself or her in that way.

The bodyguards, at a nearby table, watched her progress with narrowed eyes.

'The little *cat!*' breathed Desi, drawing a hand across her throat.

Dani shook her head, pointed to Nicolas, sitting white and dazed. With one accord, they went to stand on either side of him. Taking an arm each, they brought him to his feet and spoke in unison. 'Come, *jeune* Monsieur. Let us get you home.'

When he arrived in the hall, Lisette took one look at him and shepherded him into the empty library. '*Eh bien, Chéri,* it is time we had a little talk, I think. Do not you?'

'No.' He couldn't meet her eyes—couldn't deal with the love and concern they held. 'What do you think we should talk about?'

'Whatever you want.' Her unspoken sympathy finally broke him down.

'Oh, Sette! Talking will do no good.' He turned his head to hide tears. 'I am not even sure that there *is* anything to talk about.'

'Oh, you poor darling!' She held out her arms. 'Come here ...' Holding him the way she had when he was a grieving ten-year-old, Lisette listened as he poured out his woes. *I would like nothing better than to kick that girl,* she thought fiercely, *from one end of Paris to the other! And back again, alors!* 'Ah, *mon pauvre.*'

'Sette,' he groaned. 'What am I going to do? Why does she *do* this?'

'Because you allow it? Because she is afraid to get too close to you? Who knows the cause? But one thing is for sure, she is playing a game with you.'

'*Vraiment?* Then, if so, it is a cruel game.'

'Yes, it is.' Lisette deliberated a moment, crossed her fingers behind his back and said, 'Unless you love her more than life itself, I think you should drop her—before she hurts you even more.'

'But ...' He moved away to search for a handkerchief in his pocket and wiped his eyes. 'I do love her that much. I don't know why.'

'Then you must be ready to play a game yourself. Are you?'

'I don't know.' He made a wry mouth. 'It is against my nature to try to hurt someone I love.'

'I know, I know. And it is to your credit that you are so kind and loving. One would think any girl would appreciate it, *hein*? But, in this instance ... Believe me, I would wish for you to have those traits reciprocated. And it may happen, if you do as I say.'

'Oh ...' Nicolas rubbed his forehead. *How can I play such cruel games?*

The answer flashed into his mind. *Do as Lisette says. What you do now will set the scene for the future.*

*Very well, I will try.* 'Eh bien,' he said to Lisette. 'What should I do?'

'You must show her that she is not upsetting you by her actions; that you do not care for her quite as much as she thinks.'

'But she is. And I do.'

'Then you must pretend that she is not. Hide yourself a little; stand back from her. Show her that she is not the only one. Don't single out any one girl, of course. Otherwise you will do to them what Natalie is doing to you. Just back off a little. Can you do that?'

'I suppose that I will have to,' he agreed. There was nothing else for it: Angel's words had confirmed Lisette's. He paid attention when she spoke again.

'Yes, *Chéri*. You will have to, if you want to keep your sanity.' *And us to keep ours. What an idiote that girl is! How can she not see how privileged she is to be the recipient of the love of as beautiful a young man as Nicolas?* Lisette—doing her best to suppress uncharitable thoughts against as wilful a young woman as she was ever likely to meet (not that she had yet done so)—made soothing noises and took him off to make him his favourite cocktail. 'It will buck you up a bit. I don't like to see you down.'

Nicolas did, reluctantly, put into practice Lisette's advice; but could discern no apparent effect on Natalie. All he knew was that it was breaking his heart.

# 25 WHISPERS OF WAR

**17 April 1939**

*For years there have been whispers of war, but now it is
shouting at us. Even I can see that it is only a matter of
time. In March, Germany annexed Czechoslovakia. The
odd thing is, nobody seemed to care, apart from the duc,
his agents, myself and Lisette. Nicolas is still so taken up
with his studies and the vagaries of his love-life (not
necessarily in that order) that I doubt if he'd notice if the
world fell in on him. The question the rest of us in the
household are asking ourselves is: what is coming next?*

Nicolas continued to play his game without heart and, it
seemed to him, without particular success. His attendance
at his Uncle Luc's modern dinner-dance at the hôtel de
Villefontaine had been a last-minute decision after Natalie
had refused his latest invitation to the opera, saying that
she had a prior engagement.

Colonel Luc de Villefontaine was a much-decorated
hero from his country's involvement in Africa, the Orient
and the Great War. Lately, he'd returned to his family
estate ready to re-enter the society he'd rejected as a young
man. To this end, he sent invitations to surviving
members of his family, all their society friends, and as
many musicians and entertainers as he could scrape
acquaintance with.

Nicolas knew very little of this uncle, other than what he'd read in Godmama's diaries, never having met him. His Uncle Chris was quite a favourite with him; although he saw him rarely; but he knew better than to think that he would find him here. He spent his life with his beloved crops and animals on the estate, never coming to the hôtel de Villefontaine if he could help it.

Fleetingly, Nicolas wondered whether his Uncle Luc might treat him with reserve. But the big man shook his hand, expressed pleasure at meeting his young relative and welcomed him to his house. 'None of this "Uncle" business either: call me Luc or Colonel, whatever suits you. I hope you will make yourself at home and aid me in entertaining the troops,' he said, with a wink. 'Plenty of *demoiselles* for you to help me take care of.' He then announced to his guests that whatever might be the custom in general, tonight there would be plenty of dancing as he enjoyed a good jig. 'We'll roll back the carpets and get going as soon as we've finished in the mess hall.'

Nicolas, finding his military references rather boring, assiduously divided his time between as many of the unattached debutantes as he could (one dance only each). Leading out his fourth—a shy young girl in eau de Nil satin—he collided with a man in uniform. Turning to apologise, he didn't, at first, recognise him with his short, sleek hair clipped close to his head, chiselled features, broad chest and muscles rippling beneath the tailored dress uniform.

'*De rien!*' replied the man in a husky voice. 'It is a bit of a crush. Old Luc has invited the world and his friend … Oh, it is *you!*'

'*Gerry?*' Shocked, Nicolas could only stare at the handsome blond man and the girl with whom he danced. She looked meltingly at her partner, appearing to give him all her attention.

Gervais flicked Nicolas a smouldering glance, turned

his shoulder and steered the tall girl away. She had not given the slightest sign that Nicolas and his partner even existed. Nicolas drew in a breath. They hadn't been present at dinner; he was sure. The table had been big, but not that big. They must have come later. If he'd only seen them before, the shock wouldn't be so hard to deal with now.

'I say, are you all right?'

Nicolas looked down at the young brunette he was holding and dredged up a mechanical smile. 'Yes. Are you? I didn't step on you, did I?'

'No, but *he* did. That ogre in uniform. And he didn't say sorry, either. The brute!'

'Are you hurt? Would you like to sit out the rest of this dance?'

'No, dancing will take my mind off it. I hate men like that,' she confided, in a rush. 'He knew he stepped on me, but he didn't apologise. He is nothing but an arrogant bully!'

Nicolas murmured something and resumed their dance, feeling much more in accord with his partner than he'd thought possible. She'd summed up his rival perfectly. *The man in uniform!* he thought. *Natalie and Gerry? No … It cannot, it must not be!*

Nicolas made his apologies and left at the earliest opportunity. When he arrived home, he went straight up to his room, undressed without thought and flung himself on his bed. *What will I do? What can I do?* For long, he remained awake, eyes burning into the darkness. Just as dawn broke, he fell asleep—one hand clasping the locket on his chest.

Later in the day, Nicolas approached his grandfather about holding a Grand Ball at the Opéra Magique for patrons, cast and employees. 'We have not done so for years.'

'And for good reason,' replied the duc, looking at him hard. 'Why now?'

'No reason ...' A slight tinge of colour rose in his cheeks. He hoped his grandfather wouldn't notice. 'Just ... to thank the performers, really. The countess is very close-fisted when it comes to that.'

'I suppose we could. As long as it is held in our ballroom, here. I wouldn't trust you to the countess's tender mercies. Do not think it!'

'*Merci*, Grand-père. I will see if Sette will act as hostess for us. That will make La Reine look blue. Must we invite *her*?'

'Along with her husband, of course!' The duc gave a wry smile. 'But don't fret about it. I am sure she will be able to manufacture a superb reason for non-attendance.'

'*Bon*,' said Nicolas. 'Now I must find Sette.' He ran her to earth in her sewing room and sat down beside her to explain what he wanted.

§

The beautiful white-and-gold ballroom was looking its best when Natalie arrived with Herr Schmidt-Hesse and a number of other members of the orchestra. Nicolas congratulated himself that he'd made sure Gerry couldn't be here by making the invitations specific.

But this didn't make things any easier. Nicolas had duties as host, and by the time he was able to approach Natalie, she was dancing with the percussionist. He did his duty, making sure that he was not doing anything so crass as to watch her progress around the floor with her attention fixed exclusively on her partner.

Finally, in a progressive waltz, Nicolas managed to partner her and secure the supper dance. Somewhere, during the evening, he decided to try, once more, to find the real Natalie; the one he believed existed beneath the petulant surface; the one who could transport him to the angels.

In contrast to her vivacity when she danced with others, Natalie appeared abstracted, not looking at him when he spoke and behaving as if she couldn't hear him, so that he had to repeat his words. When he did, she didn't answer, but spoke completely at random.

'Your ballroom,' she said, looking around. 'It is a testament to opulence.'

He thought he detected a note of sarcasm. 'Don't you like it?'

'Yes, it is *exquisite*.'

*Definitely sarcasm! She's doing it again,* he thought, beginning to feel ill. 'Thank you. I believe it to be an excellent example of its era.'

'I wonder what the beggars on the streets thought of it?'

He almost flinched at the contempt in her voice. 'Do you? Why?' *It would only inflame her more if I said that they were never likely to have seen it.*

'You can't eat gold filigree panelling and extravagant ceiling paintings.'

'Perhaps the soul needs feeding too?' he offered, as a palliative.

'Tell that to those with empty stomachs!'

*Oh no, not again!* He looked at her and away. Her manner was becoming more and more aggressive. In contrast, his tone was calm and reasonable. 'If you are saying that this ballroom caused the problem, I can only add that, even today, despite our social programs, there are still beggars on our streets.'

'Yes, I know. What are you going to do about it?'

'I ...?' He'd never thought about it, other than to give a sizeable chunk of his earnings to charity. But he wasn't going to talk himself up about it. His upbringing by the duc in that regard had been simple: those privileged enough to have money gave a percentage to the poor, and they did it as a private sacrifice to their God, never mentioning it to others. That was a crudity he would not be guilty of.

'Yes, *you*,' she taunted. 'The rich are responsible for all the evils in the world.'

'*Eh bien*, you floor me, Mademoiselle.' He saw her expression and, unable to decide whether or not she was serious, murmured, 'So *judgemental!*'

Natalie gave him a Mona Lisa smile, not deigning to reply. They finished the dance in silence; his misery complete. They were so far apart on the spectrum that there could be no common ground. *Why did I think that there ever could be?*

Nicolas took her in to supper, deciding to forget his resolve. But she looked up at him as he passed her a dish of vol-au-vents, and the sweetness of her expression took his breath away. 'You look beautiful.' He cursed himself for unoriginality. 'I'm sorry, I …'

'Thank you. Nobody minds a compliment. Don't spoil it by apologising.'

The ice was broken. He found himself laughing with her. Natalie seemed to have abandoned her previous attitude, and they chatted so comfortably that he dared to say what was in his mind. 'I wonder if you and your grandmother would honour me by spending the summer at Belvoir with me and my grandfather?'

'That is so kind of you to think of Nanette!' Her smile flashed. 'Lovely of you! Thank you.'

His heart swelled. 'Then you will come?'

'I am sorry.' She dropped her eyes to her silver bracelet. 'I truly am. You see, I have a prior engagement.'

'Oh.' *Not another one!* His manners ensured that he made the best of it. 'Then, it is I who am sorry that you will not come with me to beautiful Provence.'

'*Provence!*' He heard the longing in her voice. 'I would if I could. But, you see, I have been invited to spend the summer at his château by Colonel de Villefontaine.'

'Oh …' *Do I tell her that he is my mother's youngest brother, but I have only just met him because he was stupidly jealous of my mother and had to be sent away?*

*No!*

'You won't have far to go, then. It is quite close to Paris.'

'Yes, I believe so.'

'Hardly in the country at all.'

'Mmm.' She played with a glove. 'He has invited Major l'Abbaye and I ...' She saw that Nicolas had jerked upright and was looking over her head. 'Are you *listening*?'

'Yes. Yes, of course.' His social façade was firmly in place. 'He has invited you and Gerry ...'

'Not Gerry, Gervais. He is a military friend of Colonel de Villefontaine.' Natalie concentrated on smoothing a crease in the little finger of her glove while she made her triumphant disclosure. 'He is a superb concert pianist. We are going to be entertaining the party every evening as a duet.'

It passed over his head that she was baiting him. He could almost have laughed at the naivety of it, were it not for one thing: he knew what Gerry would do to her if he got her alone—with or without her permission. And if the brute didn't get compliance, he was just as likely to beat her into submission. Gervais was not the kind of man to use as a pawn in a childish game.

Knowing that Natalie had interpreted his momentary lapse as jealousy, Nicolas didn't waste time trying to explain. She met his eyes and looked down, barely concealing her triumph. He saw a member of the orchestra approach her for a dance and made his excuses, completely missing her little satisfied smile as she adjusted the bracelet on her gloved wrist.

The person he needed now, and quickly, was Lisette. He looked up, and there she was, regarding him from across the room. Guests delayed him, wanting to talk, thanking him, requiring all his tact to pass them by without offending. Finally, he reached Lisette's side, just as she detached herself from a group.

'Sette?' Nicolas breathed in her ear. 'A word alone, when you have time?'

'*Mais certainement, Chéri.* In Armand's study,' she whispered back. 'Wait there for me. I will be with you as soon as I can.'

Nicolas stopped pacing the floor as Lisette hurried in. 'Your girl?' she asked. 'I saw your face out there. What has she done now?'

'Another prior engagement ...' he said. 'This time, with *Gerry*!'

'Oh no!' She put a hand on his arm. '*Tell* me ...'

He explained. Never had she seen him so agitated. But then, she'd been unconscious the last time.

'Of course, you cannot say it, *Chéri*. But I can. *And* will!' There was a determination about her that soothed Nicolas's inner turmoil. 'You leave it to me, *hein*? And don't worry! I will make sure that she knows all about that fine gentleman before she leaves here tonight. It is a promise.' She hugged him and turned; her gown swirling about her like shimmering fairy floss.

'Your dress: I like it.'

'There's hope for you yet! ... What is Natalie wearing?'

He shrugged; his eyes rueful. He'd noticed Natalie's lips, her eyes, her shining hair, tried to interpret the many changing expressions on her face. Whatever she was wearing, she looked superb. 'Blue? Or green? I'm not sure.'

'Then I take it all back.' Lisette laughed. 'It may have just tipped the scales in your favour, a compliment like that. Go on, back to your guests.' She shooed him out. 'And don't worry, do you hear? Leave this part to me.'

# 26 A PRIOR ENGAGEMENT

**10 May 1939**

*Nicolas has organised this ball, roping in Lisette as
hostess, just to get Natalie here without that brute, Gervais.
Poor Nicolas, he is still in the toils of this brash, capricious
demoiselle, despite valiantly playing her game: a game that
I am certain he has no appetite for. And by the look on his
face after supper, I feel that he is getting the worst of it. I
do understand his fears—as Lisette could attest—Gervais is
not what he seems. And, certainly, would be every father's
nightmare as a suitor for his daughter!*

Lisette placed three red leather-bound volumes in a calico
bag and put them with Natalie's bag and coat on the bed
in the set of apartments designated as the ladies' cloak and
powder room. Then she went back into the ballroom.

When she saw Natalie make her way there, Lisette
followed and introduced herself in front of the mirror. 'I
did try to meet you when you were playing duets with
Nicolas,' she added, with her friendly smile.

'Oh, that was a long time ago, Madame Lemaitre. I
was just a stupid child.'

'Not so long ago, Mademoiselle. Two, three years?'

'I suppose … It seems a long time.'

'No doubt. You have certainly grown up since then.
You are a beautiful girl, Mademoiselle.'

247

Natalie stiffened. Beside this delicately built woman, she felt gauche, plain and overly large. 'Thank you.'

'And beautiful girls can suffer more from unwanted attentions than their less fortunate sisters.'

'I don't wish to be rude, Madame, but *is* there a point to this?'

'Sadly, there is. Please forgive me for intruding, Mademoiselle, but I feel it is necessary. I have heard that you are very direct. That, *en effet*, you are one to call a spade a spade?'

'Yes, that is true. I hate polite drivel.'

'*Bien.*' Lisette nodded. 'That makes it easier. I have also heard that you have made a friend of Major l'Abbaye …'

Natalie raised her brows. 'I wonder where you heard that? You must forgive *me*, Madame, if I ask you what business it is of *yours*?'

'But certainly. It is merely that I care what happens to a friend and former colleague of Nicolas's.'

'Don't disturb yourself, Madame.' Natalie curled her lip. 'I can look after myself.'

'Yes,' agreed Lisette. 'As long as you have the necessary knowledge to do so.'

'Necessary knowledge? What do you mean?'

'What do you know of Major l'Abbaye?' Lisette waved a hand. 'Gervais.'

Natalie shrugged. 'He is a friend of Colonel de Villefontaine and also of my music teacher.' She looked at Lisette from under her lashes. 'He is *very* good looking.'

'Better than Nicolas?'

The younger woman raised her brows. Madame Lemaitre was certainly taking full advantage of her permission to be direct. She took time to consider. 'No. Just … different.'

'Yes, he is different. You have spoken the truth there, Mademoiselle.' Lisette studied the mutinous face in the mirror. So like her own—face shape, hair colour, everything but eye colour—yet so unlike, because it was the difference in expression that made the subtle alterations to face shape that hid their likeness from all but an expert.

'Well, he certainly doesn't need babysitters!' Natalie tossed her head. '*And* he doesn't trip over girls lining up for him ...'

'No.' Lisette's eyes began to twinkle.

'*Swooning* at his feet!' she finished, in a voice of disgust.

'He can do,' said Lisette, becoming serious. 'But under very different circumstances.'

'Different circumstances? How different?'

'Tell me, straight off the top of your head, your first thought when I ask you this question: would Nicolas beat a girl, do you think?'

'No.' Natalie answered without hesitation. 'Never!'

'You are right; Nicolas would never do such a thing. But I am sorry to have to tell you that Gervais *has*.'

'*No!*' The girl recoiled. 'I don't believe you.' She wavered. 'Who did ——?'

'Me. And I tell you, before that, he was ready to force himself onto me with little or no encouragement.'

'But *he* ...' Natalie's mouth twisted. 'I don't believe it!'

'Don't you?' asked Lisette, watching her closely. 'Why not?'

'Because he ... he just *wouldn't*!' She faced the older woman. 'He is always gentlemanly to *me*. Why would he do such a thing to *you*?'

'It was very simple: I had something he wanted, and he knocked me unconscious to get it.'

'You're lying! You're trying to help Nicolas.'

'I am trying to help *you*. And I am not lying.' Lisette lifted her fringe. 'Look here, at this scar. I was lucky that Nicolas came along when he did. With his bodyguards, *alors*, to save me. I can take you to Doctor Martin. She will testify as to what happened to me. And so can Nicolas. We are both trying to help *you*, Mademoiselle. Nicolas knows that you will think he is a pawn in your little game

…' Satisfaction entered her eyes as she saw the girl flush. 'And that is why he has asked me to warn you. Now, shall I take you to Dr Martin?'

'That will not be necessary, Madame.' Natalie straightened her shoulders. 'As I said before, I can take care of myself.'

'That could be a matter of debate. It could all depend \_\_\_\_\_'

'Depend on *what*, Madame?' The hazel-green eyes challenged.

'On whether *you* have something Major l'Abbaye wants.'

Natalie dropped her gaze and reached into her bag for her powder compact.

'Come, Mademoiselle, you who are so grown-up: What do you think? *Do* you have something he wants?' Lisette saw two spots of colour appear on her cheeks as the younger woman concentrated on her image in the mirror and made much of powdering her nose. When Natalie did not reply, she added, in gentler tones, '*Ma chère*, if you have the *slightest* doubt, then I beg you to present to them your apologies and accept Nicolas's invitation. You will be safe with us. Gervais is not a man to be trusted with *any* woman, and Colonel de Villefontaine is hardly the host for a young girl. Please, come to Belvoir with us, Mademoiselle. These are not the friends for you.'

Natalie finished powdering her nose and snapped shut her compact. 'I will be the judge of that, Madame,' she said, with icy precision. '*And* I can choose my own friends. Thank you for your warning and your kind invitation, but I have a prior engagement.'

Lisette knew that beating on brick walls was an unfruitful pastime, but felt compelled to try again. 'Can I not persuade you? Gervais is not the tame pussycat that you imagine.'

'Major l'Abbaye is an accomplished concert pianist!'

Natalie flung at her through shut teeth. 'I am honoured that he has asked me to help him entertain the guests.'

'I see that I must tell you the full story. You see, I know Gervais very well. He grew up with Nicolas.'

'Oh?' Natalie bit her lip. 'I didn't know ...'

'There is a lot you don't know, *ma fille*. Gerry was Nicolas's understudy. It is not as silly as it sounds: with a black wig and make-up it was almost impossible to tell them apart, at a certain age, you understand. And their voices: identical. One night, after standing in for Nicolas, Gerry was attacked outside the opera house and lost his singing voice.'

'Oh, poor Gervais!'

'Yes, poor Gerry. We all thought that. A sentiment that he, perhaps rightly, resented. He stole the black wig and began to impersonate Nicolas in *certain* houses, bent on ruining his reputation.'

Natalie lifted her shoulders. 'I don't understand why he did these things. *If he* did them?'

'Oh, he did them. And he did them because he was jealous of Nicolas.'

'Don't you think it could be the other way around, Madame?' said Natalie, with a little Gioconda smile.

Lisette interpreted her expression: the satisfaction of a girl who knows she is adored by a man other girls would kill for, and is not afraid to wield her power to hurt him. Shaken by a little frisson of anger, Lisette gripped her hands together. Her palm itched to slap away the triumph. 'Gerry is not a man you can use like that,' she said, 'and you will come unstuck very quickly if you try. I am sorry that you are too young to see it. Little girls should *not* play games they don't understand.'

Her words bit. Natalie gasped and changed colour.

'I went to one of these houses to stop him,' continued Lisette, as if there had been no interruption to her story. 'Disguised, you understand, so that he wouldn't suspect. At midnight, I unmasked him by removing his wig.'

'But you can hardly blame him for ...'

'I don't blame him. He is what he is.' Lisette gave her a significant glance. 'And that is the whole point of this rather sordid story: for *you* to know what he is.'

Natalie shook back her curls but wasn't given time to reply.

'One warning I can only reiterate: Gerry wants what Nicolas has. And when he gets it, is prepared to destroy it. Are you feeling strong, Mademoiselle?'

'I ...' Natalie groped for an answer, disconcerted— no, infuriated, beyond words—by the inference that she belonged to Nicolas and that her companion saw it as the reason for Gervais's interest in her.

'You wanted the truth, Mademoiselle,' said Lisette, accurately reading her expression. '*Eh bien,* I have given it to you. And now I will give you some more. In fact, I will spell it out for you.'

Chilled by an icy undercurrent, Natalie stepped back from the quiet intensity of Lisette's words. Words delivered in a way that invaded her personal space. The smaller woman followed, holding her eyes.

'You can get away with playing your cruel games with Nicolas's emotions. You know that. That is why you do it, *hein*? Because you know that you can. But don't try it with Gerry. Because with *him*, you won't get away with it. *Eh bien,* I have warned you.' As always, Lisette's compassion overrode her irritation. She went on, in kinder tones, 'Believe me, Mademoiselle, the château de Villefontaine is no place for a young girl. You will do better to let Gerry entertain Monsieur Luc's friends on his own.'

'I appreciate your concern, Madame ...' began Natalie, in freezing accents.

Lisette's eyes lit with amusement. 'You *don't.*'

'But *nobody* tells *me* what to do.' Natalie rather spoilt her air of icy maturity by snapping, 'And if you are worried about propriety, Herr and Frau Schmidt-Hesse will be there with me!'

'They'll be by your side every hour of every day, will they?' For just an instant, Lisette allowed her contempt for this naivety to show, then gave in. '*Eh bien*, I see that your mind is made up. I am sorry that I could not persuade you. But I hope that you have no hard feelings towards me for trying?'

'None at all, Madame.'

'*Bien*. Then I wonder if you would do me a tiny favour?'

'If I can ...?' There was a wary light in Natalie's eyes.

'I have left you some books.' Lisette's smile was warm and conciliating as she picked up the bag on the bed. 'Holiday reading. I think that you will find them ... educational, as well as interesting. By the way, perhaps you do not know? Nicolas's mother was a de Villefontaine. Luc is his uncle. It is all in here.' She tucked a card between the leaves of the top volume. 'Here is my address and telephone number. Come and see me when you have finished them. I would like to know what you think. You *will* read them?'

'Thank you, Madame.' Natalie could not help but respond to the warmth and charm; her resentment forgotten. 'Yes. Yes, I will.'

'*Bon*. And remember that I am here if you need me.' Lisette's lip quirked at her sudden rigidity. '*Eh bien*, Mademoiselle, you appear very sophisticated, very confident,' she said, winking as she went out the door. 'But *I* think that you are not quite as hard-boiled as you would like the world to believe!'

# 27 SULTRY WEATHER

**2 July 1939**

*I have heard on the grapevine that Mademoiselle Watson
has today gone to stay at the château de Villefontaine,
despite advice to the contrary. My wife is devastated that
she could not convince her of the danger in which she has
placed herself by accepting the invitation of Colonel de
Villefontaine: a big rough man with military habits and a
temper to match. The silly girl stood on her dignity and
refused to believe that she wouldn't be able to handle
Gervais—of a similar description to his host. I can only
hope that Mademoiselle is right, and I say it with all
sincerity. It goes without saying that Nicolas is beside
himself.*

After the first week of her holiday at the château de
Villefontaine, Natalie had almost become used to being
treated with head-turning admiration by all the men from
Gervais upward. Even the most elderly general had words
of praise for her charm and beauty. There was not the
faintest sign of anything but chivalry from all of them. It
made her feel special, like fine Dresden china. She did not
stop to analyse what it meant to be treated as fragile
womanhood and was too young to see what it might mask.

Natalie did not think of herself as particularly
feminine, nor was she a hardened feminist, despite the

smokescreen she threw up to Nicolas. Deep within herself, she despised her reaction; but it was pleasant to always be treated with such deference. The young violinist didn't just find it pleasant: she basked in it. Today she rose to dress in her favourite cream coloured trousers and tailored summer jacket, teamed with an emerald green shirt; ran a comb through her glossy curls and set off down the stairs to breakfast with a sense of anticipation and wellbeing.

The two old generals had gone to the mountains because of the sultry weather, and the colonel's party now consisted of herself, Gervais, and Herr and Frau Schmidt-Hesse. That is why she was surprised to see, sitting at the breakfast table, a stranger: A great, hulking giant of a man with kind eyes and a gentle expression. He wore a farmer's smock, liberally decorated with smudges of earth.

Colonel de Villefontaine smiled, greeted her and waved a hand towards the man who was wolfing croissants and gulping coffee. 'Here's my brother, Christian, behaving like a peasant. I don't know why he's *dis*-gracing our table now. He's usually gone with the sparrows.'

'Beg … pardon,' said the giant; his mouth full. 'Calving problem … Running late.'

'You mean, you're going to Paris? Dressed like *that*?' Luc threw up his hands.

The other nodded and poured himself another cup of coffee without speaking.

'Is the calf all right?' ventured Natalie.

'Yes, Mademoiselle,' said Christian, raising his eyes briefly as he reached for the second-last croissant. 'Mother and daughter doing well, *Dieu merci*.'

'And you haven't changed to come to breakfast: disgusting!' said Luc. 'Observe the cut of his clothes: impeccable design, wouldn't you say?' he taunted. 'Chris likes to work the land. He grows vegetables for the Paris markets and grain for his beloved sheep and cattle. *And* if there is a bit of bare earth around, he will roll in it.' He sat back, mockery in his eyes. 'Or, at least, looks as if he does.'

Christian grinned and went on eating his croissant.

Natalie could see that he was used to being the butt of his brother's rather cruel humour, but she warmed to the big, gentle creature who, so obviously, loved his land and his animals—and let the insults pass over his head. She resented them for him and tossed back her curls. 'Why should he not?' she asked, with her straight gaze.

Luc dropped his eyes. 'Why not, indeed?' he murmured. Then, as Christian left the table with a murmured apology, changed the subject. 'I am taking out a riding party this morning,' he said, looking around the table. 'Are you coming, Madame?'

Frau Schmidt-Hesse declined, pleading a headache and the heat. A large, tightly-corsetted woman, she was already showing signs of discomfort, fanning herself and breathing heavily.

'Mademoiselle?'

'I'm afraid not, Colonel.' Gervais spoke before Natalie could reply. 'Mademoiselle and I will take this morning to practise a new piece for your delectation this evening.'

'Lucky dog!' said Luc. 'Herr Schmidt-Hesse?'

The conductor's hooded gaze passed over Gervais and settled on his pupil. 'You will be all right to practise without me, my dear? Good. I would like to ride. Frau Schmidt-Hesse will be here if you need her.'

'*Eh bien*, Herr Schmidt-Hesse, I must protest.' Gervais bowed. 'We are only practising our music.' He glanced down at Natalie; a caressing light in his eyes. 'Mademoiselle will be quite safe with me, in any case.' His gaze held that of the conductor. In mounting tension, the two men stared each other down.

'Very well,' said Herr Schmidt-Hesse; his back ramrod straight. 'I will hold you to that.'

Natalie moved uncomfortably. Her eyes apologised to Gervais. Under the conductor's innuendo, her immediate impulse to protest at being spoken for without consultation and declare her wish to ride died without utterance.

'Messieurs, Messieurs! We are all gentlemen here,' said Colonel de Villefontaine, 'Except for Madame and Mademoiselle, of course. We will give Mademoiselle the say ...' He looked expectantly at Natalie.

Now, in an impossible position, she could only reply, 'I would love to ride with you, Messieurs; the heat doesn't worry me one little bit. But I cannot pass up this chance to practise with such an accomplished musician as Major l'Abbaye.'

'Very nicely put, Mademoiselle,' said Luc. He clapped Gervais on the shoulder. 'I said you were a dog.'

'I thought you said, "Lucky"?'

'That, too.' His next words sounded like an order. 'Take care of Mademoiselle.'

'*Mais certainement,* Colonel.' Major l'Abbaye saluted.

§

Natalie fetched her violin and whiled away a pleasant hour practising a new instrumental piece by Glenn Miller, *Moonlight Serenade*, with Gervais at the grand piano in the salon. Then they had fun with *The Ballad of Lydia Pinkham*, a drinking song from the trenches of the Great War; and *The Beer Barrel Polka*, the latest craze from the USA.

'Very good. You're very good,' he said, admiration in his eyes.

'Thank you.' She bowed. 'So are you.'

'We play well together, *n'est-ce pas?*'

'Yes.' It was strange: she had to take her teacher's word for it that Gervais was a far better pianist than Nicolas and perhaps, technically, he was; but, although she would not admit it to herself, his playing could not strike sparks off her as Nicolas's had. Their duets were good—excellent even—but the passion of her work as a fourteen-year-old was chronically lacking at seventeen; and she knew it, if Gervais did not.

'Oh …' The man seated at the piano stretched his arms above his head. 'I need a bit of air.' He rose, took her violin and bow from her and lay them on a settee. 'Coming?' He offered his arm. 'Why don't we take an old-fashioned stroll in the shrubbery? It will be cooler there. And I will get to know you a little better. You have been here a whole week, and this is the first time I've been able to have you to myself,' his voice deepened with satisfaction. 'And *I* am going to make the most of it.'

She glanced at him, then away. He was tall, thicker set than Nicolas; but his eyes were hauntingly similar. As they walked, arm in arm, exchanging pleasantries, the little smile on his lips could have been Nicolas's. Except that he was so fair … Natalie pulled herself together. Why should she hanker after a lean, dark aristo—always fighting off other girls—when there was a good-looking man right here who wanted her? Every one of her senses tingled with awareness of it. She met Gervais's eyes and shivered involuntarily.

He stopped. 'Are you cold? On a day like this?'

'No.' She was embarrassed. 'You know what they say …'

'No. What do they say?'

'Something about a goose …'

'You're saying that a goose has just walked over your grave?' He laughed and began to walk on, deeper into the shrubbery. 'But, how morbid of you, my dear!'

'Isn't it, just?' she agreed, laughing with him.

'Hurtful, too. Especially when I have just congratulated myself on my strategy for getting you to myself.'

'I am desolated for you, Major,' she replied, in a voice of silk. ·

'Are you?' His eyes, bright with laughter, probed hers.

'*Eh bien*, I suppose that it must fall to me to cheer you up, then, *n'est-ce pas?*'

'If you like. How will you do that?' Mischief touched her little smile. This was what she loved: fencing with words, harmless flirtation with men who knew the rules, the heady spice of danger with a man who had a reputation. She leant on his arm, looking up into his handsome face. Lisette's warning seemed so inapposite— totally inappropriate to the chivalrous, delightful man who steered her so carefully along the paths in the overgrown shrubbery.

'Let me think ...' he said. 'Perhaps the fact that I feel such joy at walking with the most beautiful girl in the world will radiate onto my companion? How is that?'

'Very good, Monsieur. I like that. I feel better already.'

'Ah ... You see how good for you I am?'

'That question, I feel, is just a *tiny* bit forward, Major.'

'*Vraiment?* Then I see I must back off a little ... How have you been enjoying your holiday with us?'

'Very much. It has been wonderful. As well as all the splendid activities, I have had time to catch up on my reading: a luxury that I have been missing out on lately with my studies.'

'You are ... what do they call it?' His eyes twinkled: more like Nicolas's than ever. 'A bluestocking, *hein?* I am afraid that I am not much of a reader, myself. More of an action man.'

Natalie eyed his lithe figure. She could feel the taut muscles of his forearm under her hand. 'Yes, I can tell,' she said, in frank admiration.

He looked down into her eyes; his own faintly patronising. 'What have you been reading?'

'*Madame Dupont's Diaries.* I couldn't put them down. I finished them last night.'

'You found them so interesting, then?'

'Yes. Yes, I did. It seems odd to say so, but ... My father is in them.'

'Really?'

'Yes. And Colonel de Villefontaine; this château ...'

'And the de Beaulieus!'

'Yes.' She looked at him with fun-filled eyes. 'Let me guess: you've read it, too.'

'Tell me,' he said, with an unexpected mood change. 'Have you, by any chance, been comparing me with Nicolas de Beaulieu?'

She started, 'No.' It wasn't a lie. Just because she had noticed a haunting resemblance, now and again, did not mean that she was making a comparison. In fact, the notion of doing so was offensive. 'Why would you ask me something like that?'

'Because you have, haven't you?'

'I said, "No!" Natalie tried to pull away from him, but he held her arm in a vice-like grip. 'Let me go. I want to go in. Now!'

'You'll go when I let you. And not before.' The husky voice held a note of menace.

Even though their stroll had begun to assume the aspects of a nightmare, Natalie was mystified but not yet afraid. 'Why are you behaving like this? What has Nicolas de Beaulieu got to do with it?'

'You tell me.' His expression grew ugly. 'It's him you want, isn't it?'

'I don't know *what* you're talking about.'

'Yes, you do. I've heard that you've been running around after him.'

She was surprised into protest. 'That is *not* true! Where would you have heard a thing like that?'

Gervais shrugged. 'You went to his ball without me.'

'The whole orchestra was invited. I went with Herr Schmidt-Hesse and the others. It was only for the artists and patrons of the Opéra Magique ...' *Why am I explaining? It is not as if he has a priority on me!* 'I don't see why you're upset about it. Or what it has to do with you *where* I go!'

'Don't you?' He kept his gaze on a bright-eyed wren,

peering at them from the foliage. He plucked at a leaf and the bird flew away with a little cry of alarm. 'Perhaps you will find out, presently.' A corner of his lip drew down into a grimace. 'I used to work there, didn't you know? De Beaulieu and I were close. Once. It used to be said that we were so alike that no-one could tell us apart. Did you know that?'

'I heard,' she admitted, feeling suffocated: suddenly afraid of where this was going.

'Then you *have* been comparing me with him!'

'No! This is ridiculous! You're *hurting* me!' She tried again to free herself, but his iron grip was effortless, making a mockery of her own desperation.

'You're hurting *yourself*.' His sapphire-blue eyes narrowed to vicious slits.

Why had she ever thought they were like Nicolas's? His eyes would never contain such jealousy; such hatred. Her heart began to pound, and she felt sick.

'And now I'll tell you what *I've* heard,' he gibed, intensifying the pressure of his fingers to screaming point. 'I've heard that you've been panting after him. And since we are so *alike* …'

Natalie drew in a breath. Now she *was* truly frightened. So frightened that she no longer felt pain. 'I don't have to listen to this. I want to go in. *Now!*'

'Very well. Go, then.'

He released her so violently that she lost her balance. His hands cupped her shoulders to right her. Then, incredibly, she felt him thrust his boot between her ankles—causing her to lose her balance again—and pull her, so that she fell against him.

'So, you *do* want me? It isn't Nicolas, after all!' He crushed her to his chest. 'That is good, because *I* want you.'

'Please!' she said, trying to extricate herself from what felt like the grip of a boa constrictor. 'I don't. You're being unfair. You *know* you tripped me.'

'I did no such thing! When a woman puts her arms around a man, it is usually because she *wants* something.'

'You *tripped* me!' she gasped, repelled by the injustice of his accusation; the duplicity of him. Then she made a fatal mistake. She knew it as soon as she opened her mouth. 'You say you're like Nicolas,' she threw at him, 'but *he* would never do something like this!'

He went white about the mouth. 'He doesn't have to, does he? He can have anyone he wants. Except *you!* If he wants you, he's going to have to take my leavings!' Iron fingers gripped her breast, burning through her summer jacket.

'Oh-h-h …!' Natalie slapped his face.

'*Salope!*' Without the slightest hesitation, Gervais returned the favour, backhanding her with such force that it almost whiplashed her neck. The pain brought tears to her eyes, and she swayed, dizzy from the blow.

'I'm sorry,' he said, grasping her upper arms to hold her upright. 'You must not fight me. I don't want to hurt you, but I will if you hurt me.' He jerked her close to whisper, 'This can be good or bad: it is entirely up to you. I have made up my mind to have you. So, what is it to be?'

Natalie couldn't believe he'd changed so much, but she fully believed him when he said that he was prepared to hurt her unless she submitted. His touch vibrated with barely leashed energy. She could feel the danger: the darkness of him. The sibilance in his whisper. It was all there: everything that Madame Lemaitre had warned her of. *What a fool I have been! But no longer!* She made a little compliant sound and relaxed against him.

'That's my girl!' Gervais's husky tones rang with triumph. 'You will find me a good lover: The best. I promise that you will enjoy it.' He held her gently and stroked back her hair from her damp forehead, murmuring endearments that chilled her to the bone. 'Oh, my darling, look at your poor face! You must have fallen over. I will take such good care of you that you will never stumble again. Poor sweet. Let me kiss it better.'

Natalie felt his tongue rake her burning cheek—his teeth pull at the painful split in her lip—and flinched, tasting blood. She shifted all her weight to her left and drove up her right knee: hard and fast. Gervais moaned, released her and crumpled, grey-faced. She looked down at the man writhing on the path and, knowing she had just one chance, turned and fled.

§

Natalie was exhausted: her legs ached, she had a stitch, she'd fallen and torn the knee of her trousers and she'd only gotten a few hundred yards from the château. She touched her lip and blood ran down her fingers, but she didn't notice, cursing her own stupidity. If she'd thought to look for a bicycle, instead of running in panic, she could have put some real distance between herself and Gervais, who was only temporarily disabled. Bent double, she stopped to catch her breath and heard a vehicle over the jungle drumbeat in her ears. Crouching down behind a bush, she saw that it was a farm truck loaded with vegetables and ran out on the road, waving madly.

An earth-stained hand pushed open the passenger-side door. She looked up into a placid, gentle face, just now, creased with concern. 'Get in, Mademoiselle. I am taking this lot to Paris. Tell me where I can drop you ...' He squinted at her injuries. 'A hospital, perhaps?'

'No, thank you ... Do you know the hôtel du Bois?'

'*Oui.*'

'Can you take me there?'

'But certainly. It is on my way,' he murmured, fishing in his pocket to proffer a crumpled, slightly grubby handkerchief for her bleeding lip. Sadness clouded his eyes. 'I am sorry,' he said, gripping the steering wheel and staring straight ahead. 'My brother is a brute. He has brutish friends. Did no-one warn you?'

# 28 CHÂTEAU DES JEUX

**10 July 1939**

*The first week of les vacances have passed, but still no sign of Nicolas, who seems strangely unwilling to leave Paris. I have had to go with the duc. He is of an age where he cannot be expected to take such a long trip alone. Reluctantly, I have taken Lisette's advice and have left her to follow with Nicolas, whenever he can tear himself away. I hope it is not too much longer! Every day that I am apart from Lisette feels like a year: barren without her sweet presence. But I know what Nicolas fears, and I do agree with my wife: he must not be left to worry on his own.*

Nicolas could not have said why he wanted to linger on at the hôtel du Bois when his grandfather had already gone to Belvoir, but he begged for a moratorium. 'Sette, I don't want to leave Paris just yet. Will you stay with me? Just for a week?'

'What good will it do, *Chéri?* Your girl has already gone.'

'I know, I know.' He rubbed his forehead. 'I cannot explain. But I just have this feeling ...'

'Very well. As long as you promise me that you will not brood?'

'I won't. I might buy a car.'

'Might you? Ooh, that will certainly lift your spirits!

Will you take me for a spin?'

'*Mais certainement.* If I buy it.'

'What is it?'

'A 1936 Bugatti. Type 57.'

'Is it a Ventoux?'

'No: Compressor Stelvio Cabrio. Four seat convertible.'

'*Eh bien*, class, eh? That settles it: I will stay. What colour?'

'Red, black trim with red leather upholstery.'

'Ooh! You'll cut a dash in that. Drama, *hein*?'

'*Sette!*' He shook his head at her.

'What?'

'It is a car, not an opera.'

'As long as you remember it, *alors*.'

'Don't worry, I'm careful. I won't let all that power go to my head, if that's what you're thinking.'

'It never crossed my mind, *Chéri*.'

'No? Then you'll be pleased to hear that I'm learning the harp, as well.'

'Are you? Why?'

'I really don't know. Grand-père and Armand suggested it when we were ... Armand has told you about the underground city?'

Lisette shook her head. 'No, he felt that it was not his secret.' She gave him an indulgent smile. '*As if* I could not have guessed from the excitement in your faces when you got back that something was afoot! It was your grandfather told me. What does this have to do with you learning the harp?'

'There's one down there, is all. But Monsieur Lorraine promised me a week of lessons if I stay here. He cannot come to Belvoir for another week because of commitments in Paris; the details of which I have forgotten.'

'Very well. After we've been for a spin in your flashy new auto, you can entertain me with your angelic chords.

The main thing is: we don't do them together.'

He laughed. 'I most certainly hope not! But don't hold your breath for either, just yet!'

But even though these plans were faithfully carried out, Nicolas still wanted to linger after the week was up. Lisette, sweet and patient—understanding of his affliction—agreed to stay with him. The weather became oppressive. Nicolas saw that Lisette was struggling with the humid atmosphere and knew that he must make a move, for both their sakes.

The new car was, literally, at the door, being loaded with luggage, when a farm truck jerked to a halt and a girl leapt out and came running down the drive to collapse on the front steps. 'Madame Lemaitre ...?' she whispered.

'But certainly, Mademoiselle,' said the man who stood over her. 'Let me help you to a chair.'

The butler carried the wilting figure inside out of the heat, and Nicolas, starting down the stairs, finished them in three strides.

'*Natalie*!' He stared aghast at her bruised cheek and split lip, the bloodstained handkerchief in her hand, her torn and grass-stained trouser suit, as he took her from the arms of the butler. 'Did Gerry do this to you?'

'Please don't ask me ...' Her face puckered. 'I want ... Madame Lemaitre.'

Nicolas glanced at Justin. 'Call Madame and bring some water.' He looked down at the girl he held. 'Come in here and rest in the cool. You don't have to say anything.'

Natalie shrank into his arms, then tried to push him away. 'I can't ...'

'It is all right,' he murmured, setting her down on the sofa. 'You're safe now.'

Lisette hurried in, ran her eyes over the distraught girl and shooed Nicolas out. 'This is women's business,' she told him. 'Go out for a while. Come back in an hour or so.'

He thought it was the longest hour of his life, but when Nicolas re-entered the salon, Natalie was sitting with Lisette, outwardly calm. Healing salve had been placed on her lip, and her bruised cheekbone anointed with arnica.

She tried to smile at him, but it turned into a kind of painful grimace. 'If your offer still stands to spend summer in Provence, I would like to take it up.'

Joy pierced his heart. He crossed the room to kneel by her side and take her hands. 'But *of course* it does. *Cela va sans dire!*'

'Thank you.' All the game playing had gone out of her. She was subdued, grateful but still trembling with shock.

'Will Nanette come with us?'

'No, she will stay in the apartment with her maid. Her arthritis makes it too painful for her to travel. She ... she does not know about this.'

'I will go with you to tell her,' announced Lisette. 'Nicolas can take us in his car after lunch. What about your clothes?' She looked the girl over frankly. 'We can save the jacket, perhaps, if it will take bleach, but not the trousers, I am afraid. It is a pity. It looks a very elegant suit.'

'Yes, it is, *was*, my favourite. But I don't think I want to ever see it again. As for my clothes, I am afraid I left them at the château. There are ... I have a few at the apartment.'

'Never mind. We will get what we can. You will only need a few casual things. We are quite informal at Belvoir. We can buy some pretty material, and I will run you up a nice little sundress or two.'

'Oh, but I *couldn't* ask you ——'

'It will be my pleasure, *Chérie*. And now, let us have lunch.'

'It is true that Sette loves to sew,' said Nicolas, taking her arm to lead her to the dining table.

'I will enjoy having so lovely a model,' affirmed Lisette.

'You're both so *kind* ...' Natalie put her head in her

hands and burst into tears. 'Sorry … Sorry! I don't know why I keep on crying.'

'It is the shock, *ma pauvre*. It will take time. Me, I know what it is like. Come, let Nicolas serve you some lunch, and we will collect your things and be on our way.' Lisette put an arm around her. 'Dry your tears now. You are safe with us; I promise you.'

'Yes.' Nicolas stretched out his hand, and Natalie put hers in it.

'I know,' she sobbed. 'That is why I came.' Her eyes— large and filled with pain—sought Nicolas's. In that moment, honesty blazed, stripping away all the cynicism, all the defences. 'I am sorry for being so rude to you.'

His fingers gripped hers. 'You can be as rude as you like if it makes you happy.' *Anything to take that pain out of your eyes.*

She looked down and fiddled with her cutlery. 'I expect I will be, sometimes.'

'Then I must take full advantage of your current penitence,' he said, cutting a slice of quiche for her. He raised a brow, waiting for her riposte.

But Natalie merely thanked him and held out her cup to Lisette, who was motioning with the coffeepot.

'There was something I wanted to ask you,' said Nicolas, passing her the sugar. 'Was that Uncle Chris who dropped you here? Why didn't he come in?'

'I am sorry. I forgot to give you his message. He was running late with his vegetable delivery, luckily for me. He begs your forgiveness and will see you another time. I …I think he was quite upset about …'

'Yes, he would be: a gentle giant, my uncle. He never stands up for himself. Just takes what the others dish out and retires to his fields and animals.'

'He is there when it counts, is he not?' said Lisette, looking at Natalie. 'That is what matters.'

'Yes, indeed,' agreed Nicolas. 'I must find him and thank him.'

'He won't want that.' Lisette shook her head.

'No,' he sighed. 'I suppose not. Just when I see him again, *hein*?' He waited until they finished their coffee, rose and bowed deeply. 'Mesdames, your chariot awaits.'

§

Frau Schmidt-Hesse was sitting with a frail and wizened old lady with deformed fingers and huge bunions that made her feet seem as wide as they were long, when Natalie arrived to introduce Lisette and Nicolas to her grandmother.

Nanette, whose gnarled fists were clasped about the heavy silver knob of a walking stick, greeted her granddaughter with a little squeak of joy. 'We have been so worried about you! Helga was sure she would find you here. But you weren't! And, of course, I had no idea ...'

'Yes, *such* a worry, my dear!' Frau Schmidt-Hesse looked relieved to see the girl and waited until greetings had been exchanged to take her hands and say what was so obviously in her heart. 'Poor, poor child,' she said, her plump cheeks trembling with concern and righteous indignation. 'From my window, I saw you running away down the drive and guessed what must have happened. Some of these military men are just brutes! *Brutes*!' She shook her faded curls and pointed to some luggage and a violin case. 'I knew that you couldn't possibly be expected to put up with that sort of thing, so I packed your things and brought them with me. Because I will *not* stay in a house where such things are allowed to go on! And when Franz comes home, I shall have a thing or two to say to him about the kinds of friends he thinks it is permissible to expose his womenfolk to!'

Natalie was amazed. Never had she seen Frau Schmidt-Hesse anything but subservient to her husband and began to think that beneath the layers of soft, maternal compliance there lurked an unexpected core of steel. 'Thank you, Madame. It is so kind of you.'

'It is nothing, Child. I am only relieved that you have injuries that will heal quickly. And have not ...' Frau Schmidt-Hesse changed the subject. 'And if you wish to holiday with your new friends, I assure you that Nanette shall be well looked after by me.'

'Go, Child,' said Nanette, stretching out distorted fingers. 'Helga has explained everything to me, so that it is not such a shock. I can see that I will not have to worry about you in the care of these good people.'

Frau Schmidt-Hesse dabbed at a tear and took Natalie's other hand. 'I am afraid that you have been very frightened, my dear. I would not have had it happen for the world! And your beautiful suit: it is spoiled!' She brushed ineffectually at the fabric, making little clucking noises and, when Natalie excused herself to change her clothes, went to Nicolas and made a direct appeal. 'You will remember that, won't you? That she has been very frightened. And not ...' Her face puckered, and she fell silent,

'Madame, you need not worry. Mademoiselle Natalie will not be coerced in any way. While she is with us, she will do exactly as she pleases. I promise you that.'

'Hmph!' said Nanette; her eyes on the ornate silver cap of her walking stick. '*That* may not be such a good thing for her, either.'

§

Nicolas's new touring car was a source of pride, but no-one would have known it. Secret lessons with Mary and a natural affinity for machinery had made him an excellent driver. The Bugatti was fast and powerful, but he controlled it without effort. Natalie, seated beside him, had shown no reaction to the car and, apart from denying that she wanted the hood up and accepting Lisette's offer of sunglasses and a scarf for her hair, remained silent.

Out on the open road, away from traffic, Nicolas opened the throttle and allowed the big bird to fly. He smiled at Lisette in the rear-view mirror and glanced at his front-seat passenger. He saw that her face was white and strained and, with his customary thoughtfulness, eased down.

'Natalie? Is the wind hurting your face? … It is.' He pulled onto the verge and parked. 'I'll put up the hood.'

'Thank you.' For the first time, she seemed to notice her surroundings. She settled back against the red leather and ran her fingers over the gleaming mahogany and satinwood dash. 'This is a beautiful car. What is it?'

He reeled off the name, in a kind of chant, as he fastened the hood.

'Heavens, what a mouthful! That is the kind of name a car would have to live up to.' Natalie was beginning to sound more like her usual self.

'A legend, *en effet*,' added Lisette, making a wry mouth, as he settled back in the driver's seat.

'A legend?' Nicolas briefly raised his eyes to the rear-view mirror. 'Perhaps. She goes well.' He flicked another glance at Natalie. 'Are you about to say: A bit too well? Don't worry. I'm not a mad driver.'

'You seem to be a very good driver.'

'*Merci*,' he said, noting the sincerity in her voice. 'Mary would be pleased to hear that. She worked hard enough on me. Our chauffeur,' he explained. 'She drove Armand and Grand-père down to Belvoir and came back on the train to stay with her husband in the hospice. He never recovered from his war wounds, poor chap.'

'No, I'm sorry,' murmured Natalie, not knowing whether she should mention that she already knew this from the books Lisette had given her.

'Mary wishes to retire,' said Lisette to Nicolas. 'Did she tell you?'

'*Oui*. She is thinking of taking her husband back to a nursing home in England and living over there with him. I hope she doesn't.'

'Yes, we will miss her ... How is our patient?'

Natalie did not answer, and Nicolas, noting her increased pallor, asked, 'Feeling under the weather?'

'A little,' she admitted, with a shaky attempt at humour. 'As a matter of fact, I feel rather like a piece of chewed string.'

'Stop for petrol at the next village,' said Lisette, 'and I will give Natalie another aspirin. *Eh bien,* a visit to the powder room and a strong cup of coffee is also on my programme, if you don't mind.'

Nicolas's charming smile appeared. 'I don't.'

After the break, Lisette re-inserted herself in the rather cramped back seat and watched, with half-shut eyes, the sweet and gentle way Nicolas seated Natalie, before closing the door and striding around to get behind the wheel. Flanked by the extra luggage and Natalie's violin, she sat with a faraway expression. It was a sign of the times that her place beside Nicolas had been taken by another. She did not smile at the thought. It remained to be seen how this girl would treat him when she recovered from her shock. Then, her lips curved a little at her next thought: *It is fortunate that the Amazons have gone home to Sweden for their holidays, otherwise it would be a little crowded with those two giants in here with me, bien sûr!*

She knew from what Nicolas had told her that Natalie was scathing of his bodyguards and was not surprised that the girl didn't understand his friendship with them. Lisette only understood it herself because of her knowledge of Nicolas's sunny temperament and unconscious charm that bound others to him: An ancestral characteristic that made those around him love and wish to serve him. A trait that, she knew, was something that Natalie was bitterly fighting. Another reason that it would, perhaps, be more comfortable at Belvoir without the two magnificent

Swedes. *Fewer misunderstandings. At least four years, they have been with us. It is about time they had a holiday,* she thought, then realised that she was being asked a question. 'Pardon?'

'Should we overnight somewhere, Sette?' Nicolas was looking at her in the rear-view mirror. 'It will be a very long day if we don't.'

'I think so. Wherever we decide to stop for dinner will do. Armand and your grandfather will just have to wait another day, *n'est-ce pas?*'

They exchanged smiles. Natalie somehow felt like an intruder. Until Nicolas looked across at her and said, 'We can't have your first sight of Belvoir spoiled by being at some ungodly hour of the night. Besides, we must take care of you and not overtire you, *hein?*' Then she felt a sudden warmth envelop her.

Fields of golden grain; vineyards; orchards, interspersed with cool, green forests continued to flash by, as the big car ate up the kilometres.

Towards evening, Nicolas turned on to the road to Chagny and, after a few hundred metres, into the driveway of an elegant little château. 'We will see if Ernesto can accommodate us. He practically twisted my arm to call in and stay this time on my way to Belvoir, and I will take him at his word. If not, we can find accommodation at Chalon-sur-Saône. Or, if we feel up to it, go on to Lyon.'

'Should we not have telephoned?' asked Natalie.

'We *should*,' said Nicolas, 'but for the fact that he has no telephone.'

'Oh,' said Lisette. 'I know! Resting, is he?'

'That is a polite way of putting it. Or hiding, perhaps, is another. His last tour was chaotic, I heard.'

'So it was. No wonder he doesn't want to be near a telephone!'

Nicolas smiled at Natalie's mystified expression as she tried to follow this exchange. 'I must apologise for talking shop. Do you know Ernesto Rinaldi?'

'Not the tenor that fell foul of Mussolini, read a lecture to the Calabrian society about not sharing their ill-gotten gains with the poor and then was thrown out of Germany by Hitler's Brownshirts?'

'For telling Herr Hitler he was the leader of the biggest organised crime gang in the world? Yes, the very one!'

'Oh good! I've seen him sing, but that's all. I've always wanted to meet a man that has the intestinal fortitude to stand up to all the establishments, especially Uncle Adolf!'

'You'd better make the most of it, *alors*,' said Lisette, with a wry twist to her lips. 'A man with such flagrant suicidal tendencies is not likely to live for very much longer!'

'He's a humanitarian, isn't he? And a socialist?'

'Yes. I believe he is a communist. You and he will probably get on so well that neither Nicolas nor I will get a word in.'

'*Ma foi*!' said Nicolas, slapping his hand down on the steering wheel. 'I ought to have thought of that! Perhaps we should turn around right now and go on to Lyon!' But he stopped at the wrought-iron gates and gave a blast on the horn. 'On the other hand, it is probably a safe bet that no-one will get a word in except Rinaldi, whoever is there.'

'This is such a pretty château!' exclaimed Natalie; her eyes drinking in the slender symmetry of the building with its ornamental mouldings and conical pointed roof structures. 'Is it like Belvoir?'

'Not … quite,' said Lisette, her lips twitching.

'Oh, that's right …' Natalie's voice trailed off. Why could she not remember Madame Dupont's description? 'Belvoir is bigger, isn't it?'

'Yes, and different,' said Nicolas, intoning, 'The château des Jeux is an elegant sixteenth century manor house, enlarged and renovated in the eighteenth century—in a very flamboyant style …'

Natalie glanced at him. 'You sound just like a guidebook.'

'Yes, well, that might be because that's where I found the description, as it happens. Belvoir is much older: medieval,' Nicolas told her, saluting the gatekeeper and driving through the gates, past a miniature lake and a paved area with a water feature like the Trevi Fountain, to the entrance with its covered portico with marble columns and statues. 'This garden is very Italianate. Perhaps that is what attracted Ernesto.'

'That and a fine sense of drama,' added Lisette. 'Perhaps you should prepare Natalie for ——'

'Nicolas! Nicolas! At last! ... Madame Lisette! My heart beats faster, I assure you ... And who is this? ... Mademoiselle Natalie? Bella, bella! ... Come in, come in, my dear fellow, with your beautiful ladies, to grace my house.' A short, solid man with raven hair and a glossy black beard that made him look like a brigand out of an opera capered down the steps; his ruddy face alight with goodwill. He kissed each of them on both cheeks, between his booming utterances and led the way inside, gesturing widely. 'What do you think of my country cottage, *hein*?'

Nicolas looked all around the grand entrance hall, its panelling embellished in fine rococo style at the door but becoming more and more ornate and bizarre as it went; its designers having apparently gone mad with gold leaf and baroque extravagance. He raised his eyebrows at the bevy of voluptuous maidens holding up lamps and leering at them from the gilded panelling and cornices. 'Very nice, *mon ami*. You do yourself proud.'

'Nice? Is that all you can say? Philistine! Do you not realise that I got this house very cheaply because of all this rampant femininity? If the artists were here today, I would throw myself at their feet! Truly! I only forgive you for your pedestrian taste in architecture because you have brought to my house, not one beautiful lady, but two! But *how* I am a fortunate man!' His limpid gaze searched

Natalie's face and adopted an expression of concern. 'And if Nicolas did this to you—which I would refuse to believe, even if a troop of angels told it to me!—then I lay myself and my fortune at your feet and beg you to accept my hospitality forever!'

'Enough, you incorrigible rogue! You're frightening Natalie.'

Natalie, who had by now realised that the Italian's sense of humour was as dramatic and flamboyant as his château, since he seemed to speak only in a series of exclamations, replied, 'Not at all, Monsieur. The tables might be turned. Are you not afraid that I might take you up on your offer?'

'One to me, Nicolas!' he crowed. 'Mature charm has it over the vulgarity of youth any day!'

It was almost impossible to believe that this frippery man could be such a *tour de force* for philanthropy and a powerful orator. But Lisette knew it was true. She made a moue. 'But what about me, Monsieur?'

'But of course!' Rinaldi, as light on his feet as any ballet dancer, waltzed between the two women to take an arm of each. 'There is plenty of room for both of you!—I cannot tell you apart, in any case!—my home will be graced by two such seraphic creatures! We will send Nicolas away. We do not need him. Go away, Nicolas! You are *de trop*, my friend!'

'Behave yourself, Ernesto. I warn you: If I go, I will take my revenge upon you. My ladies will come with me.'

The Italian assumed a crestfallen expression and heaved a great sigh. 'Very well. If that is your condition, then I suppose that I will have to put up with you. *Hélas!*'

This kind of banter went on throughout the impressive dinner. The table was spread with an eclectic range of dishes, described by their host as, 'A little something for every taste.'

Natalie, seated on Rinaldi's right, tried once to speak to him seriously. 'I just want to say how very much I admire the way you stand up to dictators and oppressors for the rights of others. It is immensely courageous and philanthropic of you.'

'Thank you.' The words were softly spoken. 'It is also spiritually exhausting. Yet, so much needs to be done that I cannot see ...' For just a second, the curtain parted and Natalie glimpsed the stature of the man behind the jocular fool. He looked at her, and his eyes were stricken. The eyes of a man who had taken upon his shoulders a burden that was, perhaps, too onerous for a nation, let alone one man. 'That is why I come here, without communication: to renew my spirit.' He patted her hand. 'I hope you will not mind if we don't talk about it? It is the only way that I can do what I do.' Then he smiled at her and said in his jolly buffoon voice, 'Life is meant to be enjoyed! And at the château des Jeux, we play, we party! We enjoy it to the full! What else can we do in a château with such a name, eh?' He banged his fist on the table and raised his glass. 'Attention, everyone! A toast! To enjoyment!'

They made that toast and many others through the fun-filled meal, until their host suddenly fell silent. After enquiring if they were all replete and required nothing more, and gazing at each of them for an answer, he pushed back his chair. '*Bien*,' he said, draining his glass in one swallow. 'And now, we must work off our dinner with a little exercise.' He spoke to Natalie. 'If you are up to it? Yes? Excellent! Do you sing, Mademoiselle? No, wait! I think I have seen you somewhere: Ah, yes, the Opéra Magique, that's right! On the stage with Nicolas. I have a photographic memory, you know. Did you bring it?'

Natalie shook her head, as if to clear it. 'Did I bring what, Monsieur?'

'Your violin, of course! I told you I have a ———'

'So. We are singing and Natalie is playing for us,' said Nicolas, ruthlessly interrupting him. 'Is that your idea?'

'I will sing! You are not singing! I don't want any competition from you, my friend. Your range is too big!

Bigger than one man has any right to! Showing up the rest of us! No! You will play the piano and Mademoiselle the violin, and I will serenade Madame; and all shall be as it should be. Unless, of course, you wish to dance for us, Madame?'

'No, Monsieur, I will spare you the spectacle.' Lisette spread wide her arms. 'Behold me: a most appreciative and attentive audience!'

Now came the moment Natalie had managed to avoid since Nicolas had shown his interest in her. But, this time, she knew that there was nothing else for it. A manservant brought in her violin, and she murmured her thanks and took it from him.

'I will now sing a song that you both know well,' grinned the rubicund Italian. Natalie could swear that he had the face of a devilish imp, as he glanced at her before turning to Nicolas. 'A song made famous by your sainted mother, Angelique.' He kissed his fingers in obeisance. 'The beautiful *Éternité d'amour*.'

'*Eh bien*,' said Nicolas, smiling at Natalie and seating himself at the piano. 'Be it on your own head. It is supposed to be a duet, you know. Not a single cockerel crowing on his own.'

'I will pretend that you did not say that,' said Rinaldi, with dignity. 'Begin!'

Natalie took her cue from Nicolas and they began to play. The tenor was good, with a voice of haunting timbre. He sang with passion and power: great emotion. Natalie's eyes met those of Nicolas, and her violin took on a life of its own; the music penetrating deep into her soul. It ebbed and flowed, taking her with it. Vibrating her body, tapping yearnings she didn't know she had; confusing her senses, so that there was only the music and Nicolas. She couldn't hear the tenor any more. The music: it was drawing her heart out to give to someone who had thousands lying at his feet. She couldn't! She just *couldn't* ... Somehow, she didn't know how, Natalie's bow caressed the strings to form the last exquisite chord.

*The music ... Nicolas ... My heart ...* Her violin and bow slipped from her fingers. Natalie crumpled to the floor.

# 29 THE BARGAIN

**11 July 1939**

*I looked in vain for them last night. Another lonely night without my love. I hope they will be here, today. If not, I cannot think that they would not make it in good time for our usual Quatorze Juillet celebrations. That would be a catastrophe of gargantuan proportions!*

Next morning, the Italian tenor sent the travellers on their way with a hearty breakfast and a profusion of good wishes. When Natalie tried to apologise for failing them the night before, he clapped his hands over his ears. 'No, no, no, a thousand times, no! It is I who must apologise and lay my heart before you in sorrow, for being such a bad host that I did not see how much your performance would exhaust you.'

Natalie thanked him and disclaimed, as he put her into the car and shut the door. She had no real answer as to what had happened—only vague memories of being carried upstairs—of Madame Lemaitre murmuring soothing words as she and the housekeeper put her to bed.

Their last sight of their complex and flamboyant host, as the big convertible turned on to the main road, was of him jumping up and down on a vantage point, vigorously plying a tricolour scarf, before he vanished behind the rows of grapevines.

'He's the most French Italian I've ever seen,' said Nicolas, waving a hand as they rounded the bend. 'But his extrovert warmth and hospitality is all southern.'

'He is a wonderful character,' agreed Natalie. 'Very colourful. Unforgettable!'

'He is a man on the edge,' said Lisette. 'We must keep an eye on him.'

§

The road became steep and winding in places, but the car took it well: purring up the slopes, taking the bends neatly and swooping silently on the downhill runs.

'It is not far now,' commented Nicolas, as they turned south off the road to Gap. 'How are you bearing up?' He glanced at Natalie then turned his attention back to the road.

'Well, thank you. This is beautiful country. Spectacular.'

'We are coming into Haute-Provence,' he explained. 'Under the shadow of the Alps.'

Nicolas turned off the road just before Sisteron onto another, then, a short while later, another. 'Look up there,' he said, and there was no mistaking the pride in his voice. 'What do you think?'

Natalie gasped. Lisette thought she looked frightened. 'Is that ... Belvoir?' she asked, taking in the tall grey fortified walls high above them to the north. 'But ... It looks like a walled city. Like ... like Carcassonne.'

'A little. It is of the same period. There is a village within the walls, as well as this one here in the valley.' Nicolas indicated the cluster of pretty period stone cottages either side of the narrow road that made up Belvoir village. 'The château was a fortress in medieval days and later. In times of threat, the villagers could be accommodated within its walls.'

Natalie twisted her fingers together. 'I ... I was not expecting something like this.'

'Were you not? Then it is one-up to me for being able to surprise you. I hope you find it a pleasant surprise?'

'Stupendous!' she replied, then seemed lost for words.

But, to Lisette's ears, her voice rang hollow. She understood that it was being brought home to Natalie just how important a family the de Beaulieus were; the fact that Nicolas, indeed, lived a privileged lifestyle. Nicolas himself was never self-aggrandising, never claimed rights for himself over others. He did not allow himself to be called 'Monsieur le marquis', was generous with his time and money, tolerant and accepting of others, non-judgemental. Easy to be with.

Lisette saw the measure of Natalie's shock and her heart sank. This girl would not be so accommodating that she would sacrifice her principles for love. Not only that, Lisette knew that she was afraid. Afraid that if she gave herself, Nicolas would move on to another of the thousands of young women ready to pick up the handkerchief; desperate to become the marquise de Beaulieu.

Lisette was certain that Natalie saw Belvoir as a symbol of wealth and privilege, of oppression of the poor by the same *ancien regime* that had lit the fuse of the Revolution. Whereas, to Nicolas, it was home. A vast, exciting home with endless treasures from antiquity; and a fascinating history.

As they passed through the portcullis and into the first courtyard, Natalie was possessed by a sense of unreality, of stepping back in time. There was no fire or ringing anvil to bring the blacksmith's forge to life, but it was there along with the stone cottages and cylindrical towers at intervals along the walls. Beaming faces surrounded them as the estate staff hurried to open gates and greet their young seigneur.

The girl at his side gasped at the fairytale beauty of the

château, tucked within its walled garden and, as in a dream, entered between the great studded doors that were standing open, as they often did in summer, into the grandeur of the great hall.

Natalie had already met the duc and Armand at Nicolas's ball. Armand gave her a friendly smile over the top of Lisette's head, then lowered his own to rest his cheek on the bright hair. There was no mistaking how delighted he was to have his wife back.

The duc greeted them with his usual charm and dignity. Natalie found him gracious, kind, hospitable. Perhaps it was her imagination that, beneath his courteous manner, there was a faint but chilling reserve. As if, in some way, her presence displeased him. Or perhaps he was waiting for her to reveal herself, reserving judgement.

Lisette emerged from her husband's embrace to greet the duc and add significantly, 'Do you see this poor girl's face, Monsieur? … *Gerry.*'

'Oh no … *ma pauvre!*' The duc was all compassion; the faint hauteur replaced by a kind of rueful sorrow. From then on, his attitude to Natalie was unequivocally warm and protective.

*Quatorze Juillet* came and went with all the usual joyful dance and celebration that characterised this day at Belvoir. In the morning, it was held in the square of Belvoir village and moved after lunch to the cooler château garden where the party continued.

Finally exhausted, Nicolas and Natalie flung themselves down on the grass in the shade of an ornamental peach.

'There used to be a maze here,' said Nicolas, 'but it got some kind of dieback or disease and had to be taken out.'

'Oh, did it? What a shame! I would love to have seen it. But this lawn with shrubs is rather nice.'

'Yes, and much easier to trim, as well.'

'There's that, I suppose.' One of Natalie's bright curls

had escaped from a side comb and fallen forward over her face.

Nicolas put out a finger to touch it. 'You're growing your hair. I like it.' He raised his hand at her expression. 'Please don't feel you have to cut it because I said that.'

'I won't,' she assured him.

'That's a relief,' he said with an exaggerated sigh. 'I never know how you're going to take what I say.'

'Oh, you big sook, you need to toughen up. It is only an Australian pastime called leg-pulling.'

'What?' He raised himself up on one elbow to look at her more closely.

'We say, "Just pulling your leg." You know: teasing someone to jog them out of their rut. Have you never heard of it?'

'No. Why do it?'

'No reason.'

'Oh … What if it isn't a rut?'

Natalie hunched a shoulder. 'It is just that … you always look so contented, so complacent with your life. I just wanted to shake you up a bit.'

'Do you mean that you don't like to see a person happy with his life?'

'No, I …' She plucked at a grass blade. 'I don't mean that.'

'The thing is: I didn't always feel that you were teasing. I don't believe you were, what, doing this "leg-pulling"? You seemed serious to me.'

'But that is the art of it: not letting on whether you're serious or joking.'

He made no reply.

'Oh well …' She shrugged. 'If you can't take it, you oughtn't to dish it out.'

'Something tells me that it might be advisable for me to tuck away in my memory that you said that.' Their eyes met. Beneath the superficial humour, all their misunderstandings stood between them: a silent barrier.

Natalie stretched out a hand. 'I am sorry, all right?'

'Apology accepted.' He held her hand in a warm clasp. In a little while, she moved to take it back; and he let go, at once. 'But ...' he said; his face serious, 'there is more to it than that, isn't there? I hope you will tell me one day. I am sorry that you don't trust me enough to tell me now.' He rose, holding out his hand again to help her up.

'Don't you dare to *presume* ...' Natalie thrust his hand away and flew to her feet; her face a mask of fury. 'Do you *hear* me?'

They went back to the party in silence: their new-found rapport destroyed.

Each of them stepped warily for the next few days, meticulously polite, until Lisette told them, with her impish smile, that she wished they would go and practise their music instead of prowling around like a couple of stray cats trying to decide whether to ignore each other or fight over the cream saucer. Natalie smiled her little Gioconda smile and left the room. Nicolas, meeting Lisette's bland gaze, lifted a shoulder and decided that he might as well take her advice.

Approaching his grandmother's sitting room, a favourite place to practise, Nicolas heard the exquisite strains of a violin in the hands of a virtuoso. He hesitated in the doorway. Natalie was at the window, softly playing *Éternité d'amour*. His heart bounded at the sight of her. How elegant was her back view, in her beige fitted jacket and tailored pants, emphasising her tiny waist, the curve of her hips, the long slender lines of her legs; her hair a bright aureole in the light from the window. How sweetly she cradled the violin, held her bow, to coax from the strings a haunting melody. She seemed to be dreaming, absorbed in the music. He stood, drinking in the vision a little longer, then soft-footed over to the piano and, awaiting his moment, began to stroke the keys.

The rippling notes asked a seductive question. Natalie swung around; her mouth forming a shocked 'oh'. It was as if she would put down her instrument, but once again, her violin and bow took on a life of their own, responding with a plaintive query. The key strokes were persuasive, alluring; the violin replied with longing, but disbelief. The piano reassured, soothed: spoke of love, life, eternity. The violin asked a tremulous question; the piano's response was compelling, passionate: a declaration of love. The violin answered with joy and abandon. Nicolas and Natalie looked into each other's soul and saw their destiny as, in perfect accord, both instruments sang together in a glorious crescendo of ecstasy.

At the end, their eyes held, dark with emotion. Nicolas rose, took the violin and bow from her unresisting hands to lay them on a side table. What struck Natalie most was the inevitability of it, as she went into his open arms to offer her lips in a long sweet kiss. At first, it seemed that they could never stop, but eventually, Nicolas raised his head to look deep into her eyes. He touched her cheek with unsteady fingers. 'You are so beautiful, my darling. All I ever want. This, what we create together, is our own special magic. There is—there can be—nothing like it.' He bent to kiss her again.

'*Don't*, please …' Natalie turned her head.

'Darling, what is it? Did I hurt your lip?'

'No, it isn't that.' Natalie shook her head, refusing to look at him. 'I can't …'

'Can't … what?' His heart began a slow, painful beat. 'My love, doesn't this connection we have mean anything to you?'

Hazel-green eyes met sapphire-blue and glanced off like a clash of swords. Natalie made a little emotional gesture of negation.

Nicolas needed a moment to overcome his pain and disbelief at her attitude. He saw tears trembling on her lashes and took a deep breath. 'Natalie, listen: *look* at me! That's better. Are you going to tell me that what we have together is not special?'

'No.' She veiled her eyes. 'You are right: it is special.'

'I knew that your honesty would come to the fore.' He sighed with relief, cradling her to him. 'Then, everything will be all right between us.'

'No, it won't.' The words were muffled against his shoulder.

'But, why ever not?' He held her away to look at her, but she avoided his gaze.

'Because I don't want it to be!' Natalie moved out of his suddenly lifeless arms.

'Don't say that,' he whispered. 'I love you. I have tried not to, but I cannot help it. You're brash, rude, self-opinionated ... You say terrible things to me: hurtful things. I don't know why I love you, but I do.'

'That is a backhanded declaration if ever there was one,' said Natalie, dabbing at her eyes with her handkerchief. She made a shaken effort at flippancy. 'What happened to the good old-fashioned red rose?'

'I can do that if you like, any number of them, but I didn't think they would be welcome after some of the things you've said.' He smiled without mirth. 'When I think about it, I suppose you have done your best to discourage me.'

'Well, I don't know why it hasn't worked. Or has it?'

'No, I am afraid not.' His expression beguiled. 'What will you do about me?'

Arched brows drew together. 'I am *not* going to join the queue!'

'I don't know what you mean?'

'Yes, you do! And you can forget it.'

'*Eh bien* ...' he stood, wordless: devastation in his eyes.

Natalie stared at him for a moment, snatched up her violin and bow and ran out of the room. Nicolas bowed his head in despair.

*Hold hard, mon fils. Doucement.*

*What have I done, this time? Why does it always end like this?*

*A china-loving bull is likely to end up on a butcher's hook.*

*What are you trying to say? I cannot decipher your cryptic
utterances today.*

*A fool will trip over himself, whereas an Angel …*

*All right, I understand: take it more slowly. But will it work?*

*It depends on you: how slowly you take it.*

Nicolas took the hint and backed off. As the days went
by—lazy, golden days—Natalie stopped fighting and gave
herself up to Nicolas's company. He was the perfect
gentleman: courteous; thoughtful, restrained. It was as if
he didn't have a passionate bone in his body. What it cost
him, he never divulged; and Natalie had no idea. She
began to feel at home, more so than she could have ever
imagined. Far more than she wanted to allow herself.

Nicolas showed her his favourite places in and around
the château, introduced her to his friends amongst the
farmers and staff of Belvoir; and Natalie could see that his
people adored him. From the roof of the east tower, he
pointed out the various landmarks.

'It is a natural fortress, isn't it, Nic? The mountain so
steep on three sides, almost cliffs to the west and north.
That only leaves the south to defend. What an amazing
place!'

'I love it up here,' he said, secretly treasuring the
unconscious way she shortened his name. 'I used to
imagine armies marching, surrounding Belvoir. Finally
defeated … by us, their conquerors.' He laughed, kissed
her hand and held it. 'I'm glad you are impressed.'

'Impressed is not the half of it!' she assured him.
Common sense urged her to retrieve her hand, but
somehow, she could not.

§

They took a run down to Grasse to see the lavender
fields, so beautiful at this time of year.

'Oh, aren't they glorious?' sighed Natalie. 'Thank you

for bringing me. This is a sight not to be missed.'

'We must call in at the *parfum* factory. I promised Sette that I would bring some back for her.'

Natalie breathed in the array of scents presented to her by the perfumer, listening to his animated discourse on the various components that gave each perfume its own separate identity and signature fragrance. How, once it was placed on the skin, it took on a different note for each wearer, being truly individual.

'Choose a bottle for yourself and one for Sette,' said Nicolas, when they had finished the discussion. 'She said to let you choose for her. Something light and floral for summer.'

Natalie swung around. 'You are *not* buying me perfume!'

'But why not? We are here at the perfumery. You cannot leave without your favourite scent.' *Please don't make a scene, my love.* He wanted to say that he thought no more of buying perfume for her than he did for Lisette, then reflected that it would be so tactless as to not help his cause at all.

*Damned if you do and damned if you don't …*

*Shut up!*

Nicolas glanced at the perfumer, but his gaze was discreetly lowered.

'I will choose a bottle for Madame if that is what you desire,' said Natalie, in cutting tones, 'but *not* for myself. Is that clear?'

At the note in her voice, Nicolas began to feel ill, just as he'd done in Paris. 'You must do whatever you think best,' he said with a little shrug and saw that the perfumer was looking at him with sympathy before he turned to present a selection of scents to Mademoiselle.

'I will take this one,' said Natalie, after a few minutes. 'I think it will be best for Madame.'

'Very good, Mademoiselle,' said the perfumer, wrapping the bottle. 'This perfume is an excellent choice

for summer. I am certain that Madame will approve it.'
He selected another and wrapped it. 'There is a special
price for the one you have chosen: two for the price of
one. Just for today. This one I have picked out for you,
Mademoiselle. It compliments your spirit. A gift from the
house.' He made a tiny gesture that Nicolas recognised,
but Natalie did not.

She regarded him suspiciously but could see nothing
beyond the courteous demeanour. 'Thank you,' she said,
at last.

Nicolas waited until Natalie had taken the packages
and turned away before handing over double the named
price.

§

Nicolas and Natalie were sitting under the oldest tree
in the apple orchard after a long, rambling walk on the
mountainside. 'Summer is nearly over,' he said, leaning
back against the gnarled trunk. 'I don't want it to end. Are
you glad that you came to us?'

'Oh yes, this place is so beautiful. Thank you. It has
almost made me forget ...'

'The thing that happened to make you come here?'
said Nicolas, covering her hand with his. 'I am so glad to
hear it.' He hesitated, afraid that she might lash out at
what he was about to say. 'I was worried that it might ...
scar you ... Your soul, I mean.'

'No ... It taught me a lesson. One that I needed to
learn.'

His eyebrows asked a question.

'It doesn't matter.' She shook her head. An insect
buzzed, disturbing the silence, before she spoke again. 'I
think they are Nazis, you know: Gervais and Colonel de
Villefontaine. I wouldn't admit it to myself until now. I
heard them once, talking about a blond master race. They

… they may have been joking, of course, because they looked at each other and laughed.'

'Perhaps, yes. They certainly do look the part.' Nicolas frowned and plucked a leaf from the tree. 'One could hardly suppose that they would—either of them—be prepared to put it into practice, even if they do agree with the ideology. Although, with Gerry …'

'A lot of people do think it is a good thing, very efficient. I can understand a military man agreeing with it, but it worries me. So … *inhuman.*'

'Yes, there are certain aspects of this jackboot ideology that would only appeal to those without compassion. What did your conductor think of it?'

Poor Herr Schmidt-Hesse didn't seem to agree with the idea, at all. I felt sorry for him having to listen to it!'

'But …' exclaimed Nicolas in surprise. 'He is one himself.'

'Oh, no.'

'Yes, I am afraid so.'

'But, Nic, he argued when they said that only those with blond hair would be allowed … *Oh!*'

Nicolas smiled and kissed her hand. 'Let us go in to lunch.'

He helped her to her feet, and they made their way back between the laden boughs.

'Nic?' Natalie put out a hand to stop Nicolas's progress, gazing at him with a little frown between her brows. 'What reason have you to say that Herr Schmidt-Hesse is a Nazi?'

'I once saw how he treated a respected conductor whose only crime was that he was a Jew. Nazis regard those of Jewish blood as inferior.'

'How unfair!' she exclaimed, eyes flashing. 'Racism is a crime! Hitler has a lot to answer for.'

'Yes, he is the ultimate Judas.'

'Is he? Why?'

'He is said to be of Jewish descent himself.'

'Well, it is true that he isn't blond or German. But Herr Schmidt-Hesse does admire his philosophies immensely.'

'Your teacher: Are you afraid of him?'

'Not exactly. I am in awe of his musical genius.'

'I found him an overbearing bully. I have been worrying that he might treat you like that.'

'No. He is formal, punctilious, very rigid in his standards. But he is kind to me.'

'What about the day …?'

'At the gate? He is always short with men who walk me home. You see, he told me that to be his pupil, I must be in love with my music and nothing else. He views my friendships with the opposite sex as distractions from my music and within a hair of breaking my contract with him.'

'Contract?'

'Yes. I signed a contract with him: like an apprentice's bond. If I break it, he will send me home—my musical career over before it even starts. He only has to see me walking with a man to become suspicious.'

Now Nicolas knew the source of her fear: not what he had thought. *But what kind of man would behave like that?* 'He must be paranoid. Does it happen often?'

'No. There are not many men chivalrous enough to walk a girl home these days.'

'How many?'

'Now you're starting to sound like him! Only … you. Is that what you wanted me to say?'

'Perhaps the good Herr has frightened the others off?'

'Perhaps. Does he frighten you?'

Nicolas shrugged. 'It is not for the want of trying.'

'Look, Herr Schmidt-Hesse is old-fashioned, with antiquated ideas of courtship. You mustn't mind him.'

'I do mind him when he comes between me and the one I love.'

'I told you: I want to remain free. I don't want to get married. *Ever!*'

Nicolas looked down at the leaf he was turning between his fingers. 'I have said that I love you,' he said, with quiet dignity. 'Forgive me, but have I asked you to marry me?'

'No,' she replied, smothering a little embarrassed laugh. 'How previous of me!'

'I won't take back what I said, but I am prepared to wait for you.' His eyes smiled into hers with compelling charm. 'Let us give ourselves time, *n'est-ce pas?* Let us just enjoy the rest of summer.'

'It is a bargain,' she said, tucking her hand in his. He kissed it, and they walked on, hand in hand, through the scented orchard—the somnolent beauty of the garden—to the château, where lunch awaited them on the terrace.

# PART II

A World Gone Mad

# 30 HELL FROM THE SKIES

**3 September 1939**

*Two days ago, Poland was invaded by Germany and that
which we have feared has come upon us. A great iron fist
ready to crush us all. What shall be the outcome?*

'It is a fact,' said the duc, taking out his pocket watch and
snapping open the cover to observe the time, 'Britain
declared war on Germany earlier in the day, and by now,
France will have joined her.'

'Can this be true?'

'Sadly, it is. Gabriel brought me the news earlier. He
said the generals are in a stew, which is the reason for the
delay. But there is nothing else to be done. The nightmare
begins.' He looked at Nicolas. 'You feel that I am being a
little melodramatic, *hein?*'

'No, Grand-père. I know that you have been worried
about something like this for some years now. You are a
prophet, *n'est-ce pas?*'

'I was hoping that I would be found to be an overly
anxious old man.'

'Pooh!' said Lisette. 'I would like to have the insights
into the world that you have, Monsieur. If our country is
at war, she will need you.'

'*Merci,* Lisette. Naturally, I will do what I can. But I am
afraid that the defence of our beautiful France will be in

the hands of young men such as Armand and Nicolas.'

'*Et moi*, Monsieur! Don't forget me!' Lisette's small features were set with determination.

'But certainly not!' said the duc, bowing. 'It would be impossible, my dear.'

'Whatever we get into, Sette will be in there with us, *cela va sans dire*,' said Nicolas. 'But my Dees have returned only to tell me they are deserting me, just when I need them.' He beckoned to the bodyguards, standing either side of the door: 'Are you certain you want to do this, girls? We make a formidable team!'

The bodyguards answered in sequence, as always, starting with Desi, 'We must go back home, Monsieur.'

'We're sorry to abandon you, but we believe our country needs us.'

'We will miss you.'

'Go with God, Monsieur.'

They hugged Nicolas and shook hands with the others.

'We will meet again after the war,' said Desi.

'Cross our hearts and hope to die,' added Dani, simultaneously making the sign with her twin.

Nicolas raised an eyebrow. 'Shall we make a rendezvous now?'

'No,' said Desi. 'Wherever you are, we shall find you.'

'That is a promise,' said Dani, kissing him goodbye.

§

Everything happened in quick succession. Nicolas was snapped up by Military Engineering with other bright young engineering students in a bid to modernise their machinery of war, well knowing that Hitler had already many years to consolidate and prepare while France had languished with what remained of guns, tanks, aircraft and a fleet of ships that had survived the Great War. The duc, ever mindful of the dangers facing his grandson, tried to use his influence for Armand to join him as his batman. But, to all their shock, Armand failed the medical to enter the army due to weakening eyesight. He thus remained at home with Lisette and the duc.

Nicolas continued his studies part-time, sang regularly at the Opéra Magique by special dispensation, and sifted through the million-and-one specifications for everything from guns to aircraft carriers that landed on his desk. He was kept busy picking holes in all the plans, reporting on the limitations of each. Via military intelligence, certain plans came his way, purporting to be smuggled out of Germany by allied spies. His skin pricked with the knowledge that everything France had to throw at the enemy appeared to be woefully inferior, and he and his colleagues worked feverishly to try to find remedies.

It all seemed rather an anticlimax, as during the winter of 1939, the German army maintained a *sitzkrieg*. Everyone was uneasy, but nobody wanted to make the first move against what some saw as an invincible war machine. New Year came and went, and winter rolled into spring before there was any activity.

Natalie used the war as an excuse to step back from a relationship that she was becoming more and more dependent on: meeting Nicolas casually for coffee, dinner or a film. Unable to admit that she found his undemanding friendship and support increasingly seductive, Natalie found a raft of other reasons for her decision to stay on at the Sorbonne and continue her contract with Herr Schmidt-Hesse and the Orchestra Magique. In the face of increasing demands from her family to come home, she tossed her head and refused to go back to Australia without her grandmother.

Nanette's reply was unequivocal. She had been born in Paris and intended to die there. But that did not mean that her granddaughter had to do so, as well.

Natalie, equally stubborn, said that she was glad of the excuse to remain in Paris.

'And that is truer than you know, my girl,' remarked her grandmother, with a sly twinkle, refusing to elaborate when asked what she meant.

## 18 June 1940

*The German army has blazed its way through Europe with what is known as blitzkrieg: a method of warfare that involves throwing everything they have at us. And they have a lot to throw! Ever since Dunkerque, we have been subjected to heavy air attack. They are even bombing and strafing the poor souls who are now refugees, fleeing along the roads.*

*Four days ago, the German army marched into Paris without a shot being fired; the government having left town. This, they said, was so that our beautiful buildings would not be destroyed. Many loyal Frenchmen have been disgusted by this attitude of our leaders. Today the duc is going about white-faced, like a man who has been delivered a mortal blow. He has just come back from a private meeting with Marshal Pétain to demand the truth of a rumour that has been brought to him by Gabriel, regarding an ultimatum we have received: become a puppet regime for Germany, or watch Paris razed to the ground. To find him, he had to chase him from Tours to Bordeaux. What a government, eh? Incredibly, the whisper is that France is about to surrender like a dog with its tail between its legs. Let it not be!*

'I have called you here to tell you to get everything that is precious to you and leave for Belvoir, at once,' said the duc. 'Marshal Pétain has asked Germany for terms to surrender France. Within days, our army will be under orders from the German army; and our friends will be our enemies.' He shrugged. 'I tried to change his mind, but I could not.'

'No!' Nicolas and Armand looked as shocked as each other.

'Marshal Pétain?' said Nicolas. 'But he was a hero in the last war! How can this be?' He bit his lip. 'The craven ____'

'Do not judge him too harshly, my son,' replied the duc.

He was silent, remembering his own similar question to the Marshal: *'You are lauded as a hero: do you want to end your days considered a coward?'*

*And the Marshal's reply, 'I cannot go there again! The carnage! The futility! My God, I had to shoot my own men! Do you know what that does to a man? And what was it for? This? Again? Have you seen the way they fight? Unstoppable! No, no, this way there will not be loss of life. This way, Paris will be saved.'*

*And his own brutal last word: 'Can a leader be such an old fool? Without self-respect? Of course there will be loss of life! How can there not be? It is time that you stepped down.'*

*Marshal Pétain had turned his back, not deigning a reply to the unusually confrontational charge from a man who had always been courtesy itself.*

'Why not? … Grand-père?' Nicolas was staring at him.

'I beg your pardon?'

'You said not to judge him harshly. Why not?'

'Oh …' The duc closed his eyes against the pain. 'You don't know what the Great War did to those of us who were fortunate enough to survive it. So many sacrificed themselves for their country, for ideals of freedom and justice. And now, it happens all over again.' The duc told them briefly of the bloodbath that was Chemin des Dames in the spring of 1917 and what Marshal Pétain had been forced to do to counteract the reversals. 'It is not something you get over lightly. If you recover, at all.'

'No …' said Armand. 'I begin to see.'

'But, I am afraid, I don't.' Nicolas eyes blazed into his grandfather's. 'If he is too old to have the stomach for it, he should step down for a younger man.'

'My sentiments also I have made clear to him,' murmured the duc, 'but it will not happen in time. Therefore, we must all get to Belvoir as quickly as possible, avoiding the air attacks on the roads. You two can put your minds to that. There will be a demarcation zone if I am not mistaken. Once we cross the line, we will be relatively safe. For now.' He turned to go, and then stopped; his head bowed. 'Italy has also entered the war. As our enemy.'

'*Mon Dieu*!' exclaimed Armand.

'Yes.' The duc looked at him sadly. 'All our friends, it seems.'

'But what about Ernesto?' asked Nicolas. 'He will be on both Hitler's and Mussolini's death lists, the way he has been going.'

'I will try and get a message to him, but it will be difficult. Gabriel and his men have been working like Trojans gathering intelligence. I doubt that they can spare anyone. Armand, you had best prepare Lisette. And you go and get your girl and her grandmother, Nicolas. We must leave tonight.'

'Nanette won't come, and Natalie won't leave her,' said Nicolas, tight-lipped. 'I don't need a crystal ball to know that. If that is the case, I won't come either.'

'You will stay here? With this going on?'

'I will have to.'

'You are a grown man now and must make your own decisions,' said the duc after a short silence, having seen the purpose in his face. 'But where will you stay? No house in Paris will be safe for you. Or any of us, after what I have had to say to Pétain.'

*Underground.*

'I'll go underground,' said Nicolas, wondering at the conviction in his voice. 'The city beneath Paris is bigger than the one at Belvoir, so I believe.'

*It is.*

'I hope you don't get lost in it,' sighed the duc.

*You won't.*

'I won't.'

Armand looked at Nicolas. He, too, wondered at the conviction in his voice.

§

Nanette's eyes flashed. 'The only way the *Boche* will get me out of my apartment is if they carry me out dead!' she informed Nicolas. 'You and Natalie may go with my blessing. Personally, I would rather die than try and make my way anywhere in this country at this time. Have I made myself clear?'

'*Mais certainement*, Madame,' said Nicolas. 'Now I know where Natalie gets her spirit.'

'Don't talk about me as if I am not here,' said Natalie. She knelt before the old lady and took her hands. 'Please, Nanette. Can we not change your mind? I know it will be uncomfortable at first. Then things will be better. Please?'

'Leave me, my child. You don't understand. Life is important to you. It is not to me. You go with Nicolas. Then we will both be comfortable. You will be safe, and I will be happy knowing that you are in the care of this fine young man.'

Natalie looked at Nicolas and shook her head. 'I am sorry. I cannot go with you. She is a stubborn old woman, but I cannot just walk away and leave her.'

'I know. You wouldn't be the person you are if you did.' He said goodbye to Nanette and asked Natalie to see him out.

'Of course,' she said. 'I don't know when I will see you again.'

'Will that matter to you?'

'Of course it will!'

'I just wondered.'

'Did you?'

'Mmm.'

'Does it reassure you to know that I will miss you?'

'Oddly enough, it does.' He smiled. 'But I think you know that.'

Natalie avoided his glance. 'I hope it is not too long before I see you again.'

'It may be sooner than you think. I intend to keep an eye on you.'

'No! You must be careful not take any risks. I will be all right.'

'You plan to become a collaborator then?'

'Of course not! You know my views. How can you say that? '

'Then, you will not be all right.' He saw her expression and opened his arms. '*Ma pauvre*. Come here, then.'

'I am afraid, Nic,' she said, going into them. 'I would be lying if I said I wasn't, but how can I leave her? You know how crippled she is. If something happens to her maid, she will starve to death ... or worse.'

'I know, my darling, I know. In the same situation, I could not leave Grand-père, either. We must take each day as it comes. Let us make a rendezvous now. I will wait every morning at ten under the clock in the Metro. If you do not come, I will try to come here to see you.'

Alarm showed in her eyes. 'I will come every day. Don't take risks, Nic. Please!'

'Kiss me goodbye, then,' he said, pleased that she seemed to care so much.

'Goodbye,' she said, with a sigh, emerging from his kiss. 'Please be careful.'

'Tomorrow, at ten,' he said, demanding and receiving another kiss before striding away to explain the situation to his grandfather.

# 31 FIGHT OR FLIGHT

**20 June 1940**

*We have made it out of Paris and its environs despite several times having the road blown up in front of us and our windscreen broken by a machine gun bullet fired from a Stuka. That one was a closer call than I care to contemplate, forcing us to take cover! They are like swarms of angry bees, buzzing out of the sky from nowhere, stinging us and departing. Then there was the added problem of avoiding all the poor souls fleeing for their lives. I wish we could have given them all a seat, but since we have taken the Compressor on Nicolas's insistence, there was barely enough room for the three of us and Monsieur Lorraine.*

*I wonder how Nicolas is faring in his new surroundings? It amazed me how sure of himself he seems, since he is a true novice in the kind of war he is getting into. I am uneasy about leaving him behind, but he is a man grown and must make his own decisions. My place is with Lisette and the duc. My hope is that Gabriel will send some news to us via the duc's radio network.*

Nicolas, haunted by the image of his family driving away, was dealing with unprecedented emotion. He was on his own in a hostile city, and for just a moment, he felt overwhelmed. Especially, when he remembered Lisette's whispered words:

'Not goodbye: *au revoir*. Remember, we will see each other sooner than you think. Until that day, *Chéri*.'

Fear shook him that he would never see them again. He buried his face in his hands. *I feel so alone without them.*

*Not quite ... alone.*

*No ... Thank you.*

Nicolas waited until dark, shrugged on a black overcoat, picked up a cigarette lighter and a box of matches and disappeared into the gloom. Hardly knowing where he went, he stumbled along, following the prodding of his inner voice; his soul consumed by worry for Natalie. No-one noticed him, all preoccupied with their own problems, scurrying off the streets before someone took a shot at them, or worse.

*Damn Nanette and her stubbornness,* he thought, with uncharacteristic ruthlessness. *If she wants to die, why does she not get on with it and let Natalie live?*

Immediately, he felt ashamed. Nanette had told them to go. His expression softened. As he had told her, Natalie would not be the person he loved if she could abandon someone because she was old and ill and unable to travel. How far could they have got with Nanette, anyway? And Nanette, herself, had been honest with them. Whatever he might think about her, she did not lack courage.

Nicolas halted, feeling suddenly helpless. All he could do was wait around, avoid capture by a German and keep an eye on them; perhaps find someone reliable to care for Nanette so that Natalie could come with him. Contemplating all this, he barely noticed that he had come to a ruin.

*The Opéra Français, or what is left of it. This wall is all that exists of the coach-house. The harness hook on the end.*

Nicolas lifted the tarnished latch and a door swung out into darkness.

*Candles on the right.*

Nicolas flicked the wheel on the lighter and, in the tiny flare of light, found a candle in a holder. He lit it and held it aloft to show a rough stone stairway descending into gloom. Without thought, he followed the stairway to an impenetrable rock wall. Obeying Angel's directions, he found the mechanism for the concealed door and went on down the passage to another wall where he suddenly noticed his cold, dank surroundings.

*Where have you brought me?*

*Open the door and find out.*

*What door?*

*Behind the curtain.*

*Ah* ... Nicolas pushed aside the musty velvet and opened a heavy door. He stepped inside and stopped short in wonder as his gaze travelled around a luxurious apartment. He lit the candles in two fabulous girandoles and set down the one he carried on a sideboard as the room came to life.

*Now, I understand: your palace.*

*Your refuge. I took precautions during the Great War to modernise it and make an underground escape route. We did not need it then, but you will find that you will not have to go up onto the streets, at all. The Paris underground is a huge labyrinth. Fortunately, I know most of its secrets. But these I will show you in the morning. For now, you must rest.*

Nicolas, suddenly impelled to stretch out on the sumptuous bed, did not realise the extent of his exhaustion until his head sank into the softness of the Master's feather pillows. He fell immediately into a deep sleep, just as he was.

# 32 THE PARIS UNDERGROUND

**22 June 1940**

*God be praised, we reached Belvoir just as the sun was coming up. We had to hide in the forest all day yesterday, as the day before, with the Stukas at their deadly work again: strafing and bombing the poor wretches on the road. I cursed the auto being red, but we cut some branches and laid them over it. Obviously, it worked; and here we are!*

*There is still no word of Nicolas. Nobody is saying much: we are all so worried about him and how he is getting on. I have left this next until last because how it hurts to write it: Today France surrendered to an enemy. Northern France is now occupied, with men and women forming an underground Résistance movement against their German masters. But here, in the south, we are governed by a cursed, puppet government. Any man who is a man is joining la Résistance (along with women of similar courage and conviction). May God bless and take care of Nicolas.*

*Nicolas.*

*Quoi?* Nicolas raised a sleepy head and looked about him. The candles were guttering in their girandoles, and at once, he knew where he was.

311

*It is time to go, mon fils.*

*Yes.* Wide awake now, Nicolas leapt to his feet, unshaven, unwashed, but with a sense of purpose. Quickly, he lit more candles and carried them into the bathroom to presently emerge refreshed.

*Eh bien, if you are ready?*

*Oui.* Nicolas passed a hand over his now cleanly shaven chin. *As ready as I'll ever be.*

*The garderobe in that corner. Behind the clothing, there is a knot in the wood. Press it.*

Nicolas opened the large, old-fashioned wardrobe and pulled aside a black cloak. On impulse, he changed his coat for it, transferred the contents of his pockets and, wrapped in its folds, set his finger to the knot.

The back of the wardrobe slid away with a little scraping sound, and Nicolas found himself in what looked like a priest-hole. In the faint light filtering through the wardrobe opening, he saw a storm lantern and some wax matches in a watertight container on a shelf and used them to fill the tiny room with a warm, yellow glow. He unbarred and opened the sturdy oak door set in the opposite wall and stepped out into a long, wide passage that led into a vast cavern. At the farther end, the great space narrowed again into a similar passage with doorways cut at intervals glowing with dim light. Inside these doorways were box-like rooms with tunnels and more rooms leading off them haphazardly.

In and around some of the openings were small, sullen groups of people. Most looked bewildered, all were frightened, some were dangerous. Nicolas huddled into his cloak, grasped his lantern firmly and wished he'd had the forethought to bring a walking cane. No-one said anything about him wearing the dress of a nineteenth century magician. No-one said anything at all, just watched him walk by with covert, sinister glances that made him uneasy.

He felt the hair rise on the back of his neck when a

small unobtrusive man detached himself from one of these groups and began to follow him. As they went along, here and there, a man fell in behind the others, until Nicolas was walking ahead of five men.

'Monsieur le marquis!'

A frisson chilled his spine. He swung round and crouched, ready to defend himself, then straightened in relief. 'Oh, Gabriel,' he said, clasping the man's outstretched hand. 'You don't know how pleased I am to see you!'

'*Eh bien, moi aussi,* Monsieur. Monsieur le duc sent me to find you.'

'Of course! Trust my grandfather!'

'*Oui,* Monsieur. He is a one to look after his own. These are my men.' He introduced them, 'Jean-Marie, Raoul, Pierre, Alain.'

'Monsieur le marquis,' they murmured, nodding.

Nicolas held out his right hand to each in turn. 'Nicolas,' he said. 'Enchanted to meet you.' One corner of his mouth lifted in the suggestion of a wry smile. 'Titles are a little extraneous at the moment, don't you think?'

They loved him instantly.

'I am taking you to meet someone: the leader of our *Résistance* movement,' said Gabriel, nodding in approval. 'He wishes to meet you.'

'Who is he?'

'He prefers to remain anonymous; for safety, you understand. We will all have to operate under aliases. We call him Colonel Rol.'

'*Eh bien,*' said Nicolas. 'Lead on.'

§

A dynamic man in his early thirties was addressing a ragged audience: men and women with hungry eyes that never left his face. He spat the name 'Pétain,' and fell silent as the group came into the room, then asked, 'Is this him?' At Gabriel's nod, his eyes roved over Nicolas. 'Too soft,' he said, dismissing him.

'For what?' asked Nicolas, meeting the contempt in his glance, look for look.

'*Quoi?*' The question was almost a whisper, but a dangerous light gleamed in the colonel's large, expressive eyes.

Nicolas's spine chilled, but he stood his ground. 'You said: "Too soft" ... I want to know: for what?' He suddenly felt hot and shrugged back his cloak.

'Let me take that for you, Monsieur,' murmured Gabriel, stepping up to receive the garment. He retreated, folding the heavy black silk over his arm.

The colonel looked Nicolas over before replying, 'You were recommended to me as a leader of men. I don't believe you're up to it.'

'Why not?'

'Hmm ...' The colonel's gaze travelled around the room and back to rest on his interrogator. 'Have you ever killed a man?' he demanded, almost menacingly.

'No.' Nicolas resisted the urge to step back. 'Not that I know of.'

'What about hunting? Have you killed an animal? *Par exemple,* a fox or wild boar?'

'No. I like animals. Why should we kill them, unless for necessity? I don't believe in hunting for sport. And so far, I have not needed to kill to eat.'

The colonel grunted. 'Well for you.' He cast up his eyes. 'Just what I need for a cell leader: a man who has never killed anything in his life.'

Nicolas shrugged. 'No, Monsieur. Well ... occasionally, a spider.'

There was general laughter.

The *Résistance* leader frowned them down. He walked up to Nicolas and jabbed a finger at his chest. 'Then you will have to imagine the enemy as a spider: a giant, venomous spider; because I know men, and you are not a killer. I saw it at a glance. It is why I said that you were too soft.' For untold seconds, he held Nicolas's eyes with his own luminous orbs. 'And I still think it. *Eh bien*, it is what you must learn before you can be of use to me.'

Startled and feeling rather sickened, Nicolas was considering this when the man made a sudden move to grab and twist his forearm. Without thinking, he responded as his training demanded; and Colonel Rol found himself on the stone floor looking up at him.

Instantly, there was a forest of deadly pistol muzzles trained on Nicolas. All humour had evaporated from the room. Nicolas stared at the surrounding faces and knew that the accusation their leader had made against him would not apply to any one of them. Each would kill at the given word: willingly. His whole being went into goosebumps.

'Put them away,' said the colonel, leaping to his feet and adjusting his jacket. A satisfied smile curved his lips. 'He's not as soft as I thought. Just not battle ready. *Yet*.' He dusted himself off and thrust out his hand. 'Colonel Rol. Welcome to *la Résistance*, Nicolas de Beaulieu.' He laughed. 'Just make sure that you see a spider when you come upon the enemy.'

Nicolas disregarded this, hearing only his name. 'How do you know me?'

'A young lady told me of you. She felt that you would make a cell leader. Her name is ———'

'Natalie!' Nicolas knew it had to be her.

'Perhaps. She is known to us by her *nom de guerre*: Juliette.'

Nicolas's head was spinning. Natalie had not mentioned a word of her underground activities. How much else did he not know about her?

Colonel Rol met his troubled gaze with understanding. 'She only joined us today, after you left her. She told me that you had made her think. I know her because she is a communist, like me. But we must be secretive. There is a fifth column ready to betray us. I tell you that it is in operation already. You, too, must have a *nom de guerre*. What shall it be?'

'I don't know … I haven't thought.' Nicolas dropped his eyes. One name clamoured in his brain, echoing and re-echoing, drowning out all others. He lifted his head. 'My *nom de guerre*,' he said, 'is Angel.'

The *Résistance* leader stared at him without blinking. 'Very well,' he replied, at last, 'Angel, you shall be. Whether you belong in heaven or hell, let us hope that you have the required supernatural protection!' He paused. 'By the way, it will not be safe to meet Juliette at the clock. She has agreed to meet you here, in our underground headquarters, every other day at the time you mentioned, beginning the day after tomorrow.'

# 33 OCCUPATION

**23 July 1940**

*Ever since the duc received Gabriel's radio message reporting a development that has compromised Nicolas's safety in Paris, we have been working with everything we have on a rescue plan. If only we can get him close enough to Belvoir, our end is foolproof. Or so I believe. It is the rest of the operation that chills my spine. Our journey has shown us that our beloved France is haemorrhaging to death, with Hitler draining her lifeblood of raw materials and food: one of the hideous terms of our equally hideous surrender. And we are facing a danger so deadly that I dare not even acknowledge it.*

A tall, blond lieutenant colonel swaggered into the Opéra Magique. He had made a stunning rise to power under the new regime, due entirely to being the epitome of the Aryan type approved by the Führer.

'*Bonjour,* Madame,' he said, in an attractive, husky voice. 'Under the terms of the occupation, I will be using the Opéra Magique as my headquarters.'

'But certainly, *mon* colonel. The Opéra Magique will be particularly honoured, *je vous assure.*' Cèline waved her cigarette in its ornate holder. 'I have an apartment that will be perfect for you.'

'That will not be your decision, Madame. You will

show me over the entire building and, I will choose my own living space.'

'Of course, Monsieur. I am at your service, entirely.'

'Thank you, Madame,' he said, flicking his eyes over her in a manner that left her in no doubt of his thoughts: *Too old and ugly to be of use to me.*

Colour flared, just visible in her heavily made-up cheeks. She drew angrily on her cigarette; the sound of her indrawn breath breaking the cold silence.

'I am also looking for Nicolas de Beaulieu.' The officer enunciated the name with distaste.

'Are you?' Cèline glanced at him briefly and flicked ash off the end of her cigarette with a painted fingernail. She kept her eyes on the glowing tip. 'Is it a military secret? Or is one permitted to ask why?'

'It is no secret that he is wanted for treason, Madame. He has also deserted his post in Military Engineering. That alone holds the death penalty. But it is his knowledge of military secrets and the machinery of war that makes him too dangerous to live. There is a price on his head: dead or alive.'

'*Vraiment?* Now, that *is* interesting. *Most* interesting. I regret, infinitely, that I cannot help you, Monsieur.'

'Does he not sing here regularly? I must warn you that you also will be arrested for treason if you are hiding him, Madame.'

She almost laughed in his face but did not dare. Besides, if she played her cards right, she would be rid of Nicolas for good and achieve her life's dream: to be the sole owner of the Opéra Magique. 'I am happy to assist our new masters in any way I can, Monsieur. I believe that I have already made that clear. I assure you that if Nicolas de Beaulieu were here, I would tell you; but I have not seen him for weeks. I, too, am looking for him to make restitution for breaking his contract with this house.'

'And you do not know where he might be?'

'Have you looked for him at the hôtel du Bois?'

'He is not there. The hôtel du Bois has been taken over by one of the German generals.'

'Ah … Then perhaps he has gone to Belvoir. That is not in the occupied zone.'

'Not yet, no.' He stroked his new moustache: an ash-blond copy of the Führer's. 'But it will be. We can move on him, then, if we do not find him before.'

'*Bien.*' Cèline paused to light a new cigarette from the stub of the old one. 'Up until now, de Beaulieu seems to have lived a charmed life. I tried to kill him myself, once, you know.' She drew deeply, exhaling with a little reminiscent smile. 'Well, actually, twice.'

'Eh?' The young officer came to attention.

'Yes. The first time, I was interrupted before I could finish the job … Cigarette?' she asked, indicating the box on the table. At his impatient gesture, she went on, '*Non?* Where was I? Oh, yes: interrupted … By the chauffeur, of all people! It was a spur-of-the-moment thing, you understand. I used a rope around his neck in the style of *le Fantôme de l'Opéra*, but before life was actually extinct, the chauffeur brought him round.' Her chuckle held wry amusement. 'You don't know how many times I have cursed her since! If only she'd been a few seconds late! Of course, the next time, I planned things more carefully: paid someone to kill him. But then, *she* died, instead. Isn't that the most unbelievable bad luck?'

He was looking as incredulous as she could have wished. 'You?' he ground out; his burred tones filled with revulsion. 'It was *you*?'

The countess's eyes widened, and her mouth opened in a soundless scream as the young lieutenant colonel emptied his service pistol into her heart. She threw wide her arms and fell backwards; her cigarette, in its ebony holder, flying out of her hand. The holder rolled in an arc around the top of her head. The cigarette was nowhere to be seen.

The officer's batman came running to stare in horror

at what lay on the carpet and at his master, standing like stone, fury on his face. He watched the blond man kick the lifeless body with the toe of one shining boot, reload his pistol and turn. Unconsciously, he braced himself to face the evil in the glittering deep-blue eyes.

'Clear up this mess.' The officer glanced at him briefly while he rammed the weapon into its holster. 'I am going out.'

The batman shivered, thankful to be released from the expression in the other man's gaze. He called servants to remove the body and clean the carpet. Shocked and terrified into automatons, none of them noticed a cigarette smouldering under the edge of the velvet curtain.

§

'I am sorry, Monsieur,' said the concierge. 'We did manage to put out the fire before the building itself was damaged, but the place will need refurbishing before it is habitable.'

Herr Schmidt-Hesse's arrogant profile showed distress at the blackened and acrid-smelling remains of the countess's avant-garde salon. 'Yes, indeed. We will not be able to perform again until it has been done. I must speak with the Countess Kireyevsky about this.'

'But, haven't you heard, Monsieur?' The concierge fell silent as a uniformed figure entered the salon. He noticed that Herr Schmidt-Hesse's expression had altered to disgust.

The man in uniform smiled and stepped forward. 'The Countess Kireyevsky was executed yesterday for treason, Herr Hesse.' He coughed. 'The fate of all those who oppose the will of the Führer.' He added, as the silence lengthened, 'How do you do, Monsieur? It is quite a while since we last met. A lot of water has passed under the bridge, *n'est-ce pas?*'

'Major l'Abbaye,' said the conductor, clicking his heels. A purple tide rose from his collar into his jowls. 'I did not expect to find *you* here!'

The officer frowned and tapped his epaulette. 'Look again, Monsieur. It is lieutenant colonel. And yes, before you ask, I was the one who delivered justice for the Führer.' He took a Turkish cigarette from a silver case in his pocket and lit it with a matching lighter. 'Seldom have I enjoyed a task more. Unfortunately, since these fools missed a cigarette under the curtain, I have no quarters until this building can be renovated.'

Herr Schmidt-Hesse made no comment; his entire face suffused with purple.

Amusement appeared in the blond man's eyes. He bowed to the infuriated conductor. 'Monsieur, thank you for your most kind invitation. Of course, you can have the joy of accommodating me until the work here is finished, *cela va sans dire*. I should not inconvenience you for long.'

'After what you did; the way you behaved at Villefontaine,' spluttered the conductor, 'do you think that I would give you more than the time of day? Let alone allow you into my apartment building?'

'It will be in your best interests, Herr Hesse, to let bygones be bygones.'

'My name is Schmidt-Hesse. I will thank you to use it when you speak to me,' said the other, in rigid tones.

'I will remember you said that, Herr Hesse. Now, shall we go?'

The conductor's barely controlled rage manifested as a sneer. 'If you think that I would allow you within a stone's throw of Mademoiselle Watson or *my wife*,' he barked, 'you can think again! There is no place in my apartment for the likes of you!'

'I think you will find that you can accommodate me, Monsieur,' purred his companion, moving his hand to his belt. 'Temporarily, of course.'

Herr Schmidt-Hesse found himself looking into the

mouth of a pistol, trained with deadly accuracy. As he watched, it transferred from his forehead to his stomach.

'Do not you?' whispered the man holding it.

'Certainly, Colonel.' The conductor spoke from a suddenly dry mouth.

'I thought so,' said the officer, holstering his pistol. 'I will organise my traps and meet you at home for lunch. I am not especially fussy. Whatever you have will do.' He shouted to his batman, glancing around the fire-damaged ultra-modern furnishings with unconcealed contempt: 'Have this room refurbished in a style more in keeping with its era. I want all trace of that disgusting old whore removed. She has blighted the earth for long enough. Then bring my gear to this gentleman's apartment. He will give you his address.'

§

Gabriel brought the news to Nicolas in the underground. He listened in expressionless silence to the story of the killing of the countess and the subsequent fire that closed the Opéra Magique, then asked a question. 'And the count? Where is he?'

'No-one knows, Monsieur. Some think he has fled to Switzerland, but no-one knows. He could even be dead.'

'He's well out of it, either way,' observed Nicolas, unmoved. It was only when Gabriel told him of Herr Schmidt-Hesse's coerced invitation that he reacted.

'*Mon Dieu!*' he said, leaping to his feet. 'Natalie must be warned! I will have to get her out of there, right now!'

'Wait until tonight, Monsieur. We will arm ourselves and come with you.'

'No! I must go, now, and get her out of there before Gerry moves in. If I am not back with her by nightfall, come after us then.' He didn't stop to explain to them the sense of urgency that drove him. He was consumed by it.

# 34 ENCOUNTER

**25 July 1940**

*The first half of our mission has been a success, and we are
back in Paris. Into the mouth of the wolf! But I must not
think of that—only of the next—the important part: dare I
hope that it will run as smoothly? All I can say is: Someone
is going to get a surprise! I pray to God it isn't us ...*

'*Bonjour,* Madame,' said Gervais, shouldering his way past
Nanette's maid without even a glance. 'I believe I have
some unfinished business with your granddaughter.'

Nanette observed both his uniform and ruthless
expression without appearing to do so: concealing her
sinking heart under an air of polite interest. 'I beg your
pardon, Monsieur, I didn't quite catch your name.'

'That is because I didn't give it. Lieutenant Colonel
l'Abbaye,' he said, dropping his peaked cap on the
hallstand. 'I am staying with Herr Schmidt-Hesse until my
quarters are refurbished. I thought it would be a good
opportunity to catch up with a fellow musician.'

'I am sure it would be, Monsieur, except that my
granddaughter is not here at present,' said Nanette,
mentally crossing her fingers; her gaze holding a limpid
innocence that changed to fear as Natalie came in from
the kitchenette.

'I have just made coffee, Nanette. Will you have some?

… Oh!' She shrank back into the doorway with a little whimper.

'Ah … Mademoiselle Natalie,' said Gervais, reaching her in two strides. 'I believe you and I have an old score to settle, *n'est-ce pas?*'

'No!' Natalie turned to run.

'Oh no you don't!' A heavy hand gripped her shoulder; jerked her around. 'You don't escape me this time!'

Nicolas heard Natalie scream and sprinted from the gate. Leaping through the open doorway, he saw Nanette mouth something urgently. One misshapen hand pointed at the room opposite; the other held out her walking stick. In one bound, Nicolas was in the room, taking in the horror that the old lady had tried to convey to him as he snatched up the proffered weapon.

Gervais had his back to him; his hands around Natalie's throat. Her eyes were wide with terror as she clawed unsuccessfully at his arms. She seemed to grow weaker by the second. Without hesitation, Nicolas raised the walking stick and brought it down on the back of the other man's head. Blood spurted, staining the cropped blond hair and the heavy silver knob, as Gervais fell unconscious to the floor. His assailant dropped his club and sprang for the victim.

Natalie fell into Nicolas's arms. 'Thank God you came,' she whispered. 'I truly thought I was dead.'

'Another half a minute and you would have been,' said Nanette. 'I do not like such close shaves.'

'No, nor I,' said Nicolas. He half-turned as Gervais stirred and groaned.

'Get her out of here,' said Nanette, in a brusque voice he'd never heard from her, 'and finish the job before he comes round.'

'Will you be all right alone, my love?' he asked, setting Natalie on her feet.

'Yes,' she whispered, 'I will be fine.' She touched his face. 'Thank you. I am so *glad* that I'm alive.'

'*Moi aussi*,' said Nicolas, his voice tender. 'Will you go to our meeting place and wait for me there?' He glanced at the man on the floor, and his tone hardened. 'I won't be long.'

'Hurry!' said Nanette, as Natalie vanished from sight. 'You go with her,' she ordered the maid, then glared at her companion. 'Now!'

Nicolas picked up the stick with its bloody silver knob and froze. The enormity of what he was about to do reared before him. He was about to break all the precepts of civilised man: the most hallowed Commandments of Christianity. The raw energy that had surged through him at the sight of Natalie in Gervais's murderous hands seemed to have evaporated. Then Gervais opened his eyes and looked at him—vulnerable, pleading—before passing out again. *I cannot*, he thought in misery and knew within himself that it was true. *This is Gerry! My friend.* He tried to remember the many evil things Gervais had done, tried to think of him as a spider to be crushed, but all he could see in his mind's eye were the entreating eyes of the innocent companion of his childhood, before he'd become what he now was.

*Kill him.* The command came directly from his inner voice.

*I cannot* ... Nicolas's breath caught on a dry sob. *I cannot* ...

*Kill him! Do it! Now!*

Nicolas felt his fingers loosen on the thing that he held in his hand. He wanted to obey Angel but knew that he physically lacked the strength to do it. *I cannot ... I cannot take a life. Especially not Gerry's.*

*You must! You will live to regret it if you don't!*

*No! I cannot!*

'What are you dithering about for?' demanded Nanette, with biting scorn. 'Hit him again! Properly, this time! Go *on*!'

'*Quoi?*' Nicolas's inner turmoil had produced a kind of

shock that temporarily made him forget his surroundings. He looked down at the bloodstained walking stick in his hand as if he didn't know how it had got there.

Gervais moved his head, half-opened his eyes again and muttered.

'You'd better run, then, before he wakes up,' said Nanette, summing up the situation. 'I'd finish him off myself, only I have no strength in my hands.'

Nicolas flinched at the contempt in her voice. 'I am sorry, I ——'

'You won't need that …' The old woman gestured for the walking stick, and he gave it to her. She issued another order in that new, hard voice he'd never before heard: 'Go and find Natalie. Take her far away. If you can keep her safe without killing, well and good. But, if not, you'd better find the stomach for it.'

*She is right.*

Nicolas felt a tinge of guilt at leaving Nanette behind like this. *What if Gerry …?* He hesitated. 'Are you sure that you will not come with us?'

'I am sure. Frau Schmidt-Hesse will be kind to me.' She looked at the unconscious man. *If he lets me live. That remains to be seen.* 'Go on, go! You and Natalie will need all your wits about you. You will not need a millstone like me around your necks, holding you down.' Her eyes softened. *'Adieu, mon fils.* Perhaps it is not such a bad thing to be unable to kill. The problem is, your enemies will not feel the same way about you. Especially not him. He would kill you, like that!' The old lady tried ineffectually to snap her fingers. 'But, *eh bien* …' She shrugged and waved Nicolas away.

Nanette sat in silence, waiting for the blond man to come around. She was glad that she'd already sent her maid away with her granddaughter. There was no point in allowing the risk that he would take reprisals on her. Nanette knew in her heart that he was the type of man that might go to any lengths to revenge himself on those he saw as thwarting his purpose.

With a groan, the man sat up and focused on the old woman in the chair. At first, he looked confused, then fury entered his eyes and his hand groped for his pistol.

'Go ahead,' invited Nanette, a disdainful look in her eye. 'Kill me … If it will make you feel any better.'

For fulminating moments, he glared at her while he fumbled with the pistol holster; then some kind of shame replaced the fury in his eyes, and he rose groggily and staggered out. She held her breath as the man turned back in the doorway, but it was only for a brief moment to pick up his cap. He didn't look at her again.

§

Nicolas slipped into the underground, guilt and self-reproach a filthy covering. *How can I call myself a man if I cannot bring myself to kill? Colonel Rol was right! But why cannot I do it?* It was an actual physical weakness: his mind was telling him to do it; it was just that his body would not obey—became so weak that he could not even lift his arm to direct a blow.

The tall young man strode along the underground corridors tortured by agonised thoughts. *Useless!* He slammed a fist into his other hand. *Useless!* There was no need to spend conscious thought on his direction. To find his way around all the twists and turns of the underground was second nature to him now. Throughout all this mental turmoil his inner voice was uncharacteristically quiet. *I expect Angel is so disgusted with me that he has abandoned me.*

*I haven't. You don't know it yet, but you have made things difficult. Extremely difficult.*

Nicolas shrugged, brushed against an old peasant woman he hadn't noticed and stepped aside with a murmured apology.

ANNE ROUEN

The woman pushed back her shawl and looked up at him. He stopped as if shot. Under the untidy grey hair was a face he recognised.

'*Sette*!' he exclaimed. 'But, can it be?'

'But, of course, *Chéri*. Did I not say that we would see each other sooner than you thought?' She emerged from his hug with an urgent expression. 'Come! We must hurry back to them.'

'Them?'

'Natalie and Armand.'

'Armand is here? Natalie is with Armand?'

'*Oui*. I will explain later. There is no time now.'

They hurried along to the meeting place. Once more, Nicolas was consumed by anxiety.

'Be calm, *mon brave*. We cannot go anywhere until after dark. Early morning, in fact. But we have much to do before then.'

Nicolas saw Natalie sitting with an old hunchback and called her name. She rose at once and came to him, stretching out her hands. 'Oh, Nic! I was so afraid! Is he …?'

'Unconscious.' Nicolas's hands enveloped hers as he smiled at her, almost dizzy with relief. 'He won't be coming after us, just yet. Where is Nanette's maid?'

'I sent her back with instructions to hide until the coast was clear,' replied Natalie, twisting her fingers out of his.

As always, Nicolas instantly released her. 'Yes, she will be needed now that you cannot go back. *Mon Dieu!* Is that who I think it is?' He looked hard at the hunchback and shook with muffled laughter. 'Armand! If you could only see yourself!'

'Don't you laugh,' warned Armand, greeting him with a handshake and a hug. 'You don't know what *she* has in store for you yet.'

Nicolas turned to Lisette and raised an eyebrow.

'We have come to take you both to Belvoir,' she answered. 'But you must be disguised. I don't know what you have been doing, Nicolas, but the whole German army seems to be searching for you!'

'Gerry!' said Nicolas, turning down a corner of his mouth. 'And it will only get worse!'

'Why?'

'Because I couldn't bring myself to kill him in cold blood. He lay there; his eyes pleading. Then he passed out again. I couldn't do it. I'm sorry.' He flushed, dark with shame.

'It doesn't matter, *Chéri*,' murmured Lisette, rubbing his shoulder. 'He is only one of many. We cannot expect to kill them all.'

'I'm glad,' said Natalie. 'The heat of the moment is one thing. Coldly dealing out death is quite another. But, how did he get into such a position of power with the Germans? They've only been here five minutes!'

'He seems to be Hitler's favourite, according to intelligence gleaned by Gabriel,' said Armand. 'I do think it argues some prior complicity with Nazism.'

'Are you saying that Gerry is a traitor?' Nicolas grew suddenly white.

'Possibly. Along with your Uncle Luc.'

'No!'

'Nothing has been proven,' soothed Armand. 'How Gervais came to meet Herr Hitler is debatable, but he does seem to have had an instant effect on the man. It would appear that he is the living image of the Führer's ideal: the so-called master race or Nazi supermen. And, as such, is allowed as much power as the most intrepid of the German generals will dare to limit.'

'*Mon Dieu!*' Nicolas stood there, paralysed. *Was this what you meant?*

*Sadly, no.*

*What, then?*

'Nicolas? Nicolas! Are you all right?' asked Lisette; her face a study of motherly concern.

'Yes. It is just that it is a shock.' His glance locked with

Natalie's. 'But it should not be, should it?'

'No. Not after the way they were talking at Villefontaine last summer. They weren't joking after all.'

'Apparently not.' Nicolas appealed to Armand. 'What about Uncle Chris? He would never ... would he? And what will happen to him if he opposes Luc?'

'He has the job of supplying produce to the occupation headquarters in Paris and surrounds. You need not worry about him. He will keep his head down and do what he can for us.'

'You mean ...?'

'Yes, he is one of us. His *nom de guerre* is *Le Petit Lapin*.'

Natalie smiled. 'Is there any more unlikely a name for such a great bear of a man?'

'Not unless it is *La Rose* or something like that.' Nicolas grinned at the thought.

'Come, you two.' Lisette called them to order. 'Nicolas: help Armand remove his backpack; Natalie: you sit down here. Now, in the backpack: that bag. *Merci*.'

Finally, Armand was no longer a hunchback, the backpack was empty and a peasant family of two old and two young people sat in the underground with a basket and a carpetbag. No-one who saw them would ever connect them with the two striking young musicians or that sweet young couple, the Lemaitres.

'I feel like a clown,' said Nicolas, squinting down at his clothes.

'You look like a scarecrow,' Natalie informed him.

'Thank you. You're not much better.'

'If you're going to say that I look like a frump, it is completely unnecessary.'

'Stop quarrelling, you two!' ordered Lisette.

'Why should they?' quipped Armand. 'They sound just like brother and sister, as we old parents want the *Boche* to believe.'

'There is that,' acknowledged Lisette, with a gapped smile. 'We must be thankful for small mercies.'

Armand nodded, sage-like, adjusted his beret over his bushy white hair and stroked his white flowing beard.

'At least you look the part,' said Nicolas, grinning at him.

Natalie collapsed into almost hysterical laughter.

'Stop being an idiot and put your shoes on!' Lisette nodded to a pair of heavy wooden sabots.

Natalie abruptly became serious. 'Sorry, I don't know why I am laughing. Nothing about our situation is humorous. Shoes? Are they ... shoes?'

'Yes, and you are going to have to learn to walk in them. Help her, Nicolas.'

'Come on, Cinderella. Try them for size.' Nicolas knelt to help her remove her brogues and place her feet in the shoes. 'Hardly a glass slipper ...'

'Don't try to be funny ...'

'Quietly!' admonished Lisette. 'Or you'll have the Gestapo down on us.'

'Oh ...' gasped Natalie, taking an experimental step. 'How on earth am I ever going to be able to walk in these?'

'Slowly, at first,' said Lisette with a twinkle.

'Blisters,' pronounced Armand, holding up a heavy workboot. 'That is what is going to happen to me in these.'

'Likewise,' agreed Nicolas, taking rueful stock of his footwear.

'I can't do it,' complained Natalie. 'If I have to run, I'll be flat on my face.'

'Persevere,' advised Lisette. 'At least it will disguise your walk. That is the one thing that will give away your identity, no matter what else we do.'

'My walk? What about my walk?' asked Natalie, in hurt tones.

'It, ahem ... has character, doesn't it, Nicolas?' said Armand.

'I would know you anywhere from your walk,' affirmed Nicolas, 'however far away from me you were.'

'Are you saying that I walk like a man?'

'Yes … *No!* No, no, of course not! You walk as if you are striding through the wide outback. Gracefully, of course.'

'Unconstrained: without a care in the world,' added Armand, trying to soothe the tension in the atmosphere.

'Hmm … Well, not any more: I now hobble along like an old French peasant!'

'*Très bien,*' said Lisette, unimpressed. 'It might just save your life.'

'Shall we go?' Armand tapped his watch. 'Time is passing, and we must allow for … the unexpected.'

'Yes, it will take quite a while to get to where we're going, I think.'

'You're telling me!' Natalie made a wry face as she tried to walk a straight line in the wooden sabots. 'I feel like a drunk.'

'And where *are* we going?' asked Nicolas, smothering a laugh at Natalie's ungainly attempts.

'Patience, *mon brave,*' said Lisette, handing him the basket. 'You two just follow Armand. I will bring up the rear.'

# 35 THE CORRIDOR

**26 July 1940**

*We travel in fear, not knowing who are our enemies and
who are our friends. These escape routes out of Paris and
occupied France for those of us who refuse to surrender
are known as corridors. They have to keep changing as the
fifth columnists find us out and drag the guides off to be
tortured. These Gestapo torturers are so good at their job
that, however strong a man thinks he might be, very few fail
to give away all that they know. Many are found out and
killed in this way. It is only limited by each of us knowing
only a few links in the chain. Our beloved countryside has
become an alien landscape: deadly, terrifying.*

'How much farther?' whispered Natalie. 'These wretched
wooden shoes are absolute *murder*.'

'These workboots are not much better; I assure you.'

'Too true.'

'Hush!' whispered Lisette. 'Stand still! Can you hear
that?'

In the silence, everyone could hear it: the sound of
marching boots behind them, coming ever closer.

'Now,' breathed Lisette, 'just do what I do, and leave
me to do the talking. Act as if you are asleep.' She slumped
into a squatting position against the wall, eyes closed, head
on arms. The others followed.

The tramping boots came around the corner and stopped. A guttural voice shouted, 'Hey, you, Peasant! Wake up! What are you doing here?' The soldier prodded Lisette with his rifle. 'Will you answer? Or do I shoot you now?'

'No, no, Monsieur! *Mais non, s'il vous plaît!*' The old woman's gap-toothed smile held a kind of gamine charm—sweet yet maternal—not lost on the German soldiers who were all young and secretly missed their mothers.

The officer held out his hand. 'Your papers, quickly.'

'Of course, Monsieur,' replied the woman, delving into a pocket in her apron. While the officer frowned over the documents in the torchlight, she gently shook her family awake and said, 'We are waiting for our lift to the fields to gather the fruits and vegetables for your meals, Monsieur. If you shoot us …' She shrugged. 'Your chef will not be happy. You will like some nice fresh *pommes de terre et petits pois* and some delicious juicy strawberries, *hein?*'

'If you say so, old woman.' The officer appeared satisfied with the papers and handed them back. 'Go and wait on the side of the road, then, if you are waiting for a vehicle.'

'No, Monsieur, I beg you.' Fear chased the smile from the old woman's eyes. 'We are afraid that we will be shot.'

'No-one will shoot you, unless it is me,' said the officer in painstaking French. '*I* will shoot you if you remain here, contravening orders. Now go, before I change my mind!'

'*Oui*, Monsieur. Thank you, Monsieur.' The peasant woman turned, picked up her basket and looked back to give a cheeky rejoinder: 'Be sure to enjoy your dinner tonight, Messieurs.' She spoke to her family in patois, unmistakably passing on the soldier's orders.

'You make sure you work hard to pick the best and freshest for us, old woman. What is the matter with your daughter? Still asleep, eh?' The soldier nudged the tottering figure from behind with the point of his rifle. 'Go on. Go along, do as your *mutti* tells you.'

Head down and crimson-faced, Natalie hobbled away in the wake of the others, followed by the catcalls and coarse laughter of the soldiers as they continued their patrol. Nicolas clenched his hand on the basket Lisette had just handed to him but kept his eyes on the ground.

Now the fugitives had no option but to come out into the open on the road. Above the buzzing in their ears from both fear and relief, they heard the faint growl of a truck engine. The laden truck roared past and swung off the road into a small copse.

'*Vite! Vite*! Run!' gasped Lisette, setting off after it.

'But … that's Uncle Chris!' exclaimed Nicolas, taking Natalie's arm and almost carrying her as he broke into a jog.

'I told you he would help us,' said Lisette, looking back at them.

Christian de Villefontaine greeted his nephew with a suspiciously moist eye, but was otherwise his inarticulate self. He let down the tailgate, pulled out some baskets of vegetables to reveal space behind them beneath the layers of other baskets. 'Hurry, crawl in there. Ladies first. That's it. *Bien*.'

Nicolas and Armand helped the two women climb into the darkness, then followed, adjusting themselves to fit into the cramped space as much as possible.

Christian thrust in the laden baskets, slammed shut the tailgate, leapt into the driver's seat and roared back onto the road.

'Good Lord!' moaned Armand, trying to brace himself against a metal frame.

'Oh,' gasped Nicolas, 'I knew these trucks were rough, but I never knew they would shake your bones loose!'

'Don't be such a big sook!' said Natalie, sliding her feet out of the hateful sabots and leaning back against him. 'You should be grateful to get off your feet. I know I am!'

'Count your blessings,' said Lisette, 'however small

you may think they are. It is probably the only part of our journey where we can possibly feel safe.'

Nicolas moved to make more room for Natalie, offering his shoulder as a pillow. 'Is this history repeating? What was that you once said? Something about a load of cabbages?'

'About your ancestor in the French Revolution? I didn't say it: you did.'

'No, no, you were the one who said it. Most definitely. I only mentioned the *Scarlet Pimpernel*.'

'Now, now, children, don't squabble. Besides, this load is lettuce and tomatoes.'

'Mmm, I can smell the tomatoes,' said Natalie.

'And cucumbers,' remarked Armand, removing one from the small of his back.

'Armand will tell you sententiously that those who do not read history are doomed to repeat it,' said Lisette.

'In the famous words of whom?' asked Nicolas.

'I don't know.'

'Numerous historians, I should think,' said Natalie.

'Drumming up business for themselves?'

'Cynic.'

'I don't think it matters one way or the other,' said Lisette. 'Some of us have read it and some haven't. But we all seem doomed to repeat it.'

'Spoken with the typical common sense of the Frenchwoman,' said Armand. 'It was George Santayana—the Spanish philosopher—and what he actually said was, "Those who cannot remember the past are condemned to repeat it."'

There seemed to be no answer to that, and they all fell silent, since it was becoming too difficult to speak over the rattling of the truck and the noise of the engine.

The rough trip went on and on; the smell of tomatoes overpowering. Natalie and Nicolas could not help but feel that Lisette's interpretation was probably the correct one. It only took one man of power who had not learnt from history to plunge the whole world into war.

'Oh ...' moaned Natalie, suffering a cramp in one foot. 'Will this trip go on forever? Don't answer that!' she added hastily.

The others chanted, 'No, it only seems like it!'

Finally, the truck turned down an even bumpier track, jolting them unmercifully as it halted.

'What now?' murmured Nicolas.

'The end of the line, if I am not mistaken,' said Armand.

They blinked in the sudden light as Christian let down the tailgate and pulled out the baskets. He peered into the cavity. 'All right, in there?' At the wry laughter, he helped them out. '*Je regrette* ... But it is the only way.'

'I know, *mon brave*,' said Lisette, 'and we are truly grateful.'

'*De rien!*' negated the big man, red-faced. He shuffled and said, 'This is as far as I can take you without giving ourselves away. We must be quick.' He and the men shoved back the baskets, shut the tailgate. 'Hear that?' he asked, as an engine droned. 'That way,' he said, pointing into the forest. 'There is a barn on the other side of the trees. To the right of the door is a hidden cellar under the first manger. Wait there until dark, and a guide will come. Go!' he said, as the growl of a heavy lorry was suddenly louder. 'Don't come back, no matter what you hear!'

They sank down in a thicket and waited, hearts thumping as Christian turned to greet the truckload of German soldiers with a respectful smile. Listening with their hearts in their mouths to his jolly answer to the clipped question of the driver: 'I was caught short, Monsieur. Needed to, um, water my horse, as they say. I am about to deliver these vegetables to the commandant.'

A further short exchange, a cheerful salute and both trucks went on their way.

The four in the thicket expelled their breaths. Christian would not be made to pay for his kindness.

Release of tension affected them all in different ways. The silence lengthened.

'First a vegetable truck and next a manger,' joked Nicolas, stretching. '*Hélas*! What have we come to?'

'We've come to save your miserable hide and you ought not forget it!' blazed Armand, shaking with uncharacteristic anger.

'*Doucement, Chéri*,' said Lisette, putting her arm around him, as the other two stared in amazement.

'I'm sorry,' he muttered, looking at the ground, distressed. 'I don't know what came over me.'

'Nerves,' said Lisette. 'It is understandable, *je vous assure*. Come, *mon cher*, it is over.'

'No, Armand is right!' Nicolas went to put an arm around each of them. 'Believe me, *mon ami*, I have not forgotten! Forgive me, I cannot tell you how much I appreciate what you and Settie have done for me—or that you ought not to have done it—because there are no words ... So, I thought of what Ernesto would say if he were here. But the enormity of what we are facing! Better to try not to think of it ...'

'A light heart makes a lighter step,' acknowledged Lisette, in the ensuing silence. 'And we have many to make.'

'Can I change my shoes?' asked Natalie, in a small voice. 'That would lighten mine.'

Her words defused the emotion-charged atmosphere. Armand rummaged in the carpetbag to hand out their walking shoes, and they changed into them with sighs of relief.

'We must stay under the canopy of the forest,' said Lisette. 'And there must be no sound, lighthearted or otherwise.'

'And if you hear a Stuka, you must hug the bole of a tree,' added Armand. 'Come along, Children! As your mama has said, from now on, we must be silent.'

It was as if his aberration had never been.

§

The cellar was clean, dry and spartan. A stone shelf held a covered jug of water, a box of matches, a lantern, and a pile of tin mugs and plates. A basket containing bread, cheese and a bottle of wine stood on a small wooden table with bench seats. Four lumpy paillasses were stacked against the opposite grey stone wall. Armand lit the lantern while Nicolas went back to close the trapdoor, ran down the stone steps, barred the heavy wooden door at the bottom, and pulled out a bench seat for Natalie and Lisette.

The silence was oppressive, but they dared not advertise their presence, adopting a combination of mime and hand signals to express wants and needs. Lisette and Natalie handed out bread and cheese; Lisette having found a napkin-wrapped knife in the bottom of the basket, while Armand and Nicolas poured wine and water into the tin mugs.

Though they had no words, their expressions said it all: a baronial feast could not have tasted better than the simple meal of bread, cheese and *vin du pays,* liberally diluted with water. Even the lumpy mattresses that Armand and Nicolas spread out on the floor felt comfortable after what they had been through as they dozed throughout the long afternoon; although, they would later swear that they could still feel the swaying of the truck.

Finally, the darkness above ground matched that in the cellar. They heard the trapdoor lift, extinguished the lantern, and waited in tense silence for the knock and the required password. When it was given, Nicolas unbarred the door.

Their guide, framed in the doorway, was clothed from head to foot in black; his face darkened with charcoal.

'Blacken your faces,' he said, handing Lisette a tin,

'and follow me closely, or you will lose me in the dark. If the enemy comes upon us, I will disappear and you will not know enough about where you are going to give away our secrets.'

'Well, of course, we would not ...' began Natalie, indignantly, falling silent as Nicolas grasped her wrist and Lisette spread blacking on their faces.

'You mean: we could be tortured?' he asked.

'*Oui*, that is what I mean. All finished?' he asked, reaching for the tin. 'We must go. No talking.'

# 36 A LONG WALK

**10 August 1940**

*We have walked night after night, hiding by day in barns and cellars belonging to good folk whom we must not know for all our sakes. Our feet, even in our good brogues, are covered in blisters. Every night we have a different guide. He (or she) takes us to a hiding place and melts away into the darkness. Good people, whom we cannot thank, for their own safety, leave us food and drink.*

*Even though I was sure I knew the way home, travelling in darkness disorients me. Landmarks we memorised are not visible at night and stumbling with blind trust through forests behind taciturn guides too afraid to speak can be unnerving, to say the least.*

*Right now, I really do not know where we are. Surely, soon, we must find some feature, either natural or man-made, that we recognise?*

A knock came; the passwords were exchanged. Nicolas unbolted the barn door and looked into the first familiar face he had seen throughout the whole long and torturous journey.

'*Bienvenu*, Monsieur. I have come to take you home.'

'*Gabriel!* Thank God! I don't know when I've ever been

more pleased to see your face. Is it …? Can it be over?'

*No. It is just beginning …*

'Almost, Monsieur. Just one more night, perhaps two if we are unlucky. They will be looking for you at Belvoir: spies, fifth columnists.' he spat. 'Traitors! We must take the face of the mountain.'

'At night? Without a torch? What about Sette and Natalie? It is far too dangerous!'

'Monsieur, believe me, the face of the mountain is the least of the dangers that face you and Mademoiselle Natalie.'

'It is true, *mon brave*,' said Lisette. 'It is why we came to get you. We have prepared ourselves for the mountain. Armand and I know every boulder. We could do it blindfolded. Come!'

The paths they trod would have been familiar in daylight, but Nicolas could find no point of reference in the dark shapes of his surroundings. Near the foot of the mountain, he recognised a looming boulder in the faint starlight and, from then on, had no trouble swinging in behind the others to begin the climb, always holding out a hand to Natalie and indicating where she should place her foot.

In contrast, Lisette took the path like a gazelle, only pausing for the others to catch up. Nicolas couldn't see her face, but he didn't need to. He knew it held a sweetly triumphant expression.

At last, after climbing boulder after boulder, a black mouth yawned in front of them, and they entered the first cave.

'Now I really do know where I am,' whispered Nicolas, sliding behind hanging vines into a narrow niche. 'Follow me.'

'Can we risk lighting the lantern?' asked Armand.

'Not yet.' Gabriel took out a hooded torch. 'Not until we get to the far wall.'

Nicolas went ahead to the stalactite forest, found and

lit a lantern, and waited for the others, smiling at Natalie's muffled exclamations. Then he led them to the passage, glancing, out of habit, at the stone block on the archway. It was no longer depressed. In fact, it bulged. 'The mechanism is activated?' he exclaimed. 'What …?'

'Of course it is.' Gabriel gave him an indulgent smile. 'We don't want *les Boche* stumbling upon us, do we?'

'But, the girls …'

'You're right,' said Armand. 'It wasn't activated when we left. Mesdames, a quick lesson. Stand well back against the wall. Nicolas, a boulder, *s'il vous plaît*. That big one over there will do nicely, thank you.' He walked over into the middle of the passage, as the duc had done, and dropped it onto one end of a large flagstone. '*Et voilà!*'

Lisette was obviously prepared to some degree and only gave a little gasp, but Natalie could not suppress a shudder as the flagstone spun soundlessly on its pivot, and they waited for the splash far below.

'And that's not all …' said Nicolas, taking Natalie's hand in a comforting hold.

'*Mon Dieu*, it is enough!' said Lisette. 'But I have also heard about the door of death.'

'Do you mean that there are more of these medieval horrors?' exclaimed Natalie. 'I don't think I can ——'

'Who is being a sook now?' asked Nicolas, leading her past the booby-trapped flagstone to shine his lantern on a nailed door. 'Are you doing the honours, Armand?'

'Just as soon as I find a stone,' agreed Armand, picking one up to toss against the latch. 'Now watch!'

'But that's … *barbaric!*' whispered Natalie, as the door opened and the bar swung down out of the roof, swished through the opening and back again. '*Truly!* Where *do* they get these things!' She shivered.

'Come away and look here,' said Nicolas, reaching into a crack in the rock. 'This is the *real* door to our underground city.'

He and Armand pulled out the massive rock door, and

Gabriel stepped inside to shine his powerful torch around the enormous cathedral-like chamber.

'Oh, my Lord! How beautiful!' Natalie's eyes filled with tears. 'I thought the other one was amazing, but I have never seen anything so exquisite as this.'

'The Cavern of the King's Mantle,' said Nicolas. 'Can you see why?'

'It is glorious, *mon brave*,' said Lisette, leading the way across the cavern and into the main tunnel, 'but Natalie must explore it another day. Time is short and Armand and I must soon go.'

'Why? Where are you going?'

'Armand and I have been away in St Tropez. We are coming home tomorrow in the Compressor. Therefore, we must get to Gap before morning, where we have it hidden … in a barn. From there we will drive up to the front door of the château. In grand style, of course.' Lisette gave him a mischievous glance. 'We had to explain our absence somehow: a second honeymoon on the *Côte d'Azur*.'

There was a moment of silence. Then, the four of them collapsed into laughter.

'You'd better have dinner first,' said Gabriel; the only one with a straight face. 'Monsieur le duc is waiting, alone. There must be no whisper that Monsieur Nicolas is anywhere near Belvoir. He knows this, but is anxious to see him this once.'

'Of course he is!' exclaimed Lisette. 'He will have been so worried.'

'Fifth columnists,' said Nicolas. 'Would there possibly be any in Belvoir? I could hardly think it.'

Gabriel shrugged. 'Nobody knows, Monsieur. One thing is certain: they are around, as *la Résistance* can attest, to their sorrow.'

'I have heard of these traitors,' said Natalie, her eyes flashing contempt. 'But why are they called fifth columnists? It seems like a silly name to me.'

Nicolas shrugged. 'I don't know. Ask Armand.'

'Some general or other in the Spanish Civil War said he had four columns of soldiers with him, and a fifth-column would rise up to fight with them in the city he was to attack,' said Lisette. 'I know that much. Is that not right, Armand?'

'General Mola,' confirmed Armand. 'He lost that battle.'

§

The duc rose from a throne-like chair at the head of a magnificent oval table to make an emotional reunion with his grandson, striding across the huge vaulted space to meet him as he emerged from the passage. '*Eh bien, mon fils*, I am overjoyed to see you.'

'*Moi aussi*, Grand-père, *je vous assure!* There were times when I thought it was not going to happen,' said Nicolas, returning his embrace with a wry smile.

'I have you two to thank,' said the duc, clasping first Armand's hand followed by Lisette's as he struggled to speak, then turned to Gabriel. 'And you, too, old friend. Words cannot …'

'*De rien*, Monsieur!' Armand turned a dull red.

'We did it for love, Monsieur,' Lisette assured him. 'But we are also glad to be here.'

The secret agent nodded.

'Yes,' the duc smiled. His social address took over, and he turned to the tall young woman waiting to greet him. He saw that she was stunned by her surroundings, glancing around with widening eyes. 'Natalie, my child,' he said, reaching out to her. 'I am delighted that you have changed your mind and decided to come to us, after all.'

'Thank you, Monsieur. The decision was rather made for me,' said Natalie with a wry smile. 'I would not be here at all if it weren't for Nic,' she added, taking the duc's outstretched hand and blinking back a sudden rush of tears. 'I am sorry. So silly of me …'

'*Eh bien*, my child, it is over now. Come to the table,' he said, steering her gently towards it.

'Oh!' Natalie gasped, staring at the heavily laden table in the vast man-made cavern. 'I have never seen such a splendid feast! If it wasn't solid rock, the table would be positively creaking!' She managed a laugh. 'You look like a medieval king presiding over a royal banquet.'

'I thought you might be hungry,' said the duc with a twinkle.

'Did …?' queried Gabriel, looking at the array of dishes in astonishment.

'Your men, yes,' affirmed the duc. 'We discovered quite a bit of culinary talent amongst us. Jean-Marie in particular. I have put him in charge of the kitchen.'

'That will make one less to gather intelligence,' said Gabriel, grimacing in resignation.

'Not necessarily,' said the duc. 'Food is not the only thing he will be gathering when he goes out with his basket. Besides, I will do my share from my secret tower.'

'You must be careful, Grand-père.'

'Pooh!' said the duc. 'I hate to say it, but you look like a group of street urchins. Perhaps a wash before dinner?'

'Oh, yes please!' said Natalie.

'I will show you the amenities,' said Lisette. 'It is a shame that Armand and I will have to put the blacking all back on again after dinner.'

'Ah, that looks better,' said the duc, when they returned. 'Now we can celebrate. Sit down everyone and eat. Nicolas, you may seat Natalie here next to me. I apologise for the hardness of the stone benches, my dear. One cannot be gentlemanly and pull them out to seat a lady, either.' He reached for a wine bottle. 'I will pour you all a drink. Only a little for Armand and Lisette. They have a very busy night ahead of them. The rest of us will be able to sleep it off in true medieval style.'

Nicolas carried out his bidding and disposed himself on Natalie's left. Gabriel sat on the duc's right at his command, and Lisette and Armand occupied the remaining places.

'Raise your glasses to France!' commanded the duc, holding up his goblet; the ruby-red wine glowing in the soft light. 'To freedom and justice!'

'To France: to freedom and justice!' they echoed.

For a moment, the wine in the uplifted glasses looked like blood to Nicolas, and he suddenly felt nauseated—as if it were a prophecy of what they would have to go through to get those commodities they so boldly proclaimed. *I cannot drink it,* he thought. But then knew that he must. For whatever was in the cup that would give them those essentials, he knew that they had to drink it. His sudden tremor of fear made the liquid shake in his glass and the spell was broken. Suddenly the wine was full of translucent light—a bright jewel—a symbol of hope for the future. He drank and was immediately hungry. When a hand nudged his arm, he turned to smile at Lisette and take the piece of chicken she was offering.

'It is hunger and exhaustion, *Chéri,* the nausea,' she whispered with an understanding smile. 'It will go away when you eat something.' She spoke encouragingly to Natalie, ate a little herself and tied up some bread, cheese and roast meat in a napkin. In a little while, she caught Armand's eye and rose from the table. 'We must go now. See you tomorrow, *hein?*'

Nicolas said goodbye to his protectors, fearing in his heart, as always, that he would not see them again.

Jean-Marie came in with a fruit pie, and the duc invited him to sit and eat, asking, 'Where are the other three?'

'Gone with the Lemaitres,' replied the agent. 'They ate in the kitchen, earlier.'

'Ah,' said the duc, 'a good thing. Pass Natalie the roast duckling. It is excellent, *mon brave.* You are a formidable chef.'

Throughout the meal, the duc talked softly to Gabriel, nodding at his replies, occasionally smiling at his dinner guests but obviously preoccupied.

'How are you holding up?' Nicolas asked Natalie, *sotto voce*. 'Another helping of pie?'

Natalie started, 'No thank you. I am so full! I cannot believe this place,' she whispered. 'My eyes are on stalks!'

'I noticed,' said Nicolas. 'It is not often that I am able to impress you.'

'Take a bow, Monsieur,' she murmured. 'Because you have now. Oh, Nic: I am *so* tired.'

'I know. The wine and the meal after what we have been through. Excuse me, Grand-père. Have you …?'

'Your sleeping arrangements? Of course!' said the duc, rising from the table. 'Wait here, Messieurs, I will not be long. Come along, Nicolas, Mademoiselle.'

'Have I offended you, Monsieur?'

'But certainly not! Why?'

'I was Natalie just now …'

'The habits of a lifetime, *ma fille*.' He looked at her closely. 'Oh, a joke: I see. It is commendable that you are in such good spirits. Nicolas, you will have the apartment that I envisaged for you. And we have been very busy with the other rooms. Armand and Lisette will have these two if it becomes necessary, and Natalie will have this one,' he said throwing open doors as he spoke and halting in the arched doorway of Natalie's room. 'The amenities are at the end of this passage on the right.'

'Thank you,' said Natalie. 'Lisette showed me when we washed the blacking off. This room looks super! A welcoming fire—in a brazier, it is true—a hipbath, a comfortable bed. It is better than the Ritz. What more could a girl ask?'

'What indeed?' said the duc, looking on her with approval.

'Only a warm bath. Does that thing work?' she asked,

pointing at the enamel structure.

'After a fashion,' said Nicolas. 'I'll bring some buckets of hot water. It may take some time,' he added, striding away.

'Fill the cauldron on the range in the kitchen,' the duc called after him, then turned to address Natalie: 'Lisette put some clothing for you in the armoire and decorated the room before she left to bring you here.'

'But ... she didn't know I was coming!'

'No ... Sometimes, I wonder,' said the duc. 'But she said, "Just in case!".'

'Oh, she is an angel! Do you know, this is turning out to be the most splendid adventure!'

'What a brave little trouper you are, my dear! A woman of courage,' said the duc. 'I met your father during the last war. Permit me to say that you are like him in that you have the ability to make light of a very serious situation. It is a gift.'

'It sometimes gets me into trouble. A lot of people take life very seriously and resent jokes being made. It is a curse, sometimes. But when things get bad, I can't help but see a funny side.'

'It is a very Australian characteristic, that: to laugh in the face of death. You are gallant, my dear. You will be good for Nicolas. He is inclined to become a little too emotional over life. Too caring, perhaps, for his own good.'

'There's nothing wrong with that!' she flashed before she could stop herself. 'I'm sorry, I ...' She waited for the Victorian disapproval shown by men of the duc's generation to such outbursts by young women.

'*De rien, ma fille!*' he murmured; a strange expression passing over his features. 'You are loyal. I think that you and Nicolas will suit each other admirably.'

'But ...' Natalie fell silent. She didn't understand the expression in his eyes. *Could it possibly be relief? But why? Did he not know that there was no 'Natalie and Nicolas'? Or had he merely chosen to ignore it?*

'Goodnight, my dear. I hope we have been able to make you comfortable.' The duc was smiling as he walked away. In his wide experience, one did not leap to the defence of someone who meant nothing.

Natalie paced about her room. Nicolas loved her. She saw, every time she looked into his eyes, that she was 'the one'. The one who held his thoughts to the exclusion of all others; the one who filled his entire being. The duc was erroneously supposing that she returned this regard. He must be made aware of his mistake.

She clenched her hands. *Why don't I trust? Why am I unwilling to enter a relationship with one who loves me so much?* She stood still, biting her lip. *Have I become arrogant in the knowledge that whatever I do to Nic, he stays with me? That no matter how I treat him, he is there waiting?*

Her face worked. She knew that she hurt him often. She hated herself for doing it, but something drove her that she could not control.

*I want to be free! I must be free!* But she wanted Nicolas to be there, too. The power of knowing that, when she looked into his eyes, she saw that she was the most important thing in his life. *How despicable I am,* she thought. *I want everything and give nothing.*

She stamped over to the armoire, dragged out an embroidered cotton nightdress without the least gratitude to Lisette's thoughtfulness and threw it on the bed; her lovely features marred by a scowl. *Tomorrow, I will show Nic that being in this place with him does not mean that he can expect anything other than friendship from me. I must be free! I will be free!*

When Nicolas came with the water, poured it in her bath—making sure it was not too hot—and went to take her hands and kiss her goodnight, she turned her head away.

Nicolas's heart sank. As he wished her a goodnight, closed her door and set off down the corridor with the empty buckets, he held no resentment that she had failed to thank him for bringing her bath water—just felt tired and as depressed as he ever had.

To lighten his despondency, he told himself that Natalie, too, was tired; that tomorrow she would greet him with love in her eyes.

§

Natalie's eyes flashed as she read the note from the duc that accompanied the priceless Stradivari that had just been handed to her by Gabriel, with apologies for waking her.

*It worries me,* had written the duc, *that you have nothing to practise on and no possible accompaniment except the harp.* Natalie glanced at the zither and accordion that had just been placed on her sofa and continued to read: *I trust that these instruments will enliven your days of forced incarceration. There is no need to thank me, as Monsieur Lorraine, who owns them and wants them kept in a place of safety, is happy for them to remain in use rather than in storage with the portraits. In fact, he has asked that you play the Stradivari as a favour, to keep it in good working order.*

Natalie sighed; her frown clearing. The duc had taken the wind out of her sails as, no doubt, he had meant to. How could she possibly refuse the opportunity to play such a priceless instrument as a Stradivari under the terms the duc had offered?

Of course, such a precious violin must have a safe place to hide in wartime. And it must be taken care of. Her fingers itched to take it up, but she determined to play it only in private. Monsieur Lorraine had been a music teacher for as long as she had known him, but now he spent his days under a bright light with a green eyeshade, etching tools and a small printing press. Monsieur Lorraine was their resident forger: his mind oppressed with the plight of all those hunted by Nazis. He came and went at all hours with a harassed expression on his face and papers sewn into the linings of his hat and coat to save those he could. It was the least she could do to care for his precious instrument for him.

Natalie knew that she should go and look for some breakfast and face Nicolas, but she set down the violin beside the other instruments and sat for a long time, brooding. It didn't matter whether or not Nicolas knew she had it. He would not be given another chance to get at her through their music! With an expression of fierce determination, she rose and went to the door.

§

'Good morning,' said Nicolas, greeting Natalie with his attractive smile. 'Did you sleep well?'

'Good morning. Yes, thank you,' she replied, seating herself at the dining table. 'If it is morning?'

Nicolas glanced at his wristwatch. 'Yes, it is. Just. Half past eleven. But I take your point. We either have light twenty-four hours a day or complete and utter darkness.'

'I'll take the light,' she said. 'What's in the pot?'

'Something that is supposed to pass for coffee. May I?'

'Is there tea? I'd love a cup of tea.'

'I'll ask.' Nicolas excused himself and disappeared through a door in the opposite corridor. He was back in an instant. 'Jean-Marie has some China tea-leaves. How do you like it?'

Natalie leapt up; her eyes aglow. 'Oh. I'll make it, can I? At home, when we're camping, we make it in a billy, you know, something like a soup carry can: a cylindrical container with a handle over the top. Once the water is boiling, we throw in a handful of tea-leaves, a couple of gumleaves and bang it with a stick. Then, after a few minutes, it gets nice and black; and we drink it.'

Nicolas pulled a face. 'It sounds poisonous.'

'Not with lots of sugar, it isn't. It is refreshing. Just what I need today.'

'Well, in that case,' said Nicolas, 'come with me. We will see whether Jean-Marie can accommodate us with a suitable container—if he does not possess a billy.'

He led the way into a cavern that was partially man-made. Above an open fireplace—festooned with various sized spits, trivets and hanging chains—and the adjoining monstrous range was a huge natural cavity, like a tall open chimney, which naturally drew the smoke upwards, keeping the air fresh and clean.

At a wide stone bench, the man who'd brought the dessert to them last night was beating eggs in a bowl. Bending a listening ear to their request, he told them to look on the shelf for an army-issue container that was close to what they wanted.

Natalie scooped it up with a little crow of delight; Nicolas filled it with water and, at her direction, placed it on a trivet over the coals. When the moment came, she threw in the tea, watching it roil around for a minute. Her eyes asked so eloquently for the chef's long-handled wooden spoon that he handed it over without a word.

Nicolas put it under the handle and lifted the billy onto the hearth. 'Is it *de rigueur* to bang it with a stick?'

'Of course. To settle the leaves. Like this,' she replied, taking the spoon from him to rapidly tap the side of the container.

'Oh.'

'Now, we can drink it,' she said, allowing Nicolas to carry it over to the kitchen bench. 'Will you have a cup, Jean-Marie?'

'No, thank you, Mademoiselle. I am not a tea drinker.'

'Do we have any sugar?'

'No sugar.' He shook his head in vexation. 'The Germans have taken everything. Everything! They are like voracious ants! There might be some honey on the shelf. Belvoir has its own hives, fortunately. Or it would

353

be like everything else. Impossible to get. Cursed Germans. But there is no use griping.' He straightened his shoulders and smiled at them. 'Why don't you take your tea out to the dining table, and I will bring your omelettes in a few minutes. The cups are out there. I cannot concentrate with you two under my feet.'

'But it is only omelettes,' said Nicolas, rummaging in the pantry shelves for a jar of honey. 'Ah … here we are.'

'Out!' said Jean-Marie, waving a spatula. 'You have forgotten that I am only an agent, not a chef, and I need to concentrate. A very simple dish but notoriously difficult to perfect.'

Nicolas poured the tea and waited for Natalie to drop a generous spoonful of honey in each cup.

He stirred his pensively with a crested silver spoon.

'What are you thinking?'

'Honestly?'

'Honestly.'

'I was thinking …' He gave a little deprecating smile. 'That it looks a fairly vile brew, to me.'

'Really?' Natalie took a deep breath, then a sip. 'Mmm, heavenly. Taste it. I just wish that I had some gumleaves. Then it would be perfect.'

Nicolas took a sip and grimaced. He felt as though his cheeks were being sucked inward and dried out. 'I will have to take your word for that!'

Natalie was distracted by Jean-Marie placing before her a fluffy omelette, flanked by buttered toast wedges and garnished with fresh parsley and coriander. 'Thank you, Chef, that looks perfect.'

'So does mine,' said Nicolas. '*Merci.*'

'*De rien!*' Jean-Marie bowed and went back to his range.

Natalie watched him go, then turned her attention to Nicolas: 'By the way,' she said, studying him with her hazel-green eyes. 'Your grandfather seems to think that we are a couple. Why is that, do you think?'

He shrugged, slicing into his omelette and pausing with a piece on his fork. 'He hasn't said anything to me.'

'Just as long as you realise that being stuck here together in this place does not give you a priority on me!'

'Natalie, please! Are you saying that you think I would use the situation to take advantage of you? You know that I would never do a thing like that.' He stretched out a hand to cover hers. 'Don't you?'

'Yes. I am not saying that. Of course, I am not.'

He took away his hand and sat back. 'Then what are you saying?'

It was her turn to shrug. 'Your grandfather said "you and Nicolas".' She tossed her head; a baleful gleam just visible between narrowed eyelids. 'Just so as you know: there is no "me and you" … Anything like that—if there ever *is* anything like that—must wait until after the war!'

'I love you,' whispered Nicolas; his eyes stricken. 'I told you before that I am willing to wait.' His fork with the piece of fluffy omelette, so beautifully cooked, clattered onto the plate. For all it stirred his appetite, it might as well have been dry leather. Excusing himself from the table, he went out onto the mountainside in the sunlight to take deep breaths of fresh, clear air.

In that moment of reckless abandon, he did not care whether he lived or died. If a Stuka came over, would he duck for cover? Or would he run out into the open, shouting, 'Here I am! What are you waiting for? Shoot me and get it over with!' *Why should I wait until nightfall to get on with this new work? Why not do it now?*

*It is commendable to be brave and reckless, mon fils. You will do well: be lauded for your courage; an inspiration to others. It is another thing, entirely, to be selfishly suicidal. There are many who will need you to stay alive. Including Natalie. Though she does not know it yet. Go back into the shelter of the cave.*

*You are right. Of course, you are right!* Nicolas flushed with shame and turned back towards the cavern.

No sooner had he stepped inside, when an ominous

high-pitched whining filled the air—a million angry mosquitoes—followed by a spine-chilling, continuous rattle as a convoy of Stukas flew over, strafing everything in their path.

Nicolas stood in the semi-darkness for a long time after they went.

*There is intrepid, and there is stupid.*

Nicolas bowed his head. *I know.*

*If you hadn't listened to me, you would be dead.*

*I know ... Merci.*

*De rien! Go out in daylight if you want. Or, more to the point, when you need. Just be sure to listen to my warnings.*

*Eh bien, it is a bargain.*

*Eh bien ...*

Nicolas threw back his head; his misery and overwhelming depression miraculously lifted. He had an enemy to defeat and, with Angel's prescience, he would do it.

# 37 THE CELL LEADER

**3 November 1940**

*This war is changing us all. Nicolas is not himself. He has
shouldered a terrible burden, and it is taking its toll on
him. He seems to have no regard for his own safety and
takes the most jaw-dropping risks. We are so worried about
him and would be even more so were it not for the vigilance
of the duc's secret agents watching his back, as they say.
Sadly, he does not have the support from Natalie that we
both get from Lisette. Natalie seems bent on pushing him
away. Nothing has changed there! I would not have seen
her as superficial and shallow, but it is true that she hurts
him often and does not seem to care. More, her attitude is
almost rebellious, as if she is looking for opportunities to
punish him for bringing her here. A fine sentiment from one
whom we all risked our lives to save! I know Nicolas feels it
deeply, but he says nothing. Just carries on with that grim
look on his face that goes to our hearts. Mine and Lisette's,
that is—not Natalie's. I sometimes wonder if she has one!*

Fairly soon, the fugitives got into a routine. It was as if
they'd always lived in darkness, mainly venturing out at
night. Except for Nicolas: he went out at all hours of the
day and night. He had also commandeered one of the
larger chambers as an operations room where they
congregated when not out in the field. Armand and

Lisette flitted in and out between carrying out their missions and spending time with the duc, who visited only rarely, mindful of the eyes that might be upon him.

Nicolas only saw him on the roof of his secret tower, ever vigilant with his radio, for urgent transmissions and prearranged contact with England if the agents were occupied elsewhere or, for some reason, out of contact. It was time that, in hindsight, Nicolas wished he had valued more.

If the agents were busy and Jean-Marie was called out, as happened more and more, they would find staples of roast meat, cheese, olives and long sticks of crusty bread, from which to help themselves, on a shelf in the massive kitchen.

Lisette, lively and cheerful, was a breath of fresh air, always making a cheeky comment or two before rushing off somewhere. She occasionally took Natalie with her. 'Women's business,' she said, refusing to elaborate. It usually coincided with a need to distract authorities from some rescue or mission being carried out under their noses. Natalie never shirked her duty: the problem was that what she saw as her duty and what Nicolas, as cell leader, wanted her to do were usually vastly different things.

There was so much to do: Messages to be passed along chains of underground fighters, stranded soldiers and airmen needing to be rescued, baskets of food to be left for others, airdrops to be monitored and cleared up before daylight so that the enemy would not find them. So many false papers had to be manufactured and given out to those at risk that Monsieur Lorraine could not keep abreast of it and had to have help. The enemy's progress had to be plotted and monitored for despatch of intelligence to England where the French command had fled. Slowly, the fragmented groups of *Résistance* fighters were turning into an army.

Overlaying it all was the continual threat of betrayal

by fifth columnists: all the more frightening because the friendliest farmer might be an enemy. On the other hand, they might equally be an ally. It was impossible to know. Through losses of many compatriots, those that were left took care not to expose themselves to possible betrayal.

Through his grandfather's vigilance on the radio, Nicolas became involved in the safe passage through the country of a small band of Australian secret surveillance agents working for the Allies. Attached to the Sixth Division that had seen service in North Africa and made its way through Greece, they'd come into France gathering intelligence ahead of the division. They had strict orders not to fire on the enemy, just see what was going on and get out. Their mission was so secret that, if caught, their government would refuse to acknowledge them.

'So, you're the Free French, eh?' had said one of them to Nicolas, with a wry grin, at their first meeting. 'Let me take a look at you. You're the first one we've ever seen.'

'Yeah, we thought you were a myth, didn't we, Ben?'

'That's right, Charlie. We did.'

'Is that so?' said Nicolas with an answering grin. 'No, no. We are here.' He hesitated, becoming pensive. 'It is a little … difficult, Messieurs, to make your mark with only the most basic of weaponry and communication. And even more difficult to decide who is the enemy …'

'Yeah,' said the one called Ben, who appeared to be in charge; although, they seemed to Nicolas to be fairly democratic about it. 'We've already found that out! Our intelligence we send back is all our mob have got to go on. But since we're not supposed to be here, secret service will deny all knowledge of us if we are caught. We are relying on your group to give us safe passage while we gather our info. Ironic, isn't it? We don't exist and you lot are regarded as terrorists. Not a great position to be in, for either of us!'

'No, indeed, Messieurs. You are very right. *La*

*Résistance* are fugitives in their own country. Fugitives trying to help fugitives. But we will do our best.'

'Yeah, appreciate it. Shame the Sixth has had to withdraw. Gets worse, doesn't it?'

Nicolas had to agree.

Pinned down and isolated by deadly Stuka raids, and the division's unexpected recall to Palestine due to the fall of France, the advance surveillance group were cut off, isolated and virtually stranded until they could find a way out. Their radio message having been intercepted by the duc, Nicolas had set up a corridor for their safe exit. He'd managed to get most of them out, one or two at a time. Now there were only two of them still in the country. So far, it had been impossible to do anything but keep them hidden. But any time now, there must be a breakthrough.

As soon as Natalie met them, she had formed a rapport with her countrymen, strengthened by the knowledge that their commander, who'd been cut off from them and had to make his way back alone, was a close friend of her fathers. No-one had heard from him, but his men were sure he'd get safely out of the country. 'He's tough,' said Ben. 'He'll make it.'

Now Nicolas had another worry: Lisette had not come in; no-one had seen or heard of her since yesterday. He and the duc's agents had searched all night. Armand had been out searching for her all day, and after a heated argument with Nicolas, Natalie had joined him.

'You can't keep me locked up!' she pointed out. 'I am not your prisoner.'

To every argument, she returned the same answer. 'No-one will know me. Thanks to Lisette: I look different now.'

It was true. Nicolas studied her with grim concern, noting that the unruly curls had been tamed into two smooth wings of hair framing her face and caught with a hairclip at the nape of her neck. She'd also dyed it mouse brown. She looked slim, but not striking, in her peasant clothing.

'Well?' she pressed him, adjusting her shawl.

Nicolas finally admitted that, from a distance, she would not be recognisable, shrugged his shoulders and went back to sorting the urgent despatches. All the worry and tension was changing him. He felt pressured, as he never had on the stage. He had to finish this as soon as he could so that he could go out and search again.

He heard light, hurried footsteps. *Not another interruption!* Nicolas didn't look up. 'Make your report and go.'

'That is not very friendly, *mon brave.*'

'*Sette!*' He leapt to his feet and crushed her in a bear hug. 'Oh, Sette, I thought you were lost. We have been looking everywhere for you. Where have you been? I thought the *Boche* had you.'

'Not this time, *Chéri*. We were pinned down under air attack and had to lie low in an olive grove,' she explained, shaking her head. 'But I think it will not be long.'

'Then someone else must do it!' he said. 'You have risked your life enough!'

'No, no!' Lisette put an urgent hand on his arm. 'Remember what I told you when you were a child? We are troupers.' She made an adorable moue. 'The show must go on. While my feet point to the ground, I will fight this scourge on our beloved country.'

'I know. But you *must* take care.'

'Like you do?'

Nicolas grinned at this reference to the daredevil exploits he was becoming known for amongst la Résistance. 'Come on. We'll go and see if we can scrounge some coffee.'

'*Bonne chance!*' she said. 'But dandelion and chicory are probably better for us anyway.'

'If you want to sleep, you mean.'

'Nothing short of benzedrine will stop me sleeping tonight,' she looked around as Armand came in; his eyes alight with joy.

'Oh, my love!' he said, holding out his arms. 'I got your message and came as soon as I could.'

'Have some coffee and relax, *Chéri*,' said Lisette, emerging from his embrace. 'Life is too short to worry.'

'Worry! Now, look ——'

'Natalie?' interrupted Nicolas. 'She came in with you?'

'No. She ——'

'She told me she was going to help you search for Sette.'

'She did,' said Armand. 'But when we heard Lisette had escaped and would see us back here, she said she would take some food to the Australians. She will be back soon.'

'You let her go *alone*?' Nicolas dropped his cup on the table.

Armand shrugged. 'I tried to reason with her, but she wouldn't listen.'

The fierce light began to fade from Nicolas's eyes. Did he not know what that was like? But, just the same, Armand showed a lot less concern than he should have. His lips tightened. 'I think … I will just go and meet her.'

§

Nicolas trod softly, taking his time and keeping to the thickest part of the forest. Normally, he looked forward to meeting the Australians; but today he was battling resentment against Armand for not staying with Natalie *and* concern for her safety. The fact that any remonstrance on anyone's part, including his own, would be unlikely to be heeded by Natalie, he ignored; buried beneath a mound of worry.

He reached the abandoned cottage where he'd taken the men and circled around it, staying within the shelter of the trees, all his senses on the alert. His brow wrinkled. There were no signs of life, no sign that Natalie had ever been there and no sign of the two Australian soldiers. Taking three stones from his pocket, a prearranged signal, he stepped out into the clearing and threw them one at a time against the door and stood still.

The silence lengthened. Even the birds were quiet. It was as if the whole forest was waiting. His skin prickling, Nicolas knew he wasn't alone. He swung around as two men detached themselves from the boles of trees on opposite sides of the clearing and came towards him, treading silently on the soft carpet of leaves. They walked with purpose and were slender and wiry. And dangerous.

One of them reached into a pocket. Nicolas knew that he was being stalked and weighed up his next move, wondering fleetingly why Angel had not warned him. Then, as the men emerged from the trees and came into the light, he could see that they were dressed in ragged Australian army uniforms. He relaxed as one of them said:

'Go easy, Charlie. It's the Mad Marquis.'

'Yeah, so it is. That's a relief,' said the other, stuffing a piece of thin cord back in his pocket. 'What's he doing here in daylight?'

They each stepped forward with a right hand thrust out.

'G'day, Mate,' said the taller, dark-haired man Nicolas knew as Charlie.

'Owyer goin'?' asked Ben, his fair-headed companion.

'*Bonjour,* Messieurs,' said Nicolas, smiling as he shook each hand. 'I see you're being careful.'

'Can't be too careful,' said Charlie, with a lazy grin. 'We like to give ourselves plenty of room to move.'

'That's right. Not much room in them little cottages. No point in taking any risks,' corroborated Ben, with an answering twinkle. 'Don't tell me you've found a way out for us already?'

'*Je regrette* ... Not yet, no. But we are working on it. We will get you out of here, so don't worry about that. Unfortunately, our latest corridor has been compromised and we are setting up another. It will take a little time to make sure that it, too, will not be compromised. A fact of life, Messieurs.'

'Plenty of spies? Fifth columnists, eh?' asked Ben.

'Sadly, yes. Too many, Monsieur. We take what precautions we can, operating in cells so that no-one knows anyone too far along the way.'

'Holy terrors, aren't they? Dunno what the world's coming to.'

'Come in. We're just about to put the billy on,' said Charlie. 'You'll have a jar with us?'

'Not for me, thanks,' said Nicolas, with an inward shudder. Stooping to enter the cottage, he saw bread and cheese on the table under a cloth. 'Did Natalie bring you that?'

Charlie straightened from his work over the fire to shoot him a look. 'Not today, she hasn't. Why?'

'You have not seen her, at all, today?'

'Nuh.'

'She was going to bring you food. She should have been and gone by now.'

'Put that fire out, Charlie. We've got work to do.' Ben took Nicolas by the arm and steered him to the door. 'We'll backtrack. Where was her last known location?'

'She would have gone to the farmhouse on the northern edge of the forest.'

'I know it. We'll take the path until the house is in sight. Then we'll split up to reconnoitre. We'll decide on somewhere to meet when we get there. Wait till we get our ironmongery.'

Nicolas waited while they unwrapped their pistols from oiled rags and shoved them in their belts.

'All ready. Lead on, Macduff!'

Since he'd known Natalie and, more recently, the two Australian servicemen, Nicolas had got used to their weird sense of humour. But he didn't have the time or the inclination, right now, to comment on their predilection for Shakespeare, striding on ahead without another word.

§

Natalie knew that she was in trouble as soon as she entered the farmhouse kitchen where Madame Dubonnet normally had a covered basket waiting by the door. Today the kitchen was empty, the big range cold, no produce on the table waiting to be washed and chopped. And then she saw the blood! Seeping from behind the bench.

Her breath catching in her throat, Natalie edged forward, knowing, in her heart, what she would find: Madame Dubonnet laying where she had fallen, shot through the head with a German bullet. A scream welled up in Natalie's throat, but she fought for control. If Madame Dubonnet was there, behind the bench, it was incumbent on her to render any assistance she possibly could if the poor woman was not beyond aid. Hand over hand, she made her shaky way around the bench and gasped. A broken jar of pickled beetroot lay on the floor, its blood-red brine spreading across the flagstones. As relief washed over her, Natalie heard a car start up and take off, revving. Too late, she remembered the warning to circle any building and reconnoitre before committing oneself to entering. All had seemed peaceful as she'd come past the henhouse and pigsty—no disturbances there. She hadn't given it another thought. Trembling, Natalie turned and made for the door, gasping as a figure loomed in its portals.

'You're going nowhere, Mademoiselle.'

Natalie took one look at the man in uniform and fled for the inner door. 'Not this way, Mademoiselle,' said a second officer, filling the aperture.

§

'Hang on a minute!' The Australians quickly caught up with Nicolas.

'Do you think we'll get that storm?' asked Ben, squinting through the canopy above.

Nicolas shrugged. 'Perhaps. This time of year, it is a little hard to say.'

'Might be snow?'

'No.' Nicolas glanced up through the trees. 'Not the right kind of cloud, I think. But anything is possible, I suppose.' By now, he'd had time to assimilate their reception of him. 'Two questions, Messieurs: Were you going to kill me if I was someone else?'

Ben looked at Charlie. 'Only if we had to. We have orders not to shoot.'

Charlie patted his pocket. 'Learnt it in Italy. Easiest thing in the world. No noise, no blood. Quick and easy. Rope around the neck, a couple of twists and that's that. Would have had to bury you, of course. Hide the evidence.'

*Listen and learn.*

Nicolas managed to suppress a shudder.

'And the other?' asked Ben.

'I beg your pardon?'

'You said you had two questions. What was the other?'

'Oh ... I was just curious as to why you referred to me the way you did. I don't use my title, Messieurs ———'

'That's to your credit.' Charlie nodded in approval.

'And my *nom de guerre* is Angel, as you know.'

'Yeah. That's a bit ironic after what we've been hearing about you lately. Isn't it, Ben?'

'Yeah, just a bit. We've been on our radio. According to all reports, you're hell's own son ... Angel.' Ben grinned.

'Natalie would not have said anything. She hates my title.'

'No, it comes from the other side. They know who you are. Our Nancy told us to warn you. She said the Gestapo are after you, the same as they're after her. That's their name for you, The Mad Marquis. Same as they call her The White Mouse. So be careful.'

'Nancy? Oh, Madame André!'

'You know her?'

'Only by reputation, Messieurs.'

'Yeah, that's what she said about you. She says you get amongst 'em. Yet, the funny thing is: you never kill anybody.'

'Oh.' Nicolas shrugged. 'We do what we have to, Monsieur. You know how it is.'

'Yeah, we do. That's why we don't understand why you let our Nat wander about the forest on her own.'

'In a war,' added Charlie, in an under voice; his eyes on the ground.

Nicolas glanced up at the trees, then met the accusing eyes squarely. 'You're right to take me to task, Messieurs. It should not have happened. One of our group was missing, and Natalie went out with others to look for her. Everyone came in except Natalie. Tell me: did Madame André mention Juliette?'

'That's Nat's *nom de guerre*,' said Ben, in answer to his companion's unspoken question. 'She hasn't been sprung yet, as far as we know.' He looked at Nicolas. 'No mention of her in the intelligence intercepted by our side.'

'Better look for Romeo, then.'

'Not funny, Charlie. Here he is, here: looking for *her*. But we get your point.'

'Yes, anything could have happened,' said Nicolas, in agonised tones. 'Just because we have not heard of it, yet …'

Ben stood still. 'Yeah, it could. We'd better make a plan. Where's the road?' he asked Nicolas. 'We'd better stay close to it. And we'd better keep schtum from now on.'

They were standing on the edge of an unpaved track just out of sight of the farmhouse when they heard a vehicle start up.

'Down!' said Ben dropping into the ditch. The other two dived behind a large, thickly leaved branch, newly fallen and still hanging by a scrap of bark from its tree.

A big tourer with two gendarmes in the front seat and a middle-aged woman, sitting very upright in the back, went by them slowly. She turned her head, as if to look for escape. Briefly, Nicolas glimpsed the terror in her eyes. He would never, as long as he lived, forget her expression.

'Vichy police,' he whispered, grey-faced, 'and they have Madame Dubonnet.' Keeping to the bushes, he ran down the road a little way, ducking behind the hedge that lined the drive. 'There is another car waiting at the house.'

The Australians joined him, watching with narrowed eyes: two soldiers, one vanishing around the corner of the farmhouse and the other entering by the front door.

'They're not the Gestapo,' said Ben. 'Same as the others. What are they, again?'

'Vichy police—gendarmes. They're just as bad,' said Nicolas. 'They are their tools. What if Natalie is there?'

'If she is there,' muttered Charlie, 'those boys will bring her out to the car.'

'Only two of them, but armed to the teeth, by the looks of it.' Ben pursed his lips. 'We'll need the odds to be on our side.'

'We'll have to jump them if they come back with Natalie!'

'Yeah, but not here.' Ben's eyes blazed with sudden inspiration. 'That branch you two hid behind up yonder. It could easily fall across the road.'

'With a bit of help,' said Charlie.

'Right!' Ben assumed command. 'You come with me, Charlie. And you,' he said to Nicolas, 'stay here and watch.'

'I'll have to go in!' said Nicolas. 'You must see that I can't leave her. I don't know what they're doing in there!'

'Now, look. This is not the time to play the hero. You

could get us all killed if we're not careful. Nat may not be there. That's why *you* are going to stay here behind the hedge, and Charlie and I are going up the road to that branch. If those two are the Gestapo's tools, as you say, they won't do anything to Nat here. They will take her to their masters, just as they have Madame. True?'

'*Oui*,' admitted Nicolas, reluctantly. 'You're right.'

'If she's not there and these boys come out on their own, you just sit tight behind this hedge and do nothing. We don't want to advertise our presence if we don't have to. We'll go up now and get ready to fall that branch on the road. If they do come out with her, wait until they are getting in the car and give us a wave when you're sure they aren't looking your way. Then you follow, keeping out of sight.'

'*Mais* ...' Nicolas was plainly unhappy. All his senses were screaming at him to get into the house. All that is, except his inner voice.

Nicolas felt a steadying hand grip his shoulder. 'I know how you feel,' said Ben, 'but you're too close to this to think straight. If we're going to save Nat, we have to do it in a way that can be put down to nature.'

'Not to mention that, if we don't, it would only compound the trouble caused by whatever poor old Madame there will be forced to tell them.' Charlie contemplated the sky. 'A few storm clouds around,' he remarked. 'Could be a bit of lightning in 'em. If they got struck by lightning, they wouldn't remember a thing.'

'That's right,' corroborated Ben. He looked at Nicolas. 'You wave if they've got her. If not, just sit tight and we'll let the beggars go. Then you'd better get back and tell everyone Madame knows to clear out because they've been compromised. We'll keep on looking.'

'If they *have* got Nat,' added Charlie, 'don't you worry about us. Just get her to safety. We can look after ourselves.'

'After you fall the branch, what are you going to do?'

'Play it by ear,' said Ben, striding away.

'Yeah,' said Charlie, following him. He looked back with a grin. 'You ought to know how to do that.'

Nicolas crouched behind the hedge, fuming. *Damned Australians! How can they joke at a time like this?* Through a sparse patch of leaves, he could see the car sitting on the driveway. He fretted as the minutes crawled by. Did they have Natalie? What were they doing all this time? Why was there no sound?

He threw up his head as the silence was split by a sharp command and two gendarmes came into view holding between them a slumped figure. *Natalie!* Was she unconscious or shamming it? *If they've hurt her ...*

Nicolas raised an unsteady hand and signalled.

The two militia, engaged in lifting their inert prisoner into the back seat of their vehicle, didn't notice a sudden gust of wind that felled a heavy branch from an overhanging tree across the narrow road, nor did they see the two khaki-clad figures that melted, wraith-like, into the forest on either side.

'God, she's heavy! What do these peasants find to eat?' said one, slamming the door and getting in the front passenger seat.

'Not much if Hitler has his way. But she wasn't heavy. You must be getting weak,' taunted the driver.

After a bit of chaffing, the two drove away: Nicolas followed as fast as he could, crouched behind the hedge, then the bushes lining the track.

The car jerked to a halt and the passenger got out, started to haul the branch off the road and stopped to beckon to the driver. The gendarme glanced in the back, then seemingly satisfied with what he saw, gave a groan, and came to stand beside his colleague, obviously giving orders as to how they would remove the obstacle. Then they both bent to the task, grumbling.

Nicolas, hurrying as best he could, had another worry. If Natalie was unconscious, as apparent from the actions of the driver, it was going to be difficult to make any pace to get her away. He'd almost reached the vehicle when he saw the two Australians dart out from behind the trees lining the road and chop each man across the back of the neck with the side of a hand. Both went down without a sound. At the same time, he saw the driver's side back door of the car begin to open and rushed around to pull it wide and hold out his hand to Natalie.

'Come on,' he whispered. 'Let's get out of here.'

'But Ben and Charlie …' Natalie tugged on his hand.

'We're right behind you. Move along. We didn't hit those jokers hard enough. They'll come round any minute now.'

'Yeah,' said Charlie. 'And they won't be happy.'

A crack of thunder coincided with a sudden flurry and spatter of raindrops. 'Good timing,' observed Ben. 'Except that it will wake 'em quicker.'

'At least there won't be reprisals because we've killed someone,' said Nicolas.

'You've forgotten Madame,' said Charlie. 'No-one she knows will be safe after those monsters have wrung all they can out of her.'

'You'd better come with us, then,' said Natalie. 'Can they, Nic?'

'Of course. There will be nowhere else to guarantee their safety. Madame knows the forest like the back of her hand. Fortunately, she doesn't know the exact whereabouts of our secret hideaway.'

'Oh blast!' said Ben. 'Our radio equipment! It's hidden in the roof of the hut.'

Natalie gave a gurgle of amusement. 'Tell him, Nic.'

'Don't worry, Monsieur. There will be plenty to choose from where we're going.'

They were all fit, but their breaths were coming in short puffs by the time they reached the shelter of the cave. The Australians were just as amazed as the others had been and laughed with delight at the medieval booby traps.

They fitted into life in the underground palace as if they'd been born there.

It was just as well, because, over time, it became clear that poor Madame Dubonnet had given up all her considerable knowledge before her broken body had been flung out of a moving vehicle in the village square. This terrible torture and murder had an equally devastating effect on her countrymen, deepening the resolve of some and frightening others into subjection. The purge was only contained, with most of her contacts escaping arrest, because they had been warned at the outset by Nicolas and the duc's agents to disappear. But it wasn't over yet.

During the interminable hours when the enemy were searching for them and they had to stay holed up, Charlie produced a pack of cards and taught them to play poker for matchsticks; Ben could play the piano accordion and sang them rollicking ballads, including one to the tune of *Colonel Bogey*, describing in ribald detail the manhood of the German hierarchy. Natalie refused to play the violin for such reprehensible sea shanties, and Nicolas could not see a harp suiting their raunchy tunes, so left it in its cover. There was a lot more laughter and good humour than anyone would have thought possible given the severity of the situation. But, somehow, it eased their misery.

If Nicolas had time, he would have been jealous of the hours Natalie spent with her countrymen; but as his inner voice told him, at least they would not allow her to go out alone.

# 38 DREAM OR NIGHTMARE?

**29 May 1941**

*Of all the words I can think of to describe our lives at the moment, nightmare reigns supreme. According to our faithless puppet government, we loyal Frenchmen are terrorists and criminals; and they hunt us down with terrifying similarity to their masters, the Gestapo. So efficient, ruthless and precise in their inhumanity. And now another shocking deviation from humanity: they have begun to round up Jews and take them away on cattle trucks to where we know not. Like animals! My heart bleeds for these gentle, educated people! Not only that: if any protest, they go with them! I don't know whether or not this dreadful betrayal of all we hold dear has caused it, but we now have another blow to bear.*

It had been a long, hard day. They were still suffering from the ramifications of Madame Dubonnet having been tortured to death. Innocent people were being rounded up and taken away to unknown destinations, never to be heard of again.

Knowing he was being hunted did not make any difference to Nicolas. He'd been hunted since the beginning, but now the search was being concentrated on the forest and in a radius around Belvoir. It was only a

373

matter of time before the caves were discovered, and they would have to defend themselves. Nicolas was surprised that it had not already happened. *With what?* he wondered. *Defend ourselves with what? A few old pistols and rifles with sabres left over from the Great War? A few scythes and hoes? Against machine guns, bombs and grenades? How will it be possible?*

This was one of their most pressing problems: lack of weaponry to fight the enemy. There were so many willing and able, and nothing to fight with. Frustrated at his forced inaction, he decided to go out and, with Angel's help, try to make these problems clear to their allies and leaders in England.

After long hours flitting through the forests, trying to make contact with those with whom he needed and learning of more and more reprisals—and his subsequent attempts to let their leaders know what was happening at the coalface, (unsuccessful for the most part)—Nicolas felt unsatisfied and depressed. He made the long climb back up the mountain, went straight to his apartment without seeing anyone and flung himself down on his bed. He lay sprawled, immobile and fell immediately into a deep sleep. The sleep of exhaustion. Sometime later, he stirred, muttered and pulled up the blankets, huddling into them.

Nicolas was dreaming. He knew it was a dream, but he could not awaken from it. He was standing in a dance studio of an opera house he did not know. It was baroque, sumptuously decorated in red and gold, embellished in the rococo style. The vast expanse of polished floor was empty. Waiting. Nicolas felt the tension. Something was going to happen. Was it good or bad? In his sleep, he twisted and turned, dislodging the bed covers. He could smell flowers. Now there were flowers everywhere, standing in vases on the parquet floor, hanging, wreath-like, from the walls, massed in the gallery. How had he not noticed them before? Red roses, love-in-a-mist, forget-me-nots and others he did not recognise. Beautiful, overwhelming in both their fragrance and their messages of love.

Through the archway strode a young man: tall and slender, dark and handsome, with an eager light in his golden-hazel eyes and a sketchbook under his arm. He glanced about, puzzled, then swung around to face the door.

Dancing towards him came a beautiful ballerina: exquisite, sylph-like, light as thistledown. She was dressed in the white costume of Giselle, and every move she made was the embodiment of perfection. She circled the room with ethereal lightness, scooped up the nearest bouquet of red roses, inhaled the scent for a moment, and passed it to Nicolas with a graceful gesture and an enchanting smile as she floated by; one of the gauze wings of her costume softly brushing his hand.

*Godmama!* Yet, it was Godmama as Nicolas had never seen her, save for the portrait that lay with the others in the underground storeroom. Nicolas moaned in his sleep, his lips forming the words, 'La Belle', as the young man threw away his sketchbook and exclaimed, 'Ma Belle,' and held out his arms. The ballerina danced right into them. The joy that flamed in his eyes was answered in hers. They kissed.

Nicolas would forever after remember that kiss. Haunting in its rapture, it heralded the end of a lifetime of yearning—of self-denial. All their love for each other, everything they'd never been able to express in life, was in that kiss. It was so beautiful it hurt. Nicolas moaned softly. A tear fell on his pillow. If only Natalie would kiss *him* like that.

The two were dancing now; their steps intricate, beautiful. The young duc providing the support to allow the ballerina to show the breathtaking glory of her dance. Nicolas saw the radiance in their faces; such joy as he'd never seen from either of them in the years he'd known them. They'd been through their tragedies; had, with honour and integrity, made the best of the cruel hand that life had dealt them. Now the love and joy that glowed in their faces would be with them forever.

Nicolas brushed away another tear. The dance was coming to an end. It was so beautiful that he didn't want it to end, ever. Too soon, it was over. The duc bowed; the ballerina curtsied; then they both turned to Nicolas, hugged him, kissed him, murmured blessings and goodbyes before leaving him and walking away together, arms entwined, through the baroque archway and out of sight. Together, for all eternity.

Nicolas glanced down at the flowers he held. More tears burnt his eyes. *This is how I love,* he thought, in anguish. *Like my grandfather. If only the one I love, loved me that way: the way that La Belle loves him.* He became aware of a kind of heavenly rustling and turned his head to stare in astonishment at the great crowd that gave them a standing ovation, then streamed from the gallery to follow the lovers, led by his grandmother. At the door, she turned to put up a hand and the crowd stood motionless. He saw his mother and father, smiling at him. *Mama, Papa,* he whispered. And the hot tears sprang anew.

Nicolas never wondered why his grandmother held back the crowd. She'd always been sweet and sensitive. Some deep instinct told him that she loved the duc enough to give him this time alone with his beloved that he'd never had in life. And why should Nicolas be surprised at the many who'd come to greet him? The duc was adored by all his people. Absolute devotion: he'd seen it for himself— and marvelled—often enough.

Nicolas could hear Natalie calling him, but he could not see her for the crowd. He struggled through the great throng to get to her, impeded by the flowers, compelled by the message he read in them. He didn't question how he could read it. He just could. He waded through them, scooping up great bunches. Fearsomely burdened; weighed down by them. But he must bring as many as he could to give to Natalie so that, perhaps, at last she would understand his message; the message written in their glorious faces: *You alone. Love eternal.* So that she would know! And never be afraid again.

It was so urgent that she should have them. The yearning to see her was a physical pain. He twisted and turned. That was her voice. But, where was she?

'Nicolas! Nicolas, wake up, *Chéri.*'

Nicolas jerked awake and then fell back. He blinked. It was not Natalie who stood by his bed. 'Oh ... Sette!' He sat up and ran his hands through his hair, trying to hide the disappointment that clouded his eyes and the shock it gave him to come back to reality. 'What time is it?'

'Early. Are you properly awake?'

'Almost. Give me a minute, will you?' He yawned and stretched. 'Now I am.'

Lisette sat on the side of the bed and put an arm around him. 'I am so very sorry, but I have some sad news for you. For us all. Your grandfather has passed away during the night, in his sleep.'

'I know,' he said; a faraway look in his eye. He picked up the embroidered top of the bedcover and concentrated on smoothing its wrinkled edge.

'You know? But, how can you know?' She touched his tear-wet cheek. 'Oh, my dear, I see that you do.'

Nicolas shrugged and reddened. After a while, he said, 'I was dreaming of him. He was young and ...' He wanted to add 'in love', but something stopped him. The dream had shown him so much that could never be spoken; that was too precious for words.

'He was a wonderful man: kind, generous, far-sighted.'

'Yes ... he was. And if my dream was right, he is now a happy one.' His eyes searched Lisette's. 'Could that be?'

'*Eh bien,*' she murmured, stroking his hair back from his forehead. 'You must believe in your dreams. That is why they are given you: to make a bridge for knowledge, comfort and understanding of the things that last forever; that cannot be seen.'

377

'You could be right. I hope so.'

'I *am* right, *Chéri*. Go and have a cup of coffee while I find out when we can pay our respects, *hein*?'

He waited until Lisette left the room, then rose to wash and change. He took time to shave cleanly—the duc would expect it—and made his way to the dining chamber, suffering confusion and loss. The first day of his life without his grandfather.

'I'm so sorry, Nic.' Natalie left the table to put her arms around him.

'*Merci*.' Nicolas pulled her close, buried his face in her hair, savouring the comfort. 'Oh, Natalie …'

But, as always, she pulled away. And, as always, he released her immediately, suddenly feeling more bereft than he had before her brief expression of sympathy.

Now that his grandfather had gone, who had he left that loved him? Only Lisette and Armand. But *they* had each other.

He sat at the table and lifted the coffeepot, offering Natalie a refill before pouring his own. Never had he felt more alone. Somehow, he must get through this day and all the others left to him. He toyed with his coffee in silence.

Lisette came in, glanced from one to the other and stood beside him, an arm about his shoulders. 'We can all go up now and pay our respects. You can come if you stay in the shadows.'

'Where is he?'

'In the chapel. The villagers are waiting outside. Family first. Then they can come in. I have spoken to the curé, and he is ready to conduct the requiem at your order. It must be your decision, of course. But, as the rest of the family cannot be here, we, Armand and I, feel it should be carried out this morning, before the enemy hear about it and start looking for you. You do agree, don't you?'

'Of course … I understand.' Nicolas fidgeted with his

cup. He raised anguished eyes. 'But … who will be here for him?'

'Not everyone who loved him can be here, *mon brave*. Just us, the villagers and the curé. But all of us that *are* here loved him. You must remember that, *hein?* And take comfort.'

Nicolas sent her a grateful glance. 'Thank you. I will keep it in mind.'

'And another thing that is most important for your safety.' Lisette's eyes were full of anxiety; her fingers on his shoulder, tightening momentarily. 'Please, *Chéri*, you *must* stay in the corner near the priest-hole for a quick escape.'

Nicolas put his hand over hers. The priest-hole led down into the crypt, where the duc would soon lie. It was Nicolas's least favourite part of the château—a place to be avoided—full of must and the bones of his ancestors: dank and eerie. But, if desperate, one could escape by various passages to the château cellar where there were plenty of hiding places. He suppressed a shudder. 'I will try.'

They made the long underground journey to the chapel in the château where his grandfather lay, at peace, in a silk-lined casket surrounded by flowers. Nicolas marvelled as he bent to the fine white hand and kissed it, that his grandfather seemed to be merely asleep, as if a slight noise would awaken him, and he would open his eyes and smile at him the way he'd always done.

There was no sign of how hastily the flowers had been gathered and arranged, and the casket constructed. Or that the silk had been found in an old wedding chest of the duchesse's and worked on through the pre-dawn hours. The duc's retainers had worked tirelessly with secret tears. Everything must be done that could be done for the honour of their beloved duc.

Throughout the simple service for his grandfather, Nicolas could not be overwhelmed by sadness, because, overlaying it all, he had the comfort of his vision of the handsome man and the glorious ballerina: young, joyful and in love; the great crowd in the gallery applauding their dance; everyone so happy, rejoicing for them.

Forgetting his assurances to Lisette, he left the dark corner where he was hidden, went to the chorister's dais and sang for them *Éternité d'amour*. He knew it was not his imagination that he felt a warm embrace and a kiss on his brow, before the others hurried him away to the safety of his underground city.

He was now Monsieur le duc but, just as he'd wished not to be called Monsieur le marquis on the death of his father, he knew that he would never be called it. For him, there had been only one Monsieur le duc: a man of grandeur and humility; nobility and compassion. A man who knew both how to rule his empire and draw the love of his people. He knew his grandfather would understand if he were to renounce the title. In fact, they'd discussed it not so long ago; although, now it seemed like another world.

'Grand-père,' he'd said, riding with him about the estate in the halcyon days before the war. 'Don't you feel that the world has changed?'

'Indeed, *mon fils*, there is not a doubt of it. The world is always changing. Every generation feels it.'

'Natalie does not believe that there should be ducs any more; that everyone should be equal.'

'It is a fine sentiment,' said the duc, pursing his lips. 'And how do you feel?'

Nicolas frowned. 'In some ways, I think she is right. There should not be privilege due to an accident of birth.'

'Where there is privilege, my son, there is also responsibility. One born as you have been has the obligation to care for his people. You must not forget that.' He smiled gently at his grandson. 'Surely, you will not allow Natalie's taunts to get under your skin?' To Nicolas's questioning look, he answered, 'It has been brought to my notice that she has called you an *aristo* more than once in a rather ... challenging way.'

'Oh.' Nicolas had forgotten his grandfather's penchant for surveillance. Doubtless, he knew a lot more about his grandson's stormy relationship than he ever let on. 'No.' Nicolas shook his head. 'But there *is* truth behind it. There has been so much bloodshed associated with th*e ancien régime.*'

'It is true that there were many who abused the privilege that they were born to. And suffered accordingly. One might even say that they paid the ultimate price.'

'That is true.'

'But there were some who have always cared for their people,' the duc reminded him softly, 'and still do so today.'

'I know.' Nicolas's hand clenched on the rein and his horse stood still.

The duc also halted, raising a brow.

'Grand-père, you have been a wonderful example to me, and I will not forget it. It is just that …' He hesitated, allowing his mount to walk on. 'I will always care for my people, *cela va sans dire.* But that can be done without a title. I don't see that the *ancien régime* has a place in this day and age.'

The duc sat his horse easily; a spark of humour in his warm golden-hazel eyes. 'Are you saying that I am an anachronism, *mon fils*? *Eh bien*, perhaps you are right.'

Thinking back on this talk with his grandfather, Nicolas felt it showed the magnanimity of the man that he accepted these criticisms with his customary patience, understanding and humour. *If I could just have his wisdom,* he thought. And with it came a sharp pain of loss, and he hurried on into the depths of the earth.

Back in the underground refuge, holding a wake of sorts, Nicolas stood at the table talking to the duc's agents and the two Australians. They paid their respects and left him standing alone. He saw Natalie, smiled and held out a hand.

'How are you holding up?' she asked, avoiding the

hand.

He shrugged and withdrew it. '*Comme ci, comme ça.*'

'I will miss your grandfather. He was a beautiful man.'

'Yes. Yes … he was.'

'So, now you are Monsieur le duc?'

'No.' Nicolas shook his head with a sad little smile. 'Just plain Nicolas de Beaulieu, as I have always been.' He cleared his throat. 'When the madness finishes and the world gets back to normal, I will be officially renouncing the title.'

Natalie was like a cat raising its fur. 'I hope you are not giving up your title to impress *me.*'

'No.' He looked at her oddly. 'Is there any reason why I should?'

'No.' She played with the stem of her wine glass; a mutinous set to her lips. 'It wouldn't work.'

'I am well aware of *that*!' Out of nowhere, bursting in his head, he felt a tiny spark of anger, an emotion that was foreign to him, and one he found uncomfortable. He suppressed it to ask quietly, 'Does everything have to be about you?'

Natalie was shaken. 'No, of course not! I am only saying …' She shrank from the unfamiliar expression in his eyes, but squared up. 'There's no need to be unfair!'

'*Unfair?*' He bit off the retort that hovered on his lips and turned away, hurting in so many ways. 'It is for my grandfather,' he said; his voice muffled. 'There can never be another duc de Belvoir. His boots are … *cannot* be filled.'

Ignoring her little cry of, 'Oh, Nic! I *am* sorry …' he strode to his apartment, shut the door and flung himself on the bed.

*Softly, mon brave,* said his inner voice.

But Nicolas could not listen. Grief had taken over reason.

§

Later, Gabriel brought the news that the Vichy government had sunk to a new low. It had made its first round up of Jews. In the midst of all the horror—chaos of feeling that the announcement brought—Nicolas could only be glad that his grandfather didn't have to know about it. *If Grand-père had not already died,* he thought, *the shock of such a terrible thing would kill him.*

§

Toiling his way to the top of the secret tower to relieve Gabriel, Nicolas found that this was where he missed his grandfather most keenly. He wondered if their traitorous puppet government had yet given up the hunt for those betrayed under torture by poor Madame Dubonnet.

He spoke softly: 'Are they still on the slope?'

Gabriel lowered the field glasses. '*Oui*, Monsieur. Swarming like ants.'

'Have they found our cave?'

'No, Monsieur. Something is stopping them climbing quite that far.'

'What?'

'I don't know. Take a look.'

Nicolas took the proffered binoculars and made a sweep. 'I can't see anything out of the ordinary. But they are definitely not going above a certain point.' Into his mind jumped a hideous thought: *Landmine? Unexploded bomb?* He was shaken. 'Can you stay here a little longer, Gabriel. I will have to take a look.'

He made all speed to the underground city, cursing the amount of time it took.

'What's up, old son?' said Charlie. 'You look like your favourite aunty just ——'

'Can it!' growled Ben in a furious under voice. 'He's

just lost his grandfather, you idiot.'

'Yeah, sorry. How can we help you, Mate?'

'Do you know how to defuse a bomb? Or a landmine?' asked Nicolas.

'Ben does. I only hold the spanners.'

'Didn't I just tell you to shut up?' said Ben in amiable tones. He turned to Nicolas. 'He's braver than he looks. Now, tell me why you're asking?'

'I'll do better than that. I'll show you. Where's Armand? I need him to relieve Gabriel.'

They made the long trek up to the top of the tower. Armand took over the radio post from Gabriel, and the Australians, viewing the enemy activity, came to the same unwelcome conclusion as Nicolas.

'We'll have to go down there,' agreed Ben, lowering the binoculars. 'We can't see anything from here but they're definitely up to something.'

'In about one hour,' said Armand, 'they will be changing shifts. That might be the best time to go. Well camouflaged ...'

'Good idea,' said Ben. 'That will give us time to collect a few knick-knacks. Now, what we need is ...' He walked away, explaining what would be required if they had to defuse a bomb.

'Do we have anything like that, Gabriel?'

'*Oui*, Monsieur. Your grandfather prepared for every eventuality, God rest his soul. I will have to sneak into the château to get them. He was going to bring them to you himself before he ... You keep going. I will catch you up.'

When he returned, Ben looked in the bag and grinned his approval. 'That's the ticket. Best bomb kit I've ever seen. Nothing will be too hard with this lot. Now, we'd better find out what is making that lot down there pussyfoot around the way they are,' he said, setting out for the cave entrance.

§

'Whew! Look at this big baby! No wonder those frog eaters are avoiding it,' exclaimed Ben. 'Kraut: Not one of ours.'

'Must have come from a Dornier or Ju 88. A Stuka wouldn't be able to handle it.'

'Yeah, you're right. Lucky it didn't go off. Half the hillside would've gone with it.'

'Yeah,' agreed Charlie. 'Would've made a big hole, all right.'

The Australians fell silent and stood back, assessing the grey cylindrical mass with its fins and scrawled messages. It lay there, menacing, unknown. Nicolas felt his hair rise as he looked at its great silent bulk with the little shiny, circular metal insert in the nose.

Charlie walked away to peer down the slope. 'Not much going on down there.'

'No. They seem to have all moved to the northern face, where they will find plenty of useless caves to distract them,' said Nicolas, with satisfaction. 'I'll watch out for them in case they come back.'

'Good thing,' said Charlie, glancing sideways at his companion. 'Can't stand about here all day, twiddling our thumbs.'

'Right. We'd better get down to it.' Ben looked at Nicolas. 'We won't need you. No sense in us all getting blown to kingdom come.' He turned away and thrust out a negating hand. 'Now, don't argue. I don't want to hear it.'

'All right. I'll keep a lookout from that big rock up there.'

'Yeah, that'll be sweet. Whistle if anyone comes. Come on, Charlie, hand me that stethoscope. Let's see if this baby has a heart ...'

Nicolas watched the two kneeling Australians

crouched over the head of the bomb, and wave after wave of tension feathered over his scalp. It seemed to take an endless time for them to complete their delicate operation and rise to their feet.

Finally, Charlie signalled; and Nicolas made his way to where they stood, deep in conversation. Relief made him light-headed for a few moments.

'Dead as a doornail, but they don't know that,' said Ben. 'Charlie and I think it might be an idea to leave it here as a deterrent.'

'Yeah,' said Charlie. 'As long as they don't drop another one on it.'

'We'll take the risk,' said Nicolas. '*Merci,* Messieurs.' He laughed. 'It must be time for *smoko* ...'

'You're learning, Mate,' said Charlie, with a grin. 'Ain't he, Ben?'

# 39 FALLEN TO THE ENEMY

**11 November 1942**

*I record this in devastation and disbelief. The Germans have swarmed into Provence, taking over the Vichy government. And our château! We have to find somewhere else for our radio transmissions. Probably moving about the forest, inherently dangerous in itself, or barns, churches, public buildings—each with their own particular difficulties. We dare not involve the people for fear of reprisals that are all too real and often for imagined slights.*

*As I am writing, the SS is turfing out the villagers from the château forecourt and marching in a unit. It is the first time in history that Belvoir has fallen to an enemy. However, like Paris, it has been left undefended for them. Lisette and I just managed to escape through the secret tower room before they crossed the drawbridge. Will they find the secret room? None of us think so, but it is a terrible time.*

*We have so many secret missions, involving so much walking at night. At any time, we may be called upon to take an ally to safety.*

*I am worried about Lisette's ankle. All this trekking we have to do is coming against her, even though she*

*bandages it for support, it still becomes swollen and*
*painful. But she always comes with me. She refuses to allow*
*me to make the return journey alone. So faithful and sweet!*
*Did ever a man have a better wife? Impossible!*

*But, next time, I am just as determined that I will use my*
*husbandly authority to make her stay here, in safety.*

Nicolas, Armand and Lisette sat at the table, Nicolas frowning over his barely touched meal; his face white and drawn.

'What is it, *Chéri*?'

He met Lisette's anxious eyes. 'Monsieur Lorraine has not returned. No-one has seen him since the day before yesterday. He has not made contact at any of his rendezvous. Just … seems to have disappeared.'

'Oh no! *Le pauvre*.' Lisette dropped her knife.

'*Has* he?' asked Armand, with dawning horror. 'You don't think …?'

'Possibly.' Nicolas crumbled his bread. 'He is a Jew.' He raised his head. 'The agents are out looking. They will report back as soon as they know anything. There is nothing we can do.'

'We can hope,' said Armand. 'That is all that we can do.'

'And pray, *Chéri*,' said Lisette. 'We must not forget to pray.'

'No. But if they have caught him with false papers …' A muscle moved in Nicolas's jaw. The silence deepened, fraught with horror. He broke it with a change of subject: 'Meanwhile, we have to get the Australians out of here and across to the Pyrenees before they close the pass for the winter.' Nicolas crumbled some more bread. 'I hate to ask, but can you do it, Armand? I can't be away from the radio for too long.'

'Of course,' said Armand. 'I should know all the paths,

by now.' He leant towards Lisette. 'But, this time, you will stay behind, my love. Your ankle ...'

Lisette lifted a determined hand. 'Save your breath,' she said. 'There is nothing you can say to stop me coming with you.'

Armand eyed her ruefully and closed his mouth. He shrugged. *So much for husbandly authority ...*

'Sorry, we're late,' apologised Charlie, as he and Ben slid into their seats. 'Been having a sing-song and didn't notice the time. Looks like you've left some for us, though.'

'*Bien sûr!* Help yourselves. We were just talking about you.'

'Thought my ears were burning,' said Ben. 'What's up?'

'Has anyone seen Natalie?' asked Nicolas. 'She hasn't come to lunch.'

'She's coming. Just putting away that swanky violin.'

Nicolas said nothing, but his eyes clouded.

'So,' said Charlie, breaking the end off a long loaf. 'What have you been saying about us?'

'*Eh bien*, Messieurs, I have some news for you.'

'I hope it is a bit better than the last lot you gave us.'

'Yes, it is a great blow to have Belvoir occupied. But they had better make the most of it, for they will not have it long.'

'That's the spirit. What about our country, eh? Bloody Japs! We've got to get home!'

'And you will, Messieurs, you will.'

'Yeah, and pigs might fly.' Ben bit moodily into a piece of cheese. 'Taking into account progress to date ...'

'Come here, you little blighter,' said Charlie, trying to stab an olive with his fork and chasing it all over the dish. 'Well?' he asked, holding it aloft and waving it in triumph before he popped it in his mouth. 'Are you going to put us out of our misery?'

'Eh?' Nicolas looked at him in surprise.

'He means,' explained Ben, 'what is this news you have

for us?'

'Ah.' Nicolas's lip quirked. 'I thought he meant something else … Only that we have found a way out of the country for you, Messieurs.'

'Oh,' said Ben. 'That all? What do you reckon, Charlie? Our trip abroad might be coming to an end.'

'Yeah … A pity. I don't think I've seen all the sights yet. How's it going to happen?'

Nicolas told them, 'We have a new corridor, but you must go tonight. For two reasons: before our corridor can be compromised, and before winter snow closes the pass. We have heard from the Greek … He is not a Greek, but that is how he is known.'

'I know: *nom de guerre* or whatever you call it. So, we're going tonight: where and how?'

'Armand and Lisette will take you to meet the Greek. He, in turn, will take you over the Pyrenees and pass you on to his next operative.

'The Pyrenees,' said Ben, rubbing his jaw. 'Hmm …'

'Yes, it is a journey *not* for the faint-hearted.'

'We'd better go and pack, then. C'mon, Charlie, get your skates on.'

'Skates?' said Charlie. 'It sounds more like it could be a ski job to me.'

'Not if we hurry. Go on!'

Natalie arrived in time to hear this exchange. 'Where are you going?' When it was explained, she said, 'Oh good! I'll go with you and come back with Armand and Lisette.'

Ben was quick to veto. 'Don't be silly, Nat. You've got work to do here. If you want to be smart about it, you can write a note to your parents. We'll deliver it when we can.'

§

At the cave door, as they were leaving, Natalie handed

Ben an envelope. Instead of saying goodbye, she said, 'I'm coming with you. I'm all packed.'

'No you don't, Nat,' said Ben, shaking her by the shoulders. 'What's the idea, eh?'

Natalie was speechless before the expression in his eyes: not that of the jolly, easygoing friend, but the remote fighting machine; the commanding officer. She writhed as his hands bit into her shoulders. 'You're *hurting* me, Ben.'

Nicolas made a move, and Lisette stopped him with a swift gesture and a headshake.

'I know I am,' said Ben, releasing her. 'I could hurt you a lot more than that, if I wanted. And so could any other bloke out there.'

'But … I'm a soldier, like you.' Her face hardened. '*And* I'm going with you.'

'Yeah?' He stood back; his eyes granite chips. 'Well, soldiers obey their commanding officer. Who is *your* cell leader, eh?'

Once again, Natalie was bereft of words.

'You know what happens to soldiers that disobey orders, don't you? … Don't you?' He held her chin, forcing her to meet his eyes. '*Don't* you, Nat?'

This time Nicolas stood still, watching. The silence lengthened, vibrated with tension.

'Yes,' admitted Natalie, at last. She tried to twist out of Ben's grasp, but he tightened his hold.

'There's just one more thing.' The Australian's flint-blue eyes looked intently into hers. 'You ought to play fair, Nat.'

Reddening, she jerked her head away. And this time, he let her go.

'Right,' he said. 'That's all: lecture over. Now, you have a bit of sense and stay here. We've got your letter, and we'll make sure it gets to your parents.' He held it up. 'We get home, so does this.' The hard light went out of his eyes as he leant forward to kiss her cheek. 'You be good, now.'

Charlie had been standing back, looking from one to the other and back to Nicolas. Moving forward to say goodbye to Natalie, he murmured, 'Not that we don't want you, Nat. But we've all got work to do.'

She could not meet his eyes.

'Been good to know you, Mate. Dunno how to thank you,' said Ben, holding out a hand to Nicolas. 'But you get the general drift.'

'Yeah, mercy bookoo.' Charlie grinned. 'Or something like that.'

'*De rien*! It was a pleasure. Go with God, Messieurs.'

With a farewell grin and salute, both men started down the mountainside. Armand and Lisette said their goodbyes and turned to follow.

Lisette ran back to hug and kiss both Natalie and Nicolas. '*Au revoir, mes chères*,' she said with her warm, cheeky smile. 'We will be as quick as we can. You two take care of each other, *hein*?'

Natalie watched them out of sight, glared at Nicolas and went back inside the cave, straight to her room and slammed the door.

Nicolas shrugged. The tension between them was unbearable. The sooner Lisette got home to lighten the atmosphere, the better. He thought of Lisette: funny, sweet and loving. If only Natalie were more like her. A feeling of hopelessness swept over him. *How can it be like this?* he wondered.

But there was no answer.

§

The rocky path seemed interminably steep and long, bushes slashed their faces, the wind tore at their clothing and made their cheeks burn with cold, but no-one complained, least of all Lisette. Stoically pressing on, she hardly whimpered when a stone rolled under her boot, twisting her ankle, and she fell back against Ben.

'Whoa there,' he said, breaking her fall.

Lisette tried to stand and, white-faced, clutched at the Australian's supporting arm. 'I am sorry, I cannot … My ankle will not take my weight.'

Armand dropped his bundle and came to put his arms around her. 'My love! What can I do?'

'You will have to go on without me.'

'No!'

'You must. Armand, you must! I will only hold you back. Get us all killed.'

Armand held her in his arms; his expression one of horror. 'Don't suggest that, my love. I *cannot* leave you.'

'Sit over here on this rock, Madame,' said Ben, 'and let me take a look at your ankle.'

'Water?' asked Charlie, offering his canteen. Lisette took it gratefully, sipped a little and handed it back.

Ben finished his examination; his face grave. 'You won't walk far on that, Madame. You will need your ankle strapped and rested. I'm not a doctor, but I think you might even have broken it. Might be ligaments, but …'

'It feels as if I have broken it,' said Lisette. 'It is the one I broke years ago in a skiing accident.'

'That settles it,' said Charlie. 'She can't go on.'

'Can you help me to the edge of the next village? I will stay with a friend until Armand returns. It will give me a chance to rest. Please, Armand, you *must* finish the mission. Madame Lebrocq will look after me.'

Armand's brow cleared. Madame Lebrocq was a trusted friend: an old school friend of Lisette's and a fierce partisan; a keeper of a safe house that had never yet been compromised. Lisette would be fine with her.

The Australians made a sling of their arms and carried her between them to the edge of the village.

'You can put me down now, Messieurs. The pain has eased. I think I can walk with help,' she said, leaning on Armand's ready arm.

Hidden in a thicket, they rested while Ben selected a branch; and Charlie cut and whittled it into a walking stick. They waited until dusk, and in the half-light, Lisette stood with help and took the stick. 'Thank you, Messieurs. This is good, very good,' she said. Her little face, pinched with pain, cleared as she put her weight on it. 'I will manage to hobble into the village without difficulty.'

She said a cheery goodbye to the Australians and reached up to kiss Armand. 'Don't worry, *Chéri*. Madame will take good care of me. I will wait here for you.' She smiled. 'Don't be too long.'

With a heavy heart, Armand watched her laboured progress into the village. He suppressed an almost overwhelming urge to go after her and took his place on the path ahead of the Australians. 'This way, Messieurs.'

The village square was crowded with villagers, peasants and refugees. Here and there towering above them were German soldiers, examining papers. *Good,* thought Lisette; her alarm at the sight of a uniform stilled. *No-one here will notice me. Sometimes it is helpful to be not so tall.* She pulled her shawl over her hair and hugged the buildings, leaning heavily on her stick. Occasionally, she rested on a stone bench, for a few minutes only. The more she walked, the worse the pain. Resting helped a little. She found another bench and sat. *Just for a moment*, she thought. *To dull the pain.* Now, there was just one more street. Only a few minutes to safety.

Lisette heard the whisper behind her.

'Sette. Settie!'

*Nicolas? Here?* She turned, without thinking.

Sapphire-blue eyes, glittering with malice and triumph, bored into hers. The blond man in the SS officer's uniform raised an arrogant hand. 'Over here!'

He watched two officers snap to attention, then turned his predatory gaze back to his victim.

Lisette looked into those merciless eyes and steeled herself to accept her fate. 'Hello, Gerry,' she said, with a meaningful glance at his uniform. 'I see that you have risen high ... in *your* world. You have become quite a star, *hein*?'

A white line appeared about his mouth, but he gave her no answer.

'This woman,' he said to the two officers that had come at his command, 'knows the whereabouts of Nicolas de Beaulieu. *Make* her tell you.'

Lisette stood up, putting all her weight on her stick. She looked him in the eye. 'I have one question for you, Gerry: How can you? How can you betray your country, your people, like this?'

His answer was to kick away her support so that she lost her balance and tumbled heavily onto the cobblestones. She reached in vain for it, struggling to rise. The two officers each took an arm and hauled her roughly to her feet, holding her between them.

The SS commander twisted his lips into a sneer. His malign glance flicked over her: amused, dismissive. 'Oh, and make sure you take plenty of time over it,' he said in a rasping voice. 'She knows ... *much*.'

Lisette looked at the tall, lithe figure: the handsome, chiselled features; the eyes that should be so beautiful, but were not. *Dead,* she thought. *Your eyes are dead; your face cold and lifeless. You are supposed to be the epitome of a superman, but you are just a puppet for your masters.* 'Poor Gerry,' she said; her voice filled with sympathy. 'Even when they've finished with me, thrown my tortured remains into the road like poor Madame Dubonnet, I will still be more alive than you.'

He slapped her so hard that, had she not been held between the two officers, she would have fallen; turned on his heel and strode away.

The officer on her left muttered something in German and the other laughed. The well-known penchant of their commanding officer for sneaking up behind small women and hissing at them had not been a weird fetish, after all.

It had finally paid off: this was a cow with plenty of milk. He took a firmer grip on Lisette's arm. 'You will come with us, Madame,' he said, beckoning to the waiting car. 'You may be certain that we will follow our commandant's orders to the letter.'

Lisette made no reply. She sat, head bowed, in the back seat of the car. Hands clasped to her breast, she was already praying for the strength she would need to suffer the coming ordeal in silence; to keep her loved ones safe.

# 40 MISSING IN ACTION

**18 November 1942**

*The Pyrenees! They stand like warning sentinels: giants
without mercy. And still we have not reached our
destination.*

*My one wish is to get back to Lisette. My head tells me that
she will be safe with Madame Lebrocq, but my heart tells
me that she needs me. My anxiety increases with every day
that we are apart.*

After a week of cold sullenness, Nicolas felt that he could
stand no more. What had he done, this time? 'Please,
Natalie ... Is there any need for this unpleasantness?'

Natalie raised her head to give him a scorching glance.
The hurt in his eyes only served to annoy her further.
'*What* unpleasantness?'

'The one you've been treating me to since the
Australians left.'

'You're imagining things.'

'Am I?'

Natalie did not reply.

After an awkward silence, Nicolas cleared his throat.
'We have to radio London tonight.'

'All right,' she said, with resignation. 'I suppose you
want me to climb a tree with the aerial again? Now that

you don't have Ben and Charlie to do it.'

'If you feel up to it. If you don't mind. That is one thing you Australians seem to be very good at.'

'I'm glad you find me useful.'

'Natalie ...'

'What if I fall? I don't have them to catch me.'

'I will catch you.'

'I won't fall.'

'I know that. I didn't know you were such a nimble climber until last time we did this.'

She gave him another dark look. 'There might be a lot you don't know about me.'

Good humour creased his face. 'I know that, too. Ready in half an hour?'

§

Ben bent a searching glance on Armand. 'Want me to try and get a radio message to Nic for you? Let him know what has happened? And that you might be late getting back?'

'Thank you, yes. Lisette and I might have to stay in the village with Madame Lebrocq until her ankle heals.'

'I'd say it was a certainty, Mate,' said Charlie, making a small fire between two large rocks in a sheltered corner of a ruined castle. 'Good a place as any to camp. What do you reckon?'

'Well, at least it is out of the wind. Shouldn't be any smoke if you keep it small.' Ben shook his head. 'Imagine building something like this up here! Those old blokes were amazing.' He turned to Armand. 'This medieval?'

'Tenth century, I should think.'

'Hmm, incredible, isn't it? The way they carried those big rocks and set them into high walls, like this. Without the machinery we've got today.'

'Like to see 'em get machinery up here,' commented

Charlie, bending over his fire.

'Yeah, you're right.' Ben turned back to Armand. 'Think the snow will hold off till we get there?'

'I hope so, Monsieur. We should make it tonight.'

§

Armand said goodbye to the Australians with relief, making all speed back to the forested edge of the village where he'd last seen his wife. With increasing disquiet, he waited until dark before attempting to contact Madame Lebrocq. Then he made the elaborate preparation, going through all the required passwords to finally stand before the *Résistance* heroine.

'I have come for my wife, Madame. How is she?'

'Lisette? You are asking after *Lisette*?' Madame Lebrocq's black eyes grew large in a face devoid of colour. She shook her head. 'But she was never here, Monsieur. I have not seen nor heard of her. Are you *sure* she was coming here?'

'But she *came* …' Armand clutched at the doorpost, struggling to remain lucid. 'She … she twisted her ankle and couldn't go on. I saw her enter the village myself!'

'A seat, Monsieur?' said his hostess, comprehending his distress. 'Some cognac? There, there, *mon pauvre* …' She put his wilting form into a chair and ministered to him with practical sympathy. *Dear God*, she prayed silently. *Please, no! Not our beautiful little Lisette!* She compressed her lips at the sudden fear that entered her mind.

Madame Lebrocq thought rapidly and spoke in the same fashion: 'What day, Monsieur? Do you remember? What time? Oh dear, that was the day the SS were here poking around the square looking for Jews. Wait while I enquire on the grapevine. It will take a little while. Patience, Monsieur.' Madame Lebrocq took a hat and coat from a peg, opened the door to the cellar and started down the stairs. 'I will be back soon. It may not be as bad as we think ...' she added; her voice floating upwards.

But Armand knew it was. And he could tell that Madame Lebrocq thought so too, despite her palliative words. His heart had been right after all.

He knew it.

# 41 FAITHFUL UNTO DEATH

**30 November 1942**

*I should have stopped her. I should have stopped her!*

Madame Lebrocq's partisans brought the news that some of the villagers had seen an SS officer strike a small woman who was leaning on a walking stick. Others saw her being put in a car and driven away from the village. So said Madame Lebrocq, in a voice holding back sobs, to a distraught Armand. Her people had been unable to trace the car from there. It had taken the main road north, which could lead almost anywhere.

'If I can find Gabriel,' said Armand in a muffled voice, 'we could set up our own search.'

'Come with me tonight, and we will try to get out a radio message. Even if it means radioing England and getting them to contact Gabriel. We have to be careful ...'

Armand gave her an agonised glance but said nothing.

§

Days went by and there was no sign of Lisette. Nicolas and Gabriel set up coordinated searches, grid patterns, radio messages. Armand, finally returning to base, was an automaton, searching endlessly, unable to respond to conversation that had no reference to his quest.

Their whole lives were taken up with finding Lisette so that anything else they had to do was by the way, finished quickly so that they could resume their feverish, fruitless search. No-one had seen the car containing Lisette since it had left the village. The mystery deepened; their fears more agonising.

Whenever they heard of a body or a prisoner killed, their hearts stopped until it was identified and proven not to be Lisette. They all knew that there was only a slender hope of escape once arrested by the Gestapo or the SS. And yet, despite everything, they still held hope.

Until a body was thrown out of a moving car in the middle of Belvoir village square. The car, identified as an SS staff car, had roared out of the château and over the drawbridge, slowed to toss out its unwanted cargo and sped away. Arrogant: uncaring.

§

Gabriel walked ahead of the covered stretcher carried by two of his agents, Raoul and Pierre. He saw Nicolas making his way down the mountain path to meet them and prepared himself to deliver terrible news.

'Are you saying that *Gerry* did this?' Nicolas spoke through grey lips. His tongue felt stiff and wooden.

'I am sorry, Monsieur.' The agent's face was etched in lines of fatigue and misery.

'Is this *true*?' Disbelief rang in Nicolas's voice. 'No ... It cannot *be*!'

'Yes, Monsieur. *Je regrette* ...' Gabriel took a deep breath. 'He sneaked up behind her, whispered your name for her; and when she turned, thinking it was *you* ... Easy, easy, Monsieur.' He grasped his leader's arm as his pallor suddenly increased and he reeled.

'Ah, *mon Dieu*!' Nicolas tore his hair: a man demented.

His eyes, burning with horror, met those of his agent. 'May God forgive me,' he whispered. 'I let him live when I should have killed him. *This* is what Angel meant. Oh, Gabriel: *how* am I going to live with this? Oh, Sette! *Sette!* I am sorry. I am *so* sorry! It is *my* fault!' He doubled over with the agony of it.

The agent, thinking that grief was making his mind wander, hastened to reassure him. 'No, Monsieur. *No* … Of course it is not. How could you have known …?'

'Oh, *Sette* …' Nicolas pulled away the blanket with trembling fingers and stood looking down at the blue-white face: so still; so beautiful in its alabaster purity. A sword pierced his heart at the sight of blood seeping from beneath the eyelashes, fanning her cheeks; and he gagged. He bent to pick up a little hand; observed with incomprehension and then increasing horror that the nails had been torn from their beds. The more he looked, the more he saw; his agony increasing at every mark of torture to an unbearable pitch so that he cried out, '*No! Settie! No!*' The raw sounds issuing from his throat like those of a wounded animal.

And as Nicolas finally comprehended what had been done to this beautiful person who had been to him as a mother, he understood his agony: something, as a placid being, he'd never before experienced. From his feet to his crown, with the velocity of a tsunami, surged a murderous rage.

He gasped, racked with the pain of it. His immediate sensation was that the top of his head had blown off. His fury tore at his muscles and tendons until they zinged with tension; it pounded his bones, crushing them to powder. It pierced his brain like a sword, hissed in his blood and burned him like fire.

The pain, the intensity, bursting in his head, flashed like a thousand-watt globe. He cried out for the last time—a scream of anguish—and fell senseless over Lisette's body.

§

Natalie closed her bedroom door and leant against it, exhausted.

Somehow, they would have to deal with the horror of Lisette's terrible death and its immediate consequences. Somehow, she and the others had brought Nicolas's unconscious body back to the underground city and lay him on his bed. They'd taken Lisette, wrapped her in a blanket and buried her on the mountainside. Armand had been in such a state that he had to be sedated. *I need something myself*, she thought, beginning to undress. *This is all such a nightmare. I don't believe it!* An edge of hysteria was rising behind the fatigue, but she controlled it with a supreme effort.

When she put on a nightdress and dressing-gown, she had a sudden fear for Nicolas and slipped out into the lighted corridor. 'Gabriel?' she whispered to the figure seated near the bed. 'Is Nic all right?'

'I don't know, Mademoiselle. I really don't know. But it appears that his vital signs are all normal, so perhaps it was the shock of … He may be better after he sleeps it off.'

'Yes. I don't suppose there is really anything that we can do.' She ran to the bed, crying; her composure suddenly evaporating. 'Nic! Nic! Wake up! I *need* you.' She began to shake his inert shoulders.

'Mademoiselle,' said Gabriel, pulling her away. 'I beg of you: Go back to your room. None of us has been able to wake him. He must wake in his own time. *If* he does.'

'What do you mean: if?' Natalie's hazel-green eyes widened so far that they showed white all around.

'He could have suffered a stroke.'

'No-o-o,' she sobbed. 'It is *not* possible. Nic … *Nic!*'

'Come, Mademoiselle,' said Gabriel, pouring a measure of cognac from the decanter on the bedside table. 'A composer for you and back to your bed. No argument, *s'il vous plaît. En avant!'*

Natalie, still sobbing hysterically, refused the cognac and ran back to her room. As the door slammed, Gabriel took the even pulse of his leader, looked at the drink in his hand, shrugged, and tossed it down.

He settled in the armchair to wait. Presently, exhaustion took its toll; and he began to snore quietly.

# 42 A MAN POSSESSED

**7 December 1942**

*The fact that I am alive to write this, twists a particular knife in my heart. And Nicolas? I never saw such a change in a personality! He is a man possessed.*

The man who was Nicolas awoke and stretched. Momentarily, his features crumpled, then hardened into clean, ruthless lines. *Nemesis.* He looked with amusement on the snoring agent and glanced around at his shadowy surroundings, felt for his locket, kissed it and slipped it back inside his shirt. He did not question the raw, baleful energy that surged in his muscles and spirit and gave him a new and deadly purpose. And a certainty: He would never have to depend on his inner voice for help ever again. He knew everything the Master knew and more. Sure in his new knowledge, he flexed his fingers: *I am Angel.*

Yet, this energy did not sit well under his skin. It gave him mental pain as well as physical. It made him restless. He tossed and turned for a while, switched on a light and looked at his watch. He waited for Gabriel to respond, but the man only turned his head and muttered in his sleep.

Suppressing an exclamation of impatience, Nicolas threw back the covers and rose, dressed all in black and went to where his dressing-gown hung on a hook behind the door. In one deft move, he pulled the silk cord from its keepers, rolled it up and thrust it deep into his pocket. He strode soundlessly along the well-lit corridor, but as he passed Natalie's door, it suddenly opened and she stood there in her dressing-gown, blinking in the light.

'Nic! Are you all right?' Then, seeing how he was dressed, cried out in alarm, 'Where are you going?'

He paused in his stride and turned. 'I am sorry. Did I wake you?'

'No. I was just going to check on you.'

'But how *kind* of you.'

'*Nic?*' Natalie eyed him uncertainly: shaken by his words, the sarcasm of his inflection and the unfathomable expression in his eyes. 'Why are you …?'

'I don't know why you are suddenly interested in my movements, *but* …?' His eyebrow asked an arrogant question.

'*Oh!*' Natalie tossed her head, spun on her heel, ran back into her room and slammed the door.

For another moment he stood there, one corner of his mouth lifting into a little half-smile.

Then he went out into the night.

§

Gabriel stirred, opened one eye and leapt to his feet at the sight of the empty bed. He glanced at his watch, muttered under his breath, and rushed out into the kitchen where Jean-Marie was preparing a rabbit for roasting with herbs and potatoes.

'Have you seen him?'

'No,' said Jean-Marie, sewing some seasoning into the carcass. 'I haven't seen anyone except this rabbit. I'm preparing it now in case I don't have time later. Coffee's on the hob.'

Gabriel grunted, poured himself a cup and moodily watched the other's ministrations. 'You'll be able to start a restaurant after the war.'

'After the war, I never want to see the carcass of a rabbit or a chicken ever again,' replied Jean-Marie, twisting the thread around his middle finger and snapping it. He looked at Gabriel and shook his head. 'This is a terrible business. How is Armand?'

'Asleep, I hope.'

'So, who is it you're looking for? The young master?'

'Mmm. I was hoping you had seen him.'

Jean-Marie shook his head and began to scrub a potato.

'If you're looking for Nic,' said Natalie, moving quickly to pour herself a coffee, 'he went out in the night.'

'Good morning, Mademoiselle.' Gabriel swung round. 'I am sorry; I did not see you there. Was he all right?'

'I don't know.' She stared into her coffee. 'He didn't seem to be himself, at all.'

'Perhaps it is the shock. A bad business all round,' said Jean-Marie, nodding a greeting. 'What about poor Armand, *hein*? How is he going to go on without …'

'I don't know.' Natalie shook her head. 'We gave him a pretty hefty whack of chloral. He'll still be under.'

'A good thing if he knows nothing for a while.'

The agent Raoul came in, went to the hob and poured himself coffee.

Gabriel shot him a look. 'Anything going on out there?'

'No, nothing.' He took a mouthful of the beverage and grimaced.

'Mademoiselle, would you …?' asked Gabriel.

'Yes, I will go and check on Armand as soon as I have finished this.' Natalie drank her coffee and decided to take some with her, in case he was awake. Entering the room, she found that Armand had a visitor, seated on the bed, talking quietly to him:

'Oh, Nic. You're back.'

'*Eh bien* … So I am.'

'Are you all right, Armand?' she asked, putting down the cup on the bedside table. 'I'm sorry. That's a stupid question. Coffee?'

Armand shook his head. Words seemed beyond him, right now.

Angel clasped his shoulder. 'We will leave you to sleep off the sedative, *mon ami*. And you may rest your mind about Toinette. I have seen to all that.' He hesitated, 'About the other: I hope that when you've had time to think about it, you will be heartened. Eh, *mon brave*.' He rose and made a gesture. 'After you, Mademoiselle.'

Outside the door, Natalie asked, with a lifted eyebrow, 'Mademoiselle?'

'Are you not?'

She gave an exaggerated sigh and ignored the question. 'What did you mean when you were talking to Armand?'

He looked mystified. 'It is perhaps my turn to ask what *you* mean?'

'You said he will be heartened ... Heartened by what?'

'Is it any of your business?'

'Yes, I think it is.'

'Point taken.' His lashes veiled a telltale glimmer. He brushed his fingers across his cheek and took a deep breath. 'Settie never said a word. She loved ... beyond death.'

'Do you mean ...?'

'Have the SS found our hideaway?' he demanded. 'Are they swarming about the mountain? Have they taken any of us, yet?'

'No,' she replied, fighting the urge to step back from his vehemence. 'The agents have reported no unusual activity.'

'*Eh bien ...*'

'Oh, *poor* Lisette!' Natalie twisted her hands. '*So* brave! Oh ...' It was her turn to dash away a tear. '*What's that?*' Natalie's eye caught a shadow behind him, and she jumped. 'Oh, it is a cat!' she said, sighing with relief.

'Yes. He followed me home.'

'I didn't know you liked cats, particularly.'

'Didn't you?' Straight-faced, he quoted her own words back at her. 'There might be a lot you don't know about me.'

'I'm beginning to think so,' she said, meeting his eyes for tense seconds. The tears had gone; they were hard and bright. How difficult it was to hold his unnerving gaze. 'Who is Toinette?'

The cat mewled, demanding attention. He bent to run his hand along its back. '*Eh bien, les chats* ... They seem to like me, at any rate.'

'So I see,' said Natalie, watching the cat's ecstatic response, conscious of relief that he had taken his eyes off her. 'Nic? You've been out all night. I—we were worried.'

'You needn't. There was quite a bit to do.'

'Where *were* you?'

He shrugged. 'Here and there. I fancy *les Boche* will be a trifle discommoded today.'

'Why? What did you do?'

'It will take too long to explain. Let us just say that there may be a few mechanical faults show up when their vehicles start climbing hills. Oh, and by the way ...'

'Yes?'

'From now on, we will call each other by our *nom de guerre*. You will call me Angel, and I will call you Juliette.'

'What? Even in here? But ——'

'Everywhere.' For the second time, his eyes showed a flicker of emotion. 'If Sette had known that I would not use her real name, she would never have been tricked like that.'

'If you'd killed Gervais when you had the chance,' she countered, 'Lisette would still be alive.'

'Indeed.' He looked down at his hands; his face white and still.

Observing his drawn features, Natalie was suddenly

ashamed of the hurt she must be inflicting on him. 'I'm sorry, that is not fair of me to say that. I didn't want you to kill him at the time; I was even glad that you didn't, but now I wish you had!' Natalie clenched her fists. 'I even wish that *I* had killed him!'

'If wishes were horses …'

'I know. We can't do anything about it now …' Natalie shook her head and backtracked. '*Who* is Toinette?'

There was a heartbeat of silence while he stared at her. Natalie stared back. Even though he never changed in expression, she could swear he was secretly laughing at her. He shifted his gaze to look over her head. 'Settie's little sister. You haven't met her. She lives in England.'

'Oh.'

'They lost touch with each other after Sette and Armand's wedding. Toinette got busy on the stage, and then the war started. They were close in their way, she and Sette.' He shrugged. 'I don't know why it happened, but Toinette is no letter writer … She *had* to be notified.'

'Of course. But …' *Why did Lisette never mention her?*

'But … What?' His gaze was back on hers: probing, intent.

'Nothing.' Natalie shook her head. 'I was just about to say … it is going to be horribly difficult to remember to call you Angel. What about the others? Must we all do it?'

He kept his eyes on her, knowing that what she said was not what she had initially meant to say. 'It is up to them. The others are not being hunted by a madman.'

'Yes, they *are*.'

He sent her a look of enquiry.

'Hitler.'

'*Eh bien*, let me rephrase it: I agree that, in general, we are all being hunted by a madman, yes. But, in particular, it is you and I that are the targets. Gerry will be after you, not only for revenge, but to get at me. You and I will only answer to our *nom de guerre* so that what happened to Settie *cannot* happen to us. Do I have to spell it out?'

'No.' Natalie flushed and bit her lip. 'I deserved that I suppose.'

'Remember it, Juliette, and try to keep out of trouble, won't you?' He watched her closely, smiling as she bristled. 'And now,' he said, picking up the cat and draping it about his neck, 'I need to sleep. You will see that I am *not* disturbed.'

Natalie bridled at this Victorian autocracy. 'Yes, *Master*!' she shot back, with sarcastic emphasis. And turned on her heel and left when he laughed.

Natalie's mind was in turmoil. *Nic! What has happened to Nic?* she wondered, wringing her hands. *I would never know him for the same person.* Of course, he was grieving. And grief could do funny things to people: make them act in all sorts of ways that they normally would not. *But to call him Angel all the time?* She shrugged.

They were all grieving Lisette. Cheeky, cheerful, motherly Lisette: sweet, brave and generous. Always making life better and more comfortable for those around her. Natalie's skin crawled when she tried to imagine what she must have suffered. It was just too dreadful! Her mind refused to handle it. *Lisette! Ah, Lisette! I will always mourn you. Poor, darling Lisette!*

§

The man occupying most of Natalie's thoughts sank down on his bed with a sigh. He unfurled the cat from about his neck and set it down beside him while he kicked off his boots and lay back, staring at the ceiling: one hand on his locket, the other stroking the cat. When the cat curled up, he opened the locket and took out the chestnut tress it contained, winding it around his forefinger. He sighed again, kissed it, returned it to its little gold and glass compartment inside the locket and continued to stare into space. In a little while, he was asleep. But it didn't last.

Soon, the restless energy forced him awake.

Thus began a new pattern of sleeping for him: cat-like, keeping vigilance, alive to the slightest alteration in his environment. He accepted the cat's devotion, thankful for its warm presence. Indeed, he understood it: did he not stalk the enemy with purpose and determination—silent, relentless—as did a cat its prey?

§

Armand had been prostrated for days, yet emerged from his chamber quietly determined to remove the great evil that overran them or die in the attempt. 'I value my life,' he told Natalie, 'only to the extent that I can use it to avenge my beloved.'

And, looking at him, Natalie had to believe him. He was ashen, seemed to have shrunk; yet it was more as if he had been refined, honed down, like a sword ready for battle. What happened to Lisette had shifted the whole axis of their world; changed all its parameters. It was a world they did not know; a nightmare existence in which they were lost, struggling for survival. Sometimes wondering why they even wanted to survive, the way the world was. Wouldn't it be easier to give up? To run outside and meet a quick end by a bullet or a bomb? The trouble was, for those captured *Résistance* fighters, the end would not be quick.

And yet, Armand seemed to have found a measure of comfort in the knowledge that Lisette had not betrayed them, even under the most skilled of the Nazi torturers. 'She has been faithful to death; *beyond* death,' he said. 'She has set the standard of courage, of valour, for us all. Can any of us not use our lives that she bought with her own— her blood; her suffering—to free our country and our people from this shocking evil?'

Natalie agreed, excused herself and went to her room,

biting her lip. *We are all killers now. In our hearts, if not in fact. Now it is real,* she thought, shivering. *Not just do or die, but do or die horribly.* Her lip trembled. Now, when she most needed Nicolas, he seemed to have gone, and a stranger stood in his place: a cold, demanding, *imperious* stranger who expected his orders to be obeyed; who was as autocratic and short-fused in temperament as Nicolas had been gentle and endlessly patient.

One day, when he seemed in a quieter, more communicative mood, she said to him, 'Nic? You don't seem like yourself. You seem ... different, somehow.'

'Do I?' He lifted her chin between thumb and forefinger, half-smiling at her predictable reaction.

'*Eh bien,*' he said, dropping his hand and turning aside. 'Perhaps I am.' He shot her a quick look over his shoulder. 'But why would you start to care now?'

'I don't understand ... What do you mean?'

'Did you think that you could treat Nicolas in any way you please? Without consequences?'

Natalie stared at him with narrowed eyes. 'Why do you speak of yourself as if you were another person entirely?'

He shrugged: proud, remote. 'A figure of speech. A slip of the tongue.' He swung back; a dangerous gleam in his eye. 'Will you hold me to account for every word? I think not!'

'*Nic!*' she protested in disbelief.

'Juliette,' he said, as he walked away. 'You must remember to call me Angel, *n'est-ce pas?*'

In that moment, she knew that she did not know him: this new Nicolas who was alight from within; who burned with unquenchable rage. This man who had an indefinable aura of menace about him that was both seductive and frightening; compelling and dangerous. So foreign to all that she believed she knew of Nicolas: his kindness, sweetness, innate chivalry. All gone before the intimidating presence of this man who made her feel uncomfortable with his penetrating glance that seemed to have her measure—weighed her and found her wanting—as if he knew all about her and was amused at her shallowness, could read her heart and didn't care.

Her mouth took on a petulant droop. *Angel,* she thought. *Angel?* Anyone less angelic, she was yet to meet. *Nic. Oh, Nic, where are you? You were more like an angel then, than you are now.*

# 43 LE CHANT DES PARTISANS

**16 February 1943**

*At last, in Vichy France, we Maquisards seem to have a
leader that is dynamic and acceptable to all. Not least
because he is a great organiser and a man of uncanny
vision. He is brave, having tried to kill himself rather than
be tortured into committing an act against his principles.
Nicolas and I both feel that he is 'the one'; the man to unite
us into an invincible force. Natalie regards him as her hero
and is crowing because she says he is a communist. A lot of
people seem to think that without any real evidence—other
than his extreme left-wing views! We even have our own
anthem: We will be an army to be reckoned with. A tour de
force!*

With the conscription of French nationals into German
forced-labour camps, there were suddenly a lot more
people hiding out in forests and ready to join the *Résistance*
movement. There was a push to unite them under one
leader and communicate more with the Special
Operations Executive based in England.

A man called Max had gone secretly to England some
time ago and returned with a swag of money and a
microfilm, and his organisational abilities were finally

becoming evident. With money from the SOE, Max was able to organise the groups into an army. If his name was attached to an order, Angel and all the other cell leaders took it seriously. Now, at last, they had means, not only to defend, but to attack.

Coordination and airdrops of weaponry and explosives sent by the SOE saw a comprehensive assault on the French rail system, key road and rail bridges and factories used by the Germans. The Maquis were up for anything to hinder their occupiers' insane bid to conquer the world. And Max oversaw it all.

At increasingly frequent intervals, Gabriel brought back orders in code. If they were from Max, Angel decoded them privately and often went out alone. He sometimes stayed away for days and did not always return alone, accompanied by one or more special operatives. He also began to bring back bottles and canisters of chemicals, which he stored in one of the small rooms in his quarters.

After one of his absences, Angel returned with a clavichord: a small, dainty instrument, its cabinet intricately worked and patterned *en grisaille*. He did not say where he got it, and none of them dared ask. After that, from time to time, delicate tunes were heard coming from his apartment, at any hour of the day or night.

As well as the spies and operatives, during this time, there were great numbers of people seeking shelter; but no-one was turned away from the underground city. The rules were simple: They were to come, singly, to a prearranged, randomly chosen rendezvous at a certain time of night; the meeting place and time were always changing to prevent betrayal by informers. There, they were blindfolded and led to an unoccupied section that was stocked with fuel and provisions, where they shifted for themselves. When it was safe to leave, they were again blindfolded and led to the operative who would be their guide out of the country. In this way, if they were caught, they could not reveal the secrets of their hideaway.

One thing they brought with them: a new song, *Le Chant des Partisans*, and Natalie was enchanted. She could not get it out of her mind. But she determined not to share it with Angel, falling silent if she happened to be humming it when she came into his presence. She knew it was childish and stupid, but she did not care.

Occasionally, Max made a surprise visit, talking with them and their temporary residents for long hours of the night. He and Angel got on well, spending a lot of time together at the map in the operations room, discussing possible strategies. He also bought a gift from the SOE: a tin containing a number of small buttons with a secret cyanide capsule hidden within that they could use to shorten their suffering if captured by the enemy. 'It is up to your own judgement,' he said, a trifle wryly, 'whether you take one or not, and whether you wish to use it. However, I have offered it, as the SOE suggested.'

All of them, including Natalie, nodded. Some took one, some didn't, but they all saw Max as their hero; their wise leader who could solve their communication problems, plan offensives and coordinate them into efficient fighting units. What Natalie particularly liked about him was that no-one's opinion was too small for him to count. At the end of the night, he would smile, set his hat at a dashing angle, tuck in his scarf and leave as quietly as he had come. Occasionally, Angel went with him, returning alone, hours, days or sometimes weeks later.

Whenever Max came, Natalie watched who he spoke with and talked to them herself: airmen, refugees, peasants, Jews and Maquisards with prices on their heads, gaining inspiration for places to blow up—to cause the maximum amount of delay and frustration to the enemy.

On a particular day, after an intense conversation, she returned to her room deep in thought. There must be some way to frustrate the enemy living above them. How it galled her that they lived there without hardship, lording it over the populace, taking all their food and comforts, killing and torturing without compunction. *If only there were some justice in this world!* How she would enjoy the captors of Belvoir being locked up as prisoners! Even if it were just for a short time. Let them find out what it was like!

She slipped out of her room just in time to see a tall figure silhouetted in an archway. 'Nic!' Natalie ran along the lighted corridor; her face animated. 'Nic! Wait!'

He put down the bag he was carrying and turned, enunciating with reproof, 'Angel.'

'Yes, right!' Natalie grimaced. *'Angel …'*

'What do you want?'

Undaunted by his tone, she rushed on: 'I have just had the most amazing idea: why don't we blow up the drawbridge of the château?'

He stared, unwinking. *'Our* château, do you mean? Belvoir? Just like that?'

'Yes, Belvoir. Just like that.'

'Why?'

'If we pick the right time, it will distract the enemy when the operatives parachute in from England. Do let us, Nic … Angel, please?' She saw his face. 'You're looking rather grim. I take it you don't agree that it is a good idea?'

'No, I do *not,* Juliette. I think it a harebrained scheme, at best.'

'But why? You've been pretty hot on blowing up bridges and railway lines whenever the chance is given. Why not the only entrance into the German quarters above us? It would annoy them no end.'

*'Eh bien …'* His expression said, *God give me strength!* But he achieved a relatively patient tone: 'Do you mean, aside from the fact that it would be destroying a structure that has stood for more than a thousand years? Or the fact that those inside the château will immediately contact outside troops for help, thus drawing attention to our skies on the

one night we must avoid it? Not to mention what they might do to the villagers in reprisal ... And you would do this just to *annoy* them?'

Natalie flushed. 'I didn't think of that.'

'You did not think, at all. And well do I know it!'

'It was only an idea. There's no need to be rude about it!' Natalie tossed her head and began to walk away.

'Juliette.'

She turned. 'Yes?'

'My answer is that I will not allow you to vent your hatred of social injustice and inequality on a magnificent edifice that has been standing for countless generations and will still be here when we are gone.'

'Oh! You *are* the limit! Do you know that?'

He stood, saying nothing.

She noticed that he was dressed for outdoors; a rucksack by the wall. 'You're going out to radio? To find out when the SOE operatives are parachuting in?'

He nodded.

Natalie eyed him darkly. 'I suppose after that prime piece of chauvinistic misogyny, you expect me to go with you to hold the aerial?'

'No, why should you? I can do it.'

'But you don't climb!'

He laughed. 'I think I can manage, thank you. No, I want you to stay here with Armand. He should not be left alone. He has the black dog on his shoulder and must have company.'

'Armand doesn't need company. He needs *Lisette*.'

*We all need Lisette.* The words, unspoken, hung between them. 'Nevertheless, Juliette, you will stay. And do not think to try and convince him of the value of your little scheme. It will be best to keep the blowing up for bridges and railway lines on strategic routes. We have to count the cost. I thought you would be able to see that for yourself.'

'I think you are *wrong!*' she said, with passion; cut by his scathing tone. 'I have enough supporters to do this without you.'

'Is that so?' He hefted the rucksack onto his shoulder and grasped her wrist with his free hand. 'Understand this: you will defy me at your peril.'

'Oh! You're just ... *unbelievable*!' She fought free of his iron fingers: furious, rebellious.

'*Eh bien* ... I will see you when I come back.'

'Don't disturb yourself, *especially*!' she flung at him, through her teeth.

'I won't. *À bientôt.*'

Natalie slammed into her room, threw herself on the bed and burst into tears.

*This is becoming a habit I could do without! Oh, Nic. Oh, Nic. Where have you gone? What has happened to you?*

# 44 THE ENGLISH SPY

**18 February 1943**

*La milice: more dangerous to us than the SS or the Gestapo. Existence is more difficult than ever because they are natives and understand our dialects and are able to gain more information from torture. Frenchmen torturing Frenchmen: how can this be? It seems that they were formed last month by the Vichy government and their German masters to combat our increased ability to harm our enemy occupiers. We must make every blow count. Yet, at the same time, protect ourselves more, so that we live to fight another day. Avenge another day! Drive these monsters from our country!*

Natalie put her idea to Armand.

At first, he did not answer, then asked, 'Have you spoken to Nicolas about this?'

She avoided his glance. 'Yes. I suppose you know that he insists on me calling him Angel? And that he will not say my name, only calls me Juliette?'

Armand played with his pen, twisting and turning it until Natalie was tempted to snatch it out of his hand.

'Well? What do you think?'

'I think we must humour him, my dear. He is suffering. Just as much, perhaps, even more ... because ...' Distress clouded his eyes. He took a deep breath and changed the subject. 'What did he say about the drawbridge?'

'What do *you* think he said?'

'Ah … I think I can guess. You must understand that it has been his home; the home of his ancestors for hundreds of years. It is also a landmark, an icon. Perhaps you do not understand …?'

'No, I don't. Quite frankly, I do *not* understand how Europeans are prepared to sacrifice people for inanimate objects of stone and wood! Just because they have stood for centuries! They can be rebuilt: lives cannot!'

'No, *indeed*.'

'Armand, I *am* sorry.'

'No, you are right. But it is not just Europeans, you know. All races have attachment to their homes and are prepared to die for them …'

'Yes. Some of us for *other* people's homes …'

He looked at her quickly, then away. 'Very well, I will think about it. What Nicolas does not know cannot hurt him. In this respect, at any rate. It will take some careful planning. If we blow the drawbridge at the end away from the château, it will not cause damage to the walls. I should imagine that they will rebuild it as soon as possible, anyway.' His eyes met hers: owlish, behind his spectacles. 'So, what is the point?'

'Distract them. Torment them!' Natalie balled one hand into a fist and slammed it into the other. 'Show them that we are not going to lie down and let them take us over! We will do it at a time that will cause maximum disruption to them and will distract them from something we are doing. We will know when the time is right.' She looked at the maps and papers littering the table. 'What are you doing?'

'Plotting enemy movements and key strategic points on the map. There are also these despatches.'

'Give me the despatches. I can do them.'

'*Merci*.' He looked up. 'Where is Nicolas?'

'He went out to meet some operative parachuting in:

an English spy; all very hush, hush. He absolutely *refused* to let me go with him. Apparently, it is a woman.' Her words edged with frustration, she exclaimed, 'I don't know *what's* got into him!'

Armand looked at her for a second, seemed to hesitate, then returned his attention to his map.

Natalie did not tell Armand how she had questioned Angel: 'She?'

'Yes,' Angel had replied with a challenging light in his eye. 'What of it?'

'Nothing.' She'd shrugged, offhand.

'Just as well.'

Her face darkened; lips tightened at the memory of that hint of warning. The man was impossible. *Impossible!*

Armand glanced at her but again said nothing. They got on with their war work in uncomfortable silence.

§

The parachutist landed and instantly began grappling with the tangle of cords and billowing silk that was dragging her slight figure across the forest clearing.

'Toinette!' Even as he said it, he cursed himself for not using her code name. Rapidly, he added the passwords that she would recognise.

The urgent whispers made the parachutist look round. '*Eh bien*, Monsieur, I take it you are Angel, who is to meet me?' she said, as he stepped from behind a tree to help her. 'Nicolas! It *is* you! They said it was. You have grown up quite a lot since I saw you last.'

'Indeed. I am now only called Angel.' He made a moue. 'They were happier times. We did not know what we had, back then.'

'No, you are right. We do not appreciate the good until we have the bad,' she replied, releasing herself from the parachute and pulling off helmet and goggles. Light filtering through the trees made her hair a silver halo.

'Your hair is shining in the moonlight,' he said.

'I can fix it,' she replied, dragging a black beret out of a pocket and over her pale head. 'How is that?'

'Fine. I am sorry that you have had to come here under such dreadful circumstances,' he said, not revealing his shock at seeing how like Lisette she was, even though he knew it and was prepared. 'I won't ask what your trip was like.'

'I'll tell you, anyway: It was hell. *Pure* hell! Especially the last bit. But I am here now.'

'And it is still hell, *hein?* But now that you are here, you'd better have a *nom de guerre.*'

'You know what my name is. Even though you did not use it.' Antoinette showed her teeth. '*Nemesis.*'

His smile just lifted one corner of his mouth. 'You cannot have that: it is already taken, *believe me,*' he added, *sotto voce.* 'Here, when you take your place amongst the *Résistance* fighters, your name will be Sibyl.'

'Sibyl?' she said, divesting herself of her heavy flying suit to reveal a lithe figure clad in a neat jacket and trousers. 'Then I prophesy that we will win this war.'

'Undoubtedly: a foregone conclusion.' He looked her up and down. 'Can you dance?'

'*Un peu,*' she said, beginning to draw in the parachute. 'Back chorus line standard only. Nothing like ...' Her breath caught on a sob. 'My sister.'

'No, but ... It is enough.' He bent to the task of reducing the billowing folds of silk to manageable proportions. 'How do you feel about a different kind of warfare? One in which we hold all the ammunition?'

Antoinette stopped packing up the chute to look a startled question.

'If we kill, they take reprisals on our villagers. Shocking ... reprisals.'

'Oh, I *know.*' Antoinette put a hand on his arm. 'Madame André, she told us when she got back. Oh, I could not believe the brutality! And poor darling Ernesto: shot because he tried to bring the poor woman water!'

'*Ernesto?* Was he? Oh no!' After a minute, he said, 'I did not know that you knew him.'

'Of course I knew him! Everyone knew Ernesto. I have sung with him more than once, but …' She shrugged, turned away, adding in a whisper, 'Never again.'

'A terrible thing! Juliette will be devastated … He was a good man.' *One more dreadful blow to take on board.* Angel squared his shoulders and began scooping away leaf litter to bury the parachute. '*Eh bien,* it will add piquancy to what we are going to do next.'

'I am here to avenge my sister. I will do anything it takes,' said Antoinette, dropping to her knees to help him. She gave a slight smile, reminiscent of Lisette. 'Being a Sibyl, I know that I should know this: But what are we going to do? What is this new kind of warfare? And why did you ask if I could dance?'

'*Eh bien,* all in good time. I have plans for you. You see, I am going to make the enemy call you Ghost Dancer.'

'Ghost *Dancer? Mais* …' said Antoinette, in dry tones. 'I have in the past been called a ghost by persons who thought they were being funny. But I must tell you that nobody in their right mind has *ever* thought of me as a dancer. Perhaps I would be better cast as a wailing banshee?'

'*Pas du tout,*' he said. 'It is not sound that will cause the effect that I have in mind; although, it might be part of it. Indeed, we could make it so. A good idea!' he said warmly. 'How do you feel about generating fear in the enemy? Fear to melt their bones and turn their blood to water: ice, even? Fear such that they have never known, against which they have no defence? That, no matter where they turn, they will never be able to escape it? How about that, *hein?*' he asked, rising to his feet.

'I think that it would be perfect retribution,' she said. 'It sounds like justice to me. And also, *pure* fantasy because

I don't know how my second-rate dancing is going to produce this effect?'

'Ah,' he said. 'That is where we differ. Because *I* do.'

'Then tell me more. Like the senate in Rome, I am all ears!'

'It will take time,' he said, 'to perfect it. We will have to work on it. How is your chemistry?'

'*Chemistry?* Well, um, not as good as my dancing.' She gave a tiny gurgle of amusement, rose and dusted the knees of her trousers while she thought. '*Eh bien,* let me see … I can mix bicarbonate of soda with cream of tartar to make bubbles.'

'It is a good start,' he said, with an answering twinkle. 'We will go on from there. Come, we must get you back to our underground city.' He looked at her. 'Armand *is* prepared, but he will still have a shock.'

'I know. I will treat him gently.' She thought for a moment. 'You know, when I look at myself, I don't see my sister.'

'The likeness is there. More noticeable with your hair covered. We must be quiet now. There might be patrols.'

They walked in silence until they were signalled by Gabriel. He was the bearer of more unwelcome news.

'Do you say so?' asked Angel, after introducing him to Antoinette and watching his predictable reaction. 'When did this happen?'

'Pardon, Mademoiselle. I thought, at first, you were … someone else …' gasped Gabriel, too shocked to take in the rest of his speech.

'*Or* her ghost,' said Angel brutally. '*Are* you going to answer my question?'

'Pardon, Monsieur, yes,' said the agent. 'Today, just before *le déjeuner*. They say he has taken the ducal apartments …'

'*Eh bien* … more fool him.'

'Just what I was thinking, Monsieur. But I must warn Mademoiselle Natalie.'

'Juliette. And *I* will warn her.'

'Very well, Monsieur, I will go back into the field.'

'*Bien*, Gabriel. *Merci.*' Angel looked at Antoinette. 'And now it begins ... in earnest!'

§

The two *Résistance* fighters made good time to the foot of the mountain and stopped to catch their breath in the shelter of the great rock that marked the beginning of the climb to their hideaway. They shrank farther into the shadows as torchlight flickered, and they heard the sound of voices. Two men appeared to be arguing in querulous, guttural accents.

'Who is it?' breathed Antoinette. 'The enemy?'

Angel hushed her with a gesture. 'Wait!' He listened; his mouth curving. As the sounds of debate receded, he said, 'German soldiers. Their car has broken down on a steep slope, and they have to walk back to their quarters in the château. They are furious about it and blaming each other.'

'Why are you smiling? Was it sabotage? Something you did?'

'Probably. Come on. We'll go carefully. As long as we don't dislodge a rock ... '

'Oh!' Antoinette's boot slipped on the path with a long scraping sound and a scatter of leaf litter and small stones. Angel grasped her arm, and they dropped into the brush as a torch waved in their direction.

A sharply raised voice spoke in German: 'What was that?'

The second man made a peevish reply. 'What was what? Come on. I'm tired.'

'Someone moving. Up there. On the mountainside.'

'It's probably a goat or a sheep. Come on!'

'Could be Maquis. If we find that nest of vermin we've

been told to look for, there might be a promotion in it.'

'Promotion, *ja*! For whom? You know as well as I do that our commandant will take all the credit for it. Come, Dieter. I don't want to spend all night on the mountain. I want my dinner and my bed.'

'Shut up, Hans. It was up here. Somewhere …' The German began to weave his torchlight, searching for a track. 'Ah, here it is! Stop grumbling and come *on*.'

Angel took hold of his companion's hand, and they made all speed up the mountainside, spurred on by the clatter and scraping of heavy boots behind them. 'In here,' he breathed, as they reached the cave entrance.

The German torchlight caught the ripple of the curtain of vines as they slid through.

'There they are, Hans. Come!' The German pounded after them.

Angel used his torch to cross the cavern and was held up for precious minutes weaving through the maze of stalactites, while the German soldier closed the gap, his boots echoing in the chamber. He, in his turn, was delayed in the same fashion, as Angel led Antoinette through the niche and into the passage, hugging the wall and lifting her bodily over the trap flagstone. They were halfway along the corridor when the German skidded through the archway.

He stood, shining his torch on them and shouting orders: 'You two! Halt or I shoot! He pulled out his pistol, aimed it and began to walk towards them as they turned, white-faced. 'Hands up!' he said. 'I would shoot you now, except that there are some who need your knowledge.' He stopped just short of the trap flagstone and smiled: 'No easy death for you two.'

'Do as he says.' Angel glanced down at Antoinette and raised his hands. 'We have no choice,' he added, watching the soldier with eyes narrowed against the light. *One more step*, he commanded, silently. *Just take another step.*

'Now turn and face ——' The German shone his torch

in their eyes and stepped towards them, putting his weight squarely on the trap flagstone. As it dropped out from under him, reaction made him squeeze the trigger; the bullet ricocheting off the limestone just above Angel's head and twanging from wall to wall with terrifying speed, striking sparks off the rock. The random motion of the bullet, combined with the man's high, drawn-out scream, made their hair stand on end. Long moments later, they heard a splash.

'*Mon Dieu!*' whispered Angel, thrusting his arm into a crack in the wall. 'That was close!'

'*Un peu,*' agreed Antoinette. 'What happened?' she asked, staring into blackness that was, a few seconds ago, German torchlight.

'Shh. There's another of them out there.' Angel dragged out the rock section just enough to allow passage, shoving her in front of him. 'In here, *vite!*' he said, cutting his torch and pulling the concealed door behind them until the latch dropped. 'Sit down and keep very quiet.'

The second German arrived in the vaulted archway too late to see the section of wall lock back into place. 'Dieter?' He shone his torch around and quickly doused it, holding his pistol, white-knuckled, the sounds of the shot and the blood-chilling scream still ringing in his ears. *Who did he shoot at? Or did someone shoot him?* He eased himself along the wall. Something had happened to Dieter, and he did not know what.

He risked a second quick flash of his torch, but found no sign of his friend. Another, longer flash showed him a nailed door at the end of the empty corridor, and he stood still, biting his lip. Was this where Dieter had gone? He had a bad feeling about that door.

The German edged farther along, then, taking shaky aim, stood back and fired at the door latch. The noise reverberated in the tunnel. Little pieces of debris fell from the roof as the door opened onto the void, and the beam followed through. The thundering in his ears was augmented by the waterfall that he glimpsed before the door swung back. A wave of goosebumps passed over him as he remembered that dreadful scream and the distant splash. 'Poor Dieter,' he muttered. 'So, this is what must have happened to him. And *this* must be the place we've been looking for.'

Once again, he shone his torch around but could see no evidence of another entry point. He decided to go back for troops to help him search the caves and warn them to keep well back from the door. He shivered as a fanciful name occurred to him. His lips framed the words, 'Door of Death.'

Overcome by a creeping horror, he turned and ran back the way he had come. Straight down the middle of the corridor.

Angel, who had tensed at the pistol shot and held his breath at the sound of ringing footsteps, switched on his torch at the agonised yell and counted the seconds until the splash. 'That is what we have been waiting for,' he said, smiling at his companion. 'No more danger of discovery by the enemy. At least, not this time. We will start a whisper that those two Germans are deserters. If they ever do find their bodies, it will be a long way from here. Probably, in a lake.' He helped Antoinette to her feet, shone his torch around the great cavern and bowed. 'Welcome to your new home, Mademoiselle.'

# 45 BATTLE PLANS

**20 February 1943**

*My wife's little sister is just as determined as I am to avenge her terrible death. I am not sure how or what they are going to do, but she and Nicolas seem to have their heads together over the formulation of a plan to create maximum distress and furore in the enemy. I wonder how much fortitude la milice will show in dealing with it?*

Natalie paled and grasped at a pillar, but Armand held out his arms to the slim woman that came in with Angel. He opened and closed his mouth, but no sound escaped.

Antoinette looked with comprehension on the shocked faces and tore off her beret. '*Eh bien*, does that help?'

'Toinette!' said Armand; his face crumpling. 'Oh, Toinette!'

'I know, *mon frère*, I know. Hush now. There, there …' she said, going into his arms and returning his embrace.

'I knew you were coming, but …'

'Ah, *mon pauvre*, never mind. Together we will avenge our beautiful Lisette, *hein?*'

'And Ernesto,' said Angel. 'Toinette has just told me how selflessly he died.' He motioned Antoinette to give the details she knew. 'One more to avenge,' he added when she finished.

Natalie gave a sigh and subsided against the pillar.

433

'Juliette?' Angel was standing over her, but his voice seemed to come from a long way away. 'I am sorry to have delivered such news so baldly. Are you all right?'

'I will be,' said Natalie, through taut lips, 'when I get over the shock of how like Lisette she is. I am truly sorry about Ernesto, but it is not a shock to hear that he died caring for others. It is only what I expected. It is the shock of seeing ... *her*. You did not tell me that your spy was her sister.'

'Why should I? You are aware that we all operate strictly on a need-to-know basis?'

'I think you should have told me.'

'Do you?'

'You told Armand.'

'Well, of course, I told Armand. *Look* at her!'

'I know! That is why you should have told me!'

'Then, here is something that I think you *do* need to know: Gerry has taken over the command of the garrison in the château.'

Natalie whitened. 'Oh, no! Gervais, *here?* Do you think Lisette could have ...?' She flushed and broke off.

'You *fool!*' Angel jostled her out of Armand's line of sight, speaking in a furious undertone. 'We've already been through this. Of *course* she never said anything! We're all still here, aren't we?'

'No! You must not say that!' The cry was filled with distress. 'She did not! She was faithful! Not just to death, but ...' Armand made a strangled sound and left the room. Antoinette cast Angel an agonised glance and went after him.

'*Now* see what you have done!' Angel controlled his fury with an effort. Then he seemed to change. His eyes mocked. 'Tell me: do you see *yourself* being faithful ... to death?' At her gasp of shock and outrage, he gathered her hands in a strong hold. 'You may find out *if* you persist in this stupidity that you have been planning.'

She began, 'What makes you think that I ...?' and fell

silent before his knowing glance. Her head drooped. 'Armand has told you. I see.'

'He hasn't … But you have just told me something that no doubt you did not mean to. As to how I know what you have been planning, suffice it to say that I know *you*.'

'Oh, you *arrogant* … Words fail me!' She tried to free her hands, but he held them effortlessly; and she stopped her futile struggle, standing tall and rigid in an attempt to maintain an air of injured dignity.

'The danger you face from Gerry is *real*,' he went on, ignoring both her interruption and her demeanour. 'If you don't want to learn the answer to my question, then you had better heed my warning.' He dropped her hands and turned away.

Natalie felt as though she had been summarily dismissed from his thoughts. A sensation previously so foreign that she could not yet take it in.

§

At breakfast, Natalie noticed Armand glance at Antoinette—a look of pain in his eyes—then quickly look down at his plate; his jaw working. He excused himself and left the table.

Antoinette went to follow, but Angel shook his head. 'You must leave him to work out this problem for himself,' he said. 'He will accept it in time.' Then he smiled at Antoinette. 'Today begins your apprenticeship.' His gaze went to Natalie—travelled over her—turned cold. 'I don't need you this morning. You may help Armand if you have nothing to do.'

'Thanks.' Natalie spoke through her teeth and got up quickly from the breakfast table. 'I've plenty of work of my own to do.' She didn't exactly flounce, but if she'd been wearing a gown instead of trousers, it *might* have looked that way.

Angel watched her retreat, then turned a bland gaze on his companion. As concisely as possible, he outlined what he had in mind for her, answering all her questions, almost before she asked them. He rose. '*Eh bien*, if you are ready, I have set up an area for your chemistry lesson.'

'I am not sure what kind of pupil I will be ...'

He shook his head. 'Simple stuff. You will have no trouble.'

Antoinette laughed. 'It will have to be very simple.'

'It will be. Then, once we have that perfected, we will think about a costume for you.'

'Yes? Where will we find a costume down here? That could be difficult.'

'It may be easier than you think.'

'Then what?'

'Then we do our rehearsals. And when I think you are ready, I send you into battle.'

'Well, as long as you don't expect me to do it *en pointe* it might work out ...' Antoinette's eyes held a hint of speculation. 'Angel?'

'Hmm?'

'Just one question: how long since you have sung?'

'I don't know.' He shrugged. 'I haven't felt like singing.' He faced her squarely. 'I don't feel any more like it now.'

'No, no, my friend, it is like this ...' Antoinette put her hand on his arm. 'If you are going to send me into battle, then *first* we are going to sing, *n'est-ce pas*?'

'*Eh bien* ...' He seemed to consider, then sighed. 'What do you want to sing?

'*Le Chant des Partisans*. Do you know it?'

'I haven't had time to learn it.'

'Then we must remedy that. Right now!' Antoinette's lips curved. 'At last, I get to sing with you, *mon brave*.'

'I don't know that *that* is such a great thing. *But* ... if you must.'

'We all need to sing, especially in these times. But *I*, and *you*, particularly need it. Now *écoutez bien*: These are the words ... And *this* is the tune.'

Antoinette's voice was well trained and sweet. Angel joined her in the second chorus.

Natalie heard the two beautiful voices raised in song— her *favourite* song—and had no idea why she felt that her heart was breaking. She *had* intended to boldly walk into the lesson, see what they were doing together. But now? She turned away, lifting a trembling forefinger to her eyes.

§

Angel led the way to the storeroom, dragged out a trunk and looked towards the heavens. 'I am sorry Elise, Georges. But needs must when the devil drives ... And he is driving us hard right now.' He flipped up the lid. 'Yes, this is the one.'

'I know that Georges is ... was your grandfather,' said Antoinette, watching with interest. 'But who is Elise? Not your aunt, I take it?'

'No.' He shook his head. 'Was, not is ... My aunt was named for her: A ballerina *sans pareil*. She was ... exquisite.'

'Did you know her?' Antoinette was looking at him curiously. 'Forgive me: you sound as if you loved her.'

'I did. She was my family.' He seemed to speak to himself. Then he started and returned Antoinette's questioning glance. 'I called her Godmama,' he said, in explanation. 'She reared my mother, and she died when I was nine. She was a lovely person.' He bent to rummage in the trunk. 'Try this for size.'

'Ah, *mon Dieu*, she was tiny! I will not fit into this.' Antoinette held up the white filmy costume; its bodice and overskirt sewn with a scattering of tiny crystals. 'Giselle: the white act. This is *very* pertinent, *mon ami*.'

'Yes, the *Wilis*, I know. Let us hope that you can dance a few Germans to death.'

'Not with my dancing, *mon brave*. I told you.'

'*Eh bien*, we will try it out soon. Then we will see who was right: you ... or me.'

'That is, if I can make this fit,' said Antoinette, examining the crystal-studded bodice. 'I will have to let it out along the side seams, add some more material. If there is something else in here that I could use? You have no objection?'

'Not in the least. Do what you have to. I will leave you now.'

Antoinette turned back to the trunk; her eyes sparkling with anticipation.

§

There it was again. Each meal time, Natalie particularly watched Armand: the hunger in his eyes every time he looked at Antoinette; the quick glance, then the pain and misery; his abrupt leaving of the table without eating. How thin and drawn he was.

Natalie's heart went out to Armand. She tried to speak to him, but he said, 'Forgive me, I cannot talk about it,' and walked away.

It was getting on her nerves. The whole thing was getting on her nerves. Poor Armand, he didn't need to be reminded all the time. *I don't need to be reminded all the time, either! I'm going to do something about this!* she thought.

In this mood, she marched off to find Angel. She found him in the operations room alone, taking measurements with a ruler and sticking pins in the map. He looked up. 'Is something the matter?'

'Yes. Haven't you noticed?'

He straightened, raised an eyebrow.

Natalie took a deep breath and charged right in. 'I want you to send Antoinette back to England.'

'Oh, indeed? Just like that, *hein?* And why is this?'

'Can't you see what it is doing to Armand?'

'Can I not see what *what* is doing to Armand?'

'Oh … need I spell it out? Her likeness to Lisette.'

'She cannot help her looks.'

'I know, but …'

'But what?'

'Oh, *why* can't you *see*?' Natalie's eyes met his, challenging at first, then pleading. Without warning, she changed her attitude, moved to go into his arms, seeking the comfort she had previously disdained. 'Oh, Nic. What has happened to us?'

He took her by the shoulders, but only to hold her away. 'The war happened. Have you forgotten?'

'Of course I haven't forgotten!' she exclaimed with a little spurt of temper. 'It has gone on for years and years. Years and years, living underground like—like *moles*. Afraid every minute of our lives! Will it never *end*?'

'It will end … One day.'

'Oh …' Natalie lost her animation, clenching her hands in frustration.

'But it could be a lot worse,' he pointed out. 'What if we did not have this place?'

Natalie made a little movement with her head but said nothing. Her eyes welled with tears.

Antoinette entered the operations room, looked from one to the other. Aware of the charged atmosphere, she had enough presence of mind to step behind a pillar, unnoticed, just as Angel spoke.

'I am sorry that I can do nothing about the way we have to live, but ——'

Suddenly, Natalie came to life, shaking with passion. 'And the one thing you *could* do to make life bearable for Armand. And me.' She struck her chest. '*And me!* And you can't see why you need to do it!' She glared at him, distraught.

He met her wild gaze with a percipience that she resented. '*Ma pauvre.* I see a lot more than you may think,' he told her. 'Including Armand and Antoinette's predicament. And here, before me, I see a child without understanding, speaking of things of which she knows nothing.' He stroked her cheek with a gentle forefinger. 'Go away, little girl. Come back to me when you have grown up.'

Natalie tried to slap the rueful smile off his face, but he was too quick for her, holding her wrist with effortless calm. 'Valerian is good for overwrought nerves, so I apprehend. Go back to your room, and I will send Toinette with a dose for you.'

There was something about him: something that Natalie could not confront, had no answer for. He was cool, in control. And she wasn't. She stumbled away, numb and rigid.

Antoinette emerged from behind the pillar. 'Well, that was edifying.'

He raised his brows. 'Indeed? How much did you hear?'

'Not much, but enough. Their nerves are shot: hers and Armand's.' She sighed. 'Poor darlings.'

'Can you wonder?'

'Not at all, *mon brave*. Not at all. We will be lucky if we do not join them. Where is this valerian you have been bragging about? I might take a dose myself ... later.' Antoinette waited while Angel measured the dose for Natalie. 'You were hard on her, just now. Are you sure this is the right way?'

He shrugged. 'What else can we do? She wants to see you. Give her this, then come back here to me. I have something for you.'

§

Natalie turned a white face to the door and watched it open on a gentle knock.

'Juliette?'

'Come in,' she called, turning her face into the pillow as Antoinette entered with a medicine glass that she placed on the bedside table.

'Angel said you wanted to see me,' said Antoinette. She indicated the medicine glass. 'Will you take this?'

'Oh, he *would*,' groaned Natalie, sitting up and making a gesture at the glass. 'Later, at bedtime.' She looked earnestly into Antoinette's face. '*Please* don't take this the wrong way,' she begged, on a long, sighing breath. 'But I told Nic, um, Angel that I think you should … go away.'

'*Tiens!* You want me to go away?' Antoinette spoke in a humorous tone that quickly cracked. 'And where would you like me to go? Out into the forest to suffer the same fate as my sister? There is no guarantee that I would be as strong as her.' She took a painful breath. 'Or anything like … It could sign all your death warrants.'

'No, oh, no! I didn't mean that! I just mean that when we get the next lot of airmen out of the country, instead of coming back, you could go with them. You see?'

'You are very anxious to be rid of me,' said Antoinette, resuming her jocular tone and smiling a little. 'Why is that? Is it because you think that I am getting too close to Angel?'

'No!' Natalie almost shouted. 'It is not that, at all. You've got it all wrong. Angel probably thinks that, too. But can't you *see*?'

'Since Sibyl is only my code name: No. What must I see?'

'That you are upsetting Armand.'

Antoinette's whole demeanour changed from gamine to deadly serious. 'You are right,' she said. 'But there is nothing I can do about it. You see, I have already offered to Armand what you have suggested, and he begged me to stay. He said that he cannot bear to lose both of us. And really, his nerves are so very fragile just now. I would not like to do anything to make things worse for him.'

'Oh, no … What can I say?' Natalie looked down at her hands, twisting in her lap. 'I am sorry.'

'*De rien*, my sweet!' Antoinette hesitated, then added deliberately, 'But for what it is worth: Angel and I are friends, comrades, that is all.'

'But, I did not mean …'

'Did you not? *Eh bien* … We will speak of it no more.' She glanced shrewdly at Natalie's averted face. 'But I will just say this …'

Natalie jerked upright, suddenly thinking she saw more than Antoinette meant to reveal. 'You mean: you do love him?'

'Angel, you mean? Yes, I love him.' She met Natalie's sceptical gaze, calmly. 'As a friend.' She hesitated. 'As a matter of fact, I do have someone I love in the way that you mean. But it has never been possible. And the way things are, it never will be possible.' She put up a hand to arrest Natalie's unuttered words of sympathy, looking and sounding so like Lisette that Natalie covered her eyes. 'The difference between you and me, *ma chère*, is that I trust Angel, and you do not.' Antoinette looked into the distance. 'Perhaps you have reason? I do not know.'

*No. No reason.* Natalie raised a stricken face. She knew she had no reason that she could explain, even to herself, except one that she could not bear to acknowledge. With a wordless apology, she leapt up from the bed and ran along the main corridor, diving into the first one that branched off it. Only the darkness stopped her headlong flight. She sank to the cold stone floor and gave way to uncontrollable tears.

Antoinette sat for a while—her face puckered—then went back to the operations room.

# 46 GHOST DANCER

**3 March 1943**

*Everywhere I look, I see a ghost. But Antoinette is real, and my darling Lisette is the ghost. And every time I look at her ... Oh, my love, come back to me!*

Natalie found Antoinette altering the ballet costume. 'Where did you get that?'

'In the storeroom,' mumbled Antoinette around a mouthful of pins, without looking up. 'Angel found it in a trunk.'

'You're dressing up for him? You're dancing for him?' *You've been lying to me, you cow!*

Antoinette straightened. She met Natalie's hostile gaze and took out the pins. 'Not for him, no. If you mean Angel? No, it is for us: the *Résistance*.'

'Why?'

'I cannot tell you. It is complicated.'

Natalie tossed her head. 'Do you mean that you and he are on a mission? And he has left me out again?'

'Are you a dancer?'

'No.'

'Then he doesn't need two of us.'

'What do you mean?'

'You know that I cannot tell you. You will have to ask him.'

'I'll go and see him right now. Where is he?'

Antoinette shook her head. 'Not here.'

'Where, then?'

'I only know: not here,' replied Antoinette, replacing the pins and bending over the filmy dress.

'I'll ask Armand,' said Natalie, beginning to leave. She swung back. 'Actually, there's another thing that has been bothering me for simply ages. Ever since you got here, in fact. Something you *can* tell me. And I might as well find out while I am here.' She squared her shoulders. 'Why did Lisette never mention you to me?'

'Did she not?' Antoinette faced her with troubled eyes. She took out the pins again and dropped them onto the delicate fabric.

'No.' Natalie watched her with palpable hostility.

'*Tiens!*' Antoinette raised an eyebrow. 'And you knew her so well that she would speak thus to you?'

Natalie was silent, pondering. 'Perhaps not,' she acknowledged. Lisette had not appreciated her treatment of Nicolas, though, since the ball all those years ago, she'd never mentioned that either. It was more a feeling Natalie got from the way Lisette had looked at her sometimes. But then she saw that what she said had upset Antoinette and narrowed her eyes. *I knew there was something!*

'I don't believe she knew it,' said Antoinette, almost to herself. 'I didn't really know it myself until they'd gone. But even if she did, she would understand the reason that I did not keep in touch.' She faced her tormentor squarely. 'I don't know what you're trying to insinuate, but I loved my sister and she loved me.'

Natalie shrugged. 'I'm not insinuating anything. I just asked a question, that's all.'

'Yes? An insensitive one, too.' A momentary anger flared in Antoinette's cool blue eyes. 'Go ask your questions somewhere else,' she snapped, jamming the pins between her small, white teeth and turning back to the delicate crystal-beaded fabric.

'Gladly!' said Natalie, storming out. But underneath she felt a tinge of guilt at the cruelty of her question to Antoinette. She tucked it away, out of mind, in her search for the answer to another question.

But when she found Armand, he had no idea where Angel was, either. 'I know he got something … a secret communication from Max,' he told her. 'He's gone out in the field. I don't know where.'

Angel was away for days. When he came back, he held discussions with Armand and Antoinette, gave a fresh set of orders to his agents and sent for Natalie.

He was writing at his desk and didn't seem to notice her.

Natalie curled her lip at what she saw as a ploy. 'You wanted to see me?' she asked: her voice harsh and metallic.

'*Un moment, s'il vous plaît,*' he murmured; his hand continuing across the page. He made a decisive full stop, said, 'Now,' and looked up.

Natalie flinched from the power in his eyes, shocked speechless. She'd always been sure of herself with the old Nicolas. But, with this one, she did not know where she was. When he shifted his gaze back to the paper, it was as if she could breathe again, freed from hypnotic tension.

Head bowed, Natalie clenched her hands: just one more thing to add to the avalanche of emotions that were beginning to tell on her, steadily eroding her self-esteem. She wanted to run and hide; had, in fact, to force herself to remain standing there in front of him. It was all adding up to something that she could not steel herself to face.

'Sit down.' He waved to a chair.

'I'd rather stand,' she muttered.

'As you wish. You know, I always liked your directness,' he said, leaning back in his chair to look up at her. 'At first, I found your honesty refreshing: a new approach. But when you are using it to hurt others … No, there must be an end to it.'

*Liked, not 'loved'?* That was the word that leapt out at Natalie with blinding clarity: the word that said it all. The loving, sweet-natured man who adored her was just a distant memory; even, perhaps, a figment of her imagination. Natalie felt that this one treated her as an errant child that he could only just muster the patience to tolerate, but she'd gone past wanting to lash out and flushed painfully, knowing that he was holding up a mirror; a mirror that she would not, could not, look into.

'This is a *war*,' he said; his words quiet and deliberate.

'*Oh* ... Tell me something I don't know!' The old Natalie surfaced momentarily.

'We, here, are all battling the same fears, the same dangers, the same enemy. You do not seem to understand that we are all on the same side.' He stood suddenly, looming over her. 'You will not take out your petty grievances on your companions. Is that clear?'

Natalie was silent, avoiding his eyes. What *was* clear was that Antoinette had been complaining about her. Was it justified? Natalie didn't want to go there. Yet, under Angel's steady regard, her skin prickled; she felt guilty, mortified, diminished. Were he and Antoinette so close? Pain slashed at her heart. She gasped, unable to reply.

When she did not answer, he said, 'I will assume that it is, until otherwise advised. And now, about the division of labour in this place: your work and my proposed mission ...'

Natalie swayed on her feet, grasping the back of the chair as Angel told her in no uncertain terms that she was not to be involved. 'It is my mission, mine and Antoinette's. You have your own work to get on with. And another thing ...' The sapphire-blue eyes flashed a warning. 'Sette was eminently practical. She lived day to day, especially in these times. If you did not know Antoinette, there was no reason why she would mention her to you. And neither is it your business to ask.' He gave her a curt nod. 'You may go.'

Fury, mortification, jealousy; any number of passions were aroused in Natalie's breast at his cavalier dismissal.

§

There was a flurry of activity when Angel pronounced Antoinette ready for their first mission and gave her five minutes to get ready. Struggling into her costume, she was feeling the pressure when one of the hooks on the back of her costume had become entangled in the fabric beside the wrong eye. Twisting and turning ineffectually, desperately conscious of time passing, she called Natalie to help her.

'You told Angel on me,' said Natalie, concentrating on freeing the hook from layers of delicate thread.

'It wasn't quite like that. We are worried about you.'

Natalie gritted her teeth. 'Don't be. I am *perfectly* all right.'

'*Eh bien*, I am pleased to hear it.'

'Look, if I have *said* things ...' Natalie spoke with difficulty as she fastened the hook into the correct eye. 'I am sorry. All right?'

'Quite, *ma chère*. We will forget it.' Antoinette wriggled her shoulders, smoothed the diaphanous silk-tulle and lace with its sparkling bodice and overskirt. 'There. That is better. *Merci*.'

'Shall I ...? Would you like me to give you a hand with your headdress?'

Antoinette gave her a quick glance. 'Thank you. That will be a great help.'

'It is pretty,' murmured Natalie, reaching for the delicate, jewelled headpiece. 'Quite ... ethereal.'

'I hope so, my dear,' said Antoinette, with a wry twinkle. 'That is why I have chosen it.'

§

Angel eyed his assistant up and down, quirking a lip at the faint luminescence that emanated from her person. 'Perfect: Even if you have kept me waiting. You look exactly as I had envisioned. I see that you have thoroughly dusted yourself with the powder I gave you. That will give an added touch: a ghostly essence. And the headdress: exquisite!' Monk-like, he was completely covered in a black cowled robe and threw her one the same. 'Put this on. We don't want to give our secrets away just yet. Ready? Then let us do it.' He led the way to the woods at the edge of the village in silence, carrying his paraphernalia in a sack over his shoulder. 'This will be a good place, I should think. In view of both the château and the village.'

'Yes,' she agreed. He had chosen well: an eerie spot, the tree branches gnarled and twisted. *Like ghostly arms reaching skywards*, thought Antoinette, and shivered. She watched him take a canister from the bag. 'Can I help you set it up?'

'No, your turn will come. This was once known as the Promethean Fountain,' he mused, hefting it in his hand. 'Although, I have modified it for our purpose. But I am hoping that the ignorant will call it *feu follet*.' He set up the canister on the edge of the woods in full view of the sentries; darkness cloaking his actions. 'Now, you know what to do: out of the flames *en pirouette*, two leaps *en grand jeté* and back into the fountain just left of centre. Remember, it is cold fire and cannot burn you, but we must be coordinated. Just left of centre, *hein? Bon.* I will be waiting with this.' He put his hands on the shoulders of the enveloping black robe she wore over the ghostly costume. 'If it is any comfort, this is the only time that you will have to do this. The rest of the time, we will use the device. Once the fear is established, the mind will fill in the details for itself.'

'So,' she said. 'If a bullet gets me, you can still carry on as if nothing has happened. Is that what you mean?'

'It is not!' A tiny half-smile just touched his lips. 'I am depending on you to set the magic fire without me after this. Even if they shoot, and you dance as I have told you, then you should be moving too quickly to present a good enough target at that distance. It will be only if they close in. But I have a little remedy for that.' He patted his pocket. 'Now: take off your over boots.'

Antoinette obeyed his order, keeping her glowing slippers hidden under the long cloak.

'Are you ready?' Angel set the timer and stood behind her. 'Five seconds,' he said. And started to count.

The canister began to spew multicoloured fire with a steady hissing. Higher and higher it rose until it responded to gravity, spreading like a brilliant umbrella.

A ripple of wonder passed through the sentries, astonishment holding them silent. The tiny light they observed on the edge of the forest was behaving in a way that set the hair lifting on their arms and scalps. From that distance, they could not hear the hissing, saw no human movement in the sudden flaring light produced by the growing flames—the colours of which they had never seen. An older man gasped, 'Can it be the angel? The Angel of Mons come to get us like it did in the Great War?'

'No,' breathed another. '*Irrlicht*. It is *Irrlicht*. I saw it once: ghostly fire.'

'Will-o'-the-wisp.'

'*Feu follet.*'

'Demon fire.'

'*Fata morgana!*'

There was a bigger gasp, then silence as the brilliant tongues leapt into a towering fountain.

'Now!' whispered Angel, pulling the cloak from his companion's shoulders and giving her a little push into the flames. '*Vite!*'

A wraith-like ballerina, glowing with unearthly light, spun out of the fiery fountain just as a great shout came from the drawbridge of the château. Her whole figure, from her jewelled headdress to her bright slippers, flashed a myriad rainbows, giving her a mysterious translucence, as if the watchers could see right through her to the flames behind. Floating out from her like wreaths of mist, a shimmering iridescence followed her every move, alternately enveloping her and being trailed behind, as she pirouetted with desperate speed; at times, there seemed to be two of her. A spirit phenomenon to bring dread to the hearts of all who witnessed it.

There was another great shout, and this time, the intent was clear: the soldiers were being given orders to shoot. Fear lent wings to Antoinette's feet, turning her into the dancer she claimed not to be. In a trice, she had performed two leaps her sister would have been proud of and vanished into the curtain of flames before the first volley of shots.

The cries of the sentries now held a note of panic. The fragile, ghostly being that danced out of the flames— transient, nebulous, a blur of fuzzy luminosity—terrified them. Especially when she danced back into them and disappeared without a sound. No human being could do that. Nothing less than the supernatural would explain it.

The longer the sentries watched, the more their senses misgave them. War made acts of unconscionable brutality permissible. Yet, in their hearts, they knew that, one day, there had to be a reckoning. Condemned by their own guilty knowledge, they each became certain that they were being forewarned of a deistic retribution for their rape of an innocent country—the sufferings of a blameless people.

Along with intense fear, each one battled guilt, remorse and an increasing dread that they were about to pay the price that was to be exacted for their heinous crimes. Some of them remembered a small, delicate woman that had been hustled up the stairs to the interrogation chamber and carried out, weeks later, a broken corpse. They felt, most keenly, a sense of impending doom: of *Nemesis* wreaking vengeance. None questioned why she leapt into their thoughts—the most primitive of reactions had overcome intellect—and the only one who could have known it was away, using his leave to dance attendance on the Führer. Their terror mounted, but that only meant that the firing increased in intensity.

As Antoinette emerged on the other side under a hail of gunfire, Angel wrapped her in the heavy cloak and rolled over and over with her on the ground. When they reached the shelter of rocks behind a large tree, he pulled the pin on a grenade and hurled it into the fire. Then, covering Antoinette's body with his own, he waited, head down, for the explosion. Afterwards, there was a strange silence: immense, almost mystical. Then a faint sigh, as if the forest had held its breath and then expelled it.

'That should give them pause for thought,' he whispered, setting her on her feet and leading her away through the empty forest. Not until they were in the cave entrance did he speak again. 'You did well; showed great courage. Sette would be proud of you. *I* am proud of you. The whole *Résistance* will be thankful for your bravery because now we can wreak hell on them without endangering ourselves, since a timer will ensure that we can be well away before it manifests.'

'Thank you, *mon brave*. That is very kind. But you may not think so much of my courage when I tell you that I hope I do not have to do something like that again.'

'That is not lack of courage but common sense,' he said, lighting a lantern and turning to face her in its warm glow. 'And no, you will not have to do it again. That was a once only: perfectly executed. From now on, we will use the device. And the next one will be even more terrifying; I promise you.'

'For them, I hope, but not for me.' Antoinette shuddered. 'That did not feel too good, being pursued by all those bullets, *je vous assure!*'

He put a bracing arm around her. 'You were protected by angels.'

Antoinette looked down at his forearm. 'But you weren't, *mon ami*. You are bleeding.'

He lifted the lantern to study the rent in his sleeve. 'It is only a graze. It doesn't hurt.'

'It will tomorrow.'

'At least we will have a tomorrow.'

'Were you worried?'

'*Pas du tout.*' He laughed, released her and led the way across the chamber. 'Are we not home, safe?'

Antoinette had to run to keep up with the tall, striding figure.

§

Early next morning, Angel was in the operations room. 'Good morning,' he called to Antoinette, as she entered the great chamber. 'And it *is* a good morning,' he added, with satisfaction. 'I had a message from the village. The *Boche* and the villagers are terrified out of their minds. They say the sentries would not stay on duty last night.' He stood up and stretched. 'Jean-Marie has managed to find some decent coffee. Come and have a cup.'

'How is your arm?'

'As I said: a scratch. Nothing to worry about. And you? No ill effects from your spectral dance?'

'No. Just happy to be alive, my friend. Although, it *was* a little difficult to get rid of your phosphorescent powder …'

'*Eh bien …*' The smile in his eyes reflected hers.

Natalie saw them enter the dining chamber together, looking very pleased with themselves, and wished herself anywhere but here. She responded in a small voice to their greetings, relieved when Jean-Marie brought in a pot of coffee and slapped it on the table with a flourish.

'You have both been very clever,' he said, smiling broadly. 'According to Alain, enemy radio chatter this morning is all about demonic fire and a mysterious ghost dancer.'

Antoinette looked at Angel. 'Then you should be called Sibyl and not I,' she said. 'Because it was your prophecy.'

Natalie watched them laughing into each other's eyes and felt so ill that she had to leave the room. It hurt her even more that no-one noticed. They were too busy talking of their exploits.

'*Merci*,' said Angel, accepting Jean-Marie's offer to pour the coffee. 'You have started the "Russian scandal"?'

'*Oui*, Monsieur. It is well on its way,' said Gabriel.

'A rumour?' asked Antoinette. 'What rumour?'

Angel checked to make sure that Armand had not just walked into the room and placed his hand over Antoinette's to hold it firmly. 'The rumour that the phenomenon is Settie's ghost out for vengeance. We had to start it ourselves because nobody knows but us that she was a ballerina. Besides, we need to impress upon them the idea of the supernatural as an explanation.' He looked closely at her. 'You are not upset?'

'No.' Antoinette made a moue and shook her head. 'It is only the truth, after all.'

# 47 FEU FOLLET

**27 May 1943**

*Nicolas has been called away to a secret meeting—top secret. Natalie is devastated, but it is more than my life is worth to let her in on it. And to be honest, I don't know where he is, either. Nor when he expects to be back. He has become a real will-o'-the-wisp. Speaking of which, his magic fire and ghost dancer (deployed by Toinette while he is away) has been more successful than we could have dreamt, allowing us to disrupt machine gun nests, convoys, troop movements. The most fearful thing—and I do not know how he has done it—is that the more they fire at the ghost dancer device, the more wildly it dances and moans and screams. Finally, when its wailing reaches the most unearthly pitch, the whole thing explodes with the force of a deadly grenade! So, the enemy do not just run from the supernatural, but they run just the same! Eh bien, it is good to wield some power, however small!*

In Angel's absence, Antoinette continued to set the magic fire and the ghost dancer device at random intervals and places according to secret codes she received by radio. The German occupiers were becoming nervous because there was no predicting when or where it might manifest, and there were serious ramifications over what the authorities saw as the cowardice of their troops. Some were shot out of hand, others imprisoned, tortured and beaten.

Those few Maquis that were let in on the secret rejoiced at these signs of emotional instability in the enemy—weakness in a war machine that for years had seemed invincible; a monster eating its own tail—and redoubled their efforts to fight back. And when the Belvoir Maquis managed to get close enough to an enemy machine gun nest to take it out with a well-aimed hand grenade, because its occupants were preoccupied with firing at the device, they were even more inspired.

§

Angel was in Paris, renewing his acquaintance with Colonel Rol in anticipation of a pivotal event in the history of the war in France. Max had called all the *Résistance* leaders to a secret meeting. Tonight, if things went well, all the *Résistance* groups in the country would be united under one flag: The Free French Forces of the Interior.

The leaders talked well into the night, and Angel brought guests to his underground palace, smiling at their expressions of admiration. But when they left the next morning, he declined to accompany them.

'There is something that I must do before I leave,' he explained, farewelling them with a little half-smile.

Some time later, he came away from an apartment door with a wrinkled brow and a stern set to his mouth and went into an abandoned garden. Then, at the Cimetière du Père Lachaise, he dropped to his knees to place two rosebuds: one red, one white at the foot of a new wooden cross.

'To a woman of courage and integrity, from Natalie *et moi*,' he said, making the sign of the cross before he rose. For a moment, he stood looking down on the freshly turned earth—a curiously regretful expression in his eyes—then, at a sound in the distance, vanished amongst the headstones.

§

Natalie worried about Nicolas every day, finally coming to the realisation that he might never come back. She began to see that her freedom—that freedom that she so prized—came from being able to expand in his love, like a flower opening in spring: nurtured, protected. It was breaking her heart to understand what she had thrown away through fear and ignorance.

*It was wrong to play games,* she thought. *Only children played games.* She didn't know how she could have been so immature. It shamed her to think of it. When—*if*—he came back, she would ask him if they could start again. Tell him that she really did love him, that she'd been too young.

Her face quivered, tears rolled; she resolved to apologise for all the times that she'd hurt him to prove she could. It was time to grow up: own emotions so huge that they frightened her. Time to take that terrible, remote expression from his beloved face. Time to tell him that she really did love him, after all.

The hours dragged, each one a day, each day a week. *Why hasn't Nic come back? He can't be dead. He can't be.* Natalie haunted the operations room, waiting for news. She was jittery, lived on her nerves, hardly bothered to eat and noticeably lost weight.

Armand and Antoinette were gentle with her, completely understanding what she was going through. They gave her space, never reacted to a sharp tone of voice, smiled and patted her hand when she apologised for her lack of control. '*De rien, ma chère!*' was a murmured phrase she heard quite often. Too often. Natalie was suffering—more obviously than she liked. But somehow, she couldn't do it in silence. Couldn't just carry on. It was her whole life, turning into nothing. How could she not be visibly affected?

And then, right in front of her eyes, there he was, coming towards her in long, easy strides, with kindness in his eyes and his arms outstretched, just like he once was, before the war had changed everything.

'Nic! Oh, Nic. You are back!' she sobbed, melting into his embrace. 'Where have you been?'

'In Paris,' he said. 'A secret meeting with Max and the other leaders. The *Résistance* is now a united force to be reckoned with.'

'Paris?' she whispered against his chest. 'You were in Paris all this time? I thought you were dead!'

'*Doucement, ma chère,*' he murmured. 'You must be brave. I have some very sad news for you.'

Natalie raised her head. 'Nanette? It is Nanette, isn't it?'

He nodded. 'Yes, I went to visit her, only to find that she had been buried the day before. I talked to her maid. She slipped away easily. One minute, she was sitting chatting while the maid prepared her supper, the next she seemed to have dropped off to sleep. Except that the maid could not wake her.'

Natalie sobbed quietly against his shoulder. 'I suppose I should be thankful that she had a good death. I know that she was in a lot of pain and that she wanted her suffering to be over.'

'Yes. She made no secret that death was her preferred option.'

'Well, at least she died in her own place, in her own time. Which is something to be thankful for in this dreadful war.'

'Indeed, *ma chère*. I hoped you would see it that way. She was a courageous woman. Remember her like that.'

'Yes.' Natalie took a handkerchief from her sleeve and

wiped her eyes. 'I will. Thank you for taking the time to … to …'

'*De rien*! It was for me as much as you.'

'Well, thank you, anyway.' She concentrated on the crumpled fabric in her hand, smoothing the lace edging. 'Nic …?'

'Angel,' he reminded her gently.

'I just wanted to say that I am *so* sorry for the way I have treated you, for all the horrible things I have said to you.' Incredibly, she felt him stiffen, distance himself.

'Are you? How do I know that you won't take the opposite stand tomorrow?'

'Oh, Nic!'

He held her away to look into her eyes. 'Well? It is a valid question. You blow hot and cold, turn and turn about. How do you expect to be taken seriously this time? How can I trust you?'

*Trust?* There was that word again. Natalie knew that she couldn't run away from it any longer. Now she must own that she had never looked at it from that point of view; never seen anyone's point but her own. As she stared into his eyes, she saw something that she had never seen before. Well, perhaps she had seen it but never acknowledged it. In that moment, she saw that the diamond-hard stranger who looked out of the same beautiful sapphire-blue eyes, smiled with the same generous well-formed mouth, lived in the same lithe body as the man who loved her, had no interest in reconciliation, whatsoever.

Natalie was shattered. But hadn't she always been fearful of this? Wasn't this why she'd been afraid to give herself, ever?

Uttering a little cry, she broke away and ran to the sanctuary—or prison—that was her room.

# 48 SACRIFICE

**21 June 1943**

*Betrayal again. And on a terrible scale. Nicolas and I feel
it all the more because it brings back the suffering of my
darling Lisette. And I feel my betrayal most of all! But all
of us Maquisards are affected in one degree or another.
The communists are outraged! Natalie is tearing her hair,
beside herself with grief and rage, and the desire for
revenge. I am afraid that she will do something stupid. The
fact that Nicolas seems to have abandoned her in favour of
Toinette appears to be adding fuel to the flames. Because,
despite German pragmatism, their macabre ruse does still
seem to be working. Unbelievably, no-one has yet got to the
bottom of it. Although, it may be the cleverness of the
design that ensures the device selfdestructs so that there is
no evidence left to find. There is nothing like a hint of the
supernatural to arouse all humanity's irrational fears—no
matter what beliefs (or lack thereof) they hold. Especially
when, deep down, they know that they are guilty of the
worst crimes against humanity. And now the news of more
betrayal!*

The agent Raoul sped along the corridor, ignoring the
questioning faces at the big table in the main operations
chamber. He came to a skidding halt in Angel's doorway.

'Monsieur, Monsieur, you must come at once!'

'Raoul, what is it?' Angel leapt to his feet and put a steadying hand on his agent's arm.

'Gabriel and Jean-Marie, betrayed! *La milice* have them in the village lockup: not Belvoir, the next one, St. Étienne-les-Bains. They are waiting for the train to take them to Lyon, where the SS have taken Max.'

'Max? The Germans have Max?'

'*Oui*, Monsieur. Betrayed with others in a meeting in Caluire. You know, the one you couldn't get to because _____'

'Don't worry about that now. Timely, it seems, for me, but not for Max and the others. First, we must free Gabriel and Jean-Marie; then all of us must see what we can do for Max. Where is Armand? Come on.'

'But, Monsieur, there must be a breach. So many betrayed …'

'We will find them, these traitors. Be assured that they shall not escape. But first, we must free our men.'

He strode into the operations room, where Armand, Antoinette and Alain were bending over the big map. 'Quickly, give me your place,' he said, moving Antoinette out of the way with his hands on her shoulders. 'Now, Alain, see this railway bridge? I need it blown up before morning. Find whoever you can to help you. Armand, get on the radio to the Maquis at Lyon to try and find if there is any chance to spring Max. If we don't get him soon, it will be too late, you understand?'

Angel looked around. 'We must go. Are you up for this, Raoul?'

'But of course, Monsieur. Need you ask?'

He smiled and shook his head. 'Where is Juliette? You can tell her about Max but not about the others. That news will be bad enough as it is. You will keep an eye to her, Antoinette? *Bien*.' His eyes met those of Raoul. 'Let us go.'

§

Natalie was having a terrible day. In fact, it was the culmination of a run of terrible days. And the news that Max had been betrayed whilst in a meeting at Lyon and was, even now, under torture by that butcher Klaus Barbie made her physically ill. She knew that there could only be one end: it was only a matter of time before they heard that he had been tortured to death. She knew that Max, like Lisette, would never reveal their secrets. And like Lisette, he would die horribly.

His dear face rose in her mind: dashing in his fedora and scarf. A handsome man and in the prime of life. *God knows what those monsters are doing to him!* she thought and began to sob. *It is just so unfair! So wrong! How can such evil exist, let alone prosper?* 'God!' she shouted. 'Can you *hear* me? *Why* have you let this happen?' Natalie's hands balled into fists, tears streamed down her face. 'Why? Why? *Why?*' She collapsed, moaning, on her bed.

'Juliette. Dear child ...' Antoinette sank down beside her and began to stroke Natalie's damp hair back from her forehead. She spoke soothing words, exactly the way Lisette would speak. Gradually, Natalie's sobs quietened. She became stoical, accepting of whatever came. God had not done this evil: the mastermind was Hitler.

'We will pray for Max and we will sing *Le Chant des Partisans* for him, *hein?*'

Natalie agreed. 'Not that I am much of a singer.'

'You don't need a big voice. You can hold a tune can you not? *Eh bien*, that is all that is required.'

The singing definitely helped. Natalie managed to pull herself together and follow the song with only an occasional hiccup.

When they had finished, Antoinette asked, 'Will you be all right now?'

'Yes, thank you. I suppose we must all ... accept our

fate.'

'Whatever we cannot change, sadly, we must accept.'

'Yes ...' Natalie plucked listlessly at her bedcover. 'Where is Angel?'

Antoinette decided on a half-truth. 'He has gone to meet his agents and see if he can find out who betrayed Max ... And if there is anything that can be done. He said not to worry if he is away for longer than he anticipates.'

'And how long does he anticipate?'

'He didn't say.' Antoinette patted her hand. 'I should go now to see if I can help Armand in the operations room. He is alone ...'

'Yes, please go. I will be all right.'

'Are you sure?'

Natalie made a gesture. 'Of course. And thank you.'

'*De rien, Chérie*! Believe me, I know how you feel.'

*No, you don't ...*

As soon as Antoinette had gone, all Natalie's fatalism evaporated. Her face hardening, she got up, dressed in black and sneaked down the mountain to the village. *Antoinette is right: to a point. But there is a further point where you get beyond fear,* she thought, striding out boldly. *A point where fury and disgust take over. Well, let them do their worst! I am going to do mine!*

§

Calling in to see how she was a little later, Antoinette was alarmed that Natalie was not in her room. Even more so, when she had searched all the usual places Natalie might be found. She went back to the operations room. 'Armand?'

'Toinette. What is it?' Armand responded to the quaver in her voice. 'Have you heard some news?'

'No. I was about to ask you the same thing.'

'No. Nothing. I hope he ——'

'I cannot find Juliette.'

'Oh, no!' Armand clapped a hand to his brow. '*No* ...'

'What is it?'

'I believe I know where she has gone, and it will sign her death warrant. We must cause a distraction so that they do not get her.'

'If I knew what you were talking about, perhaps I could help you.'

'The magic fire. The ghost dancer. Can you ...?'

'Yes, yes, *mon brave*. Of course, I can. Calm down and tell me all about it. Then we will make a strategy, *hein?*'

§

The garrison commandant was writing his nightly letter to the Führer. He started to write the truth: the bleakness of the future, the slow but steady eroding of their command by terrorist underground organisations. Then he changed his mind. It would only upset the Führer to read this, and upsetting the Führer was something that did not pay. He fingered his pen thoughtfully. One might even say that he had a vested interest in *not* upsetting the Führer.

The commandant threw down the letter, swept it off his desk, took up a fresh sheet and began again. All positives and light. All lies. They were stifling him. Suddenly, needing air, he flung down his pen, strode out of the château, crossed the two courtyards and climbed the ramparts to the top of the gatehouse where the giant portcullis lay sheathed in its ancient stone, ready to drop on the unsuspecting at the whim of a commander. He glanced at the medieval machinery, oiled and waiting—his bloodied soul enjoying the thought of those it impaled struggling ineffectually only to die in indescribable agony—and stood idly watching two sentries laying down the law to a group of peasants caught in the shadows beneath the château drawbridge.

'You, peasants! Come out of there. What are you doing?'

'Collecting herbs and mushrooms, Monsieur. By moonlight, as is best for medicine.'

'Assemble on the road! Why were you hiding?'

'We were afraid that you would shoot us, Monsieur.'

'And quite rightly. Next time I find you here after dark, you will be shot on sight. Put down your baskets. They have been confiscated. You have one minute to get out of range of my pistol before I start firing. Now, march.' The officer watched them obey, then turned to his fellow. 'Help me with these baskets. I fancy some mushrooms for my supper.'

No sooner had he bent down, than a ghostly fire flared in the moat, reaching giant proportions in seconds and bathing the whole area in an eerie glow. A translucent white figure emerged from it, floating over the top, dancing in and out of the fiery fountain.

The commander gave a husky exclamation and bounded down the stairs. One of the sentries screamed, '*Irrlicht!*' and fled for the sanctuary of the château. The other, who had given the orders, stood staring, struck dumb.

'Halt! You coward!' growled the commandant, hitting the drawbridge at the same time as the terrified man. When the sentry didn't stop, he jerked the rifle out of his hands and jabbed him under the chin with it. He stepped over the fallen man and went to stand by the other.

'Demonic fire,' breathed the sentry.

'Balderdash!' grated the commander. 'That fire has human origin! And when I find it …' He shouldered the rifle and started firing. The dancing figure began to moan, louder with each successive shot, eventually giving out a spine-chilling wail.

Despite himself, the hair rose on the back of the commandant's neck. It was the first time he had seen this phenomenon, but he had heard about it more than he liked. It had been having a ridiculous effect on the men. He stopped shooting and watched the eerie display in silence.

'You see, Mein commandant? Bullets have no power! Flesh and blood we can fight. But not this witchery. This … I never believed in the supernatural. But this! We are not safe anywhere. Spirits can walk through walls ——'

'Stop your snivelling you lily-livered fool!' The commander backhanded him across the face. 'It is trickery! A ruse! And it is working because you are *all idiots*!'

'But, Colonel, it has only been happening since ——'

The commander swung around with a menacing sneer. 'Yes? Since?'

*You tortured a poor little woman to death!* Sweat broke out on the sentry's brow. A hunted expression crossed his face. 'Erm … Nothing.' He averted his eyes to exclaim, 'Look!' It is gone! The dancer is gone!'

The commandant's gaze followed the sentry's pointing finger into sudden darkness. 'There must be something left there. Get a searchlight and see what it is,' he grated. 'Hurry!'

The guard stared at him in horror. 'But what if it explodes?'

'Then we can be sure, dolt, that it is *not* supernatural! Get on with it!'

The sentry called for a searchlight; the commandant raised his rifle, but the intense light flared too late to show a black cowled figure throw a sack over the unexploded canister and spirit it away behind the bulge of a tower in the ancient wall.

'There is nothing there,' whispered the sentry. 'Nothing! Look!'

'Trickery! We will examine the area more closely for evidence in the morning.' The commandant grunted and turned his attention to the peasants caught in the glare of the searchlight. 'I wonder if this lot had anything to do with it?'

Most of them had run from the ghostly fire in panic like the first sentry, but a few were made of sterner stuff, only running at the sound of gunfire. They had slowed to a fast walk when they realised they were not the targets.

The commandant lowered his rifle and cast a speculative eye over what was left of the ragged group, in particular, a couple of women bringing up the rear. '*Mon Dieu!*' he gasped, poking the sentry with the rifle barrel. 'Quickly! Bring me that woman! Not that one, imbecile! The tall one. That's her.' He watched her capture with satisfaction. '*Eh bien,*' he muttered. 'I would know that walk anywhere.'

The cowled figure, hidden behind the fortification, raised clenched hands to heaven in a gesture of futility and despair.

§

Angel and Raoul made their way to the village watch house, picking up a young man on the way. 'My nephew, Roland,' said Raoul. 'He has been watching the movements of the sentries.'

'Three sentries,' said Roland. 'They make their patrol on the hour. This first one, he goes around the watch house clockwise. The others go anticlockwise and pass him on the other side. There is one who always stays inside at the desk.'

'There are four? Only four?'

'*Oui,* Monsieur.'

Angel nodded. 'Very well; we will wait. We must be coordinated. I will take the first one. When you two take the others, I will be there to help.'

Silently they hoisted themselves over the stone wall surrounding the lockup and dropped into some bushes.

Concealed in the shrubbery, they waited, tensing as a uniformed figure opened the door and looked around, before stepping out.

'That is the first one,' whispered Raoul. 'He will come this way.'

'When he gets around the corner of the building, I will have him,' murmured Angel, taking a cord from his pocket and flexing it between his fingers. 'You be ready for the others. Good hunting, *mes braves*. And remember: no sound when you take them. Otherwise we are finished before we start.'

The sentry paused in the lee of the building to light a cigarette. Angel needed no other invitation, waiting until the man's hands went to his pockets before leaping on him from behind. The silken noose dropped over the sentry's head, pulled tight as Angel lifted him bodily into the garden. The cigarette fell to the ground, extinguished by a flailing boot. In a few seconds, the man lay still. He had not uttered a sound.

The other two were despatched in similar style; the small scraping noise of their boots inaudible to their fellow, writing painstakingly at the desk. Perhaps he had heard a boot scraping on stone, but it meant nothing without a cry or a gunshot.

Angel signed to his men to arm themselves with their victims' pistols, and the three men stepped inside the watch house, guns drawn. The desk officer looked up; his jaw sagging.

'Keys,' said Angel, holding a pistol to his head. 'We want your prisoners. Now.'

In the space of seconds, the officer was locked in his own jail, and Gabriel and Jean-Marie stood smiling and shaking hands.

'I can't thank you enough,' said Gabriel. 'We thought that was it for us.'

'No, you live to fight another day. It is Max that we now have to think of.' Angel turned to Raoul. 'Find out if

Alain was able to do that job. You may take your nephew with you. My thanks for a fine effort,' he said, shaking their hands. 'We will wait here for you.' When they had gone, he said, 'Gabriel, we must make all speed to Lyon, forming a strategy on the way.'

Gabriel shook his head. 'Time will be tight, Monsieur. And we will need the others.'

'They will not be long,' said Angel, raising his head. 'In fact, I think that they are back already ... Over here,' he said, as Raoul appeared with Alain and Roland. 'That was quick.'

'Alain was already on his way with a message for you, Monsieur,' said the young man, handing Angel a piece of paper. He held a lighted match for him to read it by. Angel read it twice, swore softly and stumbled over to lay his forehead against the stone wall; his hands either side, clenched against the rough surface. He stayed like that for long moments. 'Max ... Oh, Max,' he breathed. 'I am *sorry* ...' He straightened and turned, beckoned to Gabriel, waiting in respectful silence with the others. 'Get everyone you can and go to Lyon,' he said. 'Do what you can for Max.'

Then, he sprang over the wall and vanished into the darkness.

# 49 RETRIBUTION

**Late, 21 June 1943**

*Now Natalie has disappeared. My ruse to help her seems to have backfired in the most unfortunate way, so that I will have her death on my conscience if we cannot find her in time. Sometimes I wish I could have died with my wife, then all this would be over. I know it is a cowardly sentiment, but true, nonetheless.*

The SS commander frogmarched Natalie up the stairs; her arm cruelly twisted behind her back. Every few steps, he jerked it until she gasped with pain.

'*Mon* colonel!'

The commander turned; his lip curling into a snarl. 'What do you want? Can you not see that I am busy?'

'The peasants' baskets, *mon* colonel: they are full of explosives!'

'So …' The snarl became an ugly sneer. 'You did not get your mushrooms?'

'Well, yes. Just not as many as we thought.'

'Ah … then my prisoner will have a lot to tell us.' He bared his teeth in a grin that made his hardened sergeant shudder. 'So as not to waste bullets, we will delay reprisals until we have the full story. We don't want to risk any of them getting away. In here, you.' He jerked Natalie's arm again, threw open the door to the ducal chambers and thrust her inside.

A girl in a white satin peignoir was lying on the carved four-poster bed; her full, red lips opening in surprise as she saw Natalie. It was Yvette, a girl from the village; and Natalie did not miss the preening smile before it turned into a sullen pout.

The officer narrowed his eyes and jerked his head imperiously. 'Get out!'

The girl gave Natalie a dagger look and bounced up off the bed.

'And you can leave that here.'

With another sultry pout, she divested herself of the robe and pulled on a simple print dress.

'Wait! Light the fire before you go.'

Yvette obeyed, crouching to set a match to the small logs laid with paper and kindling. When the flames caught, she rose and turned. The commandant jerked his head towards the door. She started to speak, thought better of it when she met his eyes and fled the room.

He kicked the door shut behind her and turned his prisoner to face him. 'Now, you,' he whispered. 'I have been waiting a long time for this.' He dragged her over to the fireplace and shoved her into a bentwood chair.

§

Armand sat hunched in the operations room, biting his nails. Occasionally Antoinette made soothing sounds and patted his shoulder, but they both looked white and ill.

Then, Antoinette heard something. 'Listen,' she said.

Armand raised his head; a sudden hope stirring the sad cast of his features. A smile lit his face. 'Gabriel, we are so thankful to see you! Jean-Marie, is he …?'

'*Oui*, Monsieur, we are both safe. Angel and the others saw to that.'

'That is wonderful news.'

'Yes, wonderful!' agreed Antoinette. 'But we have another problem now. Juliette has been captured by the SS. She is ——'

'In the château, I know.' Gabriel stroked his upper lip. 'There's a girl in the village swearing Juliette is a collaborator, but I do not believe she went willingly.'

'No, she didn't go willingly,' said Armand, wringing his hands. 'She went to blow up the drawbridge. She'd been keen to do it for quite a while, but Angel vetoed it. When I found out where she'd gone, I got Toinette to set a diversion; but it backfired on us, and Juliette was caught. I sent a message to Angel, but I don't know if he got it.'

'He did. That's why I am here. I've come to get you and Toinette and anyone else I can find to help free Max and the other leaders.'

§

Natalie sagged in the bentwood chair. Her captor hadn't tied her, but she knew he was waiting for her to make an attempt to escape; and she refused to give him the satisfaction of thwarting it with violence. She had tried to put a brave face on it, tried not to let the fiend see how utterly terrified she was. But then she realised why the fire had been lit and began to tremble as Gervais thrust the poker into its glowing depths. And now that another officer had walked in, he had the gall to say that he believed that this was the *White Mouse* herself and would be made to talk.

'Of course I am not. You know who I am.' Natalie's tone was scornful.

'Not entirely …' he drawled. 'But I will before we are finished. Or, should I say, *you* are finished.'

Natalie knew what she had to do. She wasn't strong like Lisette. She was afraid that she would give them Nicolas. Betray them all. *You expect to die for your own country, not someone else's,* she thought, bitterly. But then she knew that France was her country just as much as Australia. She couldn't bear the thought that, after all the emotional pain she had caused Nicolas, she would be the instrument of his torture and death. Her thoughts were rambling. She remembered what Max had tried to do so that he would not betray the innocent. Knowing that the German torturers could crack you before you died horribly, knowing that she was very close, that she had no more choices left, her hand flashed to the second button on her blouse.

'No you don't,' said the visiting officer, knocking her arm so that the cyanide capsule flew across the room. 'What a spitfire! We'll have some fun with her. But we'll have to tie her hands first.' He did so with leather straps, then laughed. 'Nice hair,' he said, and ripped out a great clump, oblivious to Natalie's hastily suppressed whimper. He stared down at it; his jaw working. 'But she isn't the *White Mouse.* These roots are the wrong colour.' He turned to Gervais, accusation in his voice. 'What kind of game are you playing? Why did you lie about who she is?' *Trying to get more credit with the Führer, I'll bet!*

'Do you know,' purred Gervais, 'I have rather a fancy to play a lone hand.' He straightened and moved towards the other officer, brandishing the red-hot tip of the poker in his face. 'And I find you just a little *de trop,* my friend.'

The officer looked into his eyes, changed colour and speedily effaced himself. Gervais followed him to the door and locked it. 'No more interruptions,' he said with satisfaction, thrusting the poker back into the fire, then turned, smiling, to his prisoner. 'And now, my dear, you must help me decide ...' he said, deliberately prolonging the moment. 'Which eye would you like to lose first?'

'No,' she whispered. 'Please ...'

'What? Lost your bravado? Dear me!' He straightened and brought the glowing tip into her line of vision. She met his eyes bravely. It was so incredibly hard not to show fear and revulsion. And then, behind him, she saw something: something that made her think that she must be hallucinating.

Natalie's eyes flicked away and back to his. They held, despite the darkness she encountered. Desperately, she tried to think of something to stall him, keep him talking so that he wouldn't swing around and see the unbelievable sight that had come into her field of vision.

The tip of the poker moved nearer, ever nearer: the heat off it searing her eyelid. A part of her noticed he had chosen her right eye. She shrank back in the chair, twisted convulsively against the leather straps, closed both eyes and waited for the agony.

She knew Gervais was grinning—his handsome face wholesome and fresh, his eyes pure evil—holding his instrument of torture close enough to burn, yet not making contact. 'Not so scornful now, are we, Mademoiselle?' he crooned. 'Now that I have the upper ____,'

The words broke off in a muffled grunt. Natalie opened her eyes as the poker clanged on the hearth.

'Keep them closed,' said Angel. 'This won't take long.'

§

When Natalie risked a glance, Gervais's short struggle was over. He was lying still and silent, eyes half-closed: his face an unmistakable mask of death. Angel removed the silk cord from his neck and put it in his pocket. Then he released Natalie from her bonds.

'Oh, Nic! I am sorry that I went against you. Didn't do what you said,' she whispered, rubbing her wrists.

He stood; his face averted. A muscle moved in his jaw. 'Not as sorry as you might have been ...'

'I know. Thank you.'

'Later. We have no time for that now. There is much

to do, and we are not out of danger yet.' His eyes searched the chamber, as if for inspiration. He moved to pick up the discarded letter from the floor, made a suppressed exclamation and switched it for the positive version on the desk, which he tossed into the flames. 'This may give them some explanation for his disappearance. Bring his torch,' he commanded, dragging the body by the shoulders into the dressing-room, surprising Natalie when he vanished into the garderobe.

'What?' she said, diving after him and shining the torch around. 'Another secret escape route? This place must be riddled with them. Is this the way you came?'

'Shh. Give me a hand to get him onto the staircase, if you can.'

'Gladly,' mouthed Natalie, taking first one boot and then the other as Angel heaved the corpse onto stone steps set in the wall. 'Where are we going?'

'It comes out in the passage that leads to the crypt,' he told her, grunting with the effort of carrying the heavy body. 'At least it is all downward; otherwise, I would have my work cut out.'

They went the rest of the way in silence; Natalie helping where she could. It was a test of endurance, and when they finally dragged their macabre burden into the crypt and hefted him in to the catafalque of a medieval priest, they were too exhausted to talk.

Back in the ducal apartments, Angel closed the garderobe and took the torch from Natalie. 'Now comes the hard part,' he said. 'We will have to walk down the main hall and one flight of stairs. There will almost certainly be a sentry at the head of them.' He put on Gervais's greatcoat, muffler and peaked cap. 'How do I look?' he asked in sinister tones that made Natalie shiver.

'Too much like him for my piece of mind, muffled up like that,' she said.

'In dim light, I may get away with it,' he agreed, doing something to a light socket that plunged the château into darkness. 'Come. Say nothing unless I press your arm; then, I want you to moan as if in pain. *Tu comprends? Bien.*'

Natalie walked beside him as if in a dream.

'Who goes?' demanded the sentry.

'It is I,' said Angel, in husky tones.

'Herr Commandant.' The soldier saluted.

'You may let us pass,' he grated, shining the torch in the sentry's eyes. 'Mademoiselle is showing me a secret of the château. I don't know how long I will be. You had better go and wake up an electrical engineer to find out what has happened to the power.'

'At once, Herr Commandant.' The sentry saluted and felt his way down the banister.

The supposed SS commander and his prisoner had no more interruptions, reaching the duc's study and the secret room without incident, making their way down the stone tower and through the underground passages. Finally, they stood in the empty operations room.

'I don't know where the others are,' said Natalie, looking about. 'But at least now I can thank you.'

'They went to Lyon to try and help Max,' said Angel in dry tones, ignoring the latter part of her speech.

Natalie put her hand to her mouth. Somehow, with all she had been through, the *Résistance* leader's plight had been pushed to the back of her mind. 'Oh … *Max!* Could you do anything?'

'No. I was needed … elsewhere.'

'Do you mean that I ——'

'Yes.'

'But aren't you going back?'

He shook his head. 'No. It is too late.'

'How do you know? I could go with you.' She shook his arm with urgency. '*How do you know?*'

He turned; his face dark. 'Don't ask me that question: I *know*.' He grasped her shoulders. 'The question you need to consider is: were you worth it?'

'*Nic!* What do you mean? Don't you love me any

more?' She could hear herself, like a panic-stricken child. Shame coloured her cheeks. Had he not already made it clear? And here she was, blurting out a question with an obvious answer. Suddenly, she wished that she had died in the château, that she didn't have to stand here and face him—and the bleak, terrible truth.

His hands on her shoulders loosened; he looked over her head; his flash of anger abated. In his eyes was an ancient wisdom and a hint of amusement for her childishness. Otherwise he gave no clue to his thoughts. Gently, he kissed her on the forehead. 'I want you to do me one small favour,' he said. 'Ask me again when the war is over.' And then, as if to the child he thought her, 'You've had an exhausting night. Go to bed.'

'But what about you?' she cried, once again panicking at seeing him turn away. 'Aren't you staying here with me?'

'No,' he very faintly shook his head. 'I must go.'

'But … Where are you going?'

'Wherever I am needed.'

'Why?'

'I owe it to Max.'

Dumbly, she watched him stride away.

# 50 SAVING PARIS

**15 August 1944**

*There has been so much bloodshed, so many terrible battles and even more terrible reprisals. We have been driven back so many times! And now, when at last it looks as though we might prevail, when we have had our greatest breakthrough, Nicolas has not been seen or heard of for months. After all that we have gone through, all those we have lost, must we prepare ourselves for news of Angel's torture and death? Let it not be!*

*Gabriel has just returned without our hoped-for news: only that Hitler has ordered the destruction of Paris. My God: Where will it all end? And is Nicolas dead or alive?*

'Perhaps we are winning, after all,' said Armand. 'The Germans have abandoned Belvoir and are making for Gap, from where, I believe, they are going to make their escape into Italy.'

'Does Angel know?'

'I don't know. No-one has seen or heard from him for months.'

'*No* ...' Natalie left the chamber, stuffing the ends of her scarf into her mouth so that she would not disgrace herself more by wailing like a child.

'What do we know of him, *mon brave?*' asked

Antoinette, with a compassionate glance at Natalie's running figure.

'Nothing concrete since the Battle of Glières in the Haute-Savoie, where he joined the Maquis des Glières to take a stand against the Germans. There have been rumours of him fighting with different groups, but ...' he shrugged. 'They are only rumours.'

'There were dreadful losses in that battle. We *do* know for certain that he survived it?'

'Yes, thankfully we know. The agents confirmed it.'

As if on cue, Gabriel entered the chamber, greeting its occupants with a deprecating salute. His delivery of stunning news was fairly low key. 'We have the enemy on the run. The local Maquis plan to surround Gap, cut off the enemy's retreat and force them to surrender. They have asked us to join them. Are we up for it?'

'*Bien sûr!* Is there any news of Angel?'

'No, Monsieur. But I have hope. No news is good news, as they say. If the enemy had killed him, they would have advertised it. He is a big catch.'

§

A dark figure crept along the rue de Rivoli, keeping well back in the shadows, to stand looking up at the swastika decorated façade of le hôtel Meurice. The faint light showed his face curiously set. He took some time to determine the apartment he wanted, then leapt for an ornate pillar and up onto a first-floor balcony where he vanished into the building. Minutes later, he reappeared, climbing the wall with reckless grace to slide over the required window sill. The curtain swayed with a slight hushing, and he stood still, not daring to breath.

General von Choltitz heard the tiny sound and began to look around, but was interrupted by the imperious demand of the telephone. He turned back and picked up the receiver, holding it away from his ear with an expression of distaste.

His interloper smiled grimly at the series of parrot-like squawks emanating from the handpiece.

The general listened impassively until the high-pitched screaming ceased and said, 'I have heard you, Mein Führer.' For a few seconds, he stood there, a troubled expression in his eyes, then put down the receiver. Just as it dropped into its cradle, a silken noose descended over the general's head and instantly tightened to discomfort level.

'Stand still, General, and you will not be hurt. I would prefer not to have to kill you, but if you move, you are a dead man.' While he spoke, Angel relieved him of his pistol. 'Now ... Sit down and make yourself comfortable. Over here, away from that bell.' He loosened the silk cord, drew it over the man's head and sat in a facing chair, holding the German's pistol with his finger loosely on the trigger. 'We have a lot to talk about.'

'You might well have killed me, but if I had managed to press that button next to the telephone, you would be dead, too,' the general pointed out, rubbing his throat. 'I don't know how you got in here without alerting my men.'

'You cannot think rationally with a noose biting into your neck, cutting off the essentials for life, General.' His visitor shrugged. 'But the question of my death is of no moment. There are many loyal Frenchmen prepared to die for their country, as I am sure you know. For none of us wish to live under the brutality of a regime such as yours.' Out of the ensuing silence, he added, 'No, I need you alive, General.'

'Should I be thankful?'

'If you mean, am I going to resort to your methods for obtaining information: No, I am not. I expect to conduct this discussion like a civilised man.' He glanced at the pistol apologetically. 'Insurance.'

The general flushed. But he curled his lip. 'Do you

think that you are the only man who has come here to try
and reason with me?'

'No, General, I am sure I am not. But, you will allow
that I am the only one who could have killed you out of
hand.' He moved the pistol slightly. 'And I still could.'

The general did not answer. But since he gripped his
thin lips together and grunted under his breath, Angel
took it as agreement.

'So ...' His visitor indicated the telephone. 'That was
a communication from your leader?'

The general made a moue. 'He wanted to know why I
have not yet razed Paris.' He watched his captor cast up
his eyes and added in a mimicking tone, '"Is Paris
burning? Is Paris burning?"' He shook his head. 'That is
all I hear from him.'

Angel looked down at his hands. 'I take leave to tell
you, General,' he said, levelling his gaze squarely on that
of his prisoner, '*if* you do not already know it, that your
leader is insane.'

The general expelled a long breath, loosened his collar
and pointed. 'A drink?'

'No, but you go ahead.' Angel pushed the well-
equipped drinks trolley towards him.

The general selected a bottle, and it clinked against the
glass before he spoke. 'I have already come to that *most*
unwelcome conclusion, myself,' he said, concentrating on
pouring a measure. 'And I find it quite ... terrifying.'

'And?'

'And what?' asked the general, swirling the clear liquid
but not drinking. 'Isn't that enough?'

'More than enough, I should think,' agreed Angel. 'My
question is: what are you going to do about it?'

'I? ... Me?' The general looked up, startled, to meet
the compelling eyes. A man of power himself, it shook him
to find that he could not look away.

'Yes, you, General. You are the only one who can end
this madness.'

'I think you have an exaggerated idea of my authority,' said the general, with a thin smile. 'I command Paris, not the Third Reich.'

'*Eh bien*, if that is so, why have you not carried out your leader's orders to destroy the city?'

'There are two reasons.' The general toyed with his glass; his small mouth wistful. 'Because, in the short time that I have lived here, I have grown to love Paris: a city of culture and beauty, made for art and romance, not war.' A bitter twist replaced the wistful set to his lips. 'And because, as you have so rightly said, our Führer is insane.' He sighed and went on. 'You don't know what happened to those of us who realised it and tried to end his unholy reign.' It was almost as if the general was impelled to share his confidences with the man who sat so casually holding a gun on him. Yet the general, well-versed in warfare, knew that his captor was not as casual as he seemed. He sat facing the door, while the general had his back to it. And while he held the pistol loosely, it never wavered.

'Go on. I am interested.'

'After the July bomb plot—a purge of thousands—imprisoned, sent to concentration camps, awaiting execution. Von Stauffenberg executed by firing squad the next day; von Haeften, loyal fellow, stepping in front of him and dying, too. Terrible reprisals and not finished yet! So many attempts have been made to eliminate the Führer and end the war, to show the world that all Germans are not vicious animals like the Nazis; but every one has failed. The man seems to have the luck of the devil!'

'I sympathise with those of your countrymen who gave their lives in this quest, believe me. But even though your Führer has, so far, seemed to lead a charmed life, his luck is about to run out.'

'If one could hope!' exclaimed the general.

'A man may think that he has the power to escape earthly justice, that he can do what he will, no matter how evil,' said Angel quietly, in tones that raised the general's hair on his scalp. 'But let not that man think that he can escape the justice of the universe.'

A silence fell, broken only by the ticking of a clock and a sharp gulping sound as the general suddenly tossed down the neat spirit.

'Before I go, General, I will have your word that you will not go further with this monstrous plan to destroy Paris, that you will do your best to broker a surrender in which you hand it over in good order.'

'You have my word. Believe me, I see no sense in destroying a beautiful city, nor in wasting any more lives. But, I must warn you, you will not get it without a fight.'

'So be it.' Angel rose lithely to his feet. 'Don't ring your bell, General.'

A blur of movement, a tiny swish of the curtain and the general found himself alone. Freed from the compelling presence, he leapt up, went over to the window, closed and bolted it. Then, realising the enormity of the other man's actions, he rushed back to his desk and slammed his fist down on the bellpush. He waited for the clamour of the alarm system, the hurried tramp of boots, but nothing happened.

General von Choltitz lowered himself into a chair, head in hands, a rueful smile on his lips. So, the man had disabled the alarm system. He'd been two steps ahead from the start, had always had him in his power. That talk about not ringing the bell had all been a ploy. *A worthy foe,* thought the general. *Yes, a worthy foe. But he has forgotten one thing!*

The general started to reach for the telephone, then changed his mind. It was certainly better to surrender to a civilised man than to face execution or forced suicide over his refusal to obey an insane order. The French people would treat him well. He knew that he was already being hailed as the saviour of Paris. *I could spend my time in prison writing my memoirs,* he thought and determined then and there to surrender to his uninvited guest. But then he sat up straight, frowning. *But I cannot: I have no idea who he is!*

§

The Maquis surrounding Gap had done their job thoroughly, blowing up every road and rail link and communication line, completely isolating the enemy forces that had congregated in the town. Then, finally in a position of power, they called for the enemy to surrender. And were stunned at the reply.

'They will only surrender to a proper army and not a bunch of terrorists,' said Gabriel, with a wry grin. 'They refuse to believe that the Free French are a proper army.'

'I don't know what options they think they have, stuck where they are and surrounded by us,' said Armand. 'I wonder who they consider constitutes a "proper army"?'

'I don't know. But we don't want to be *stuck* here for God knows how long, living in tents and whatever,' said Natalie. 'I want to go *home*.'

'A *proper* army?' laughed Antoinette. 'Who do they think has been chasing them out of France all this time?'

'Yes, but how do we convince them?'

'We'll have to find someone with a tank to fire a few rounds over their heads,' quipped Antoinette. '*That* might convince them.'

'Do you know, that is a very good idea,' said Armand. 'It might just work. I will get on the radio and find out the closest allied tank division; get them to send one over.'

'One?'

'One will do. The Germans know the Maquis don't have tanks. We have to end this. Didn't you hear? Natalie wants to go home.'

'She won't do that in a day. Australia is a long way off.'

'Don't blame me for it,' said Natalie, tossing her head.

'I bet I am not the only one that wants to go home. But I mean home to Belvoir. And *that* we can do in a day.'

Later in the day, the tank rolled up to a high point. The driver shared a joke and a meal with the French troops, fired off a few shots and settled down to wait.

§

'What is de Gaulle doing?' fumed Colonel Rol. 'Dithering about like an old woman! We can take Paris ourselves. Who is with me?'

Amidst the overwhelming roar, Angel stepped forward. 'Good evening, Colonel. Your troops look to be in unanimous agreement. Can I be of assistance to you?'

Angel! Just the man I need.' Colonel Rol pumped his hand. 'Now, let us make a strategy for battle—the battle for Paris—for I will not rest until every one of those filthy swine are thrown out of my city!'

The two men retired to the colonel's headquarters, reaching agreement on their strategy in quick time.

'Sniper fire from high windows and the tops of buildings is going to be a major problem with street fighting,' said the colonel. 'They are hard to take out, and even one can do a lot of damage. And of course, they move on before we can get to them.'

'That is something that I can help you take care of. But warn your men that if they see me on the wall of a building, not to shoot me. Although, I might appreciate a bit of covering fire.'

'Very well, I will tell the men not to fire at a cat-burglar if they see one. But I can do better than that. I will send two men with you, specifically to provide the covering fire to allow you to reach the sniper's nests. Now, I'd better arm you. What would you like? Something nice and light? What about this one?' he asked, proffering a light machine gun.

Angel moved a negating hand. 'I prefer my own method. It is quieter. Besides, I already have a gun,' he said, showing the pistol.

'A Walther! Very nice! P38, too. Where did you get that?'

'Von Choltitz.'

'*Mon Dieu!* I won't ask how! Is he still alive?'

Angel's mouth lifted at one corner. 'Need you ask, Colonel?'

§

'Tomorrow,' said Antoinette, settling into her camp bed in the tent she shared with Natalie. 'That allied tank did the trick. The Germans will surrender tomorrow. Only one more night in this awful tent.' She looked over at the other bed, saw that its occupant seemed to be asleep, and snuggled into her blanket. But soon her eyes flew open.

Natalie was whimpering in her sleep. When she started to cry out, Antoinette knew she had to wake her before one of the others thought that someone was attacking them and barged into the tent.

'Juliette. Juliette!' Antoinette leapt out of bed to shake her by the shoulders. 'Natalie!'

'Oh … Oh, what?'

'You were crying out. Are you all right?'

Natalie shivered. 'It was a nightmare. Horrible.'

'I'll make us a hot drink, and you can tell me about it,' said Antoinette, reaching for a thermos flask and two mugs. Into them she broke up some chocolate, added hot water and handed one to Natalie.

'Chocolate? *Chocolate* …?'

'I know—Luxury with a capital L,' agreed Antoinette. 'From the Americans. The tank driver gave me a bar. Here.' She tossed Natalie a spoon. 'It will soon melt into a heavenly drink. Now tell me!'

Natalie stirred and sipped her chocolate. 'I was running through a maze of dark corridors, looking for a way out. There was a woman sitting with her back to me. When she turned, at first, I thought it was myself I was looking at. But when I looked more closely … her hair was really long and she was dressed in the fashion of the nineteenth century—a long white gown. She looked at me with sympathy and said, 'Are you lost, Child? You look as if you are.' Then she said …' Natalie shook her head. 'Oh, I *can't* tell you. It is too *utterly* preposterous!'

'Nightmares always sound ridiculous when you try to describe them, but tell me anyway,' said Antoinette, savouring her drink. 'Talking them out always helps, I find.' She smiled encouragingly. 'Go on …'

Natalie was silent, remembering what the woman had said to her. 'Angel is mine,' she said. 'That is why you cannot have him. Nicolas could have been yours had you treated him with the love and respect he deserves, but you have spurned his precious love.' Her eyes flashed. 'Trodden it under your feet. Let me show you what your life will be without him.'

Natalie only told Antoinette about the last part of this speech. 'She … she told me she would show me what my life would be like without Nic,' she faltered. 'And it was so cold and dark, so horrible and frightening, so unbearably desolate that I cried out and woke you up.' Natalie shivered. 'I'm sorry.'

'*De rien, ma chère*! You're cold. Drink up your chocolate.'

Natalie gazed at her with wide, terrified eyes. 'Do … do you think it could mean that Nic is … Could he be … *dead?*'

Antoinette looked down into her cup; her face inscrutable. 'My sister believed in dreams,' she said, at last. 'But I think it is your own anxiety at the bottom of it.' She stood and took the empty mug from Natalie's nerveless fingers. 'And no, since you ask, I do not think it means he is dead.'

'But you don't know.' It was a bald statement.

'No,' said Antoinette. 'I don't. None of us knows.' She put a comforting hand on Natalie's shoulder. 'We must just hope.'

# 51 FREEDOM

**26 August 1944**

*At last, our beloved country has been liberated: the scourge removed from our land, sometimes with methods as evil as theirs. But I will not dwell on that: every man must face his own demons—his own judgement—in his own way. But after so many years, what will I do with my freedom? Is it not just a slow form of death? Waiting to be with my love? I dare not think of Antoinette, because if I close my eyes ... And what of Natalie? She looks so unhappy, so pale and drawn. I know how she feels but can do nothing for either of us.*

Nicolas stirred and opened his eyes. The first thing he noticed was that his body felt relaxed and comfortable—his mind calm—no restless energy to force him up and out of bed. From habit, his hand found his locket before he started to look around. For long moments, he wondered where he was, then realised that he was in Angel's underground palace. *Paris! I am in Paris,* he thought. *But how did I get here?*

He saw a man standing with his back to him in the candlelight, and his heart skipped; yet he neither moved nor called out. Just watched as the man moved around the room, touching its effects with an air of reminiscent sadness, as if he were saying goodbye to things he truly loved and would see no more. Then the man turned in profile and Nicolas bounded up, startled.

'Angel?'

The man turned fully and smiled in recognition. 'Hello, *mon fils.*'

For a moment, there was silence as the two men surveyed each other—both tall and athletic—their eyes dark pools in the dim light.

Nicolas moved a hand. 'I have known you all my life, yet it is the first time that I have seen you outside of your portrait.'

'And it is the last. I am going now.'

'Are you? Why?'

'Because you do not need me any more.'

'Don't I?'

'No. You can do all that I have done—and more, if you need to. I know it, if you do not.'

'Oh … You have been with me so long: a part of me, my inner voice, my wise counsel. I have depended on you so much … that you seemed to take me over. But I am confused: did I become you, or did you become me?'

Angel shrugged. '*Eh bien,* if you want to think of it that way …'

'But, which?'

Again, he lifted a shoulder. 'However you wish to see it, *mon brave.* You may please yourself.'

'But I don't remember … Some: I remember some. Not … all.'

'Perhaps it is for the best. There were many things that I had to do … Otherwise you and Natalie would not have survived.'

'Because I would not kill! Is that why you did it?' Shame, misery and horror suffused him as he thought of what had happened to Lisette because he'd been too squeamish to finish a job. 'Oh, if *only* I had ——'

'Peace, my son.' Angel gripped his shoulder. 'It is too late, now, for that. Only you and I know that it was not you who made retribution, but me on your behalf.' His lip lifted in a little half-smile. 'You see, it was something I could do very easily, and under those circumstances, without compunction. Pursuit of justice has always been my driving force, no matter to what lengths I had to go. Whereas, you found it impossible to reconcile certain things with your heart. Is there any shame in that? But you could do it now, if you had to: *au fond* you know that. *Eh bien,* I am not going to tell anybody that it was me and not you.' He paused. 'And I would advise you to do the same.'

Nicolas said nothing. He could just imagine the kind of glances and whispers he would get if he did try to explain. Especially when he had no idea himself. 'But I don't … How did you do it?'

'You are better not to know. It is a power that you do not want.'

For an instant, Nicolas caught a glimpse of suffering—raw, terrible suffering—and tried to grasp the enormity of what this man had given up to help him. Tried … and failed. '*This* world,' he said, with bitter emphasis, 'so … flawed. So much destruction. So much death. So many atrocities. How can people *do* that to each other? Tell me … How?'

Angel shrugged but did not reply.

'I have not even lived for more than a quarter of a century,' murmured Nicolas, in despairing tones, 'and I feel like an old, old man. If you had not been here to help me, I would be dead. I know that, but … How can there be hope? How can we go on? After all that has happened?'

'There is hope. If you are alive, there is always hope. Tomorrow is a new day. Be thankful for it,' Angel spoke again. 'The only way forward is to put the past behind you. You must look to the future. Promise me …?'

'I promise. But …' Words were wrenched out of him. 'You gave so much to me, helped me so much. How can I ever thank you?'

'By living a full and happy life with the one you love. The way that I never could.'

'But Natalie doesn't ——'

'Go back to Belvoir and ask her. I think she will say yes. I have paved the way a little for you there and so has ——' He turned; his eyes lighting with joy. Nicolas saw them flash sapphire-blue in the candlelight. 'Oh, you are here, my love! I have been waiting for you,' he said, holding out his arms to the tall, slender young woman with chestnut hair and a loving, radiant smile. She melted into his embrace and they kissed: long, tenderly, fulfilling. He stroked her hair back from her face, winding a chestnut curl around his forefinger. 'You have done as I asked?'

'Yes,' she replied with a sweet, conspiratorial smile. 'All done.'

'Then we can go.' He held out a hand to Nicolas. '*Au revoir, mon brave*. Take care of Natalie and your people. After you have lived a full and satisfying life, I will see you in the greater wide.'

The woman freed herself and held out her arms to Nicolas. He felt the love and warmth of her enchanting smile. 'Katarina,' he said. 'My sweet grandmother that I never knew. You are even more beautiful than your portrait.'

She placed a gentle kiss on his forehead. 'And you have grown to be a very fine young man. I am *so* proud of you. Goodbye, my darling.'

Angel put his arm around her waist, took a last look around and, with his little half-smile, saluted Nicolas. He looked down at his companion. '*Eh bien*, shall we go, my dearest love?'

Nicolas watched them walk out the door together, drawing a sharp breath as Katarina lifted her gaze to Angel's and smiled back. So much love was in their eyes, their faces, every line of their bodies, that Nicolas felt the pain of it. It was a new dimension; the kind of love that he thought he knew, but now realised he'd never had an inkling of. Yet had he not already glimpsed it in a dream? A love to transcend all others: so beautiful, so powerful that it would last forever.

Nicolas felt tears well; at the same time, he was conscious of an overwhelming tiredness. But then he jerked awake as a tiny ballerina pirouetted into the room, obviously looking for someone. She gave Nicolas an enchanting smile when she saw him watching her. 'The Master is right,' she said. 'You will be well-equipped to look after your own from now on.' She looked at the far door and made as if to leave. 'Master, wait. I am coming.'

'Please,' said Nicolas. 'Who are you? You look like an angel,' he added, taking in the plaited coronet of pale gold hair and her ethereal lightness.

'I am Sprite, the Master's assistant. Do not forget to take his advice: the Master is always right.'

'Yes,' agreed Nicolas, watching the delightful little creature make a magnificent leap *en grand jeté* to cross the room in the wake of the others.

At the door, she turned; her eyes brimful of laughter. She made an adorable gesture. 'She will say yes,' she promised; a finger to her lips. 'Sleep now.' And with that, she was gone.

He needed no prompting. In a few minutes, he was asleep. When he woke in the morning, he did not know whether Angel, his beautiful lady from the portrait and the gorgeous little ballerina had really been there, or whether it had all been a dream.

As he dressed, he asked a tentative question in his mind: *Angel?*

But his inner voice remained silent. Nicolas went up on the street, feeling as bereft and lonely as if he'd lost his best friend. Celebrations were in full swing, but to him, it meant nothing. He just felt empty. Empty and sad.

On a corner, watching the victory parade, he met the *Résistance* leader he had only the haziest memory of fighting alongside the previous few days and nights.

'You'd think that *I* should be a part of that, wouldn't you?' said Colonel Rol with a bitter gesture as Generals Patton and de Gaulle went by. 'I mean, who was it who did all the work and handed them Paris on a plate? And you! You did your share and more!'

'Peace is enough for me, my friend,' said Nicolas, suppressing a shudder. 'Let them strut around taking all the glory. One day, they will know who really did liberate Paris, *hein*? By the way, what happened to von Choltitz?'

'He surrendered. To me and Leclerc at la Gare Montparnasse.'

'There you are, then. He knew who it was. It will come out one day.'

'He said he wanted to surrender to the man who was brave enough to beard a lion in his den, but since he did not know his name, he had to make do with me. Of course, *I* know who it was. So that was how you got his pistol, *hein*?' Colonel Rol glanced at him, admiringly. '*Eh bien*, I always believed that I knew men, but I admit that I was mistaken in you. You were everything a cell leader should be, acquitted yourself like a seasoned commando. I am sorry that I misjudged you.' His eyes went back to the victory parade and narrowed. He turned again to Nicolas. 'We *Résistance* fighters, we who were at the coalface suffering the losses, will have our own victory celebrations. Will you stay a while with us?'

'No, thank you. I must get back to my sweetheart.'

'Oh, of course. You told me that last night.' Colonel Rol held out his hand. 'Goodbye. Have a good life.'

'*Merci, et tu.* And, Colonel, you were not mistaken: you *do* know men.' With a smile and a handshake that said what words could not, Nicolas left one of the bravest men *he* had ever known.

The rest was easy. He hitched a lift with some allies travelling to Provence.

§

Natalie was in the great hall of the château with most of the women from the village, down on their knees, scrubbing. From time to time, they called to the men to bring them more water for their buckets. Natalie was scrubbing, too, working to remove all vestiges of enemy occupation: doing her best not to think.

Unheeding, she heard a truck draw up, muffled goodbyes, then the truck move off. She'd given up looking for Nicolas: always, *always* it was someone else coming home, and it hurt so much to expect to see someone who never came. It was easier not to hope, to pretend that she could not hear a vehicle … She scrubbed more furiously.

One of the women crossed herself. '*Nom de Dieu!*' she whispered. 'Can this be who I think it is?'

Natalie straightened, leapt to her feet. She dropped her scrubbing brush into the bucket with an unnoticed 'plop', and her eyes widened at the tall figure that strode across the carriage drive. Transfixed, she stood staring. She didn't notice the peasants glance at each other, gesture and melt away one by one until she was left alone in the great hall to meet—whom?

Would it be Angel with his compelling eyes and his stern mouth, who treated her like a tiresome child? Who'd told her to ask her question after the war? Who couldn't be hers because he belonged to someone else? Or Nic with his gentle sweetness, who may or may not love her? Who, quite rightly, may have turned away in disgust from her capricious and heartless behaviour?

Either way … She pushed back hair dishevelled from her work and wished she was made-up and tidy. But what did it really matter? Because, now it *was* after the war. And her question? Was it even relevant? She bit her lip, knowing she would never ask it. Her legs trembled. Her whole body shook as if with fever. *I dare not ask it*, she thought. *There is only so much hurt one can take.*

Her breath snagged in her throat as she realised anew what she had done to Nicolas—beautiful, kind, loving Nicolas—who she had discovered too late that she adored with every fibre of her being.

Tension mounted, feathering her scalp, constricting her heart. Who would it be?

The man coming towards her bounded up the steps with a springy, athletic stride. In the doorway, he paused for a moment, then opened his arms, his face lighting with joy. 'Natalie … darling!'

*Nic! It is Nic!* There was the love in his eyes; the gentle, deprecating smile. And yet there was something of Angel about him—some implacable core. A man who knew who he was, who had commanded an underground unit, taking the war to the enemy; a man who would not be pushed around. A man who could say, 'Take me or leave me: as I am.'

*We're not the same people,* she thought. *We're never going to be the same people ever again. The war has changed all that—so brutal, so hard to survive. We've all had to do things that …*

But she didn't have to ask if he loved her. The answer was in the tender light in his eyes, the deepening timbre of his voice and the arms that reached out to hold her: loving, protective, asking nothing, yet giving all.

'Oh, Nic! Oh, Nic,' she said, crying and laughing all at once as she fell against his chest. 'It *is* you. I was afraid you were never coming back. I thought you were *dead* …' Natalie's voice broke up in sobs. She clung to him as if she couldn't believe in his substance.

'Hush, my darling,' he said. 'I am here now.' He glanced around the empty hall. 'The others: are they …?'

'Yes, yes. We are all here.' Pain filled her eyes. 'What is left of us.'

He held her closer. 'I know …'

'Oh, Nic, I thought I'd given you a disgust of me. You didn't seem to even *like* me any more.'

'Impossible!' he declared, smoothing back her hair with gentle fingers and smiling into her eyes.

'But in the war …'

'The war is over, *Chérie*. And everything *I* want is right here in front of me.' He bent his head.

'Oh, Nic,' she sighed and raised her lips to his. Their kiss was as she remembered it: exquisite rapture. They stayed so for a long time, savouring the joy, the indescribable comfort of the touch of their bodies, loath to leave the haven of each other's arms.

But, in the end, it was Nicolas who took Angel's advice and asked his question; and Natalie who gave a joyful assent.

The great hall of Belvoir, enveloping them in a thousand-year embrace of love and approval, stood a silent witness to their engagement.

# EPILOGUE

**30 September 1945**

Armand lay dozing in an armchair in the library—something that he often did lately on somnolent afternoons when he was supposed to be writing his account of the Belvoir Maquis during the war. Then he began to dream: a familiar dream that his consciousness abhorred.

'No, no,' he moaned, shaking his head and making repelling movements with his hands. 'No, I cannot!'

'What is it, old friend? What is the matter?' Strong, insistent fingers gripped his shoulder.

Armand opened his eyes to see Nicolas's concerned face hanging over him.

'Oh, nothing …' He cleared his throat and looked away. 'Just a dream.'

'One you have often?' asked Nicolas with shrewd perspicacity. 'About Sette?'

'Yes.' Suddenly, Armand broke down. 'It is a wicked, *evil* dream! And it is always the same: Lisette brings Toinette to me, puts her arms around us both and tells me to take her as my wife.' Perspiration broke out on his brow. 'I will not be disloyal to my beautiful Lisette! I cannot, *will not* replace her. It is *unthinkable!*'

'Hmm. *Doucement, mon ami.*' The hand pressing his shoulder conveyed comfort. Its owner's expression was thoughtful. 'And yet, you know, you could look at it another way: might it not be a message to you from Sette herself?'

'What do you mean?'

Nicolas stroked his upper lip. 'She told me when my grandfather died that dreams were sent to bridge the gap between this world and the next.'

'You mean, she really does want me to ...'

'I think she might. She loved you very much, and knowing her, she would not want you to be lonely. She would see it as a perfect solution, don't you think? Sette was very much a realist. I ——' He broke off as Antoinette rushed into the library and breathed a sigh of relief when she saw Nicolas bending over Armand.

He straightened and stepped back. 'Is something the matter, Toinette?'

'No, nothing ... Silly, really.' She grimaced. 'I thought I heard my sister's voice saying that Armand needed me.'

'Toinette! Oh, Toinette ...' Armand spread wide his arms.

She went into them without question.

Nicolas, backing out the door, almost ran into Natalie. 'I think we are just a little *de trop*, my darling,' he said, shepherding her in to the corridor. 'Why don't we go and hang the portraits. The agents have brought them up from the underground store.'

'Yes,' she agreed, with a twinkle. 'I can tell we are not needed here. And I have never seen your portraits.'

'That's right. Grand-père put them into storage before you came to Belvoir. Even then, he was worried about war.'

'Really? Well, he was right. Lucky for us that he foresaw what might happen to Belvoir. He was a great *seigneur*. I am glad I got to know him.'

'Yes, indeed. So am I,' said Nicolas warmly, divesting the duc's portrait of its protective packaging and hanging it in its original place, as he did with each of the others.

He made only one change: the ballerina he placed one side of his grandfather, the duchesse the other and all the rest of the portraits he moved down a place.

Natalie looked a question.

'I can't explain,' said Nicolas, 'except to say that he painted her when they were both very young.'

'You don't have to say anything,' said Natalie. 'First love: I can see that he must have loved her. It is beautifully painted: full of light and spirit.' Her gaze was arrested by another portrait. 'And this is your mother? So beautiful. And your father: like you ... yet not.' She drew in a breath, staring at the next portrait he was hanging. It was a face she had seen before, and it shocked her. 'And this? *Who* is this?'

Nicolas was surprised at the urgency in her voice. 'It is my maternal grandmother. Her name was Katarina. Why?'

'Oh ... No reason.' Natalie gathered her wits. 'Do you think she, erm, looks a little like me?'

He took her in his arms to study her face. 'Well, yes, she does a little ... Actually, a *lot*—if you discount the hairstyle and the eye colour. Perhaps that is who you reminded me of when we found each other in the Tuileries Gardens?' *The day I fell in love with you.*

'Perhaps,' she said demurely, though a little frisson ran up her spine. She disengaged herself and moved on to the next portrait. 'Oh, Nic! Who is this handsome man?'

'Can't you guess?'

She stared at the portrait, looked into the compelling eyes and shivered. 'No.' Yet wasn't that touch of ironic humour about his mouth familiar? And his expression? Had she not seen him before? She turned back to Nicolas. 'Who is he?'

'Let me introduce my mother's guardian and your father's friend: the marquis du Bois.' He touched the portrait almost reverently. There was an infinitesimal pause before he added, 'Angel.'

Natalie gave a little gasp. A phrase flashed into her mind, something that Madame Dupont had said about the young Nicolas in her diaries. *What had she called him? Angel without the darkness: that was it.* Perhaps that accounted for the inexplicable likeness she perceived, even though, apart from their build and colouring, it was only superficial. *Angel without the darkness.* In the war, when it was needed, the darkness had come; and now it was gone again. Her mind struggling with a concept; she looked from the portrait to the man she loved and back again, started to speak, but thought better of it. *There are some things,* she thought, *especially in war, that we can never understand: that cannot be explained.*

It was a day of surprises and, little though they knew it, one that set the course for the future. Nicolas turned around and gave a great shout, '*Mon Dieu!* What are you two doing here?' He ran to the tall blonde women coming along the gallery and hugged them. They lifted him off the ground. There was a burst of delighted laughter and Nicolas's eyes widened at the two magnificent men of African descent who followed, muscles rippling beneath their uniforms.

Natalie smiled. How ridiculous to think that she had been so jealous of these bodyguards back in the days when they had shadowed Nicolas everywhere.

'We told you we'd find you after the war,' said Desi.

'We never break our promises,' said Dani.

'Did you know that we joined the French *Résistance?*' Desi smiled. 'We've been fighting up in the north with the communists.'

Nicolas gave another great shout of laughter. 'The *communists!* Oh, Dees ...'

'We didn't approve of our country's neutrality,' explained Dani. 'So, we came back to help out.'

'These are our husbands, Woodrow and Wilson,' said Desi. 'They are also twins. We met them when they parachuted in.'

Nicolas, shaking hands with the two grinning Americans, collapsed into mirth. 'Desdemona and Othello doubled!'

'But with a happy ending,' reproved Dani, with a twinkle.

'Also doubled,' added Desi.

'*Bien sûr!*' he said, still laughing, then became serious as he saw the man behind them; a man whose face was lined and old, with sparse white hair and a frail, painfully thin body. 'But it cannot be … Monsieur Lorraine?'

'Yes, *jeune* Monsieur,' said Desi, becoming serious. 'We have brought him to you.'

'He has something he needs to tell you,' added Dani, her white-tiger eyes glowing with a fierce light.

'But come and sit down, Monsieur. Have some refreshment.' Natalie and Nicolas were gentle with him, horrified by his condition. Only his eyes, bright and feverish, seemed alive. The rest of him was dried up and wispy: brittle, like dead summer grass.

Armand and Antoinette were summoned, and over coffee, Monsieur Lorraine told them the terrible story of the Nazi death camps. 'Beaten. Starved. Herded like animals into extermination chambers after being stripped of all human dignity. So many dead,' he mourned. 'They say it is in the millions.'

There was a moment of appalled silence.

Then Natalie whimpered, 'Oh, no!'

'It is so,' said Monsieur Lorraine. 'Had it not been for the timely arrival of the Americans, especially these two with your erstwhile bodyguards, I would be one of them. But I was determined to stay alive, if only to testify to the criminal mass murder of Jews.'

'Genocide,' said Nicolas; a grim set to his mouth. 'That is what it amounts to.'

'The master race,' gasped Natalie; her eyes dilating. 'Remember, Nic?'

'I do,' he replied, and for a moment, he was Angel,

*Résistance* commander.

'Yes,' said Armand, watching his face. 'When men allow themselves to believe that they are superior to others, they likewise give themselves permission to commit atrocious crimes against humanity.'

'*Précisément,* Monsieur,' agreed Monsieur Lorraine; his eyes like burning holes in his cadaverous face. He turned to Natalie and addressed her on an entirely different subject: 'Mademoiselle, I want you to keep my Stradivari. It is yours.'

'Oh, no,' said Natalie, taken by surprise. 'It is far too valuable to give away.'

'You mistake, Mademoiselle. I want something from you both.' His fevered gaze included Nicolas. 'Something far more important than money. I want your support: your aid.'

'But of course,' agreed Nicolas. 'Anything. What do you want us to do?'

Monsieur Lorraine took a breath that shook his frail body. 'Your ex-bodyguards, their husbands and I have joined Simon Wiesenthal in a bid to hunt down the perpetrators of this great evil, flush them out of their hiding places and bring them to justice at the war crime trials. I have made the vow to never rest until every last one of these cursed devils has been caught.' He banged his bony fist down on the table. It made a dry, rustling sound. 'Will you join me?'

Natalie and Nicolas agreed instantly, as did Armand and Antoinette.

'We can give concerts and recitals to raise money,' said Natalie. 'Can't we, Nic?'

'That is an excellent idea, my darling. They should be very special with the Stradivari.' He put his arm around her shoulders and beamed on his companions. One and all, they felt the warmth of his charm. 'You have come at a very good time, you know. Our wedding is next week. We are waiting for Natalie's family, and they should arrive in a day or two. I propose that you all stay here and celebrate with us. Meanwhile, we will fatten up Monsieur Lorraine a little and draw up a plan of campaign. How does that sound?'

'Wonderful,' said Desi.

'Perfect,' added Dani.

Their husbands smiled and nodded.

Monsieur Lorraine clasped Nicolas's hand, too emotional to speak.

'Ah,' said Armand. 'The hunted become the hunters: an eminently satisfactory proposal, in my opinion. To spend the rest of our lives in the pursuit of justice would seem a praiseworthy ambition. And we must never forget that we, too, have a poignant reason for bringing these canaille to justice.' For just a moment, his voice faltered in grief; a grief reflected in the surrounding faces. He kissed the steadying hand Antoinette held out to him and threw back his head; his eyes gleaming almost as fanatically as those of Monsieur Lorraine. 'Is there any reason why we cannot start our plan of campaign right now?'

'No,' said Nicolas, watching him closely. 'I don't think so. Do you?' He looked around the group. 'Does anybody, *hein? Non, bien sûr!*' A little half-smile just touched his lips. '*Eh bien, alors*, let the Nazi hunting begin.'

# ABOUT ANNE ROUEN

Anne Rouen is an award-winning historical fiction author from Australia, who is inspired by the opulent operatic age of 19th century France, the classic Belle Époque era and the dark times of the world wars. This passion was ignited from her own heritage, combined with a lifelong love of historical fiction writing, particularly those of a similar ilk to Georgette Heyer.

This is where inspiration for the *Master of Illusion* series was born.

Anne Rouen is the alter ego of Lynn Newberry: a country woman from the New South Wales New England region, who breeds Brangus cattle by day and is a dedicated, passionate horsewoman.

The lady behind Anne Rouen has completed a specialist teaching degree in the Rural Sciences department of the University of New England, and has spent most of her years involved in the agricultural industry—twenty of them as an educator.

Throughout her career, Lynn has escaped the everyday demands of work through the hand of Anne Rouen. *Master of Illusion—Book One* was her first published novel, and it, along with its sequels, *Master of Illusion—Book Two* and *Angel of Song* have been nominated in several award programs, most notably, the *Global Ebook Awards* where Anne won the Silver Medal for *Modern Historical Literature Fiction* in 2014 and the Bronze Medal for *Modern Historical Literature Fiction* in 2016.

Lynn has also seen success with her short story writing, achieving a Highly Commended in the *Rolf Boldrewood Literary Awards* (2011) for *The Scent of a Criminal*.

With a broad range of interests, Anne Rouen writes a regular blog where she chats about her firsthand experience beating breast cancer, her love of horses and other current issues that are close to her heart.

You can keep up with the latest information about Anne Rouen on social media and through her website at www.annerouen.com.

# ALSO BY ANNE ROUEN

*Master of Illusion Book One*

*Master of Illusion Book Two*

*Angel of Song (Book Three in the Master of Illusion Series)*